I0564236

Mark of the
Tiger's Stripe

Revised Edition

Joshua Yoder

ISBN: 978-1-7329138-2-0
ISBN 13:
Library of Congress Control Number:
LCCN Imprint Name: **City and State (If applicable)**

Cover art by Joshua Yoder

For fans old and new who travel the seas of

Geekdom

Author's Note

It has been quite a journey since I first published *Mark of the Tiger's Stripe* in 2017, and I like to think I've learned some things along the way. That is what this book is about. I couldn't help but see the glaring errors in the narrative every time I reread my old manuscript. As a self-published author, I have a unique opportunity to revisit my first published work and make it "better".

If you are new to the series, know that the plot of this book plays out much like the original. However, you will find altered dialogue, altered scenes, and overall better pacing that I hope will enhance the story and bring it more in line with my more recent work.

This version should be considered "canon", but I certainly won't stop you from reading the original and fully appreciating the changes made.

I sincerely hope you enjoy this revised version of *Mark of the Tiger's Stripe* as much as I enjoyed rewriting it.

Josh Yoder

1 – The Hunters

Night shrouded the city of Kairran, capital of the nation of Pytan. Midori, the night moon, shone pale green in the eastern sky. Yet the city didn't sleep; in many respects, it was just waking up.

Whether in the clubs and bars of the bustling downtown, the hectic northern dockyards, the ancient palace where Sultan Abdülkadír entertained a bevvy of foreign dignitaries, or the international airport, with its late-night arrivals and departures, life continued much as it did during the day.

Except in the Kahmir District.

It sat like a blight on the city's northeastern edge, crowded between the markets of the Dahley District and the formidable bulk of the city's outer wall. The great bulwark, built to protect the city from the harsh sandstorms and roving bandits in the surrounding desert, loomed ominously over ramshackle sheds and buildings slowly crumbling under the weight of decay.

The moon cast deep shadows over twisting streets, and only a few pitiful flickering lights attempted to penetrate the gloom.

Kahmir was home to the old, the infirm, and the dregs of Kairran society that had not yet been cast into the harsh desert sands beyond the walls. Row upon row of crumbling buildings lined its crooked streets. Once brightly painted, the sandstone-and-stucco walls had faded to ashen grey and were littered with the remnants of old posters and obscene graffiti. Loose bits of trash fluttered between the skeletons of long-dead vehicles resting on cracked pavement. They were leftovers from a bygone age that even the oldest residents no longer remembered.

This night, the district felt even more abandoned than usual. A string of grisly murders had plagued the inhabitants for several weeks. Death was nothing new to the Khamir District, but these crimes had been so violent, so savage, that many residents had moved to the outer edges of the market, as far away as they could get without the local authorities forcing them back to their tenements.

Barely anything was left of the victims—if they were found in the first place. The scene was always the same: copious amounts of blood, spattered everywhere, and claw marks much larger and deeper than any Amarthian inhabitant could make.

Some even claimed they'd seen the killer and that it was not a living being but a hideous beast, a daemon sent from the underworld to punish the city for its wickedness.

A blood-curdling scream split the night.

On a rooftop not far from the waterfront, two anthropoid figures suddenly stopped and sank into a crouch.

The first was a feminine feline, her athletic frame toned by rigorous exercise. Soft white fur striped in black covered her exposed flesh, and between her rounded cat ears was a shock of black long-fur, layered and bobbed at her neck.

The tigress's companion, while roughly the same height, was obviously a different species. A short blue plume crowned her skull, and her bright green scales bore the pattern of a basilisk. A long whip-like tail swished in agitation behind her, mirroring the twitching striped tail of her companion. As was typical with reptiles, amphibians, and all other nonmammalian sentient species on Amarthia, the basilisk had no body hair nor true mammary glands. Her gender was physically distinguished by the lack of laryngeal prominence in her neck, the curve of her narrow hips and the subtle build-up of fatty tissue over her pectoral muscles, which created a pair of false breasts.

Both women were examples of Amarthia's sentient inhabitants, *Homo Sapiens Anamalis*, or "wise animal", often shortened to Hom-An. They were also clearly not residents of the Kahmir District. They dressed in almost paramilitary fashion with dark pants made of tough denim, a dark long-sleeved shirt with patches of thick leather sewn into the arms, chest, and back, and a nylon harness supporting numerous pouches.

The similarities in their equipment ended there.

The tigress travelled light with only a matte black hunting rifle over one shoulder and a large semiautomatic pistol on her left hip.

Over the basilisk's shirt and harness, she wore a heavy, high-collared flak jacket similar to what a bomb disposal crew would use. The pouches on her hips carried all the tools of her destructive trade: grenades, blasting caps, detonators, and small blocks of what appeared to be clay. Her primary armament was a pistol-grip shotgun, and she carried a semiautomatic pistol as backup, although hers was a smaller calibre than the tigress's weapon.

It was a formidable arsenal should they come up against mercenaries or—Aaba forbid—the local authorities. But against the beast they hunted, they could only hope it was enough.

The tigress pressed the transmit button on the radio clipped to her harness. A wire connected it to an elastic earmuff.

"Did you hear that?" she said in a low, husky voice. She spoke in Locken with the pronounced lazy clip of a United Plains accent. Locken was not the local language.

"Like a bell," came the response. The voice at the other end had the same accent but was masculine and much deeper. "Keep moving, Kitty. The hotel on the waterfront is the most likely location for the nest. I want Rizzo to get her charges in place before we get there."

Kittina Katral gave an affirmative and turned to her companion. Emperatriz "Rizzo" Vega nodded that she was good to go. The tigress adjusted her rifle and moved forward.

They didn't know exactly what they were hunting yet, but the beast had chosen its nesting ground well. The Khamir District was a sea of loose rubble and broken glass, and most of the sentient inhabitants of Amarthia preferred to go barefoot; the tough pads or scales on the soles of their feet offered more than enough protection against most surfaces.

To combat the treacherous footing, Kitty and Rizzo wore thick rubber soles that slipped on like sandals. While not uncomfortable, the loss of touch with the ground could be unsettling, especially to people whose surefootedness relied greatly on surface contact.

Kitty paused again and turned her deep sapphire eyes northward. Distant lights twinkled on the far banks of the Hutsepth Canal; the Kirque city of Arbai was

5

blissfully unaware of the peril that plagued her southern cousin.

After the death scream, the Khamir District had settled into a listening silence. The area was devoid of any common nonsentient vermin—what the Hom-Ans would consider animals. No darzl or munski to skitter under the trash and disappear into the warren of sewer pipes under the district, and no nocturnal avians swooped through the air seeking insects for dinner.

It made the hunters wary.

Kitty gave the all-clear signal, and they vaulted onto the roof below. The building was at the head of a narrow lane leading out to the main street, paralleling the canal. Rusting balconies jutted into the alley, casting deep shadows on the ground below. Even the tigress's feline night vision couldn't pierce the gloom beneath them; it might as well have been a bottomless pit.

Kitty laid down near the roof edge and cradled her weapon against her left shoulder, resting the rifle barrel on a lip of broken wall and sighting on the intersection at the end of the alley. Rizzo crouched behind her patiently, her large gold eyes, spaced far apart on her reptilian head, focused on the ruins ahead of them, comparing their location to the map in her head and thinking of the best placement for her explosives.

The tigress spoke into her radio, "In position. I can see the hotel but not much else for all the bloody shit in the way. Not a clean shot."

Several blocks away, an enormous tiger pressed the transmit switch on his radio again, "If you see one better, by all means move. But I reckon if the roofs are as bodgie as these bloody streets, that's easier said than done."

There was no response, and the massive tiger shook his head. Mohan Katral was the leader of their little band, a hunter team they had lovingly nicknamed the Scrappers. Who they worked for and why they were there was a carefully guarded secret, but if the killer beast was what they thought it was, that spelt big problems for the city of Kairran.

Mohan rolled his shoulders to shake off the annoying itch coming from his back. The movement caused the padding of his armoured shirt to bulge even further as it strained against the corded muscles of his massive 220-centimetre frame. His orange-and-black stripes might be starting to whiten at their edges, but he was in great shape for fifty years old.

The tiger's basic gear mirrored the scouts on the roof, but aside from team lead, he also served as fire support. This was punctuated by the intimidating squad assault weapon he carried, its hundred-round ammo belt packed into an attached box magazine—an empty satchel was attached opposite to catch the spent brass and belt clips. A spare ammo box was strapped to his back like a backpack, and the bandolier across his chest was loaded with large-calibre bullets for the equally large revolver on his hip. In the unlikely event that he ran out of ammo, he could always resort to the curved kukri knife strapped to his other leg.

Like Rizzo, Mohan had augmented his armour protection by strapping on a rebrace and vambrace of segmented steel plates to his left arm. It was heavily scratched and scarred by use and made him look like a gladiator from the ancient Meccinai Empire, but instead of a basket-masked helmet, he covered his head with a wide-brimmed bush hat with the left side pinned up. A short ponytail of greying black long-fur fell out from underneath.

Unlike most common headgear, the tiger's hat had no earholes, and he wore it cocked to the side with one ear exposed and fitted with an elastic earmuff. The ear twitched as the steady drone he had forced to the background reasserted itself. He glanced back at the cause of the disturbance.

The jackrabbit hare averaged 165 centimetres, but the ears poking through the crown of his battered white fedora made him appear much taller. As he hop-stepped along, his ears bobbed and swayed, twitching now and again like electrified antennae.

Vincenzo Nieves had a melodious baritone honeyed by the strains of upper-class Banton heritage, far away in the West United Kingdoms. Or at least it would be melodious if it wasn't constantly ringing in his teammates' ears.

"So there I was, just enjoyin' a nice breakfast salad," the hare babbled, keeping his voice low so only his companions could hear, "Actually, it kinda reminded me of the carver's salad they serve at this quaint café in Clairmount, but never mind. I'm sittin' there, and in from the kitchen walks this absolutely gorgeous leopard girl. I mean you've never seen spots like she had. She had this cute little bob cut that showed off her earrings and a cute top that showed off…well…." He trailed off with a lascivious gleam in his golden-brown eyes, but no one was actually paying attention to him.

Most of the hare's stories went this way; he had a bawdy sense of humour, and if there was one thing Vince appreciated more than fine food, it was fine women. One could easily say he was the guy with ten girls in every town. Mohan guessed he could see why; he could be a charming fellow at times, and with his wavy blond long-fur and matching goatee, he was the very picture of a southern gentleman.

"All right, Vince," Mohan said, "I'll bite; what happened next?"

The hare's face changed abruptly, and he seemed concerned. "Well, I wanted to invite her to a candlelight dinner and see where things went from there. But as we got to talkin', she opened up about her previous relationships. The poor girl had a string of bad luck and had run into some real creeps. I knew right away it just wouldn't have been right to take advantage of her like

9

so many others had. So, I left her with some words of wisdom and my best wishes." He perked up a bit. "But she did give me her number, so maybe we can catch up later."

Mohan nodded; that was also how a lot of Vince's stories ended. The hare really wasn't a bad sort; he might chase after the ladies, but he had rules. Not that Mohan—or anyone else on the team—particularly agreed with his lifestyle, but at least the hare owned up to it. And he never flirted with women he worked with—much to the disappointment of some at the Sanctuary, their home base.

With his gift for conversation, it was only natural that Vince be their communications and infiltration specialist and general jack of all trades. The radio receiver unit he carried on his back was their lifeline to Watch Command at the Sanctuary, and at his side was a bag of tools that no lock could resist when in his skilled hands.

The hare was about to start another story when the figure behind him tapped the radio box.

"You sure these new radios are secure, Vince?" the petite female bullfrog asked. She had a high sing-song accent from the suburbs of Bells Point, New Port, which almost drowned out the glottal clicks and hums common to all frog speech regardless of language. "Ya know, I bet the Golden Eye would love to listen in on what we're doing."

Vince chuckled and adjusted the compact submachine gun he carried, trying to balance it against all his other equipment. "Oh, I'm sure our opposite numbers would love to know what we're doing on their turf. Especially after we contracted them to handle the PR." His fellow agents understood that PR stood for public restoration, which cleaned up any collateral damage they left behind. "Not to worry, darlin'; I secured these channels myself. But if you don't want to go by 'Vicki', we could whip up a few aliases: Agent Twenty-Three, Sergeant Major, Snaps...."

While Victoria Littlepond didn't have eyebrows, the folds above her bulbous speckled eyes wrinkled similarly. "Snaps?"

"Yeah," the hare replied, grinning, "You're our medic, right? You snap us back together!"

Vicki giggled at the suggestion and adjusted the straps on her own backpack. The massive bag, marked with a cross on a white circle, practically dwarfed her. Unlike her teammates, the frog's clothing was cut in amphibian style, a loose fit that kept the material from sticking to her moist skin except where it couldn't be avoided. She secured the outfit around her waist with a broad belt of red plastic fastened by a big circular buckle. The belt was about thirty years out of fashion, but it complemented her ensemble.

"Ya know, medicine's not the only thing I've got stashed in here," Vicki said, patting the side of her pack.

11

"If there's one thing I learned watching *MacTavish*, it's always be prepared! Plus, my dad's an electrician; that's what he used to frame all his life lessons for me and my brothers. Ya know, there's actually quite a lot in common with how circuits and the Hom-An body works."

"If you say so," Vince replied warily, "Just don't go tryin' to hotwire my heart. Might end up with some important parts not workin'."

The frog knew exactly what he meant and clamped a hand over her mouth to stifle her laughter.

"I am certain none of us would want to be deprived of your delightful conversation, Vincenzo, even if it was an octave higher." The low, cultured voice came from the figure bringing up their rearguard. While not much taller than Vince—minus the ears—the striped badger was nearly as broad as Mohan.

"Oof, Zed, I didn't know the Soketh liked to hit below the belt, too," Vince said, wincing as if struck a physical blow.

Zed, whose proper name was Ezekiel, nodded courteously, but a sly grin across his face.

The badger adjusted the sky-blue keffiyeh that covered his head and brushed dirt from the chequered blue and gold scarf that hung across a thawb robe made from the same material as his companions' clothing. The light colours stood out against the dark environs but represented his heritage and family lineage: the Clan of Nashim in the Tribe of the Brown Paw.

The Soketh were a collection of nomadic tribes of varied species connected by an enigmatic past that they rarely shared with city dwellers. They traded survival techniques and small trinkets for supplies, but many in the "civilised" world still thought of them as scavengers, only slightly less savage than wasteland bandits.

The hunters and their organisation knew that the Soketh only traded that they deemed "safe" to give to the rest of the world. There were many artefacts from Amarthia's ancient past that they shared with no one.

Zed carried two such archaic devices with him on every hunt: a bracer of finely crafted gold on his left forearm and a broad-headed axe that hung at his waist. With its indecipherable script and stylised figures engraved into the handle, the axe seemed more ornamental than functional at a glance, but the badger kept its edge honed to razor sharpness. The bracer was similarly fancy, adorned with the raised image of a winged serpent eating its own coiled tail. Only his companions knew the secret behind these items.

Zed's primary weapon was a modern-looking carbine chambered in 7.62mm. A firearms expert might recognise its similarities with the assault weapons used by the Kirque military. However, the optics attached to the top rail had been heavily modified by the Soketh.

The badger gave the hare's name-game another moment's thought. "I would hate to hear what sort of ghastly sobriquets Vincenzo might come up with for the rest of us," he said. He never referred to anyone by their nickname.

"What could I possibly call you except 'Zed', Zed?" the hare chuckled.

At the front of the column, Mohan shook his head but couldn't suppress a grin. He was grateful for the light conversation; it helped relieve the tension of their situation. If the signs they read were correct, the Khamir District was terrorized by something much more dangerous than your typical bahnger or ceravaag. This was a monster straight out of cautionary folk tales and ancient legends. Collectively, they bore many names: roulin yeshou, bhairavi, drekavac, aluka. To the Tiger's Stripe, the organisation the Scrappers represented, they were called fiends; how one had ended up in the Khamir District was still a puzzle they were trying to solve.

"I wish you packed something more powerful than that pistol, Vicki," Mohan said.

The frog idly palmed the 9mm on her hip. "Well, that's what I have you all for, right?" she laughed nervously. She didn't like guns and could never use one against another Hom-An. She carried the pistol to ward off wild animals in the bush; how well it worked against a fiend would depend significantly on its type.

Mohan smiled reassuringly at the frog, then turned his attention to his radio. "All right, Kitty," he said, "I think we're getting close to where that scream came from."

Back on the rooftop, the tigress slowly moved her scope to take in the building fronts two hundred metres away, trying to get a better view of the hotel lobby. It was a short distance for her rifle; the problem was all the clutter.

"Think you can drive it through here?" she asked into the radio. "This is a really narrow window."

"You'll make do," came the reply, "You're the best shot we've got."

Kitty frowned but said nothing. Though perfectly accurate, she found the remark patronising, especially coming from her father.

"Rizzo," Mohan continued, "go set your charges."

"*Oui*, they'll be ready in five minutes," the basilisk answered. Her mezzo-soprano carried the leathery hiss common to all reptiles, but she also had a heavy Neuf Maris accent. While it was usually a melodious language, Rizzo somehow made it sound slightly pompous.

"Finally, something fun to do!" Rizzo said, rising to her feet.

The radio clicked, and Mohan responded, "Remember to keep it neat: that's plan B."

The basilisk sighed in disappointment over the open channel, and the radio clicked again.

"Rizzo, much as this neighbourhood needs renovating, I'd rather not arse this up any more than we need to." It wasn't that Mohan didn't trust the basilisk's expertise; he just knew Rizzo believed a judicious use of explosives could solve any problem.

Rizzo acknowledged and turned to Kitty. "You have my back, *non*?" she asked.

"Trust me," the tigress responded without taking her eye from the rifle scope.

The basilisk made her way silently to the alley floor, carefully picking and choosing between rusting pipes and rickety balconies. Upon reaching the ground, she unslung the shotgun, checking the chamber to ensure a round was racked.

She moved forward cautiously, fighting the growing sense of dread punctuated by the faint burning sensation coming from her left side just below the ribs. A peculiar birthmark marred the scales there, and she always felt it in situations like this; it was something she was born with, a kind of sixth sense that warned her of impending danger. Of course, it also made it difficult for her to bluff at cards.

They had already lost two agents, who had been sent to monitor the area several days ago, but the basilisk tried to tell herself there was nothing to worry about. Their whole team dynamic was built for hunts like this through urban territory. Kitty would warn her of any impending threats she couldn't see.

Rizzo stopped twenty metres from the intersection at the end of the alley. She moved up to the wall and quickly removed several lumps of grey putty from the pouches on her hips. This close to the suspected lair, she began to hum nervously and was thankful reptiles didn't sweat.

She gasped sharply as the radio clicked in her ear.

"Easy there," Mohan said calmly, "We'll be there in a minute, Rizzo. What will you have waiting for us?"

"Concussive shaped charges," the basilisk replied, thankful for the distraction, "The overpressure should crush anything in the alley but leave the buildings intact." She pounded her fist into her palm for emphasis despite the tiger's inability to see her. "Eh, mostly anyway. Why set explosives if you don't wish to use them?"

"We still don't know what we're dealing with," came the reply. "If Kitty can't bring it down—"

"Fair go," the sniper cut in. "I'll bring it down."

"Not if we're up against anything larger than a sjörå," Mohan said shortly. "That three-aught-eight packs a punch, sure, but not against armoured hide. Remember, the Playground was still working on the new coated rounds when we loaded up."

Kitty was frowning up in her perch. The Playground was the affectionate nickname for their R&D department, and she didn't welcome the reminder that someone else would get the first crack at testing the new hardware before her. Technically, her Shepherds Sport Model 8 had the same ammunition as the belt-fed machine gun her father carried, but .308 was a high-pressure load specifically designed for hunting rifles. However, Mohan was correct; fiend hide could be as tough as tank armour, and they had few soft points.

"We really should have planned for that," said Rizzo.

"No time," Mohan replied. "By the time we found out what was really going on here, we had to load up with whatever we could. Rizzo, when you finish up there, get back and spot for Kitty. Once we're in the hotel, I don't want either of you near the ground in case we really get in the shit."

Both parties acknowledged, and the line clicked off. Vince had started another story, which the tiger interrupted, "OK, keep it down. We're getting close to the last victim."

The huge tiger skirted the burnt-out shell of a small car and rounded the corner onto a narrower street. Most of the lights were broken, and the moon was too low on the horizon to cast its glow into the lane. There was barely any breeze, and the air in the alley was surprisingly stuffy.

Ahead, just where the street made a sharp bend to the right, lay a pool of light cast by a lone street lamp. Something lay propped against the well there.

Mohan could feel the itch return to his shoulder blades as they drew closer, and he snorted as the stench hit his nose. His ears flattened as much as they could with the radio earmuff and his hat, and he growled deep in his chest.

"Problem, Major General?" Vince asked, still cheerily playing codenames with his companions.

"Shut it, Vince. But yeah, the body's still here. In most of the reports, the victim was never found. Just…pieces." Mohan turned from the grisly scene and gulped fresh air. "Zed, what do you make of this, mate?"

The badger moved forward and knelt before the corpse, looking more at the spore around it than the body itself. Regarding tracking, Mohan always deferred to Zed's superior skill over his own modest abilities. The tiger was good, especially out in the bush, but what the Soketh could do was something close to magic.

"This is the one we heard screaming," Zed said, his brow furrowing over his coal-black eyes. "He cannot have been dead more than a few minutes. Though it is very strange, the blood on this wall is at least two days old—from a different kill entirely—yet the blood spatter on the ground and the tracks surrounding the corpse are fresh. This body was moved here recently. It is taunting us."

"Yeah," Vince said, looking up at the dark buildings surrounding them as if the creature might drop from the shadows at any moment. "Anyone else just a mite creeped out at how intelligent these things are? I mean, it's almost like they can get in your head and—"

Mohan clamped a massive paw over Vince's mouth and spoke into his radio. "Kitty, Rizzo, status."

"All quiet still," Rizzo reported, her voice much calmer now that she was perched next to Kitty, high above the cloistering shadows below.

Kitty confirmed the report, and Mohan turned to their medic. "What's your progno, Vicki?"

The bullfrog leaned over the corpse, being careful not to touch it. "Victim was vulpine, probably one of the local fox species. No spines or barbs—doesn't look like our creature used poison. Head is partially severed, and the chest cavity torn open from the left clavicle down to the right abdomen. There are three distinct claw marks and a fourth lighter tear on the anterior side, so the paw was likely larger than the torso. Large bite marks on the arms, legs, and part of the internal organs." Her voice was disturbingly matter-of-fact throughout the diagnosis. "Not a pretty sight, for sure."

"Is a mutilated corpse ever a pretty sight?" Kitty's voice crackled over the radio.

Vicki ignored her and continued. "Whatever it was, it was big! Probably grabbed him from behind. See the angle of these anterior lacerations? That indicates—"

Mohan held up a paw to stop her. "I think we get the picture, Vicki. Well, no barbs or poison rules out a chimera or nagai. Most of the attacks were near water, so we're probably dealing with an amphibian fiend. What do you think, Zed? Seahagin?"

"I do not believe so," the badger replied as he studied some nearby markings. "These prints indicate a creature with four legs, not two, and there are no drag marks from a tail. Furthermore, the toes are widely spaced and do not possess the webbing of an aquatic fiend. I would say the scale pattern resembles that of an ahuitzotl, yet it lacks the aforementioned toe webbing. It is also entirely too large."

As if on cue, a series of heavy coughs echoed through the streets, followed shortly by an eerie shriek.

Vince clutched his weapon tighter and stared cooly at the shadows above them. "That was not a weet-zol."

Mohan hefted his heavy machine gun, his face grim. "No. It's a tiamat."

"That fits the damage to the corpse," said Vicki. "But this far inside city limits? Not to mention half a globe from their normal stomping grounds?" She checked her 9mm, keenly aware of how pitiful it would be against the armoured scales of a tiamat.

"Well, that's why we were here, right?" asked Vince. "To see if that crimelord, Alabwaq, was rounding up fiends for his new gladiator arena?"

Mohan frowned. Assad Alabwaq—whose name meant "the Black Horns"—had become a major player in Pytan's underworld over the past several years. Most of his business centred around arms smuggling, gladiators, and the slave trading that accompanied the latter. Based on his psychological profile, Mohan suspected Alabwaq was searching for a new thrill in his arena. However, higher authorities within the Tiger's Stripe feared he meant to branch out, possibly into biological weapons, because, in addition to being highly destructive, many fiends were known to carry a deadly and incurable plague. Either way, both roads led to the monster they hunted.

"We don't know for sure yet," the tiger said. "Tiamats might be more popular in South Contéga, but we've found them elsewhere. And they love to swim; it might have just wandered upriver and crawled into the sewers. We can find out for sure after it's dead. Alabwaq would probably brand it if it's his, and if he's holding it here, we should search for a stockade. Tag this corpse for disposal; we don't want an infection spreading."

The radio crackled to life. "You heard that, *non*?" Rizzo asked, trying to mask the nervous click in her voice.

22

Kitty's response was far more enthusiastic. "Ace! I was getting bored shitless up here."

"Steady on," Mohan admonished. "Keep your knickers on; we still got another block to cross before we hit the water. Keep eyes in the back of your head."

The sniper and spotter acknowledged. Mohan rechecked his machine gun for what felt like the hundredth time. His team was waiting for him to give the order. Finally, he nodded and took the first step into the gloom.

2 – Hotel Nest

They had to navigate several narrow streets before reaching the canal's edge. Nothing moved save for the gentle bobbing of a few dilapidated fishing boats, abandoned long ago and left to collect barnacles. The buildings around them were dark, devoid of life after their occupants fled the waterfront. Two blocks away, the old hotel rose through a gathering fog.

It was once an elegant structure ten storeys tall—large for that district. The flowering chutes around the shattered dome roof and arches were a classic representation of the art deco style from the early fifties. Kairran had been a different place then, adopting customs from Locke and the West United Kingdoms. That is, until radical religious fanatics started another territory war, throwing the country back into poverty.

The fog lifted slightly as the team crept up on the hotel, revealing the remains of an outdoor café facing the canal. In its heyday, foreigners would have played bridge at the tables while listening to the dulcet tones of some local starlet singing on the outdoor stage. Now all that remained were the skeletons of wrought-iron tables and weathered paving stones.

Mohan held up a hand and brought the squad to a halt. A wall of twisted rubble blocked the path to the portico, save for a single opening barely large enough for the tiger. Another corpse lay spread across the threshold, this one a rodent.

The tiger inched forward, whiskers twitching, eyes trained on every shadow, until he crouched over the body.

Vince wrinkled his nose and whispered, "Anybody home? Looks like he left us a housewarmin' gift. Should really tell them rose petals are much more becomin'."

"Indeed," Zed said. The badger moved up next to Mohan and examined the barrier. "This was constructed recently, a defensive wall to protect the nest. From the stench, I sense we are very close; however, this is not the main entrance to the lair."

Mohan peered through the recess and could just make out the wall of shattered windows that had once lined the hotel's sunroom. The faint stench of rotting meat drifted from the inky blackness inside. His back began to itch; this was a bad place to be, and he could feel it.

"It's trying to lure us in," he said quietly. "We're in his territory now. What better place for an ambush?"

He turned back and examined the nearby structures. The tenement next door wasn't even half as tall, but one of the walls had collapsed outward and fallen against the hotel.

"Up there," Mohan said. "We might be able to get in through the upper floors. Everyone, stick close. Vince, you're rearguard; make sure he doesn't round on us."

The hare gave a mock salute. "Righto, sah! Say, you know it's a good thing this isn't the movies. Everyone knows the guy in the back always dies first. Like the movie they showed on the plane when we flew in—can't remember the name of it. I could tell right away that—"

Everyone chimed in to tell Vince to shut up.

Beneath the hotel, cloaked in dark and damp, a massive shape stirred.

It had been waiting in the shadows beneath the floor of the great cavern—or what its prey called the sunroom. But something was wrong. Its prey had not taken the bait it had set out for them.

It sensed something different about these intruders, a peculiar scent that sparked genetic memories of pain and fierce battle. This prey would not stumble into its trap like the others.

Their scent moved away, becoming obscured by other scents from the surrounding labyrinth. They were looking for another way in.

With swift and stealthy purpose, it slithered into the maze of tunnels that branched off from its lair. Though it could not express emotion, a peculiar thrill shuddered through its body. The thrill of the hunt.

The apartment building neighbouring the hotel wasn't in much better shape than the rest of the district. Half the stairs were missing, and the hunters wasted precious time searching for a way up. Eventually, they crossed the section of the wall that had fallen against the hotel and found themselves on the third floor.

Everything above them had rotted to the point that it was impossible to continue upwards; in several places, they could see straight up through the structure's skeleton to the night sky above. Going down proved just as hazardous, and they had to keep constant watch for weak floorboards lest they crash through all the way to the lobby. Aside from mouldering carpets and drapery, there was very little that looters hadn't taken long ago.

They found the first signs of their quarry on the second floor: scattered pools of old blood, deep claw marks in the floors, and gaping holes torn right through the walls. A mountain of debris blocked the main stairway. Apparently, the tiamat had tried to climb higher, only to find the rotten structure would not support its weight. The hunters made their way down a rear service stair into the kitchens.

The room had been stripped of everything that wasn't bolted down. A thick layer of dust lay over the counters and dented preparation tables. The doors hung limply off the cold ovens, giving them the appearance of wailing souls cursed to never again feel the warmth of life.

A faint path of Hom-An tracks—mostly rodents— led from the dining area to the rear entrance. It was the only disturbance in the dust, but so faint it was obvious they were weeks or perhaps months old—probably made before the apartment next door collapsed and blocked the side door.

The hunters moved through the room swiftly and silently. Even Vince had ceased his endless prattling in favour of the low, tuneless humming he always did when he was nervous.

The dry Pytian atmosphere had kept the dining room remarkably well preserved. There were bare patches in the mouldering carpet, and the wallpaper, with its sweeping art deco flutes, had peeled away from the plasterboard. Loose wiring on the walls showed where the ornate sconces had hung, most likely stripped off and sold for petty cash. Moth-eaten tablecloths still covered several tables, the flatware and utensils pilfered ages ago.

At the entrance to the dining area, a sign written in the squiggly characters of Netib—the local language— and a flowing Locken script announced several evening specials catered to a variety of species. It also introduced the evening's entertainment, provided by a local jazz trio. Mohan, Vince, and Zed each made a mental note to look up the band in the future; Vicki was far more interested in what 'beetle tabouli' tasted like.

The hotel lobby was a cavernous space open to the second floor, flanked by fluted pillars that flared out near the top in a shower of gilded fireworks. The floor was a maze of interlocking geometric shapes in bronze-and black marble. The main desk was also marble and stood opposite the dining hall—to the right of the main entrance. A weather-worn ledger still rested on the counter. Half the pages were missing, and the remaining ones were so faded that even the last entries were illegible. Amazingly, many of the room keys still hung on their rusted pegs, waiting patiently for guests who would never return.

Unfortunately, the passage of the fiend had marred the lobby's grandeur. Deep scratches from heavy clawed feet scored the floor tiles. A small seating area sat between the dining room and the main entrance, which some local vagrants had converted into living space. They didn't need Zed or Vicki to tell them what had happened to the former occupants; the entire area was soaked in old blood.

A broken caged elevator at the back of the lobby rose, twisted and useless, into the darkness of the floors above. The staircase wrapped around the shaft showed signs of continued use and repair and the same heavy claw marks as the floor tiles. The damage caused by the tiamat's rampage completely blocked the upper floors.

The radio crackled in Mohan's ear. "Peekaboo," Kitty said mockingly. "You should be happy I'm on your side." Obviously, she could see them through her rifle scope.

Mohan looked out the glassless door and made a face. He searched the profile of the rooftops across the way, but despite knowing Kitty's general location, the tiger couldn't pinpoint her exact position. He allowed himself a small sense of pride, knowing that if he couldn't spot her, no one else would. Until it was too late, of course.

Vince leaned back and gazed at the faded mural on the lobby ceiling. "Ya know, this was probably a nice place in its day."

"If only walls could talk, huh?" Vicki said, mirroring his interest in the old structure.

Zed was carefully observing the refuse of the seating area. "These signs are many weeks old, but I believe the residents of this structure were more than squatters. They had a firm establishment in this building before the tiamat arrived."

"A local gang?" Vicki suggested.

The badger nodded. "That is my assumption. The tiamat likely saw them as the greatest threat and established dominance by claiming their territory. Now that it has taken up residence, it is testing its boundaries."

"Is it just one?" Mohan asked.

The badger shook his head. "I am uncertain. If there is a mate, it has not ventured outside the nest."

"Close to the young," Vicki said soberly.

"Perhaps," Zed said. "However, a tiamat will secure its territory before laying a clutch."

Mohan nodded. The blood and ruin throughout the rest of the hotel were exactly what he had expected to find, but they would need to move fast to prevent the fiend from making any more of them.

The only rooms left unexplored were the laundry and the sunroom, located towards the hotel's waterfront. Unfortunately, both entrances were also blocked by debris.

"It looks like the only way in is from the side street or underground," the tiger said. "The street is more accessible, but I'll be damned if we walk right through the front door. There's got to be a basement entrance around here somewhere."

Vince was leaning over the main desk when he spotted a glint near the elevator. "How about back there?" he asked, heading for the alcove.

A heavy metal door secured with a stainless-steel chain blocked their path. Vince examined both carefully.

"Now this is interestin'," he said, rubbing at his goatee. "This lock is new—well, relatively speaking. I'm

31

guessin' it hasn't been touched in a couple weeks, but a Gatemaster Nine Forty is a pretty heavy lock for this part of town. Somebody didn't want the locals getting into the basement."

"There's a pretty active black market in the next district," said Vicki. "Maybe the local gang was working it, and they keep their stash in the basement. Can you break it?"

Vince held up the open lock and chain, giving a slight bow as he stashed a set of lock picks back in a harness pouch. "Already done, darlin'. Like I said, tough security for squatters, but it's a pretty common item at your local locksmith. Shall we have a peek inside?"

Mohan smirked and motioned to the blackness ahead with his machine gun. "You're the one showing off, mate. You play tour guide."

Vince gave a resigned shrug and hopped into the darkness. He tried the light switch out of habit but wasn't surprised when it didn't work and whipped an electric torch from his belt.

"Watch your step," he called behind him. "Looks kind of damp near the bottom."

The faint drip of water became steadily louder as they crept into the hotel basement. The stairwell ended in a long, low room with many arched tunnels leading off in every direction. A good five centimetres of water covered the floor, and a steady gurgle came from somewhere in the distance. The air was heavy with the stench of mould, decay, and rotting flesh.

Even with the beams of four powerful torches, it was difficult to see in the gloom. They saw stacks of old hotel goods piled alongside newer boxes containing electronics, imported clothing, video equipment, and various entertainment media with cheaply printed labels.

Clearly the most comfortable in the damp surroundings, Vicki splashed boldly up to a nearby pile of merchandise.

"Yup, looks like the gang was doing a bit of smuggling," she said, patting one of the black-market stereos. "Must be small-timers with this type of loot. You wouldn't find Alabwaq or Mody Nahas storing their goods in an old seedy hotel."

Vince shook out a wet foot. "Somethin' tells me it's supposed to be a mite drier, though."

Zed examined the tunnels branching off the main room, his nose quivering at the end of his striped snout. He paused at a point along the northern wall.

"This tunnel leads straight to the canal," he said. "The smugglers must unload their goods at the other end and store them here. The scent carries for some distance down here, but the canal tunnel is wide enough for a tiamat; I believe the others are too narrow to permit the creature's passage."

Mohan nodded. "The narrow tunnels probably go all the way to the market next door. Their size is probably the only thing that's kept the fiend here: the older tunnels are easier to move through."

Vince leaned against a pillar to shake out his feet again, and it shuddered slightly under his weight. A faint groan came from the building above.

"Well, that doesn't sound good," the hare said.

"Yeah," Vicki muttered as she peered at the rotted roots of the structure, "we better make this quick; this place looks about ready to collapse."

"Right," Mohan growled, "nobody touch anything, or we'll bring this whole bloody place down on top of us."

"This way," said Zed. "I believe I have picked up the trail."

The badger led them down a short hall that ended in another large room. The shelving was more haphazard and broken, interspersed with the rusting hulks of industrial washing machines. The upper floor had collapsed to create a crude ramp into darkness, a steady stream of water cascading down it like a waterfall. Zed shifted his light upwards.

"We're under the laundry room," he said. "The tiamat must have broken through here and fractured the main water line."

Vicki pushed against one of the washing machines, but it wouldn't budge. "I'm surprised there was still water running in this place," she said.

Vince was about to reply when the coughing shriek they had heard in the alley drifted down to them from the blackness above. Zed backed away quickly, levelling his carbine at the head of the ramp.

Mohan growled deep in his chest. "Clever bugger! The sunroom above is the lair, all right, but this basement might as well be its front porch." He braced himself against a pillar and levelled the machine gun at the ramp. "Best not be rude; let's give 'em our own housewarming gift."

3 - Tiamat

In the depths of an abandoned residence, a shadow separated itself from the darkness and slithered into the street. The other had moved and now lurked in the shadows of the hotel entrance.

The air had shifted again. The prey had breached the lair.

It sent silent signals to the other. This prey must not escape; the time was near, and more food would be needed if they were to produce young.

A new urgency sparked its movement. It must act quickly to close the net. It coughed the call for the hunt, and the other replied.

They would feast. They would survive.

Up on the roof, Kitty tensed as a massive form separated itself from the shadows across the intersection from the hotel lobby. It was so large she had mistaken it for the remains of one of the dilapidated cars until it moved.

Rizzo whispered next to her, "Do you see that?"

Kitty didn't answer as she scanned the heavy shape through her scope. Over many long years, Tiger's Stripe had catalogued over a dozen base types of fiends, but new species were starting to evolve from those foundations. The tiamat was one such hybrid, a larger cousin of the ahuitzotl found in the jungles of South Contéga.

This specimen was at least eight metres from head to tail. The head was broad and angular, with four bright gold eyes, each possessing two verticle pupils set under bony brows. Rows of short horns lined the jaw and crest of the skull, but its mouth was the most terrifying feature. A membrane of ochre skin pulled back to reveal four great tusks, curved inward like the mandibles of a spider, protruding from either side of a cavernous maw lined with so many razor-sharp teeth they looked like the baleen of a whale. The tusks wiggled independently of one another, and it was easy to guess that their primary use was grasping prey and dragging it into the hideous mouth.

The body that supported this head was equally hideous. Two ridges of serrated bone ran down its back on either side of the spinal column, ending at a thick short, tail with another segmented bone ridge on the horizontal axis. Its appearance was reminiscent of a sword, and it was equally as effective. Four sinuous legs supported its barrel-like body. Each ended in a five-fingered lizard-like hand tipped with claws fifteen centimetres long; as Zed had observed earlier, there was no webbing between the toes. Mottled greenish-brown scales with a peculiar diamond shape covered its thick hide. The skin pulled tight against bones and muscle, the thick muscles on its legs even seeming to protrude through the skin like dull red blisters. It gave the creature a sickly emaciated appearance that belied the incredible strength in its limbs. Initially, it was thought that the exposed muscle resulted from disease and may be a possible weakness, but they proved just as tough as the scaly hide.

This was the first time Kitty had seen a fiend in the field, and she was thankful to do it through the scope of her rifle. There was something unwholesome and alien about the creature, a sense that it didn't belong. It made her chest and left arm itch, and she could not repress a slight shudder of horror.

Even with its great bulk, the tiamat moved with swift and stealthy purpose towards the hotel.

"On the left," Rizzo called out.

A slightly smaller tiamat appeared from Kitty's blind spot, also headed for the hotel. They seemed to pause in the intersection, their heads swaying back and forth, almost as if they were discussing their next move; the conflicting signals in the air currents confused them.

Eventually, the larger of the two slunk around behind the hotel, heading for the sunroom entrance. The smaller beast cautiously poked its head into the lobby, where the scent of its prey was stronger, but it was uncertain how to proceed.

The first beast was out of sight before Kitty reacted. She fired two rounds in quick succession, the first severing an electrical wire overhanging the street and the second driving into the monster's back above the shoulder.

The high-powered round made the creature grunt and turn towards the alley, making it hesitate long enough for the wire to slap against its hide. Unfortunately, the wire was dead and slid off to the side without even a spark.

"Shit!" the tigress muttered and clicked on her radio. "Mohan! Get out of there! You hear me? Get out! There's two of them. I'm trying to pull one off, but it's being stubborn. The other is coming your way from the canal side. I don't have a shot!"

She slammed two more rounds into the back and shoulders of the tiamat, and it screeched in annoyance. She didn't want to admit it, but her father was right: against the armoured hide, her .308 might as well be a pointed stick. They needed a way to weaken the creature.

"Rizzo," she said calmly, "get down there and see what you can do to bring it this way."

"Are you crazy?"

"We have a surprise waiting for it, don't we?"

The basilisk got a wicked gleam in her eye. "*Oui*! I'll see what I can do."

As the sniper and demolitionist prepared to face the smaller tiamat outside, its mate cautiously sensed the air inside the hotel sunroom. The room was pungent with the stench of previous kills, but the intruders still lay somewhere beyond its reach.

The sunroom was once an opulent space, walled on two sides by floor-to-ceiling windows. The glass had long since shattered and been spread almost evenly across the area. The floor in the centre had collapsed, creating a bowl in one of the utility rooms beneath the hotel. It was here that the fiends brought their prey, and it was evident from the number of remains that many more had fallen victim to the fiends than were initially reported. In the far wall, a ragged hole led into the room beyond—the laundry room.

The hunters crouch in the darkness at the bottom of the ramp leading to the sunroom. Faintly, they heard the crack of a high-powered rifle, followed a moment later by a garbled transmission.

"Moh..of there! Do..ear me? Get out!...two of them!"

Mohan placed a hand over his ear, worried that the transmission might be overheard by the creature lurking in the next room.

Bits of rubble tumbled down the ramp, followed by a deep-throated growl.

The tiger reached into a pouch and produced a small black disc the size of a hockey puck. He tossed it up the ramp with one powerful underhand swing and whispered, "Brace, everyone! Vince, Zed, frag it!"

The hare and the badger each lobbed a grenade into the darkness above and sought cover behind nearby crates. Mohan's flash device went off first, and he hoped it would stun the creature long enough to let the grenades finish the job. The explosion silhouetted a massive form in the room above, and the creature shrieked in pain and fury. A violent shudder shook the cellar, and another section of floor collapsed. The beast vanished in a cloud of dust and debris.

Rizzo crept towards the intersection, using the abandoned vehicles as cover.

Less than ten metres from the monstrous creature, she paused behind a burnt-out economy car and took several deep breaths. She told herself this was no different from fighting royalist nationals in her distant homeland, as she had many years ago. With a muttered curse, she quickly dismissed that comparison as stupid.

A muffled explosion rumbled from the hotel, and the fiend turned towards it in confusion. Rizzo saw her window and rose, pumping several rounds into the thick hide.

The tiamat screeched in fury and swiped at the car with a massive foreleg, throwing the rusted hulk halfway across the street. Steeling herself against the approaching nightmare, Rizzo unloaded three more shells into the head and shoulders of the beast as she backed towards the alley. Ragged chunks of flesh tore away and began to ooze oily orange fiend blood, but overall, the shotgun was as ineffective as Kitty's rifle had been.

The membrane covering the beast's mouth slid back as it spread its tusks wide to screech at her. Its teeth parted, and a thick forked tongue lashed out, snapping at the air mere centimetres from Rizzo's face. She lept to the side, avoiding the spray of hot, sticky saliva as best she could.

Disgusted though she was, she fought trembling hands as she reached into her pouch to grab a grenade. Her throw was off, and the projectile bounced harmlessly off the creature's head, rolling down the street towards the hotel. The explosion that followed momentarily distracted the tiamat, and Rizzo wasted no time using the window to get further down the alley.

Vicki covered her mouth to stifle a cough and croaked, "Did we get it?"

Mohan peered into the fog of debris, the dust stinging his eyes. "Hard to tell. Zed, check it out. On your toes, mate."

Zed nodded and crept up the ramp. The floor's collapse had altered the stream from the broken water main, and now a fine mist obscured the air before him. He heard the thunder of Rizzo's shotgun somewhere outside and breathed a silent prayer to Mbektar to protect his teammates.

Suddenly, another explosion rocked the building from outside, and part of the outer wall collapsed inward. In the faint glow of exterior light, the badger caught the gleam of weathered bone and oily orange blood on a massive form only four metres away from him. Four alien eyes blinked into focus. A deep growl rumbled from the shadow.

Zed dived to the side as the tiamat lunged towards him; he could feel its fetid breath against his fur as its claws raked the air centimetres away from his head. It crashed into a shelf of old hotel supplies in the basement below, starting a domino effect that led all the way to the back wall.

Before the beast could recover, Mohan opened up with his assault weapon. The heavy 7.62mm rounds tore into the tough hide, but it only made the creature even madder. Vince and Zed added their own firepower, but they had little effect.

Vicki cowered behind one of the industrial washers, watching helplessly as the creature shook off the initial barrage and sought cover behind the other heavy machines on the far side of the room. It was trying to find a way to reach its prey and avoid the punishing onslaught of the machine gun. If Mohan reached the end of his ammo box, she, Vince, and Zed could do very little to keep the creature at bay while he reloaded.

The bullfrog blinked as a speck of dust fell into her eye, and she remembered the support pillar Vince had leaned against earlier. Her brain went to work, recalling long-winded handyman conversations with her father and too many *MacTavish* reruns. She picked out all the load-bearing supports in the room and connected them with the structure above them. In a few fractions of a second, she had an idea.

"The support beams!" She fired a few rounds from her pistol into the nearest one to give Mohan the idea. "Blast out the support beams and run!"

The tiger caught on quickly and redirected his machine gun's superior firepower towards the pillars, tearing several of the beams to shreds in seconds.

The tiamat paused as a heavy groaning echoed from the hotel above. With a great chorus of snapping and creaking, the structure above began to collapse.

Suddenly aware that something had gone horribly wrong, the creature attempted to leap away from its doom, only to be impaled through the skull as a heavy I-beam came crashing down upon it.

Vince opened his mouth to deliver a quip about the creature's demise when more creaking from the hotel above cut him off.

Vicki was already scrambling up the ramp into the sunroom. "Like I said. Run!"

Rizzo ducked as the tiamat sent the remains of a broken scooter hurtling over her head. Kitty kept unloading volley after volley with the .308, but the high-powered rounds ricocheted harmlessly off the creature's thick skull.

"Reloading," Kitty said over the radio, her voice deceptively calm.

"Even these damn slugs aren't doing anything," Rizzo mumbled as she nearly tripped over a dustbin.

"Just a little further," the sniper encouraged.

Rizzo was getting the uncomfortable feeling the creature was toying with her. The beast hadn't charged her yet, and it seemed to purposefully maintain a five-metre gap between them. She prayed silently that the creature would keep the pace up just a few more metres.

A deep rumble shook the ground beneath them. Across the street, the hotel began to collapse.

The tiamat twisted around, suddenly concerned for its mate. There were barely ten metres left before it would be in range of Rizzo's explosive trap; she couldn't let it turn back now.

The basilisk cursed under her breath and plucked a second grenade from her pouch. Her hands were much steadier this time, and with an expert toss, she rolled it right under the creature's front legs. She emptied the last two slugs from her shotgun into its head to distract it.

The explosion blew the creature off its feet and right towards her, sending her scrambling to an alcove for cover. The blast tore several ragged chunks out of the beast's thick hide, and oily orange blood spattered the ground beneath it.

But the tiamat was still standing. It was stunned for only a moment before it let loose a furious bellow and charged forward, noxious orange blood streaming from the shrapnel wounds. The ropey tongue lashed out again, but Rizzo was already on the move and dodged it easily.

"*Merde! Merde!*" she muttered over and over again as she ran headlong down the alley towards the base of the building. Kitty waited patiently above, a fresh magazine ready.

Rizzo prepared the detonator as she plastered herself against the wall and called up to the sniper, "Fire in the hole!"

The thunderous thump of the shaped charges drowned out the tiamat's roar, and a thick cloud of debris clogged the alley. Rizzo shielded her eyes and coughed against the dust.

Slowly, the haze cleared. The creature was no longer standing. The blast had crushed one side of the skull and tore the chest cavity open on the opposite side. A lumpy mass of colourful internal organs and offal spilt into the alley. One leg was missing above the elbow, and the tail nearly severed from its base.

Rizzo crept towards it while reloading her shotgun. At less than a metre away, the tiamat gave a final shuddering lunge towards her. The basilisk toppled backwards over a trashcan, spewing a string of curses in Marisian while Kitty finished the creature off with a final rifle round through its fractured skull.

With a choked gasp, the creature shuddered and lay still. Whether it had been alive in that final lunge or the movement was just a muscle reaction, the tiamat was certainly dead now.

Rizzo stumbled to her feet and spat on the beast's corpse. "*Fils de salope!*" she swore, following up with a very rude gesture.

Mohan, Vicki, Vince, and Zed scrambled over the edge of the ramp and spared barely a moment to orient themselves in the sunroom. Rizzo's wayward grenade toss proved their salvation because the new hole in the wall was their closest exit. They dashed frantically towards the opening, dodging shards of plaster and ceiling as the building collapsed around them.

As soon as they entered the street, they dived behind the wreck of an abandoned vehicle. A great cloud of dirt choked the air as the old hotel came to its end.

As the dust settled, they made a quick headcount to ensure everyone was accounted for and brushed themselves off.

Vince shook out his ears and blew the dirt off his hat. "Well, I declare that was quite a soirée. I think there's goin' to be some smugglers that are just a mite upset in the mornin'."

"Nope," Vicki said. "I think they got eaten."

The hare frowned. "Well, that's gruesome."

"Come on," Mohan said. "Time to regroup."

They found Rizzo and Kitty in the alley near the corpse of the smaller tiamat. Upon seeing the orange gore spattered everywhere, Vicki immediately busied herself preparing six syringes filled with bluish liquid. They had taken a dose of the medicinal cocktail earlier as a precaution, but a booster wouldn't hurt in such close proximity to the creature's toxic blood.

"Bloody hell, Rizzo," Mohan said, scratching under the brim of his hat. "Did you leave anything?"

The basilisk shot the tiger an indignant look and accepted a syringe from Vicki. After passing out the booster, Vicki examined the creature's remains.

"Difficult to tell," the frog said, "but I don't see any kind of branding on this thing. There's some vegetation caught in the claws, bits of river grass. Looks like it crawled in from the canal just like you said, Mo."

Zed also examined the creature. "This beast is several seasons old. Alabwaq would have faced great difficulty attempting to capture an adult, let alone contain it. I do not think he is responsible for its presence here."

Mohan frowned. "Bugger. No time to dig up the other one, but I feel safe betting it was also wild. Fortunately, I didn't see any eggs or young."

"Nor did I," Zed agreed. "However, based on the number of corpses they had gathered, I believe they were close to clutching."

"We'll make a sweep of the tunnels just to be safe," the tiger continued. "Maybe Caz can dig up some reports on any missing water traffic, see if we can find out where it came from. Beyond that, all we can do is wait for Alabwaq's auction in a few days. Hopefully, our intel boys will have narrowed down his real identity by then."

He turned back to the monster's corpse. "Let's wrap this up. Locals will be all over this site any minute. A ruckus like this is bound to draw attention, monsters or not. Vicki, snap some pictures for further study. Rizzo, well, you know what to do when she's done. PR will have to deal with the second one." He glanced at the ruin of the hotel. "Assuming they even bother digging it out."

Vicki pulled out protective gloves and smocks for everyone from her massive bag, and they carefully gathered what bits and pieces of shredded monster lay nearby. Once they were placed in a neat pile around the fiend's corpse, Rizzo rigged a special incendiary charge to dispose of the remains.

Despite Mohan's warning, it was almost half an hour before the sound of approaching sirens reached their ears. Rizzo set off her charge, and the Scrappers slipped back into the shadows, accompanied by the stench of burning monster.

Their departure was not silent, however. Vince reverted to his usual chatty self again, embellishing a story about how burning fiend somehow reminded him of a beach party in college. There was a shark selling fried clams where he happened to meet a lovely young harbour seal and her sorority sisters.

4 – Investigation

The following morning found the site teaming with local police, rescue services, civic engineers, and occupants of the devastated slums who had summoned enough courage to return home.

Clean-up of the site was practically nonexistent. The rescue services were only there to provide a token response. The civic engineers—mostly foreign contractors—were there to survey property they wanted to demolish anyway. And the police were there to hold off looters, as if there was anything left worth looting.

Between them all, it was clear none felt like performing the assigned duties. After all, Khamir was still a slum.

Unbeknownst to the local officials, several of the workers present were actually agents of Pytan's *Walaeyn Aldhabiah*—the Golden Eye—a clandestine organisation contracted by yet another clandestine organisation to handle just this type of situation.

They had arrived on the scene with the first responders, focusing their attention on a pile of white ash in a nearby alley and the collapsed remains of an abandoned hotel, which had mysteriously caught fire sometime in the night. With that task complete, their primary goal was now to cause as much bureaucratic red tape as possible.

It started with rolling in a few cranes and other heavy equipment while dropping hints to the engineers that it might be a good time to start a revitalisation project in the district. Then, suggestions were made to the rescue services that there may be survivors beneath the rubble, and they needed the equipment to dig them out. Finally, someone tipped off the police that the engineers didn't have the proper permits to use the equipment for any work one way or the other.

The result was a delightful mess that hindered the site's clean-up and confused the press.

Currently, an irate police commandant of the genus Camelus was busily arguing with a trio of figures: a jaguar from the West United Kingdoms who represented the foreign contractors, a lynx journalist with shaggy dirty-blond long-fur, and the journalist's vulpine photographer, who looked decidedly uncomfortable with the situation even though he never seemed to stop taking pictures.

"I don't care if you're documenting the historical value of lice in modern society," the dromedary commandant argued with the lynx, speaking in the precise rolling tones of Netib. "This is clearly a hazardous area, and no unauthorised personnel are allowed in. That goes double for the press!"

"I beg your pardon, sir, but the entire Khamir District is a hazardous area," the journalist continued, undaunted, pen and notepad firmly in hand. His Netib was good, but he had a distinct trace of a clipped Locke accent. "Haven't your own local newspapers reported that the Khamir District was, and possibly still is, suffering a string of grisly murders?"

"Speakin' of unauthorised," the jaguar foreman cut in, his voice marred by the lazy drawl of a southern WUK accent, "I swear we had all the paperwork signed and ready this mornin'. We got three hundred tons of debris to clean up here, and your guys are tellin' me my people can't move an inch!"

"All I know is that I have seen no such authorisation since I arrived on scene," the dromedary huffed angrily.

"Sir," the lynx addressed the jaguar, "Sedric Barnes, *LBC World Press*. What can you tell us about the state of the Khamir District? Are you concerned for the safety of your workers, especially considering the rumours that the murderer is some nightmarish monster and not a Hom-An serial killer?"

"That is pure conjecture!" the commandant interrupted.

The jaguar foreman held up a hand. "I'm just trying to get some work done here. No Comment."

"You heard the man," the commandant growled. "No comment! Now remove yourself from the premises or I will have you removed by force!" The dromedary turned on his heel and huffed off towards the far end of the site, his hump bobbing slightly beneath his green uniform shirt.

The jaguar followed in his wake, continuing to argue about his work permits, but he scratched at the back of his neck and spared a curious glance at the lynx.

"Well, that went swimmingly, Ric," the photographer said in the same clipped accent as the journalist. He focused the expensive-looking 35mm camera on the retreating foreman and commandant and snapped several shots.

Ric sighed. He hated using the pushy reporter tactics common among his fellows, but sometimes, there was no other way to get a question in. Your average person may give a less guarded answer under stress, but they are also more likely to blurt out unverified conjecture.

"I know there's something going on here, Ed," Ric replied, switching to his native Locken. He scratched the shirt sleeve covering his wrist. "I'm getting that tingle again."

Ed Sanders frowned and continued shooting.

Their original assignment in Pytan was to investigate rumours that the barbaric gladiatorial games and slave trading still persisted despite the platitudes of Sultan Abdülkadír. So far, Ric had learned that the Sultan, though a kind equine by nature, was a bit too trusting of some of his ministers. The trail quickly led the journalist down into the country's criminal under-world, where the name Assad Alabwaq was everywhere.

Then Ric heard the rumours about the gruesome murders in the Khamir District and that Alabwaq sought the creature responsible — the same rumours that had drawn six hunters to the district last night.

Ric spoke absently to his partner. "The local papers have been going on for weeks about a terrible beast lurking through the slums, killing indiscriminately. The locals we interviewed this morning swear they saw a group of heavily armed foreigners heading for the waterfront late last night. Several explosions and devastated buildings later, all the local officials act like it was just a tremor, a natural disaster."

Ed ran a hand over his spikey black long-fur and looked around them. "Well, it is a disaster, Ric."

The journalist ignored the remark; he'd known the fox too long to take any lip from him. With a quick glance, Ric noticed the commandant was still busy arguing with the foreman and had been joined by several construction workers. Their conversation was heated, but the lynx doubted it would come to blows.

Seeing no one was watching, Ric ducked under the yellow tape blocking off the entrance to an alleyway. Having worked with the journalist for too long to try and stop him, Ed merely rolled his eyes and followed.

Donning some discarded hard hats from a utility truck, they moved further into the alley. For some strange reason, this section was the least populated.

Ric stopped at a prominent mark in the centre of the alley. The crews had swept most of the white ash and carelessly dumped it into a large dustbin. A fire hose was used to wash the rest away, but a large white mark with black edges still marred the concrete. He studied it a moment, taking in the amorphous shape and trying to make sense of what might have been burned there. He knelt down and scratched at it with a finger claw. Flecks of white residue came off, and he sniffed at the substance.

"This wasn't any normal fire," he said. "We covered this stuff in the Academy. It's white-phosphorus residue, military-grade stuff. But to have it concentrate in such a localised area? Somebody wanted to burn something quick, and without damaging the local buildings."

"Something like what?" Ed asked. "Your monster?"

Ric stood slowly. "Maybe. Look, Ed, you weren't with me in Barju, but I know what I saw. If Alabwaq is still trying to get a hold of one of these things, and one of them was here…" He paused. "What if one of them could get back to Locke?"

The fox shifted uncomfortably. "Look, Ric, I want to believe you, but we've really gone a far step off of slave trading. And if all this damage is any indication, it looks like someone already killed the thing. So there's nothing to worry about, right?"

The lynx turned and examined the buildings nearby. On one wall, a three-metre blackened semicircle framed by shattered chips of stucco marked the outline of an explosion.

"Are you sure about that? Look at this. No fire, only minor collateral damage. This blast was directed into the alley at this spot."

Ed continued snapping pictures. "And?" he asked, trying to feign boredom.

Ric thought for a moment. "This trap was set by professionals. They lured it down the alley, away from the hotel, and blew it up. Then they cleaned up the mess with a military-grade incendiary."

The photographer reached the end of his roll and started winding it up. "All right, but who are 'they'?"

The journalist moved over to the opposite wall. The blast had pushed loose stones, trash, and similar detritus into the corners. There were bullet holes all over the wall, which wasn't exactly strange for the Khamir District. Something glinted in the dirt, and Ric picked it up, holding it between thumb and forefinger. It was a heavy-calibre bullet, smushed and deformed after impact.

"I don't know," he said, "but I really want to find out."

On the other side of the scene, another figure was making his own assessment of the situation.

The well-dressed dromedary made several inquiries of the workers, but they all gave him the same vague answers. Finally, he pulled a bulky cellular phone from a deep pocket of his gold-trimmed thawb.

"Yes?" the high-pitched but unmistakably masculine voice answered in Netib.

"Rashid here, sir. Both animals have been destroyed. I'm afraid someone else got to the site before our capture team."

"That is unfortunate. I had hoped to supplement the stock that we already have en route. I hope those specimens will prove adequate for our presentation. Were you able to find any information on the other party?"

"No, sir. The locals claim six foreigners entered the district around midnight last night, but the details were vague and smelled of old hashish, if you take my meaning, sir."

"Drunken fools," the voice on the phone spat. "But without them, I wouldn't be in business. Was there any possibility it may have been a competitor?"

"I do not believe so, sir. None of Nahas or Weis's operatives were in the area."

"Very well, you're done there." The line went dead.

The dromedary dropped the phone back into its pocket, wrapped his fashionable robes around him, and melted back into the growing crowd of gawkers. He didn't see the female basilisk and bullfrog slipping cautiously behind one of the canal-side buildings, where they subsequently vanished into the tunnels beneath the Khamir District.

5 – The Market

Three days after their midnight raid, the Scrappers huddled in a white transport lorry swerving slowly through the cobbled streets of the Dahley market. The blue and gold markings on its sides read "Kaulsk Shipping Co."

Even this late in the winter month of Ferrus, the noonday heat had climbed to thirty-two degrees Celcius. The locals considered the weather pleasant, as was evident by the throngs of people crowding the streets.

Druna, the day moon, hung its pale-orange face high in the eastern sky. It was always opposite its nocturnal cousin, the pale-green Midori, and it lagged behind and slightly to the right of Fos, Amarthia's sun.

The search of the sewers beneath the Khamir District had turned up nothing but the corpses of the tiamats' first victims. Other agents were still sorting reports of missing vessels, but all signs pointed to the creatures having wandered into the area on their own, although from where was still a mystery. The Hutsepth Canal was heavily trafficked, and until recently, the fiend creatures tended to avoid the larger cities.

However, some good news had come their way: their intelligence teams had narrowed the list of possible identities for Assad Alabwaq. Their goal today would be to confirm that identity by attending his latest auction.

Rizzo sat behind the wheel, with Kitty riding shotgun. The rest of the team was crammed into the rear compartment along with racks of various field equipment. Mohan, who took up the most space, sat on the floor near the rear door. He proved surprisingly adept at maintaining his balance without the handholds, and he leaned into each turn as the basilisk swerved through the streets.

The lorry's horn blared yet again as Rizzo narrowly avoided a pair of tourists purchasing some local garments along the roadside. Most people in the region lived within walking distance of the basic necessities and didn't need to travel far in their day-to-day lives. Consequently, there were few automobiles in Pytan and even fewer traffic laws. But there was an abundant number of small scooters. Few were newer than ten years old, and they zipped carelessly in and out of the throngs of pedestrian traffic. One would often zoom in front of the lorry and its irate green-scaled driver.

"Steady there, Speedy," Vince said, grabbing at a handle in the back. "The exhibition doesn't start for another half hour."

"And we need to get Vicki and Zed in place before then, *non*?" Rizzo said.

She braked hard again and sent a vendor diving under his counter of live aukies. The bird-like feathered lizards squawked in terror, and their jackal proprietor shook his fist in anger.

Rizzo leaned out the window and slapped the side of the lorry, shouting a string of curses at him in Marisian. The jackal didn't understand a word of it but responded in kind in his own language. Fortunately, this was standard behaviour for most drivers in the Kairran markets, so nobody around them even noticed.

"The warehouse is only a couple blocks away," Mohan said. "We'll be fine. You aren't driving the Gran Prix anymore."

Rizzo gave an exasperated sigh and slowed to a more reasonable speed, batting at the Buru'Nadi prayer beads hanging on the rear-view mirror. She was not particularly religious, but they were a memento of her father, and she insisted they brought her luck whenever she was behind the wheel.

"Now," the big tiger continued, "everyone remember the game plan for today? This op is strictly observation-only. At this point, we're ninety per cent certain our friend Alabwaq is the alias of one Jirair al-

62

Seif, a local business tycoon. Alabwaq has been one crafty bastard, and we've never gotten any pictures of him. In fact, it came as a surprise when we heard he would make an appearance at the gladiator auction this arvo." His companions knew this was Plainsman slang for afternoon.

"Vicki and Zed are going to scout out al-Seif's warehouse and see if they can make the connection there. The warehouse has undergone some recent construction, which coincides with our intel that Alabwaq wanted to build a new arena here in Pytan. I can't think of a better way to cover up a project like that. Meanwhile, the rest of us will take a peek at the exhibition and see if he really is going to show."

Repeated mentions of the exhibition brought more than a few expressions of disgust from everyone in the lorry. Despite the advancement of civilisation, there were still remnants of the blood-and-glory impulses that had shaped Amarthia's ancient past. A natural bloodlust still flowed in the veins of most Hom-Ans, and the desire to assert dominance was an instinct not easily overcome. The most common outlet was gladiatorial combat—a series of violent and brutal contests that were not viewed favourably by more "civilised" nations. Their behaviour bordered on the feral, and indeed, constant exposure to that base animal bloodlust had driven many to become ferals, the very lowest of Amarthia's outcasts.

Moreover, the exhibitions often went hand in hand with slave trading, a practice that was even less tolerated. For that reason alone, most governments had banned the games altogether, making the negative stance on gladiatorial combat one of the few issues most nations could agree on.

Mohan mirrored his team's disgust on the subject and continued. "I know we all want to string this bastard up by his balls just for that, but he's complicated matters. Even though we didn't find anything in Khamir, there are still concerns that Alabwaq wants to use fiends in his games. That's what we really need to look for today. We need to know where and how he intends to use them, if he has them already, and, more importantly, who his suppliers might be. The chances are pretty good he'll show his hand at today's festivities, and we're bloody lucky he's still going through with it. After what happened in Khamir, he's got to know there's somebody monster hunting in his backyard. Any questions?"

There were none; Mohan only repeated what they had already gone over that morning at their safe house. They might not have spotted Alabwaq himself yet, but they had his operations under observation for almost six months. Even if they couldn't get him to reveal he was trafficking fiends, they'd uncovered a string of arms deals and drug trafficking that should put him away for a good long while.

Assuming anyone is willing to try him in court, the tiger thought darkly.

Sultan Abdülkadír was a fair ruler but remarkably naïve. He had unwittingly stuffed his cabinet with a host of corrupt figureheads, many of whom had ties to Alabwaq or one of the other Pytian crime lords. There would be no justice carried out in that part of the world.

However, there was no world court or league of allied nations to indict international criminals. Many countries would extradite foreign criminals if caught, but they still preferred to keep to themselves. The law of the land remained the law of *that* land, and as far as most nations were concerned, their neighbours' troubles were their own. Assad Alabwaq would only be prosecuted overseas if he had violated the law on foreign soil.

There was one slim chance. If they could prove that Assad Alabwaq was Jirair al-Seif, they would have a greater foundation to work on. Al-Seif had expanded his business ventures into Medocci, on the northern continent of Aerenia, and had married Yursa De Palma, daughter of shipping magnate Vigo De Palma. It was suspected, but unproven, that De Palma was the top player in the Medoccian mafia. Tiger's Stripe assumed al-Seif was well aware of this; however, his holdings in the region remained tenuous and all perfectly legal. Still, if they could link him to any illicit trading overseas combined with De Palma's suspected ties to the mafia, al-Seif's nefarious dealings might come back to haunt him.

On the other hand, his alter ego, Alabwaq, had made many enemies; some would just as soon put a bullet through his head.

Mohan honestly hoped it wouldn't come to that. Despite their tendency towards isolation, he still believed, as did the Tiger's Stripe, that the world's nations could dispense justice on their own. The world was perfectly capable of balancing itself out, and the ultimate goal of Tiger's Stripe was to ensure no one intentionally tipped the scales one way or the other.

The tiger's train of thought broke as the lorry lurched around a final corner, and the waters of the Hutsepth Canal appeared on their left. Ahead, a series of storage warehouses lined the water's edge. The sprawling Port of Kairran, further west, handled the larger international freighters and cruise ships, but the warehouses of the Dahley District dealt with the local traders and private merchants. And since the local customs agents were more interested in the larger international shipments, they were less likely to interfere here.

Rizzo pulled to the curb near one such warehouse emblazoned with the faded logo of Golden Seas International: a stylised gold avian carrying a wrapped package by its string. The structure rose in three tiers composed chiefly of glass and corrugated tin, occupying several acres of property. On the roadside, next to the main entrance, was a loading bay capable of holding four heavy freight trucks. Aside from the emblem and signage, the building looked like its neighbours.

A newly constructed section was attached to the northwest corner, which appeared to be a climate-controlled storage space.

The warehouse had its own private pier, currently occupied by a small freighter offloading a shipment of live bolvin. The docile quadrupeds crooned as they lumbered down the ramp, swinging their broad heads from side to side. With their thick tails and large eyes, the domesticated animals looked like a bizarre mash-up between a brushtail possum, a kangaroo, and a cow. Of course, no sentient Amarthian ever thought about this, nor would they ever indulge the barbaric notion of testing whether bolvin and bovine tasted the same. Only fish, insects, and—to a much lesser extent—birds and reptiles would resort to what was tantamount to cannibalism.

"Well, it certainly looks legitimate, *non*?" Rizzo said as she eyed the structure.

Mohan shifted his weight. "It is, mostly. Al-Seif has quite the reputation as a reputable businessman. Of course, we're pretty sure that's just a front for his less legal activities. All right, Vicki, Zed, you're up."

The frog and badger had substituted their field gear from the other night for less conspicuous dock worker's clothes—although Zed refused to give up his keffiyeh or bracer. Vicki didn't like leaving her medical pack behind, but she had stuffed the pockets of her coveralls with a few essential odds and ends—which, to her, meant bandages, duct tape, and a multitool knife. They concealed small pistols under the loose clothing, but neither had any thought of actually using them.

The badger pulled open the lorry's side door, and the smell of farm animals, fish, and industrial smoke grew more pronounced. Even at the outer edge of the market, the streets and sidewalks were crowded with pedestrians. Most were lugging burdens from within the warehouses to shops and stalls buried deep within the maze of the market proper.

Mohan tapped the badger on the shoulder. "Remember, you're just looking around. If there is something buried under that warehouse, it might already be stocked, but I don't want any heroics."

Zed knew what he meant. If he and Vicki found any slaves held prisoner, they couldn't help. It made him feel awful, but another team was already waiting in the wings to assist with that problem.

"If things get bodgie, you might have to make your own way back to base," the tiger continued. "Otherwise, just meet us at the lorry when you're done. Good luck, mate."

Zed nodded grimly and grabbed Mohan's arm at the wrist. "Strength and Honour."

"Wisdom and Justice," the tiger completed the phrase, citing four of the Six Pillars, the foundation of Tiger's Stripe's code. The remaining two were Mercy and Loyalty, but Mohan never thought they sounded as good when returning the salute.

The badger and the frog vanished into the crowd, and Rizzo pulled away and headed deeper into the market.

The Dahley District was a stark contrast to the neighbouring Khamir District. All around them rose the brightly painted sandstone-and-brick buildings of modest shops and residences, broken now and again by the glass and steel of some enterprising foreign business—mainly of the fast-food variety. Sculpted archways joined one side of the street to the other, and occasionally, a hanging plant or branching palm would add a touch of greenery to the scene. Bullet holes were also less frequent in the walls.

The people hustling back and forth were also vastly different; they were more finely dressed and held themselves with more self-confidence than their poorer neighbours did. Pytan's population comprised primarily mammals and reptiles more suited to the dry climate. Still, one could also distinguish the locals from foreigners by the darker colouring around their eyes, concave cheeks, and longer faces. However, thanks to the proximity of the docks, the markets also had many tourists and traders from around the Medean Basin.

Uniformed police were present enough to make the tourists feel safe, but if anything happened, they would quickly learn how ineffectual the law really was in Pytan.

After several twists and turns through crowded streets, Rizzo parked outside the arched entry of a narrow side alley. Cement pylons barred vehicle traffic from proceeding into the lane.

Kitty climbed out of the passenger seat. She wore a loose cotton robe of a fine cut similar to those worn by the local women, and she quickly wrapped a blue silk hijab around her head as she stepped out. The head garb was more to hide her radio earmuff than to conform to local customs, but it would also help her blend with most of the other women who were out to market.

Vince put on a far different appearance as he stepped out the side door. The hare was dressed head to toe in a fine white linen suit that must have cost a small fortune. A dark-blue pocket handkerchief complimented a silk shirt of the same colour. He even somehow managed to spruce up his battered white fedora so it didn't contrast with the fine threads—the hat also helped conceal his own radio.

Rizzo came around the front of the lorry and eyed Vince with amusement. "Where on Amarthia did you get that outfit?" she asked.

With a wink and a grin, the hare replied, "It's easier to *be* a millionaire playboy than to fake one, darlin'."

The basilisk raised an eyebrow, suddenly remembering that Vince was one of the Banton Nieves, a very influential family in the West United Kingdoms who had amassed a substantial fortune in the cotton trade. Vince had been disowned many years ago after learning some of his father's business practices were less than ethical, leaving him little access to the family coffers. However, before joining the Tiger's Stripe, he'd made a small fortune running a high-end security systems business—something that morphed out of his love for opening locks he shouldn't.

Rizzo shrugged and gazed around the market. "Mohan, I'm going to secure the area quickly."

"Good idea," the tiger replied, positioning himself in front of the radio equipment in the rear of the lorry and strapping on a headset.

"Now it's your show," he said to Kitty and Vince. "Alabwaq's reserved the central market square for his exhibition. His mercs use the buildings nearby to house his merchandise." He spat the word. "Remember, observation only. We'll get those slaves freed after we scout the area. Strength and Honour."

Vince clasped his arm at the wrist as Zed had. "Wisdom and Justice."

Kitty barely mumbled the reply and didn't even look in her father's direction before vanishing into the crowd.

The outer rings of the Dahley District consisted of cheap tourist attractions, food vendors, and traders for everything from cloth to household appliances. The hunters' interest was the inner market. The entrances were well-hidden deep within the maze of twisting streets, and only those who knew what to look for could find them. The uniformed police swapped places with intimidating figures in army fatigues whose primary function was to keep out naïve tourists and other less desirable clientele.

Naturally, one could prove you were the desired clientele with a simple judicious use of carams, the local currency.

In these darker, narrower alleys, the kitsch and baubles, the cry of food vendors, and the scent of exotic perfumes competed alongside the bark of arms dealers and the sickly-sweet stench of opium dens, prostitutes, and slaves. There was something surreal about seeing tables laden with handguns and portable rocket launchers right next to crystal flatware, home entertainment systems, and exotic pieces of local artwork carved from pachtaur ivory, wood, and precious stone.

Vince was several paces behind Kitty, doing an expert job of simultaneously looking suitably awed and purposeful. He was a tourist who knew exactly where he was going and why. He rounded a corner and came face to chest with a bejewelled female giraffe draped in nothing but veils and reeking of scent. She twisted and gesticulated as she ran off a rehearsed advertisement for the best opium in the market. Her offer was countered by a similarly dressed jackal vixen across the street. The blatant degenerate display didn't seem to bother the throngs of richly dressed pedestrians that jostled this way and that through the narrow lane.

The hare smiled politely and tipped his hat to both women before continuing down the street.

Ahead of him, Kitty was not blending in quite as well. Her eyes strayed too many times to the balconies shading the street, marking the location of both guards and casual observers.

"I'd feel a lot more comfortable above this crowd about now," she said into her radio, covering her mouth with the hijab to avoid looking like she was talking to herself.

Vince surreptitiously snagged a bulky cellular phone handset from a stall, leaving a large caram note in its place. Moments later, a street urchin pocketed the money—it never saw the hand of the proprietor.

"No worries, darlin'," the hare said, holding the handset to his ear as if talking into it. "After all, you've got me to watch your back!"

"I'm just overwhelmed with confidence," Kitty said, rolling her eyes.

"I bet that wasn't all you were watching," Rizzo chided from the alley entrance.

"Tut, tut! I never get involved with coworkers. Especially not with so many other lovely distractions around." His eyes strayed to a pair of richly dressed serval cat women passing by. They giggled coyly as he tipped his hat to them.

"Or when their father is two hundred and twenty centimetres of tiger," Rizzo said.

"Depends. Although I did just pass a lovely seven-foot giraffe girl." He sighed wistfully. "Mmm, all neck and legs. Anyway, just take in these sights and smells! This is the heart of the Pytian economy."

Kitty frowned. "Yeah, a regular hive of scum and villainy."

In the back of the lorry, Mohan adjusted a dial. "The roofs are too closely guarded here. Alabwaq's not going to take any chances. His goons will be all over the place."

Vince continued to ramble. "You know, some of these buildings are hundreds of years old. The tradition of a common market goes all the way back to the Fahir'Jin empire, I think. The king, I forget which one, encouraged traders to—"

Once again, everyone on the radio chimed in to tell the hare to shut up.

"Vicki, Zed, how's things?" Mohan asked before Vince could ignore them and ramble on again.

Back at the Golden Seas International warehouse, the bullfrog and badger loitered around the main floor

74

of the loading bay. The bolvin shuffled in a pen outside, waiting for the trucks that would haul them away. Inside, forklifts and hand carts shifted pallets of dry grain, fresh fruits, and other foodstuffs every which way. Nobody noticed two more workers securing the shelving near the side entrance.

Zed whispered into his radio, "Victoria and I are inside. No complications to report. There are employee notices posted everywhere about the new refrigeration units; apparently, there have been several refrigerant leaks, and only authorised employees are permitted inside."

"Sounds a little too convenient to me," Vicki added. "It's the perfect cover if they're still building something underneath the warehouse."

Back in the lorry, Mohan nodded. "Good. Keep me posted."

The tiger glanced up as Rizzo climbed back in the driver's seat. She nodded to indicate everything was clear, then settled back into the chair and began to idly flick the safety catch on an explosive detonator with her thumb claw.

"Um, Rizzo? What are you doing with that? You didn't actually plant anything, did you?" He always got a little nervous when the basilisk started playing with explosives, especially in a market filled with innocent civilians.

Rizzo looked over her shoulder and batted her gold eyes innocently. *"Moi?* But it's just some little smoke bombs. We might need them to make a quick getaway, *non?"*

Mohan sighed, exasperated and tried to remind himself that Rizzo wasn't about to endanger civilians. Everyone knew the story about the Neuf Marisian rebel who bombed a royalist regional headquarters without shattering a single window on the school next door.

"We're almost there." Vince's voice broke his chain of thought.

Mohan sat up a little straighter. Time to get to work.

Deep within the market, Kitty and Vince passed under an ornate archway into a wide square. Four streets intersected here at the heart of Kairran's black market, and it was practically wall to wall with pedestrians.

From a bird's-eye view, the square was roughly three blocks from the banks of the Hutsepth Canal, but the twisting streets cut off any direct path to the water. The proximity to the canal and multiple exits made the square ideal for carrying out any number of nefarious deeds in broad daylight; there was simply no way a police raid could reach it before warning was given and everyone cleared out.

Just as Mohan had warned, heavily armed mercenaries occupied the balconies and roofs of the surrounding buildings. The hired muscle came from as many varied species as the crowd below. Money and violence held no preference when it came to species. They were armed with everything from simple submachine guns to military-issue rifles. The only consistency in their uniform was a purple and gold sash that identified them as part of Assad Alabwaq's private army of thugs.

A large stone fountain of a robed feline woman dominated the square's centre. She stood on a platform ringed with stylised nonsentient fish, which spouted water from their mouths while she poured water from a large pot carried in her arms. Age and bullets pitted and chipped the stonework, but the anonymous owners had kept the waterworks in good repair, and it was suitable for drinking should the market's guests need to refresh themselves.

Most of the patrons still moving through the square stuck to the outer edges, where market carts and shopfront vied for their attention. Those gathered near the fountain focused their attention on a large wooden stage in the north corner.

The stage was cater-cornered to a large apartment building fortified with iron bars and razor wire; it looked more like a prison than your average domicile. Towards the front of the stage, two dozen muscle-bound men and women—most of whom were of carnivorous or omnivorous species—displayed their physical attributes for the cheering crowd. Behind them, several small groups of mixed gender hung chained to wooden posts, watched closely by armed mercenaries. Most of the slaves came from herbivore species or obvious mixed breeding, and the mixed-breeds clearly shouldered the brunt of the crowd's jeering.

Kitty's snout curled in an involuntary snarl. As if the slave trade wasn't enough, the Pytians still clung to the old tradition of mistreating mixed-breeds. Gazing at the crowd, she wondered with disgust how pure their bloodlines really were.

Which sentient species could cross-breed was not an exact science. Broader classes, such as Aves and Mammalia, were proven to never produce offspring; likewise, certain diametrically opposed families—such as Canidae and Felidae—could never procreate. But even among mixed species that could produce young, the chances of it being physically obvious were rare. Most often, a child developed the characteristics of one parent or the other, and their true heritage could only be determined through blood tests, freeing them from the ridicule of their peers.

Many cultures still viewed the mixing of species as impure—and, in some religions, even heretical. Even in the more "civilised" nations, mixed-breeds were subject to unfair political rulings and cruel and distasteful jokes. After all, why would a kangaroo want to marry a possum? Their kids would be garoo-sum.

Kitty stifled an angry growl and turned her attention to the exhibition itself. It was a relatively simple arrangement: each gladiator was paired with a slave or slaves they thought would appeal to their target patrons the most. Once sold, the gladiators fought in the arena for the prestige of their sponsors while the slaves served as concubines, sometimes to both sponsor and fighter. Not every contest was to the death, but most involved bloodshed, and if the gladiators survived, they would advance to the next event. Experienced gladiators could even retire and go on to train younger generations. And if they went feral, they could also provide sport for those who hadn't.

The fate of the slave was even worse. If they pleased their new masters, they might get upgraded to a house servant or even a mistress; if not, well, their owners could toss them in the pit. Unruly slaves armed with sticks versus a deadly ceravaag or a pack of jungle bahngers was always a crowd favourite. If they were lucky, a slave might even win and go on to become a gladiator themselves.

It was a barbaric practice, and had no place in a modern, enlightened society. But the animal hunger for dominance was always there. There were always those who desired to feed it and those who were more than willing to provide the carnage.

Kitty's anger rose within her, and she could feel it spreading across her chest and arm. Vince was undoubtedly experiencing the same thing, but they both needed to keep their cool. The exhibition's host was still nowhere in sight, and they would have to endure the sickening display awhile longer.

The tigress made her way around the outer edge of the crowd while the hare pressed right in towards the fountain. More than a few foreigners in suits mingled with the locals in fine robes.

"No Alabwaq," Kitty said as she idly sorted some brass cookware, sinking more into her role as a market patron. "Would've thought the bastard would want to oversee his ill-gotten gains."

"Patience," Mohan said. "If he is going to show, it'll be towards the end."

"Shameful," Vince said, shaking his head disapprovingly and still holding the cell phone to his ear. "Just shameful. Those poor dears don't belong in chains."

"Oh? You would prefer furred handcuffs, *non*?" Rizzo retorted.

The hurt in Vince's voice was genuine. "This is no laughin' matter, darlin'. How could anyone take advantage of such a despicable situation?" He broke into a sly grin. "But now that I know that you're into that, I—"

"You guingin!" Rizzo blurted furiously; with her accent, the word sounded like *gwan-gheen*.

"You know, darlin', it's pronounced *gwin-ghin*," Vince corrected.

"That is what I said!"

The animal in question was a reddish-scaled, medium-sized quadruped with a bizarre similarity to a giant pangolin with a bear's head. Guingin meat was a delicacy in many parts of the world, but since they were wallowing animals, they were considered unclean in certain religious diets, particularly in Pytan. Due to their slovenly nature, it was also a common insult.

The basilisk continued to fume in her native Marisian. "*Je le ferais jamis dans un million d'années—*"

"All right, knock it off!" Mohan cut her off.

Vince didn't take the hint. "I was just sayin' it would be horrible if—"

"I said shut it. Both of you." The tiger let out a low warning growl. "Kitty, give me an update."

"Normal so far," the tigress said. "If you call selling people's lives normal. Hang on."

A furtive movement near the stage had caught her eye. She peered over the heads of the crowd towards a minor commotion near the fountain. A lynx and fox dressed in badly fitting robes were pushing their way through the throng.

The fox was covertly snapping photos of the auction with a camera hidden in his robe while the lynx brushed off anyone who confronted them. The average person might see a pair of rude, well-to-do tourists, but Kitty had been trained to spot people who were trying to be ignored by being as annoying as possible. For all their arrogance and dismissive-ness, the fox and lynx were a little too focused on what was happening on stage and not as buyers.

"Oh, you're going to love this." The exasperation was clear in Kitty's voice. "Got a couple of civvies up near the stage. They're making a big show of being rude tourists, but I'm pretty sure they're journos; at least one has a camera."

Journalists. Great. Mohan sighed and rubbed his eyes.

If there was one thing he hated dealing with, it was spontaneous do-gooders butting in while they were trying to do good themselves. They were always on the lookout for rogue elements, but once you found one, it was a bloody guarantee your op could go arse-up real quick. They'd need to isolate them before the whole mission got flushed down the loo.

"No doubt attemptin' to expose the reality of the slave market to the sheltered masses in Locke or the WUK," Vince said in an irritatingly pious tone. "I saw this documentary about—"

"Vince, quit the ear bashing," Mohan growled again, wincing as if from a physical injury. "Stay focused on the auction. Kitty, keep tabs on our new friends. See if you can find a way to give 'em the boot before we have a mess on our hands."

The tiger's back was starting to itch. He didn't know what the masquerading journalists were after, but he was starting to get that nagging suspicion that something wasn't right. For now, all he could do was sit and wait, and hope they didn't end up in the obituaries.

6 – On Ice

While the market team debated how to handle this sudden development, Zed and Vicki casually strolled towards the refrigeration unit on the north side of the Golden Seas International warehouse.

The freezer unit took up nearly half a soccer field of real estate, and that was still only a fraction of the warehouse's total acreage. On the outside, it looked like a standard grocery freezer: blue-grey walls of thin stainless steel wrapped in thick insulation and covered with white plastic. The hum of the roof-mounted fans floated faintly into the hall, where the badger and the frog walked casually up to a latched sliding door. There were no windows to the interior of the unit.

Zed spoke into his radio. "Mohan, we have reached the freezer unit and are heading inside."

"Got it," came the brief reply.

As Zed opened the door, he shivered slightly as a blast of frigid air hit them. He glanced at his shorter companion. All Hom-Ans were warm-blooded, but reptiles and amphibians lacked fur or feathers to trap body heat. The poor frog would suffer the most from the freezing temperatures, but she produced a woollen scarf from a pocket and wrapped it snuggly around her head.

"I can search in here alone if you wish to stay," he said.

"No, no. I'll be fine." She smiled gamely up at him. "Lead on!"

Inside, plastic curtains separated the freezer into three sections. The first and largest was primarily composed of frozen foodstuffs arranged on pallets lined in neat rows from one end to the other. Half the stacks barely reached their knees while others flirted with the ceiling. A few signs cautioning to look out for spills stood in the aisles. Nothing appeared out of the ordinary, so they moved on towards the next section.

More foodstuffs, this time in the form of frozen slabs of nonsentient animal meat. There were the standard sides of bolvin, racks of rabbit-like ahlnem'rey, hanging columns of large fish, and wrapped aukies, the same small flightless avians Rizzo had almost run over in the market.

Despite eating a good breakfast, Zed found his mouth watering a little at the sight. The crane-necked, gecko-headed aukies were a particular delicacy and came in a variety of flavours depending on what species and region of Amarthia they came from.

Finding nothing of interest here either, the badger and the frog moved on to the last section. It only took up a small corner of the freezer unit, barely three metres to a side. The curved metal cases stacked on the pallets bore long, unpronounceable names of several chemical and medical compounds.

"Looks like al-Seif is diversifying into pharmaceuticals," Vicki said.

Zed nodded and moved towards the rear corner. Several plastic sacks hung from the ceiling, almost like the sides of meat they had just passed. Further back, a large cabinet nearly as wide as the curtained section stood against the wall. Its doors were chained shut.

Zed inspected one of the hanging bags first, carefully undoing the zipper front.

"By Mbektar!" He gasped as the shrunken face of a doe slumped out. "Victoria, I believe you should see this."

Vicki examined the hanging corpse, paying careful attention to the arms.

"I find it odd al-Seif would also store medical cadavers," Zed said.

"That's how they're marked," replied Vicki, "but I don't think that's why they're here. Their arms show multiple needle marks, and look at this."

She tilted the doe's head towards him. He could see a neat hole at the base of the temple, with a much larger exit wound on the opposite side.

"Capped execution style."

Zed spoke into his radio as Vicki examined the other bags. "We may have stumbled onto something, Mohan. I will let Victoria explain."

"Well, either al-Seif is into cannibalism, or he's found a great way to dispose of dead slaves." Vicki's voice again assumed the methodical calmness reserved for medical examiners. "Still looking for a brand, but I'm almost certain these were rejects from the gladiators. Most of the bodies look malnourished and show signs of forced doping. They were also executed with a single gunshot to the temple. Not a pretty sight."

"Did you ever see a corpse that was a pretty sight, darlin'?" Vince said.

"I'm sure yours will be dressed to the nines," Rizzo retorted.

"Don't start that again," Mohan growled.

Vicki ignored the interruption. "They're flagged as medical research cadavers, but I bet that's just to avoid prying officials. I don't know about you, but it's starting to look like al-Seif and Alabwaq are one in the same."

"And dead slave might make a tasty and convenient menu item for a fiend, wouldn't it?" added Vince.

"Now there's a charming thought," Mohan said. "Good work, you two. But he could also be feeding them to ceravaags or bahngers. We need more than that if we want to nail him. See if there's a manifest lying around."

Zed had already moved away from the grisly scene to examine the large cabinet against the wall. Aside from the chain securing the doors, there was also a biohazard symbol on each panel. He looked through the plastic curtains and sized up the other sections they had been in.

"There is a missing space here," he mumbled to himself.

"How's that?" Mohan asked.

"The sections we have been in do not account for all the available space in this unit. There are at least fifty cubic metres of space missing."

"That's enough for a small elevator," Vicki commented, voicing what the badger had already suspected.

Zed rapped on the door with a thick knuckle. "It is hollow. More than that, I believe I heard an echo." He tugged on the chain. "Hmm, this is too thick to cut through without tools. I wish we had a pair of Vincenzo's lock picks."

Vicki studied the heavy padlock for a moment and then vanished into the maze of pallets. She returned moments later with a small canister and a pair of heavily insulated gloves. After slipping on the gloves, she gingerly unscrewed the cap and poured a measure of clear smoking liquid onto the lock hasp. It frosted over almost instantly. She stepped back, made a chopping motion, and gestured towards the lock like a game show host.

Divining her meaning, Zed brought out his pistol and gave the lock a sharp tap with the butt of the gun. The hasp shattered, and both chain and lock fell to the floor.

"Good old LIN." The frog grinned widely. "Liquid nitrogen. I figured they'd have some stashed away with all these chemicals." She studied the bottle for a moment, then sighed as if coming to a conclusion and put the bottle back on a shelf. "Won't be able to carry this far without some cold storage," she explained. "Oh, but this might come in handy later!" She grabbed a second bottle of unknown content and stashed it in her pocket.

The badger smiled and slid open the cabinet door. As he had suspected, it was empty. There were no shelves, but he did notice some odd seams in the back panel. He knocked on it and discovered it was hollow, but it wouldn't move to his prodding. Muttering to himself, he looked around until he saw a small button recessed above the cabinet doors on the inside. Pressing it, he was rewarded with a dull click, and the cabinet's rear wall slid aside.

The room beyond was barely three metres on each side. There was no elevator; however, a hook and winch were mounted next to a stairwell winding down into darkness.

"Bingo!" Vicki said, snapping her fingers.

Zed spoke into his radio. "We have definitely discovered something here, Mohan. We have found a hidden room with a stairwell leading beneath the warehouse."

"Bonza!" the tiger replied. "But be careful down there."

The stairs were barely wide enough for Zed, and the badger and the frog had to keep a firm grip on the bright red railing due to the steep angle. The shaft walls were featureless grey cement, and each metal step was marked with black and yellow caution stripes. The paint was practically brand new. They made several switchbacks before finally hitting the bottom.

"We must be halfway to Amarthia's core." Vicki panted, leaning on the railing; the steep and narrow stairs didn't agree with her long frog legs.

"I estimate we have only descended seventy metres," Zed replied. He was barely sweating, but he did welcome being on level ground again.

They stood at the end of a short corridor that opened into a long room with a high ceiling. The only light came from fluorescent bulbs widely spaced from one end to the other. Both hunters removed torches from their pockets to help compensate for the low lighting. On their right, a tiled mosaic depicted a graphic gladiatorial match against a fearsome beast that was too stylised to identify. Along the opposite wall were large metal cages reinforced with thick safety glass, heavy bars, and magnetic locks. A corridor ran behind the cells, and the doors on that end were much larger.

Vicki banged on the side of a cage. "What is this? It's not regular steel."

"I am not certain. Perhaps a tungsten alloy of some sort."

"Well, you don't build a cage with three-inch bars and bulletproof glass for a bunch of doped-up slave girls."

"Indeed. And, barbarians that they are, I doubt these are accommodations for the gladiators. However, I would not think such precautions necessary for your average bahnger or ceravaag."

Vicki crossed her arms and tapped at her lips with a finger. "But I'm still not sure this would be enough reinforcement to hold a fiend. Not a big one at least. I'm guessing that winch in the stairwell is to lower food down to the cages."

They followed the row of cells to an enclosed medical area. At the centre stood a low table fitted with heavy leather straps and chains. Bandages, antiseptic, and surgical tools filled the cabinets along the rear wall. The space could easily be adapted to operate on both Hom-An and animal patients.

"Nice to see Alabwaq cares about his employees' health," Vicki muttered.

"Indeed."

The medical suite had two large exits at the back, comprised of heavy double doors with the same security as the cage doors. One connected to the corridor behind the cages and the other to a long tunnel gradually descending into darkness. Fencing divided the tunnel in two, and a series of gates could direct traffic into the medical suite or back to the cages. Obviously, the intent was to segregate beasts from Hom-An combatants.

Vicki and Zed followed the downward passageway briefly before it terminated at a heavy steel gate. Fortunately, there was no power to the magnetic locks, and they stepped through it and out into a broad room with a sandy floor. The only light came from a single lamp high on the ceiling.

"This must be the arena floor," Zed said. He shined his light around, but it couldn't penetrate beyond the high walls of the enclosure.

"Hang on, I think I saw a passage to the master control room back there," Vicki said, hopping back down the corridor.

"Do be careful," Zed called after her. They had seen no signs of life, so he wasn't too worried about splitting up to search the arena.

Several long minutes passed before Zed heard a hollow click echo through the cavernous space, and suddenly, the arena was flooded with light.

"Well, they have full power." Vicki's voice drifted over the stadium's PA system. "But they've got everything switched off. I've disengaged all the locks, so we should be free to roam around. Be down in a sec."

Zed studied his surroundings while he waited. The arena stage was roughly ten metres across, octagonal, with smooth walls rising six metres before merging into thick glass that angled inward and stretched to the height of the ceiling. Each pane must have cost a fortune and was fitted with a thin latticework frame for added stability. Beyond the glass, rows of plush seats marched up to the back wall, broken here and there by VIP lounges. Zed estimated the space could easily accommodate close to five hundred spectators, and there wasn't a bad seat in the house.

Vicki rejoined him through a tunnel opposite the one they had initially entered. "You gotta see this place, Zed! The rooms over here are for the gladiators. I swear they used a whole square mile of velvet."

"Indeed. This is quite an impressive setup, but while Jirair al-Seif may be the owner, it is not proof that he is Assad Alabwaq. And, unfortunately, we are no closer to proving that he intends to use fiends in his events." He paused a moment. "We also do not know why he constructed this arena at all. Alabwaq has a similar venue in Khet, along the Median Basin. He runs the risk of exposure by opening a second location."

Vicki nodded. "True, but Khet is also a good eight-hour drive from here. Don't forget Alabwaq's ego. Sultan Abdülkadír has openly denounced gladiator combat and is trying to come down hard on the rampant criminal activity across Pytan. I'd say setting up in the capital would be Alabwaq's way of showing off just how much power he really has here."

"That is unfortunate," Zed said. "I knew Abdülkadír many years ago when he was but a foal prince. He is a good man but far too trusting. If this is the extent of Alabwaq's influence, I fear the Sultan's cabinet has become more corrupt than we previously believed."

"And he just goes along with it?"

"It is quite difficult to convince Abdülkadír that his friends are actually his enemies. His desire to see the good in all Hom-Ans is an honourable trait, but I fear it will be his downfall." He spoke into his radio. "Mohan, we have discovered the arena under the warehouse. Mohan?"

Static was the reply.

"We must be too far underground," Vicki said. "We won't be able to radio in until we get back outside."

Zed frowned. "Indeed. We should search for other items of interest."

Vicki nodded. "I doubt they'd bring the clientele in through the freezer, and they couldn't bring animal cages down that winch."

The badger and the frog split and began their search. Vicki had shut off the primary security system, but neither knew that a third party was behind the arena's construction, and they had put their own security in place. Even now, hidden mechanical eyes recorded the hunters' every move.

7 – Rollaroo

Outside, the sun had passed its zenith yet was still high overhead, flooding the crowded market square with its merciless heat. Several contentious bids had already passed—one almost leading to a brawl—but so far, the only lots were for gladiators and slaves.

Despite her best efforts, Kitty hadn't found an opportunity to corral the meddling journalists out of the square. However, they had toned down their act and were at least aware of their own precarious position. They seemed to be waiting for something.

Vince felt the tingle coming from the birthmark on his thigh before he felt the presence at his shoulder. He turned to discover a dromedary wearing an expensive white thawb with gold embroidery and purple tassels on the hem. Perched on his long nose, pince-nez was a pair of dark glasses with circular lenses that flashed in the sunlight. He was slightly taller than the hare, mostly because of his neck but also because of the tall white and gold turban atop his head.

"You are a foreigner here, sir." He spoke in Locken with a stilted accent.

Vince quietly opened his radio channel and instantly fell into the persona he had constructed for this op. He had decided to swap his Banton twang for a harsh Dollan inflexion. "*Ja, ja.* On vacation in your charming little country. Anyone can go to the beaches of Medocci, skiing in the Zeichlind Mountains, diving the reefs of East Benai. Bah, beaches and casinos bore me!" He dropped his voice to something a little more conspiratorial. "I was told that this market could provide something a little more…exciting. And I am pleased to see I have found it."

The stylish patron raised an eyebrow. "Indeed? What could be more exciting than combat on the field of glory? But I have not seen you place any bids, sir. Are the contestants not to your liking?"

Vince sighed. "*Nein.* While I enjoy the blood sport, why should I waste my marks on contenders of such inferior stock? None of these can compare to a proud son of the Zeichlind Valley. I trust you understand?"

"But of course." The dromedary continued to smile graciously. "We try to cater to a variety of tastes, but I regret we so rarely get visitors from the Dollan Empire."

The Dollans of Zeichlind were notoriously fastidious when it came to breeding and pedigree. Of all

97

the nations on the Aerenian continent, they were the only ones who still had their own secret gladiator games. They were also particularly cruel towards mixed-breeds.

Vince continued to feign boredom. "Surely you can offer more than this? Tell me, do you hunt in this country?"

"Hunting, sir? Most of Pytan is sand in rock. Unless you plan to hunt the scyllian sandworms?"

"Worms? You insult me, sir. I do not see any sport hunting something so large and cumbersome. Have you no jungles in Pytan?"

"Yes, yes. And they are rife with Pytan's own voracious breed of bahngers and ceravaags, but they are also thick with bandits. No place for a gentleman of your stature." He said nothing about the unusualness of a herbivore wanting to hunt. "If you are bored with typical gladiator games, my employer may be able to supply the excitement you seek. Right here in Kairran."

"Is that so?" Vince asked, raising an eyebrow. "I was under the impression that this stock would be fighting in Khet next week. A sort of preview, as it were."

The dromedary rested a hand on his shoulder. "That is true. It is necessary to keep attention away from the arena in Khet when we host such exhibitions. However, my employer seeks to change that very soon. In fact, he has arranged for a special event, only a few days from now, and you will not have to travel far.

"There will be a special lot—number forty-six. Bid if you wish, but be sure to catch my eye and make this gesture." He displayed this by placing three fingers to his head above his right eye. "Then I will know you are interested in what my employer has to offer."

The well-dressed patron vanished into the crowd before Vince could question him further. The hare again held the phone handset to his ear and spoke into his radio. "You heard?"

"Every word," Mohan replied. "There's only forty-five lots listed, so this last one is a surprise. We're only on twenty-three. Play along, Vince. We're close to nailing this bastard; I can feel it!"

Deep beneath the warehouse, Vicki and Zed were finishing their first sweep of the arena. The venue was still in a state of undress; unopened boxes of stationery and linens were stacked in the offices and bathrooms. The larders were still bare, but stacks of utensils and kitchen paraphernalia were waiting to be set in order. Only the medical suite near the holding pens was ready for use—as if that had been a priority all along.

Now that they had light to see by, they discovered that the mural in the cage corridor cleverly concealed a large freight elevator. By Zed's estimate, the upper platform must be somewhere just outside the freezer unit, possibly hidden by a pair of freight containers stacked close together.

Vicki frowned. "This place is squeaky clean. But it would only take a couple hours to get it ready for guests."

"Indeed," Zed replied. "The lights and elevators are working, but there was no water in the kitchen or the lavatory. It appears their first priority was to prepare the medical facilities and holding cells. Unfortunately, I have seen no evidence of what they intended to contain there."

"Me neither. Let's make one more sweep back the other way. I think I found the elevator the guests would use; we'll take it and find out where it pops up."

The mechanical eyes watching them ceased their observation. It sent the data to the warehouse above, where it was relayed over a phone line to a computer in a remote location. Task complete, the automated security system switched functions and waited.

The auction continued until the sun began to sink towards the edge of the roofs. Only a few slaves remained chained to the stage as their gladiator guardians paraded before them. At last, the serval cat auctioneer addressed the crowd.

"Friends, our exhibition is drawing to a close. However, your gracious host would like to thank you personally for your custom and make a special announcement. My esteemed guests, please welcome Assad Alabwaq."

"There's the bastard!" Kitty growled as a figure took centre stage.

Assad Alabwaq was short-statured—not uncommon for a mouflon—but he appeared immaculate and confident in a white and gold linen suit with a purple feather pinned to the lapel. He kept the long greying goatee on his chin neatly brushed, and his slate-grey long-fur, streaked with white at the temples, swept straight back from his high forehead. Despite his namesake, his horns were polished alabaster and curled until their tips were level with his cheeks. Gold and purple tassels dangled from them, bobbing enthusiastically as he strode across the stage.

Two enormous bodyguards completed his ensemble a muscle-bound rhinoceros and a female mixed-breed of the genus Panthera. The cougar-tiger woman was several years older than the rhino and bore many scars on her greying fur. At least when it came to security, Alabwaq was an equal-opportunity employer.

Kitty and Vince matched the mouflon's features to photos of Jirair al-Seif gathered by their intelligence agents. There could be no doubts now: he was indeed Assad Alabwaq.

He was greeted by rounds of applause from the gathered patrons, and many seemed just as interested as the agents to finally meet the man who had remained in the shadows for so long.

The mouflon addressed them in a clear and surprisingly high-pitched voice using his native tongue of Netib. "My esteemed colleagues! I cannot express my gratitude for your attendance this afternoon. Indeed, you have run through the lots with such remarkable speed we must end things much sooner than I had anticipated. I assure you that you have spent your money well and will soon be able to see the results in glorious combat. If you have any complaints, hmph, you know where to go."

This brought an uneasy chuckle from the crowd. Jirair al-Seif, under the guise of Assad Alabwaq, was not only a purveyor of exotic—if less than legal—goods but also had a notoriously lethal temper. No doubt, any complaints would be resolved by having the objector locked in a small room with the mouflon's bodyguards. Unless he decided to throw them into the arena instead.

"I have one special announcement to make before we conclude the day's proceedings and a special item for you to bid on," he continued. "As you know, now that your purchases are in hand, you must travel to Khet to see the fruits of your labour. Many of you have seen what I have to offer there, and it is not to be rivalled by any other arena in Pytan.

"That is, until today! I am proud to announce that I will be opening a new venue right here in Kairran!"

The crowd erupted in roars of surprise and approval, and it was several minutes before al-Seif could quiet them down again.

"I will not bore you with the details of this achievement, accomplished under the very snout of our *beloved* Sultan." A chorus of derisive laughter followed this. "Suffice to say, it would never have been possible without the donations of a gracious sponsor, who has asked to remain anonymous. Moreover, this sponsor has promised to provide a new spectacle, the likes of which have never been seen on Amarthia. A challenge so terrible that even Garik, our reigning champion, may tremble before it!"

The enormous rhino at al-Seif's shoulder laughed defiantly. Obviously, he was the champion in question.

"You weren't kiddin', Mo," Vince said into his radio. "He's practically givin' us everythin' we need."

"Yeah," the tiger replied. "I don't like it. And who is this 'sponsor' he keeps talking about? Maybe we were wrong. Maybe al-Seif is standing in for the real Alabwaq."

"There will be a special event tomorrow night to commemorate the opening of the new arena," al-Seif continued. "I regret that this event is invitation only, and special instructions have already been given."

The crowd baulked at this unusual announcement; many felt slighted for not being told about this arrangement. A murmur began to roll through those gathered.

Al-Seif held up his hands to silence them. "Come now, my friends. This is still Kairran, and I must ensure your safety above all else. This preview, organised by our sponsor, will ensure that we can operate without any undue interference."

This statement only slightly mollified the crowd; they had to admit they wouldn't want to confront the local authorities at the grand opening of such a prestigious venue.

"I understand this is highly irregular," al-Seif continued, "and I assure you I am only operating under the wishes of our sponsor. However, they anticipated your displeasure and have supplied one final lot to placate you. A prize of such beauty and purity that you will, hopefully, forget that you will have to wait a little while longer to experience the new games." Another nervous chuckle went through the crowd, but several were clearly not impressed. "May I present, for your every enjoyment, lot number forty-six!"

"OK, here we go," Mohan said, eagerly leaning over the radio equipment.

The crowd shifted in anticipation. Many remained confused by the awkward announcement, but almost half the patrons had been waiting for this lot in particular. The guards near the entrance to the apartment complex parted while another dragged the unfortunate victim on stage. It was a young gazelle, barely on the cusp of womanhood. She was tall for her age and seemed much healthier than the earlier slaves, but she still required the aid of the guard to stagger towards the centre of the platform. Her eyes peered uncomprehending at the crowd around her, glazed by the fog of an opium high. There was no gladiator to accompany her; the prize was the slave girl alone.

"Poor girl is barely old enough to drive," Vince said, shaking his head.

Kitty moved nearer the northwest entrance arch, where the two journalists had taken up positions closer to the stage. The lynx seemed particularly interested in this new lot and spoke animatedly with his photographer. The din of the market was too loud to make out what was said, and the tigress didn't have the skills to read lips. She looked towards the stage to study the gazelle girl herself. Even in her drugged state, something about her bearing recalled an air of pampered entitlement.

"Call it a hunch," she said, "but I don't think this girl has ever had to drive herself anywhere."

"Good eye, Kitty," Vince said. "Now that you mention it, I'm almost certain I've seen her somewhere before."

The bidding began almost immediately, and it quickly became apparent that al-Seif's dromedary representative had been working the crowd for some time.

"I'm seein' that hand gesture pop up all over," the hare said. "That snazzy dromedary is going to each one and handin' them somethin'."

"Better give it a go," Mohan prodded.

Vince saw the dromedary turn towards him and raised three fingers to his forehead above his right eye. On cue, the dromedary began making his way towards the hare, a small piece of paper in his hand.

He was only metres away when the sharp *crack* of a high-powered rifle drowned out the bidding process. Time seemed to slow to a crawl. Vince, Kitty, and the rest of the market patrons watched in horror as the slave girl collapsed onto the stage, her dead eyes still wide with shock as a pool of crimson began to spread beneath her. Blood spattered over al-Seif's face, who stood less than a metre away. His bodyguards closed in as they rushed their employer into the secured confines of the apartment building.

The sudden stillness that spread over the crowd after the shot lasted only a moment. Then panicked screams filled the air as dozens of people hastened for the nearest exit.

Vicki met Zed at the lift near the main entrance. It was much fancier than the freight elevator by the cages and adorned with small murals that must have shown a history of gladiator combat through the years.

Neither had anything new to report, and Vicki took the first step towards the lift doors.

They didn't see the electronic tripwire, but Zed's sharp ears picked up the high-pitched beeping noise it emitted when set off.

"Get behind me!" he shouted.

The badger dragged the frog back and held up his left arm—the one protected by the ancient and ornately carved golden bracer. A dome of glowing blue energy enveloped Vicki and Zed seconds before the blast hit them. The holding pens, arena, elevator, and half of the warehouse above them vanished in smoke and flame.

Mohan and Rizzo had only heard echoes of the shot back at the lorry, and now the tiger roared into his headset, "What the bloody hell was that?"

"Sniper!" Kitty replied, her eyes instantly going to the rooftops and balconies. "I see him! He's headed north. I got him!"

"No! Kitty, hold position and—dammit, she's gone. Vince, do what you can to minimise civilian casualties—"

A larger explosion shook the ground beneath them, cutting him off. Mohan glared at Rizzo.

"That wasn't mine!" the basilisk said.

The tiger looked out the front window to see a black cloud of smoke coming from the direction of the docks.

"My God! The warehouse! Vicki? Zed? Come on, dammit, answer me. What the bloody hell happened?"

The concentration required to maintain the shield against the blast had forced the badger to one knee. When the smoke cleared, Vicki and Zed were left at the bottom of an enormous crater that had once been the parking lot of Golden Seas International Inc. Zed lowered his arm, and the field vanished.

"We're all right!" he answered Mohan's frantic cries.

Vicki stared at the devastation around them, then looked to the bracer. "Ya know, I forgot it could do that. How's it work again?"

"Forgotten secrets from another age," the badger replied as if that explained everything.

"What happened?" Mohan was asking.

"The warehouse must have been rigged against intruders," Vicki replied, still slightly shaken. "I admit, we weren't expecting that either."

"And the arena?" the tiger pressed.

"Well, al-Seif's gonna be pretty upset when he sees what's left. And his employees aren't going to have a place to park for—"

She suddenly coughed on some dust, and Zed finished for her.

"Unfortunately, we did not find anything to confirm that al-Seif wished to use fiends in his events. The cages installed were of substantial fortification, but that may have been a new improvement over an older design. Regardless, now it is all gone."

"Bugger all!" Mohan slammed a fist into the lorry's roof, causing a dent in the thin metal. After fuming a moment longer, he said, "Glad you're ok. Our location is hot, so make your way back to the safe house by the prearranged route. Watch your backs; something about this still doesn't feel right."

Zed acknowledged, and Mohan turned to Rizzo. "You think al-Seif set that off? Some kind of remote security device?"

The basilisk shook her head. "*Non*. Even the brief look we got at the Khet arena showed no such security measures. That is not Alabwaq's method of dealing with a compromised facility. They are too expensive to simply destroy them when discovered."

The staccato of gunfire echoed from deeper in the market.

Mohan slid open the side door and climbed out. "Things are getting bad in there. Keep the engine warm; I'm pulling Vince and Kitty out."

8 – Sniper

Kitty had barely heard her father's orders. At the sound of the shot, the younger Katral's first instinct was to scan the rooftops for all the spots she would have chosen, quickly discounting those too close to al-Seif's mercenary patrols.

She saw the sniper climbing a third-level balcony down the alley behind her, heading for the roof. All she could discern at this distance was that the shooter was male, lean, dark-furred, and canine.

Something about his position made Kitty pause, and she quickly calculated a trajectory. The results confused her; even with her skill, such a shot seemed damn near impossible. Moreover, the exit strategy was wrong. Why was he climbing up the outside when he could have slipped back into the apartment?

There was no time to consider these facts; if she didn't act now, her quarry would escape.

She tore the robe disguise aside, revealing she wore her hunter clothes underneath. Her heavy pistol rested in its holster on her hip.

Using an abandoned cart as a springboard, she vaulted up to the nearest balcony and scrambled after the sniper.

She poked her head over the roof's edge and quickly ducked back down to avoid a hail of gunfire. Drawing her own weapon, she blindly fired several rounds over the ledge and then leapt up and rolled onto the roof. The retreating figure was already several rooftops away, searching for a path to street level.

Kitty ran after him, ducking under clotheslines and dodging TV aerials. It must have been laundry day for half the residents of the market. Every other line seemed to have bed sheets and clothing strung across it, making it difficult to track her target.

The obstacles didn't prevent the sniper from blindly firing in her general direction, and she ducked behind a roof access as the ricochets sprayed her with bits of plaster and mortar.

They were running out of rooftops. The end row of apartments was undergoing renovation, and several scaffolds and small cranes snaked up the side of the buildings. The sniper grabbed one of the crane ropes and began rappelling down to the street. Kitty paused at the roof edge and took aim, but there were too many civilians below to get a clean shot.

She took a breath, leapt for the rope, and swung out into space above the street. However, her target reached the ground first and turned to shoot out the counterweights for the crane.

Kitty felt a moment of weightlessness as her support failed. She reached desperately for the nearest scaffold as she tumbled through the air, gasping in pain as she barely grasped one of the steel poles, nearly dropping her pistol.

Curiously, instead of using his pursuer's difficulty to gain further ground, the sniper crouched behind a flower cart and assailed her with bullets. She was a proverbial sitting duck out on the scaffolding and rolled to the side, dropping through the awning of a cloth vendor to avoid the gunfire.

As Kitty climbed free of the shattered tables and scattered linens, the sniper took off running again, tipping the flower cart and sending hyacinths, daisies, and orchids tumbling through the air.

As the yellow and white heads of the daisies danced in front of Kitty, a stab of pain lanced through her chest, and she could swear she saw a face flash before her eyes—a face she would never forget. A surge of repressed memories followed, and she staggered under a sudden wave of emotions.

"The hell…" She shook off the ghostly images and continued the pursuit.

Her quarry had gained a lead of several metres, but the crowd was scattering at the sound of gunfire. The waters of the Hutsepth Canal appeared around the next bend, along with a small marina sheltered between two stone quays. A string of light pleasure boats bobbed at anchor along the piers jutting from the manufactured embankment.

The sniper was leaping over a low wall on the water's edge, perfectly silhouetted against the picturesque backdrop of the bustling canal. It was a perfect shot, and with a smooth motion aided by feline agility, Kitty slid into a balanced stance, aimed, and pulled the trigger.

The gun jammed.

"Bloody hell!"

She lowered the temporarily useless weapon and dashed towards the wall as the roar of an engine reached her ears. Too late, she leaned against the wall in time to see a sleek speedboat racing away from the dock.

Briefly, she considered following, but she knew her quarry must have had the boat waiting for him. By the time she managed to hot-wire a similar craft, he would be well ahead of her.

As the sniper's craft began to merge with the other water traffic, he turned and, to Kitty's astonishment and growing anger, looked straight at her and delivered a pretentious bow.

Then he was gone.

Kitty pounded her fist on the wall and swore again.

Reluctantly, she spoke into her radio. "He...he got away."

Back in the twisting alleys, Mohan paused in his efforts to push through the panicking crowd fleeing the market square. Only his sheer size prevented him from getting knocked over.

"Right," he said flatly. "Regroup with Vince; he's pinned down. Apparently, some of the bloody patrons were planted by al-Seif's rivals, and they thought now would be a bloody good time to start a little gang war. It's a bloody regular shitstorm in there. I'm already on my way."

Ignoring the bewildered stares of the few civilians watching her, Kitty cleared the jam from her pistol's chamber and dashed back down the lane towards the market square.

9 – Marked

Vince would have debated whether he needed help, but he was trapped behind a counter laid out with ornate rugs and pottery. He idly thought some of them might make a nice addition to his apartment in Banton—minus the bullet holes, of course.

"Goddam guingin swill eaters!" he bellowed, taking potshots at the mercenaries cowering behind the stage. He had purloined a 9mm pistol from one of the weapon dealers on the edge of the square. "Go cry into your nanny's teats! Hey, watch the ears, asshole!"

Southern gentleman or not, when he was under fire, he threw as many insults as he did bullets. His genteel mother and sisters would have blushed to hear the filth streaming from his mouth, but by hell, he would give as good as he got.

Nearly all the civilians had cleared the square, leaving only those who actually wanted to fight and those who were already dead or injured. A few of the slaves attempted to use the confusion to escape, but in their drug-addled state, they only succeeded in providing easy targets. The gladiators joined readily with al-Seif's goons; they lived to fight and didn't care if it was here or in the arena. If any of them made it out alive, their employer would likely chastise them for risking a valuable commodity.

After the initial panic, the mercenaries finally sorted out who was on whose side, but not before killing or injuring several of their own. Their rivals—marked by sashes of blue and red—had started out as a small group on the south side, but it was apparent that their goal had been to secure an entrance for reinforcements.

A trio of mercenaries appeared behind Vince, and they spotted him instantly. The hare sighed in exasperation and raised his hands as they levelled their weapons in his direction.

Three shots rang out, and Vince flinched, but when he opened his eyes, he saw three bodies falling. Kitty stood behind them, smoking pistol in hand.

"May I say, darlin'"—the hare grinned—"you have impeccable timing."

"Stuff it," she growled, crouching behind the counter beside him. "What's the situation?"

"I believe your father would say we're bolloxed. Seems the assassination attempt was a cue for some of Mody Nahas's boys to start a little chaos. Oh, and that journalist and his photographer are still huddled up near the fountain. Might want to help them out a bit."

Kitty frowned. "Mody Nahas? I thought that bloody orangutan actually knew Alabwaq? I hope none of his other rivals decided to come play."

She peered around the edge of the cart. The lynx and his fox companion were huddled between an over-turned cart and the lip of the fountain, which had picked up a few more chips from stray bullets. One of the fish spouts had shattered, and now it sprayed a curtain of water up and out. The bodies of two unfortunate patrons lay face down in the pool, their blood turning the water crimson.

The journalist and photographer appeared unharm-ed but frightened. Or at least the fox was; he kept rocking back and forth with his hands over his head and shouting hysterically. By contrast, the lynx appeared remarkably calm and had even managed to get his hands on one of the fallen mercenary's SMGs. How he carried the weapon showed Kitty that he had at least a little training, but clearly not military, and his aim was more to keep the mercenaries' heads down. His attention kept going back to the murdered slave girl between bursts of return fire.

Kitty ducked back behind the rug stand. Taking several quick breaths, she counted to three and dived out from her hiding spot, sprinting headlong towards the fountain, dodging bodies and bullets along the way.

As she slid into cover next to the fox, he shrieked in surprise, which she silenced with a paw over his mouth.

"Shut it. You want to get out of this, do as I say—Oi! Get your head down, nutter!"

Kitty grabbed the lynx by the shoulder and forced him behind the fountain's rim just as a bullet clipped the stone where his head had been. The lynx grabbed her as she pulled him down, and she saw the pattern on his forearm.

Beneath her armoured shirt, a strange burn flashed through a similar mark that covered her left breast and arm.

"My God!" Kitty gasped. "You're... you've got a mark!"

"What? My arm? I—"

She cut him off and spoke into her radio. "I have a birthmark here!"

Vince poked his head over the lip of the rug stand and shouted, "If that don't beat all. Here? Which one—" He ducked back as a hail of bullets peppered the frame.

"Later, Vince," Mohan shouted over the radio. "Kitty, keep them alive, understand? I'll be there shortly."

The wail of sirens reached the tiger's ears as he stood in the alley. Local authorities would be there soon, and they needed to be long gone by then. Mohan glanced around and spotted a table abandoned by a local arms dealer. A wicked grin spread over his face as his eyes roamed over the hardware. He grabbed several items and continued towards the square.

Mercenaries continued to pour into the market. From the alleys came the blue-and-red-clad Nahas thugs and from the apartment the purple and gold of al-Seif, né Alabwaq.

"Where do y'all guys come from? Villains for less?" Vince muttered. "I wonder if their insurance package has coverage for *intentional* death and dismemberment."

Several thugs took refuge on a balcony above and behind the stage. It was reinforced with iron plates and was clearly intended as a defensible nest in case of such a battle. The doors behind them suddenly burst open, and a pair of muscled mercenaries came out onto the landing, carrying a heavy belt-fed machine gun between them, which they mounted onto the railing.

Vince's eyes widened. "Aw shit!"

He flattened himself against the ground as a stream of .50 calibre bullets obliterated the top of the counter, showering him with broken pottery and pieces of carpet. The mercenaries then aimed for the fountain, severing the sculpted feline woman at the waist and shattering the top edge of the cart Kitty and the journalists hid behind. Then they seemed to wave the gun around randomly, shooting at anything and everything that might be hiding an enemy. Eventually, their belt ran dry, and they paused to reload.

Vince peered over the shattered countertop just in time to see the balcony erupt in a fireball.

"Right, time to go!" Mohan bellowed from the south entrance to the square, a rocket-propelled grenade launcher balanced easily on one broad shoulder. He dropped the empty tube and lifted a second one, aiming at a group of thugs on the other side of the square. They scattered for cover as the explosion blew a cart into the air.

Vince dashed over to Kitty and the beleaguered journalists and helped drag them to their feet. Angry shouts signalled that the two groups of mercenaries were quickly recovering from the sudden onslaught by this unknown third party.

Mohan crouched in the archway, fiddling with a lumpy canvas bag.

"Much as I hate to do this, we need to buy some time," he said as he pulled the pin on a single grenade and dropped it into the pouch. "Run!"

They raced down the narrow alley, silently thankful that most of the civilians had cleared out when the fighting started. A thunderous explosion followed seconds later as the bag full of hand grenades erupted and collapsed the archway leading into the square.

They sprinted towards the waiting lorry as soon as they arrived at the outer market entrance. The local authorities began to arrive in armoured personnel carriers, which pulled up onto the curb in front of and behind them. The rear hatches opened, and groups of large mammals clad in heavy riot gear poured into the street. The hunters tensed as a small group headed in their direction.

"Fire in the hole!" Rizzo cried from the driver's seat as she triggered her detonator.

There were several muffled *thumps*, and the street filled with thick grey smoke. The basilisk donned a pair of high-tech goggles from beside her seat and slammed the lorry into gear, laying on the horn to clear anyone in front of them. Through the goggles, she could see the vague outline of the street by the variations in the heat it had collected over the day. Pedestrians and police appeared as brighter red and blue blobs against the surrounding environment, allowing her to swerve around them as they were left choking and blinded.

Amid of the confusion, Zed radioed in. "Mohan, Vicki and I just sighted al-Seif boarding his private yacht. They are making headway for the Median Basin. We may be able to place a tracker on the yacht if we act now."

"No," the tiger said, rubbing his temples. "No, let him go. He'll probably flee to his villa in Medocci, and that boat of his is pretty hard to miss. Get back to the safe house; we'll meet you there."

Rizzo slowed before they broke through the smoke screen and spotted a pair of police cruisers waiting outside. Several other vehicles were also trying to escape, and the authorities had their hands full trying to block the street before any more could avoid a search. They offered a few angry shouts as she forced her way through the cordon, but none gave chase—it didn't matter if they caught the tag numbers; they would be wiped clean by the morning anyway.

The basilisk spent a few extra minutes driving down seemingly random streets just to be certain they weren't followed.

The sun and the day moon were beginning to set in the western sky when Rizzo pulled to the curb, and all eyes turned towards the journalist and his photographer.

The lynx returned their gaze coolly. He still carried the mercenary's SMG, but the magazine was empty. He let it drop to the floor with a sigh. "All right," he said, "just exactly what the bloody hell is going on here?"

The two tigers seemed amused by his accent, which was more refined than their Plainsman Locken.

Vince picked up the lynx's arm and studied the strange pattern with a gleam in his eye. Instead of spots, the lynx had a series of stripes arranged in the distinct image of a roaring tiger's face.

"The story of your life, brother," the hare said. "Adventure! Excitement! And all yours for the—Ow!" Kitty cuffed him over the ears.

"What were you doing in the market?" Mohan asked.

The journalist looked the massive tiger up and down; in the cramped confines of the lorry, he seemed to fill the entire space. With so little distance between them, the lynx quickly concluded that playing games with his rescuers wouldn't be wise.

"My name is Sedric Barnes. I'm a writer for *LBC World Press* in Grettasburg, Locke. This quivering mass of orange fur used to be my photographer, Ed Sanders."

"Screw you, Ric," Ed managed to stammer, "We've been in shit before, but not like that."

Ric nodded slowly. "Maybe you're right; sorry, mate." He turned back to the tiger. "We were following the trail of Assad Alabwaq's slave trade all through this region; it's a lot bigger than just this market in Kairran. But somehow, I think you already knew that."

"And now you're just starting to realize how big, is that it?" asked Kitty.

The lynx glanced at the faces around him. "Much bigger. I hope you have an exit strategy to get out of the country."

Mohan raised an eyebrow. "And why would we want to do that?"

Ric stared at him incredulously. "Because of the dead girl in the market. You don't know? That just happened to be Rijay-din-Aden, only daughter of Abdul-bin-Aden, royal ambassador for the kingdom of Barju."

Kitty cursed. "I knew I'd seen her before. It was all over the local papers last week; something about an abduction on her way to school in the palace district. To be honest, I thought we were going to find her in Khamir."

"So that was you in there," said Ric. The tigress shut her mouth tight, realizing she may have said too much. "In any case, when it's discovered she was about to be sold into slavery and subsequently murdered? Well, the excrement is going to hit the rotary device, as they say."

"No shit," Vince said, rubbing his bruised ear. "Wait a minute, you don't suppose she was really the target and not al-Seif?"

"Possibly," Mohan said. "There've been rising tensions between Pytan and Barju for decades. Both were on a path to peace recently, but after this? It might just be the straw to break the proverbial camel's back."

"I didn't think either side would have the balls to pull something like this," Rizzo said. "As you say, the peace talks were starting to work. The whole thing just feels…off."

Mohan nodded. "Bloody oath it does. On top of that, our mission is scrubbed for now, and al-Seif is still on the loose."

"Who?" Ric asked.

The huge tiger smiled mischievously. "And now for something you didn't know. The mouflon you know as

Assad Alabwaq is really Jirair al-Seif, one of Pytan's most upstanding businessmen."

He yanked open the side door, dragging Ric and Ed into the street. "This is where you two get off. But don't worry; we'll be seeing you again very soon."

Sedric Barnes thought there was something ominous in how the tiger said these last words. However, he felt a strange thrill that made the birthmark on his arm burn with a peculiar intensity.

As he watched the lorry speed off into the growing twilight, he began feeling strange amity towards this odd group of Hom-Ans. He didn't really believe in fate, but he still thought he had just had a brush with destiny.

A groan from Ed snapped him out of his reverie.

"What's up?" he asked.

Ed waved helplessly at the departing vehicle. "They still have my camera!"

10 – Hunter TS Three

The southern end of Kairran's Nayhadjin International Airport was a sea of warehouses and converted hangars, which hosted a variety of small businesses that directly or indirectly served the needs of the airport itself.

One such warehouse was a solid three-story structure of glass and cinder block emblazoned with the gold and blue logo of Kaulsk Shipping Co., care of Knight's Cross, Eisben Fens, Locke.

The hunter's white lorry pulled into an empty car park next to a fleet of similar vehicles, and they disembarked.

They unloaded their gear before heading inside, and a pair of agents were already moving towards them. They would remove the radio equipment, switch out the plates and remove any exterior markings that might be used to identify them. In minutes, the vehicle would be nothing more than a typical transport van again.

The spacious interior of the warehouse contained rows upon rows of cardboard boxes and wooden shipping crates of all shapes and sizes; several people were still busy making the place look like the legitimate business it was, but none looked twice in the hunter's direction. At the back, a metal staircase led to a sparsely furnished second-floor office overlooking the main floor.

Clearly, the office served a purpose other than the day-to-day operations of Kaulsk Shipping. Whiteboards along one wall were plastered with a cascade of photos, shipping documents, and diagrams pertaining to Assad Alabwaq and Jirair al-Seif. A few rows of folding chairs faced the boards, and a slide projector had been set up between them. A fresh pot of coffee was brewing on a small table along the back wall.

Zed was already waiting when they arrived, and the first thing Mohan did was grasp the badger's proffered paw.

"Zed," he said with a grin, "glad to see you made it back in one piece, mate."

The badger slapped him on the shoulder. "Indeed, my friend. Though this has been a dark day, I fear."

The tiger sauntered over to the coffee pot. He would have preferred tea, but he wasn't about to complain — that is until he took a swig of the strong brew the Soketh were famous for.

"Strewth, man. How can you drink this?" Mohan said, choking.

Zed simply laughed and poured himself another mug.

Rizzo was next into the room, followed closely by Vince. As usual, the hare was prattling on about a woman he had met at a local bar. "I'm only sayin' the hips on Darjay were exquisite. I mean, she was a squirrel, so it probably goes without sayin'. Squirrels do have such wonderful thighs."

Rizzo's disgust with the conversation was obvious. "You really are such a *gwan-gheen*!" she said.

"I told you, it's *gwin-ghin*, darlin'."

The basilisk glared at him.

Vicki hopped in from the back room, which served as sleeping quarters. She was just in time to catch the end of the argument.

"So, how many broken hearts are you leaving behind this trip?" she said with a wink.

"I don't leave broken hearts," Vince said indignantly. "I'll have you know that's one of the rules, and a very important one! Every one of my lovely consorts is treated like a queen durin' the time we're together. I even leave a personalised card on the nightstand."

"How thoughtful," Rizzo mumbled.

"And not all of them are one-night stands, I'll have you know," the hare continued. "For instance, after listening to Farrah's woes about her previous relationships, she just happened to drop the names of some of Alabwaq's most used business fronts, which brought al-Seif to our attention. Rebecca mentioned the Golden Seas warehouse during our delightful—and rather expensive—dinner. And Namay..." He paused, a far-off twinkle in his eye. "Ah, Namay."

Rizzo threw up her hands in exasperation. "Ugh! Enough already! I need a shower." She stormed off to the rear room.

"Didn't mean to make you feel dirty, darlin'," Vince called after her. "And of course, I can't join you. That's one of the rules."

The basilisk turned and delivered an obscene gesture before disappearing through the door.

Kitty was the last to enter the office. Out of habit, she checked to see if they were drawing any unwanted attention, but the night-shift workers continued their tasks as if the hunters weren't even there. She appeared to ignore her teammates' ranting, but she thought Rizzo was jealous of Vince's carefree activities. The basilisk made it no secret she had once lived a similar lifestyle, but as she matured, she had decided to put it behind her. If anything, the hare's antics were an uncomfortable reminder of her lusty past.

Kitty paused as she caught the look from her father. "What?"

The big tiger nodded to the rear balcony exit. "Outside," he said. "Vince, get Watch Command on the line for an update." He passed Ed Sander's camera to Vicki. "Wrap this up and get it shipped to PR. Everyone, we debrief in one hour." He followed his daughter out onto the rooftop balcony.

The night was warmer than their hunt three evenings ago—a sign that winter was waning in this part of the world. Midori was rising on the eastern horizon; on the far side of the globe, people would see its cousin Druna rising with the sun. The moon cast a long shadow over Kitty as she leaned against the low wall, her back to her father.

"What the bloody hell were you thinking?" the elder Katral admonished. "I gave strict orders for you to stay put. Vince could've been killed out there without your backup."

Kitty turned and crossed her arms, but she refused to look him in the eye. "I just reacted. We needed an ID on the shooter—"

"Which you didn't get."

"He was tall, dark-furred, and canine—greyhound, I think, but his ears were straight. He was also an impossibly good shot."

"Not the bloody point," Mohan growled, his muzzle curling in a snarl. Then he softened. "Look, Kitty, I know this wasn't your choice of posting. Most of us may have more field experience, but you don't have to prove anything; this isn't a contest for the most daring deed. We have to work as a team out here; everyone at their assigned post doing their assigned duty. I'm only trying to keep us all alive. Your mother would never forgive me if I let anything happen to you."

Kitty bristled slightly at these last words. They recalled a similar conversation not so many years ago when Mohan had told her the truth about the birthmark covering his chest and arm. The face in the daisies flashed in her mind again, and now she did look at her father, the fire in her eyes fuelled by past memories.

"You don't protect people by keeping secrets, Mohan," she growled.

He knew the incident she referred to and resented her remark bitterly, but he understood her anger and controlled his own. "No. No, of course you don't. I just—"

Zed knocked on the door and poked his head through. "Mohan, Watch Command is on the radio, and Gallows is on his way."

The tiger sighed. "I'll be right there." He opened his mouth to say something further to his daughter, thought better of it, and left.

Kitty turned back towards the view of the airport and fished out a cigarette. Her father wished she'd never picked up the habit, but all she had to do was mention his occasional cigars to point out his hypocrisy.

The face from her past invaded her thoughts again. As she inhaled, she imagined the cloud of tobacco smothering the face. As she exhaled, she blew the images away in a puff of acrid smoke and firmly closed the lid on the emotions that threatened to overwhelm her, locking them behind a seal of bitter ice.

Inside, Mohan picked up the radio receiver and pressed the transmit switch. "Hunter Tango Sigma Three to Watch Command. Repeat, Hunter Tango Sigma Three to Watch Command. You read me OK, Kane? Over."

Thousands of kilometres away, deep beneath the frozen peak of a lonely mountain, a youthful grey fox answered the call. "Loud and clear, Hunter Tango Sigma Three." Andrew Kane was just one of the dozen or so operators who huddled in the dimly lit Watch Command room, deep in the heart of the Sanctuary.

Mohan could almost picture him seated in front of his workstation, the giant world map projected on an enormous screen covering the far wall, its blinking dots marking the locations of every agent they had in the field. Knowing Kane, he probably had his feet propped up on the console, a mug of lukewarm coffee in one hand.

The fox spoke with a slight South Fields twang, a little edgier than Vince's smooth Banton. "We got a satellite blackout comin' in about fifteen minutes. What's your sitrep?"

Mohan acknowledged. While several nations had satellites circling the planet, keeping them in geosynchronous orbit had proven difficult. As a result, their course around the globe often intersected with the large dead zones that covered several continents. Whatever phenomena kept modern electronics from working within them, the effect lingered at the edges of low-Amarthian orbit, causing all satellites to go into a forced stand-by mode while they passed overhead. On the plus side, it taught scientists much about electronic shielding and fast-booting computer systems.

The tiger recounted the events of the market, letting Zed fill in the details about the warehouse. Mohan finished with the assassination of the slave girl and the ensuing firefight. "After the last lot was called, it all went Rollaroo. A sniper caught us off guard; identity unknown."

Kane furiously typed the data into his terminal, adding brief notes to the recorded transmission. "Are you confirmin' that a third party was operatin' in your theatre?" he asked, his voice carefully controlled despite his concern over these new details.

"We think there were four, actually. Several of al-Seif's rivals were hiding in the crowd—blue and red sashes from Mody Nahas—but I don't believe the sniper was part of their group. After the girl was hit, Nahas decided it was a good time to pick a fight, but the sniper fled the scene. Al-Seif escaped to his yacht; we'll need it tracked."

"Already on it. Was al-Seif the sniper's target?"

Mohan paused. "I don't think so. Turns out al-Seif was about to sell off the daughter of the Barjan ambassador. I don't know if he knew it, but the sniper bloody sure did."

"Good God," Kane muttered, then regained his composure. "Your region is about to get hot. Local assets will assist with extraction. Anythin' else? Maybe some good news?"

"As a matter of fact, yes. We found a new recruit! Send me everything you can on one Sedric Barnes, a journalist with *LBC World Press*. He was birthmarked."

"Interestin'." The curiosity was obvious in Kane's voice. "We'll have it to you by mornin'. Going dark. Over and out."

An hour later, the team gathered around the whiteboard for the debriefing. They were joined by a jaguar with sandy long-fur. Thomas Gallows had assisted them in the Khamir District by posing as the construction foreman who constantly argued with the dromedary police commandant. He was surprised by the news about the journalist but hadn't noticed the birthmark because he was wearing long sleeves at the time.

Mohan finally got some hot water and made himself a proper cup of tea; unfortunately, there wasn't any lemon. He stood in front of the whiteboard, mug in hand, and stared at a grainy satellite photocopy of the market square, playing the events of that afternoon over and over again in his head.

It shouldn't have got so mucked up. He'd been with the Tiger's Stripe for over thirty years and had never seen an operation turn bad so quickly. It didn't help that this was the Scrappers' first real mission — a sort of trial run. Fiend hunting was one of the Tiger's Stripe's traditional roles — among others — but it had always been on the frontiers, where the march of civilisation couldn't help but blunder into the territories already occupied by the fearsome beasts. The monsters were not native to Amarthia, but they had been there a long time. To make matters worse, they also carried a deadly plague that had stumped even their most highly skilled virologists looking for a cure.

And recently, they had begun to push back.

More and more sightings were beginning to happen, some of them within the fortified cities of the world. Tiger's Stripe needed teams that could not only eliminate the threat but investigate how and why the threat existed in the first place. The Scrappers were meant to determine if they were truly prepared to deal with this paradigm shift.

So far, the answer was no.

After two years of investigating seemingly random attacks across the continent of Estan, they thought they had caught a break when they heard about Assad Alabwaq and the Khamir District murders.

Mohan doubted the crime lord was responsible for attracting the fiends himself, but they couldn't ignore his growing interest in them. Halting his operations would have gone a long way towards proving his team's effectiveness.

Two years, Mohan thought. *That's how long we've been on this aukie shoot.*

He'd hand-picked most of them. Zed was the first. He was only two years younger than Mohan, but they had worked together in various task forces since they'd first signed up. They came from vastly different cultures but had bonded over shared values of hard work and family—although Mohan couldn't fathom handling five kids and two wives when he could barely keep up with two daughters and their mother.

The badger sat near the slide projector, sharpening his axe with a whetstone. He had removed his keffiyeh for the evening, revealing black long-fur with a streak of grey down the left side; the Tiger's Mark was tattooed on the back of his right ear. He was the only member of the team who hadn't been born with the tiger-face birthmark but was no less trusted by any of them—and not only because he was Soketh.

Tiger's Stripe had been founded and almost exclusively staffed by those with birthmarks—people who felt born to serve a greater destiny. But as the generations passed, those numbers were starting to dwindle, and the Elder Council—their ruling body— knew they needed help.

Agents marked with the tattoo underwent intense vetting before receiving the Elder Council's blessing. There was never a doubt they were just as loyal and capable as those born with the mark.

Rizzo, Vince, and Vicki had been Mohan's next choices, each bringing skills he thought would be invaluable to their environment.

Vince was a master with locks and security systems, and with his charming personality, he had naturally eased into the role of their face man. Rizzo knew practically everything one needed to know about explosives and had spent a too-brief stint on the Neuf Marisian Gran Prix circuit, making her an obvious pick for demolitionist and driver. Mohan had not expected the friction between the middle-aged basilisk and the younger hare, but at least their bouts were mostly verbal. And they never let their arguments interfere with their work.

Vicki made up for it by getting along with everyone. The bullfrog was in her early thirties, old enough to be wise and young enough to not be jaded. Although

Mohan seriously doubted she would ever reach that point, it wasn't in her nature.

While she had never finished medical school, she retained an incredible knowledge of Hom-An anatomy and how to keep it in one piece. And her self-professed love for the television show *MacTavish* had helped nurture her intellectual mind, teaching her to look for solutions that weren't always obvious.

That brought Mohan to the last and most recent member of the Scrappers.

Kitty was his eldest daughter, just a few months shy of twenty-one. She had joined the team barely three months ago, having just finished her training as an agent squeezed between several classes at a trade school for computer science. But she would fill a different role.

Mohan had received specific instructions that she would join the team as their scout and sniper. He felt it an odd choice, but she was an exceptional shooter—no surprise, considering she'd been able to handle a rifle since she was twelve. Some skills came as a necessity when you grew up in a compound on the frontier.

Mohan still wondered what had possessed Elder Chang to put her on his team, especially considering the bad blood between them. He had kept the true nature of his profession a secret from her for many years, believing he was protecting her. The revelation that she was destined to share in his clandestine life didn't go over well. To make matters worse, it indirectly resulted in the death of someone very close to her—to the whole Katral family. Kitty held him responsible for the incident, and in a way, he was, but they both refused to discuss the matter.

She had focused her bitterness on every aspect of her training, scoring top marks in nearly all her combat classes. Yet each of her instructors noted that she had a tendency towards recklessness, a potentially lethal flaw for any team.

Mohan had asked Elder Chang directly why he had made such a choice for him, but the answer had been as cryptic as ever. "The bonds of family prove stronger when faced with adversity." Mohan wondered if the ancient tiger was just moving pawns again.

No, that was the wrong metaphor. There were no pawns in go, the Elder's favoured game. Instead, every piece in play had its importance, and some needed to be sacrificed so that greater territory could be claimed later. And an intelligent player—which Chang was—knew they were also a piece on the board.

Mohan chuffed and refocused on the issue at hand. They had a lot to unpack before escaping the country, and Gallows would fill them in on the rest of the details.

He cleared his throat and addressed the expectant agents. "OK, you lot, the Elder Council was less than pleased with our little show this arvo. Of course, they agreed there was nothing we could've done. They were, quote, 'certainly the most unforeseen of unforeseen circumstances.'"

"Sounds like Elder Hati." Vince chuckled as he leaned back on two legs of his chair, his huge feet propped on the empty seat in front of him.

Mohan ignored him. "They also share our concerns that this act was not carried out by elements of either Pytian or Barjan radicals but by a third party seeking to destabilise the region. They don't know how things will play out, but our part here is done."

"What of al-Seif?" Zed asked without looking up from his task.

"Gone walkabout. At least for now. But that bloody big boat of his won't stay hidden for long, and if he's scarpered back to Medocci, we'll hear about it soon enough. He won't abandon his business ventures for too long. He'll need to reorganise quickly if he wants to keep his assets in line. Don't worry; we'll bail him up sooner or later.

"In the meantime, we actually got some good oil on a freighter making its way here when it was suddenly diverted." Mohan stopped himself and mentally went back over his last sentence. "I mean to say we got good info; it wasn't carrying oil. Gallows has the details."

The jaguar stood and went to the board; he barely came up to the tiger's chest. "First, I've got an update on the tiamats you took care of," he said in his mid-west WUK accent. "Several weeks ago, a small fleet of fishing

140

boats left Carmir in Nanca Fier. Their last reported position was just north of the borders of the Saran Waste. Why they had ventured so far south is unknown, but the Ferriers are a little crazy anyway."

Zed's eyes twinkled at this, but he said nothing. His tribe was native to Nanca Fier, but what Gallows said was true. The deserts in Pytan's southern neighbour were even more dangerous than what was outside Kairran's walls, and how its scattered inhabitants had managed to put together a cohesive government was among the region's great mysteries.

Gallows continued, "After the initial disappearance, several other fishing trawlers and pleasure boats went missing between Carmir and Khet. We're not sure why the tiamats bypassed Khet and went on to Kairran, but that's what they did."

"So, no chance al-Seif actually brought them here," Vince said.

"I'm afraid not," the jaguar answered, "But now the good news. Your guess that al-Seif meant to hold a gladiator fight as early as tomorrow may have been on the nose, and we think fiends were still involved. The freighter Mohan mentioned, the *Resthoven*, was coming here when it suffered an accident. The captain made a sudden detour towards the Tharsian Sea"—he gestured at a map of the Median Basin hanging on the board, pointing to an area between the Medoccian provinces of Pacé Acqua and Mata—"and was very distressed when he made an emergency broadcast asking for medical aid. All he would say was that it was an incident involving some of their cargo. Three crew members were airlifted to Pacé Acqua with unspecified injuries."

Vicki leaned forward with interest. "Oh really? Any more info?"

"Only that the injured crew members had suffered major lacerations and appeared to have been mauled by a large animal—the *Resthoven* was not supposed to be carrying live cargo. There were also veiled concerns about Daeminox syndrome."

The room went deathly silent; even the noise from the warehouse floor outside seemed muted.

The virulent sleeping sickness was the same plague carried by fiends. It had been a ghostly threat terrorising the frontier borders of every nation. Few outside the Tiger's Stripe knew the source of the disease; you usually didn't survive an encounter with a fiend. Most cases came from spore left behind by the creatures—a spatter of blood or an infected animal carcass—and while the infected tissue decayed rapidly, there was still a high risk of exposure during those brief hours.

Symptoms could take hours to manifest and appeared without warning. One moment, you were fine, and the next, you suffered severe disorientation and short-term memory loss, followed by a deep coma while the bacteria slowly ate away your vital organs. Depending on individual constitution, a living victim could remain in this state for years before the body finally refused to function. After death, the deterioration process increased dramatically; there usually wasn't even enough tissue left for a cremation.

Contact with an infected victim's blood or saliva raised the chances of the disease spreading considerably, and with symptoms taking hours to manifest, containment was a very real problem.

Those born with the Tiger's Mark had a different story. Their own research couldn't explain it, but they were naturally more resistant—but not immune—to the plague and many other diseases.

They had tried to use this resistance to their advantage, hunting down the fiends and keeping them contained in the wilderness. Above all, they had tried to keep the origin of Daeminox syndrome a secret, not only to avoid widespread panic but to keep less scrupulous organisations, or individuals like al-Seif, from turning the disease into a terrible weapon.

"Where is the ship now?" Zed asked.

Gallows tapped the map. "Your next stop: Mata, Medocci. The ship is making its way to the port city of Kalegos. We don't think it will be there very long, so we need to move on this fast. You're to go in, confirm if the ship was carrying fiends or not, and report in."

Kitty raised an eyebrow. "What about Sedric Barnes?"

"You and I will be paying him a visit tomorrow after brekkie," Mohan said, holding up a hand to stall her objection. "No buts; you know how this works. I don't much like having to drag around an uninitiated recruit, but we don't have much choice. We don't need the whole team to scout the ship, and we shouldn't be in Kalegos long. He can tag along, and then we'll stop in Locke so he can put his affairs in order before we take him to the Sanctuary. Who knows, as a journalist, he might sniff out something we missed."

"Your first field assignment and your first recruit," Gallows said. "I must say, agent Katral, you're starting your career with a bang." The tigress ignored the comment. "Let's go over the extraction plan for tomorrow."

Another hour passed. The sounds of the warehouse died down as the night shift hit a lull, but it would pick up again soon; the world of international packaging never truly stopped.

"All right," Gallows said, "I think you've got it. Your flight is scheduled for eleven tomorrow morning. We think we've got a lid on the Barjan ambassador's daughter, but keep on your toes. Someone knew she was there, and they probably had a reason for killing her. We're cutting it real close; by morning, the reports of the market massacre will be all over the local news, and they'll try to lock the country down tight."

Mohan nodded soberly and began wiping off the whiteboard and gathering their old intel notes. "That's why you're in the PR department. What's the word on our friends with the Golden Eye?"

"None the wiser," Gallows said, producing a box to shove the outdated information in for disposal. "They still think KLAWS was the major operator here."

Mohan grunted, then looked back at his team. "Well, don't just stand around with your thumbs up your arses, mates. We have to get this place cleaned. Then get some sleep; I have a feeling it'll be the last decent rest we get in a long while."

11 – New Recruit

The Hayden Suites was a cheap but relatively clean establishment not far from the main terminal of the Nayhadjin International Airport. Sedric Barnes leaned against the desk of his hotel room with a growing mixture of apprehension and excitement. Moments ago, the front desk had called to tell him he had visitors. He could almost picture the diminutive field mouse behind the front desk staring open-mouthed as the giant tiger politely asked her to page him.

There was a knock on the door, and he quickly rose to answer it.

The tiger practically filled the narrow hallway. Fortunately for him, the ceiling was tall enough, and the lights recessed, so he didn't have to hunch over. Gone were the tactical harness and the peculiar padded shirt. The trophy necklace made from long, jagged teeth—from what animal Barnes didn't know—was still present, but he wore it over a casual buttoned shirt and a pair of tan cargo shorts.

Barnes noticed with interest that he carried a green folder in his massive paw. He also noted the more comfortably sized white tigress who accompanied him—the one who had rescued him and his photographer at the market. His eyes lingered on her now that he could get a good look at her. She was a few centimetres taller than he, wearing a black T-shirt with a yellow lightning bolt across the front, which he recognised as the emblem for the heavy metal band Current. She wore a studded bangle on her left wrist, and the stems of a stylish pair of shades were fitted into her ear gauges, which she had obviously got in lieu of the more common elastic straps or lobe clips. She brushed at an errant lock of black long-fur that swept across her brow. It promptly fell back into place over her left eye.

The tigress removed the shades and returned his gaze coolly, making her own assessment of the lynx. He kept himself in shape, probably a regular runner. His shaggy, dirty-blond long-fur was lighter than his body-fur and appeared as if it had never seen a comb in his entire life. Yet his eyes struck her the most: luminous green pools that radiated inquisitiveness and sharp intelligence. They also had that distinct roundness common to Hom-Ans from the northern regions of Aerenia, a contrast to the subtle Benese folds and inward slant that her own eyes displayed, a trait she received from her mother.

Despite the warming weather this time of year, he wore khaki cargo pants and a blue cotton polo shirt under a canvas vest that seemed made of pockets. Overall, Sedric Barnes's appearance fit Kitty's stereotypical image of a foreign news correspondent.

"Ed left early this morning," Barnes said as he ushered them inside. "Even you still holding on to his camera couldn't keep him in this country any longer."

"What about you, Mr Barnes?" the larger tiger inquired, moving to the window. The tigress followed him and began searching the hotel desk and light fixtures.

"Call me Ric. To be honest, I'm not really sure why I'm still here. You said you would see me again; I suppose I assumed it wouldn't matter where. With the camera?" He added hopefully.

The tiger finished his scan of the parking lot below and moved to check the radiator. "Sorry, mate, but we'll mail it back to you...eventually."

"Are you...are you looking for bugs?" the journalist asked.

Mohan nodded, and the two agents silently went over the room from top to bottom, but they found nothing more than Ric's personal recorder, which was off and didn't even have a tape loaded.

Mohan raised an inquiring eyebrow at this.

"You would have taken the tape anyway," Ric said.

"Somebody's been watching too many bloody spy movies," Kitty muttered.

"Or not enough," the lynx answered, indicating he heard her.

After their search, the tigress leaned against the wall next to the closet while the tiger sat on the edge of the desk; the only chair in the room wasn't built for someone his size.

"How long have you had that mark on your arm?" the tiger asked, folding his own massive appendages across his barrel chest.

"From birth, of course." Ric held up the arm in question. "As if you didn't know. I've never encountered anyone else with a birthmark resembling a tiger's face; I always found that curious."

Mohan nodded. "Bloody oath, it is." He eyed the lynx appraisingly and added, "You've made some shrewd guesses so far. You would have made a fine policeman."

Ric's eyes narrowed ever so slightly. He had expected these strange people to dig into his past, but he wondered how much they knew.

"Who are you?" he asked, evenly meeting the tiger's gaze. "Some kind of secret police?"

The white tigress let slip a derisive laugh, and her companion shot her a look.

"No," the larger tiger said. "At least not in the way you think." He handed the folder to Ric and let him leaf through it. "Sedric Percival Barnes the second, age twenty-four, born in Grettasburg, Locke, tenth of Aegius nineteen sixty-nine. Son of Detective Inspector Sedric Percival Barnes the first of the Grettasburg Royal Police Force, killed in a drug raid roughly six years ago—my condolences.

"You were set to follow in his footsteps until his death when you suddenly quit the academy and decided to become a journalist. Might I ask why?"

Ric looked up at him. "Answer my question first: who are you?"

The tiger's eyes betrayed nothing as he waited patiently for an answer. *He's persistent*, he thought. *But he's got a lot to learn.*

Ric turned back to the folder. *OK, if you want to play it that way.*

"I'm sure it's all right here," he said. "My father was working a bribery case that happened to involve some city officials and one of the Locke crime families. There was some miscommunication, and he found himself following up a lead at the same location as a government drug raid. When everything went to pieces, he ended up on the wrong end of a junkie's gun."

"And that's it?" Kitty scoffed. "Daddy gets killed, so you decided policework was too dangerous?"

Mohan growled at her sharply, but Ric held up a hand. He walked up to the tigress and stared into her eyes. She held his gaze for a long moment, fire burning behind the sapphire pools.

He wouldn't turn away, and Kitty suddenly felt uncomfortable under that emerald gaze. Only one other pair of eyes had been able to look at her like that, and she had seen them flash before her yesterday in a cloud of daisy flowers. Painful emotions began to rise, feelings she had sworn she would never allow herself to experience again.

Ric thought he caught a flicker in her eyes, a faint crack in the ice, but she turned away with a growl.

"My father was a good man, a good cop," he said evenly. "If he'd gotten all the information he needed, he would still be alive."

Behind him, the tiger gave him a warning chuff, and Ric backed away from the tigress. In doing so, he missed the look she flashed him—not one of anger but of respect.

"Sorry," Ric said. "My father's death ended up being a huge embarrassment to the department. He was well-liked both on and off the force, a real local hero. Rumours that his murder was purposefully orchestrated by corrupt city officials began to spread. The department did everything they could to save face and practically destroyed the legacy of his career in the process. It's a rather…touchy subject."

"We all have sore spots," Mohan replied. "But go on; tell us how that led to journalism."

Not enough, eh? Ric thought, but he obliged. "They say knowledge is power, but my father taught me there's a lot more to it than just knowing. Understanding is just as important if you're searching for the truth." He picked up the folder and stared at it thoughtfully. "And even more important is understanding that your perspective isn't the only one people see.

"Like everyone else, my first instinct was conspiracy, that my father had been planted in front of the gunman because he uncovered something dangerous to some powerful people. I still haven't proved it one way or the other. The drug case wasn't his, but when he was told who was involved, he thought it might be connected. Ministry Intelligence never informed the local constabulary — and, by extension, my father — that they had planned the raid. Once you add it all together, it seemed my father was destined to wind up in the wrong place at the wrong time, and a twitchy junkie shot him. In the aftermath, neither department ever came clean on who bungled what.

"But the more I thought about it, the more I realised it was more than a series of convenient events that got my father killed; it was a lack of communication. And I began to fear what else could happen. I became obsessed with the dissemination of information. The world might not always be a cheery place, but people need to know what happens beyond their rose gardens and tea trays. Maybe if they understood that, they would learn they could actually do something about it."

He laughed humourlessly. "Of course, it didn't take long to figure out that idealism goes right out the window when you're trying to sell papers."

"Don't sell yourself short, mate," the tiger said. "I've read some of your articles. They're thought-provoking and fairly objective, from what I've seen. Too few people actually take the time to examine the world around them anymore."

"I would think that would be bad for you. After all, an intelligent person is often more observant and can pick out what doesn't fit. Like how you know my name but haven't offered yours."

"Mohan."

Ric raised an eyebrow. "Interesting. Buswan name, but your accent is clearly from the United Plains. New Dunsbrook or Bourne Bay?"

Very sharp, Mohan thought, then answered. "I was born in West Plains in New Dunsbrook." He pronounced it *duns-brick* compared to Ric's *duns-brook*.

"So, Mohan," the journalist said, "next I suppose you're going to tell me some secrets need to be kept."

Mohan's ears twitched even so slightly. *Kitty was right; he's seen too many bloody movies.* "Or perhaps," he said quietly, "that you can't force people to believe the truth. You can give them all the information you want;

153

it's up to them whether they accept it or not. Of course, they have to deal with the consequences when they're wrong."

Ric's eyes narrowed sharply, and the tiger held up a placating hand.

"That's not a dig at your father, mate. We checked his records; he definitely got the shit end of the stick. Unfortunately, we'll have to pick up this discussion another time. Why were you in Pytan to start with?"

The journalist stared at him a moment, then decided honesty was best. "I already told you I think people have gotten too comfortable with life inside the city, at least in what you might call 'western' civilisation. Life is a lot different here. Slavey and gladiator games are alive and well, and the people accept them because they've lived with them for so long." He paused and looked out the window. "But things are changing. The sultan has been trying to bring more positive influences to his people. I figured if I could help expose some of the criminal elements, it would go a long way towards giving people back home a reason to care."

"A noble sentiment," Mohan said, "but how exactly did you plan to pull that off at the market?"

"Well, I was just going to ask Alabwaq—er, al-Seif for his views on the sultan's recent antislavery legislation." His tone was perfectly serious, and Kitty stifled a laugh.

Mohan broke into a grin. "Well, that's ballsy, mate."

154

Ric shrugged. "No more so than hunting monsters in the Khamir District."

The tiger stopped laughing abruptly. *Oh, you cheeky bastard!* "Monsters?" he replied nonchalantly.

"This is probably yours." Ric dug into a pocket and tossed something to Kitty, which she caught deftly. It was a flattened bullet from her rifle.

"I'm not talking figuratively like our mutual friend, al-Seif," the journalist continued. "I mean honest-to-God monsters. Creatures that have only been recorded in the *Arx Monstra* or *Grimoire Gothique Bestiary*. Not the tales you tell your kids about so they behave. I mean the ones that give adults nightmares."

"How do you go from exposing the slave trade to looking for literal monsters?" Mohan asked, still unwilling to give ground.

Ric stood and went to the window, staring at the scattered groups of travellers entering and leaving the airport across the street. "I learned a lot of things following al-Seif around, things I didn't think were connected at first. Like, there's been a steady rise in sleeping-plague victims both here and in the border settlements."

"Daeminox syndrome."

Ric nodded. "I'm guessing whatever terrorized the Khamir District also carried the disease. You were sent to kill it, and burned the corpse to prevent any spread.

155

And since you were at al-Seif's market, I assume he was also interested in the beast."

Mohan raised an eyebrow. "That's a tough sell, mate. He makes an awful lot of money on weapons, but trying to weaponize a creature that spreads Daeminox is a bit of a stretch."

"That's not why he wants them at all." Ric leaned against the wall and crossed his arms. "The gladiator matches are his most prized spectacle. They're a symbol of his wealth, power, and influence. And his ego. He always has the grandest locales, the most brutal fighters, the healthiest slaves." He paused. "And the fiercest beasts."

"Nutter," Kitty spoke up suddenly. "He'd never be able to contain a fiend."

Mohan looked at her sharply.

"So the beasts exist," Ric said. "Don't deny it. I've seen one."

The tiger raised a questioning eyebrow.

"I tracked al-Seif, under his assumed name Alabwaq, to an old mining compound on the edges of the Aizlgeist," the journalist explained. "Except he wasn't mining for minerals. He found something—something living—deep in the tunnels. I still can't believe what I saw down there. These aren't rix, or bahnger or some other wild predator that frontier farmers have to deal with."

He shook his head emphatically. "As soon as I got out of there, I felt like I had to warn somebody, tell them what I saw. But who would believe me? The governments are too concerned with trade negotiations and border disputes to pay attention to a second-string reporter."

Mohan nodded to the file on the bed. "I'd hardly call two Reginald Clark awards the achievement of a second stringer."

The lynx gave a derisive laugh. "Sure. For covering the opening celebration of Medocci's new rail line to Vösleis and for my glowing review of the Queen's Golden Jubilee, which I admit were some amazing events. But they're fluff pieces, mindless drivel to lift the public's spirit. I've received more criticism for my articles on disease in Gat-Bahar or the struggles of frontier settlers in Caiman's Desert than praise for my award winners. Which do you think was actually more important?"

He was growing increasingly agitated with the subject, culminating in a low growl, which was much higher pitched for a lynx than a tiger. Kitty was surprised to find herself thinking it sounded almost cute but was careful not to let it show.

"You asked why I was in the market," the journalist continued. "The real reason is I had heard about Rijay-din-Aden's kidnapping, and when I learned there was going to be a slave auction, I thought al-Seif would be just arrogant enough to pull off something stupid like selling an ambassador's daughter." He paused and looked at the birthmark on his arm. "But maybe it was something more." He squared himself in front of the enormous tiger and crossed his arms. "Now, I answered your question; you answer mine: *who are you*?"

Mohan nodded to Kitty, and she rolled up her left sleeve while he removed his shirt and turned his back to the lynx. "Look familiar?"

There, spread from shoulder to shoulder across his broad back, was a peculiar arrangement of stripes not unlike the one on Ric's forearm. All the other stripes surrounding the mark seemed to flow around it, throwing it into sharp relief against the orange fur. The roaring tiger face stared back at him, an eye on each shoulder blade with a broad S-shaped stripe down the centre.

"We are the *Laohu Tiaowen*, the Tiger's Stripe. We hold no allegiance to any government, but acknowledge their sovereignty. We uphold the free will of all sentient beings and fight evil forces across Amarthia. Evil not unlike the monster you saw. We have hunted them through a thousand generations, and you, Sedric Barnes, were born to be one of us."

Ric blinked. "Are you having a laugh?"

Mohan turned and began to put his shirt back on, giving Ric another glimpse of the three large, jagged scars across his chest. There were two matching sets on his left arm—the one he kept protected by the vambrace when they were on the hunt.

"What, too melodramatic?" the tiger chuckled. "It's fair dinkum, mate. I'm Major General Mohan Katral, and this is Lieutenant FC Kittina Katral."

Ric nodded to Kitty. "Related?"

"My daughter."

"So you *are* military. Benese?"

"That's ancient history. Like, really ancient. Much of our history and traditions come from East Benai, but we've been international for a really long time. The ranks help us establish a chain of command in the field. We're not mercenaries; you'll find we're fairly normal when we aren't on a hunt."

Ric studied Kitty's mark before she covered it over again. It appeared to be only half a face.

"They are similar to mine," he said thoughtfully. "Does it always make a full tiger's face?"

"It's different from species to species," Mohan replied, "but yes. We tigers have the most dramatic arrangements; some show up in peculiar configurations." His eyes narrowed. "And some can't be shown in public to strange men."

Kitty growled, and Ric held up his hands defensively. "I meant no offence!"

"Right," Mohan went on. "I admit you're pretty sharp. My team is tasked with hunting fiends—your 'monsters'—and if you haven't guessed it already, they

159

aren't native to Amarthia. We've been keeping them in check for a long time now, but they're tough bastards. You're also correct that they spread Daeminox syndrome, and the recent rise in cases is because the fiends have gotten a lot bolder."

Ric leaned on the windowsill and thought for a long moment. He hadn't expected them to admit everything immediately; typically, he had to fish around to get the whole story.

"Say I believe you," he said at last. "Suppose this Tiger's Stripes or whatever you call it is really dedicated to 'fighting evil'. Why didn't you take care of al-Seif and others of his ilk a long time ago?"

Mohan motioned to Kitty and began pulling clothes out of the dresser. Kitty threw Ric's suitcase on the bed and turned to the closet.

The tiger spoke as he worked. "I know you've got a dozen questions right now, mate. We all did when we first started out. To answer that particular one, it's not as simple as good versus bad; there's a balance that needs to be maintained, or else it all goes Rollaroo. We follow a strict code: Justice, Honour, Strength, Wisdom, Mercy, and Loyalty. You'll learn more when we get you some formal training, but the important one right now is Justice.

"We can't just 'take care of al-Seif.' He'll pay for his crimes, but he must be held accountable to the law. It's important to us that every government be able to handle its own affairs; otherwise, you become nothing but a dictator treating people like puppets."

Ric thought he heard a faint growl of disapproval from Kitty. "Noble, but is it feasible?" he asked Mohan.

The tiger shrugged. "Worked in the past, and we're gonna give it a burl now. There may not be a world court, but there's at least some general concept of good and evil shared by all Hom-Ans. That's what we're trying to uphold. I'd say our biggest concern would be slipping into the grey too much and letting evil blind us into thinking it's good. But we can talk philosophy later. Right now, we got a plane to catch."

"You're kidnapping me?" It was more a statement than a question, and Ric made no move to stop them from packing.

Mohan frowned. "Turns out your prediction yesterday was spot on. We're sitting on a bloody powder keg in this charming little corner of the globe, and we've had to cut our operation short. It'd be bloody difficult to shut down al-Seif's gladiator games while trying to dodge artillery shells. Don't worry; we'll get you out safe. You may even be able to help along the way."

The tigers moved with the alacrity and skill of people who had learned to pack in a hurry. When the work was completed, Mohan zipped up the suitcase and threw it into the lynx's chest.

161

Ric staggered under the sudden weight. "Now wait just a minute! I'm not exactly a hunter. What happens if I decide not to join you?"

The tiger chuckled as he moved towards the door. "Oh, you will, and you'll be happy to. But hypothetically?" He turned on the lynx and loomed over him, a menacing voice rumbling out of his massive chest. "We won't kill you. Oh, no. We'll just make sure no one ever reads your articles again. In fact, we'll crumble your newspaper. You'll be the laughing stock of the printed word, reduced to writing gossip columns and supermarket tabloids about alien invasions and conspiracy theories. Your friends and family will weep for you and wonder how such a brilliant mind sunk so terribly low."

The journalist stared up at him wide-eyed and gulped. "You must be joking."

Mohan grinned broadly and turned to open the hall door. "Too right, mate! Sorry, I have a wicked sense of humour; get used to it. But I am serious when I say your life will never be the same from here on. Honestly, don't worry about it. The more you learn about TS, the more you'll be proud to be a part of it."

That or you'll be dead, Kitty thought. She gave an exasperated snort before following them out of the room.

12 – Escalation

The terminal at Nayhadjin International Airport swept two graceful wings out from a large central structure crowned with numerous domes and spires. It appeared more like a royal palace than a major travel hub. The sun gleamed off the aluminium skin of the aircraft as they waited on the tarmac, their propellers oiled and ready to take to the skies.

Pytan didn't possess any runways large enough to support the massive six-engine Aerlift 540s, which were used to cross the Basilisk Ocean to the eastern shores of West and South Contéga. Still, it did provide flights to almost everywhere else on the continents of Aerenia, Estan, Marinaris, Mwungo, and Saeria.

In fact, the centralised location of the nations of Estan made them a hub for most commercial travel across four continents by air and sea. If war broke out in the region, it would affect much more than just Pytan and Barju.

The airport's main concourse lobby was almost as impressive as the building's exterior. Broad geometric landscapes and sweeping cascades of black-, tan-, and sand-coloured linoleum tiles spread across the floor. Cheap but regularly cleaned burgundy rugs provided more stable footing for the thousands of padded, scaled, or taloned feet that crossed it daily. Plastic chandeliers provided soft pools of light at night and wide, tinted skylights filtered in the harsh desert sunlight.

From the main lobby, travellers could turn right and be greeted by the plastered professional smiles of the airline ticket clerks, turn left towards a large food court with an assortment of eateries for all species, or continue straight on to the first-floor baggage claim and the escalators up to the main concourse on the second floor.

The open space between the entrance and the escalators was broken by several islands of cushioned metal benches and small potted palms.

Thomas Gallows sat in the middle of the seating area facing the main entrance, casually reading a local paper. He nodded to Mohan and the Scrappers as they entered and headed towards the second floor, where the waiting utilitarian grey frames of the metal detectors guarded a few magazine stands and last-minute convenience stores before visitors could make their way to the terminal gate.

"The hunter assets have arrived," the jaguar said quietly into his concealed radio.

After a brief acknowledgement, he went back to his paper. They were still missing a few intelligence operatives who would be flying out; the rest would leave by land or water. He wished they could have all gone the northern route. One would think crossing the Hutsepth Canal into the port of Arbai would be as simple as getting in a boat, but Kirque was a bit more vigilant than Pytan when it came to border security, and it would be even more so once the threat of war started brewing. There just hadn't been enough time to alter their previous extraction plans and get the proper passes distributed to so many agents.

Personally, Gallows hated to leave. Kairran had much to offer that wasn't illegal, and he had hoped to expand his collection of exotic cooking spices.

Several minutes passed before a slight movement caught his eye and made him pause his surreptitious crowd searching. A hunched janitor was entering an employee entrance on the far side of the lobby, nothing more.

So why did Gallows have warning bells going off in his head and feel a tingle from the birthmark on the back of his neck?

At a glance, there wasn't anything out of the ordinary about the amphibian janitor's appearance; he even passed another employee who greeted him in a somewhat familiar manner. Perhaps TS-3's encounter with the unknown element in the market was making him paranoid.

Well, it wouldn't hurt to check it out, he thought as he folded the paper and rose.

He spoke softly into his radio. "Raislin? Medev? Meet me at the service entrance to the southwest terminal."

"Something wrong?" the soft, slightly raspy voice of Raislin asked.

"I don't know, but I'm going to check it out. Everyone else, hold positions." Several additional voices acknowledged the jaguar's orders.

Within minutes, Gallows was met by Anita Raislin and Yusef Medev—a female gecko and a male ostrich, respectively. The three of them were the extraction specialists for this stage of the operation, charged with ensuring that all assets were accounted for now that it was time to pack the bags and go home. They had worked together before and had established several contingencies to ensure everyone made it out safe and sound. This went double when they had to pack it in early.

Gallows and Raislin were clothed as tourists, but Medev wore the uniform of an airline clerk. The stubby, flightless wings sprouting from his shoulder blades protruded through special holes in the back of his shirt.

The sentient avians of Amarthia had the same basic anthropoid form as their mammal and reptilian cousins, but their species could add lots of variation to the length of arms and legs. Medev's lanky ostrich legs and long neck gave him a significant height advantage over his fellows, and he had to bend almost double to get on eye level with them.

"How do you want to play this, Tom?"

Gallows thought a moment. "The Waltons. You've got the uniform; Raislin and I will play the lushes. We're looking for a newt janitor. Get us as close to the utility tunnels as you can; if there's trouble, that's where it will most likely be."

Medeve nodded and opened the door. Gallows stumbled forward, affecting a drunken stagger and dragging an equally woozy Raislin behind him.

The offices were symmetrical along a wide hallway. Gallows quickly glanced through each cubicle and open door as they passed, but he saw no sign of the janitor he had seen earlier. They passed through without challenge until they reached a door at the far end of the hall. Beyond lay the utility spaces and baggage sorting area underneath the terminal gates.

A small wild cat appeared at one of the office doors and gave a start. "Uh, can I help you?" he asked in accented Locken.

Medev, who had purposefully kept a few paces behind them, stepped up, calling loudly. "Sir. Please, sir. This is a restricted area."

Gallows went straight into his drunken tourist routine. "Look here, shir, I jesht need to get my bag'sh. Dolly left her camera in there, and we can't take pictersh of our trip if it'sh in there, can we?"

He rushed for the door, dragging a giddily giggling Raislin after him.

Medev acted appropriately shocked and shouted after him, "Mr Walton! No, you can't go back there. Sir!" He turned to the stunned wild cat. "Could you please contact Mousavi in security? We may need a little help getting him out." Then he ducked through the door himself.

The utility tunnels were much narrower than the previous corridor. Ceiling-mounted signs announced each gate and marked exits directly onto the tarmac. Exposed piping and ductwork sprawled across the ceiling. Off to their right, they could hear the hum of the conveyor belts as they carried luggage from the ticket counters to the gates and from the gates to the baggage claim.

Gallows and Raislin nearly ran into a baggage handler headed for the closest tarmac exit.

"Hey, watch it," he grumbled in Netib.

Gallows kept up his drunken persona. "What wash that? Why can't anyone shpeak proper Locken around here?"

"Damn wook," the handler muttered as he vanished out the door. The term was the short form for citizens of the West United Kingdoms.

Gallows stared after him a moment. The handler was a newt, but he couldn't be sure whether it was the same one he'd seen in the lobby. Despite being on the edge of the desert, the airport seemed to hire quite a few amphibians.

Medev caught up to them. "I've bought you about five minutes; Mousavi will delay things for a bit."

The jaguar nodded. "More than enough time. Raislin, follow that baggage handler. Medev, you're with me."

Above them at gate eighteen, the far end of the southwest terminal wing, Mohan's Scrappers and their new charge waited for their flight to Medocci.

Ezekiel and Vicki watched the planes outside, the frog chatting excitedly about the various principles of avionics she had picked up through books and documentaries; of prime note was the fact that jet engines were rarely used because of the cost of fuel and the difficulties in constructing a stable airframe. Mohan and Ric lounged in the row behind them, idly watching the TV, while Kitty stood near an ashtray, smoking. Vince was, naturally, flirting with the demure lemur woman behind the check-in desk while Rizzo stood nearby, giving him a death glare but saying nothing.

The group was inconspicuous among the crowd of travellers. Even Mohan's great size went unnoticed, thanks to several other commuters. An elephant family was waiting nearby; both mother and father were at least two and a half metres tall. Two gates over, a lion couple sat making doe eyes at each other; the male could easily match the tiger centimetre for centimetre, and the female was only slightly shorter. An old, tired-looking rhinoceros in a rumpled business suit snorted fitfully near the fire exit at gate twelve, mumbling in his sleep about missed flights. He was easily over two metres tall, even hunched in a chair.

Surprisingly, the TV displayed an international news broadcast instead of a local channel. Twenty-four-hour news was a recent concept for Amarthia; Tiger's Stripe wasn't sure if it was a good thing or a bad thing yet. Reliable reporting within one's own country could be difficult enough; knowing that foreigners were looking over your borders was another matter.

Ric naturally took a particular interest in the development of constant news access. If it proved successful, perhaps his concerns about people's lack of interest in world events might prove unfounded. Of course, there was also the problem of them becoming *too* interested in foreign affairs. There was also the potential for widespread misinformation; all he had to do was look at the state-run media in countries like Mosvia.

For Mohan's Scrappers, the news was about to prove injurious.

The reporter—a glassy-eyed mongoose—confirmed their worst fears with his latest bulletin: "…received early reports of violent protests outside the Pytian embassy in Barju's capital city of Faradin. The outbursts come after the reported assassination of Rijay-din-Aden, daughter of Barjan ambassador Adbul-bin-Aden, whose body was discovered at a market in the Pytain capital of Kairran yesterday afternoon. Unconfirmed rumours state that the market was hosting a gladiator auction at the time, but it is uncertain if the ambassador's daughter was a victim of the in-Hom-An slave trading practices associated with such events."

Kitty snuffed out her cigarette. "Bloody hell. I thought Gallows said they put a lid on that? And doesn't al-Seif have enough pull with the local media to keep stuff like that from prying eyes? We haven't even had time to get our arses out yet."

Mohan crossed his arms and chuffed. "Buggered if I know. As soon as that sniper hit, we all felt something was wrong. The Barjans certainly have a yarn to chew with Pytan, but I didn't think they'd get violent so quickly. I think there's something more to this game than a political assassination."

Gallows and Medev began searching faster now. Security would arrive any minute, and they needed to finish their sweep and get out of there before then.

The jaguar was halfway down the long passageway when he skidded to a stop near gate twelve. A pile of discarded clothing lay on the ground at his feet.

"How much you want to bet these belonged to that baggage handler we bumped into?" he said with a frown.

"I'm on the tarmac," Raislin said over the radio. "I don't see him. I stick out like a sore thumb here. I'm going—Eek!" She let out a sudden terrified shriek, there was a brief scuffle and her radio went dead.

"Raislin? Raislin!" Gallows turned to head back down the passage.

"Uh, Gallows?" Medev tugged at his shoulder and pointed to the ceiling.

Strapped to the pipes above them was a suitcase-sized object composed of wires and blocks of explosive compound. No physical timer was visible.

"My God!" the jaguar breathed.

"Should we try to move it?" the ostrich asked.

"I can't see any radio triggers or pressure switches from here. No liquid canisters, just standard solid compounds. He didn't have much time to plant it before we arrived. I think it's safe to say he just stuck it up there and ran."

172

Gallows reached for the device, closed his eyes, and plucked it from the ceiling.

The reporter continued, "The Pytian Defence Minister, General Rousel Ach'eman, cautioned that, despite the horrific events of the past few hours, Sultan Abdülkadír is doing everything in his power to stem hostilities with the Barjan people. He also announced that his intelligence bureau had identified a possible suspect for the attack in the market: a terrorist group calling themselves KLAWS."

Kitty's eyes widened. "Mohan…"

The big tiger stood. "Yeah, not good."

Ric glanced from one to the other and asked, "What's happened? Do you know this KLAWS group?"

"You could say that," Mohan answered quietly, flexing his fists and scanning the crowd as if looking for possible danger. "It's a public agency that we use when we're out and about. We're not the only secret organisation out there, ya know. It's a complex game of spy versus spy. Fortunately, we're old enough to have written most of the playbook. Anonymity is key to moving around discretely."

Ric still looked confused, and Kitty gave an irritated snort. "KLAWS is us, and you can be bloody certain we weren't involved in any terrorist activity."

Zed came up behind them, attracted by the news. "Whoever released that report to the media knows it is

173

false information. KLAWS is too highly regarded in intelligence circles; they will clear their reputation easily. That name was mentioned specifically as a message to us."

"Should you report it?" Ric asked.

Mohan nodded. "Maybe Gallows is still in the lobby."

The bomb didn't go off.

"OK," the jaguar said as calmly as he could. "Not pressure sensitive. There's a receiver on the other side. Damn! The bastard with the detonator probably got the drop on Raislin. Medev, get up to the terminal, see if you can find Hunter TS Three. They have Vega with them; she should be able to disarm this better than I can. I'm going to move this thing outside and as far from the terminal as I can get."

The ostrich nodded grimly, and they parted ways.

Gallows barely made the door leading to the tarmac when the device began to beep.

Vicki, Vince and Rizzo joined the group watching the TV. A hand reached from off-screen to give the reporter a recent bulletin.

"We have just received reports of an explosion at the Nayhadjin International Airport in Kairran…"

Seven voices gasped in unison seconds before the explosion ripped through the terminal wing at gate twelve and threw them to the floor.

13 – Change of Plans

Ric gasped for breath and choked on the dust. The explosion had knocked the air from his lungs, and he had no idea how long he had lain on the floor, but from the noise, it couldn't have been long. Smoke and flames were everywhere. He was barely aware of figures moving around him.

The explosion had severed the south terminal from the main building several gates away, but there was still a great deal of structural damage at their end. All of the glass had blown out, and large sections of the ceiling had collapsed. The fire exit and the rhinoceros sleeping next to it were gone.

Somehow, the agents of Tiger's Stripe were on their feet again. Vicki was instantly at the side of the nearest victims, offering whatever medical assistance she could without the benefit of her kit. Mohan and Zed struggled against a fallen beam while Kitty and Vince pulled out those trapped beneath. Rizzo attempted to comfort a child from the elephant family who had gotten separated in the confusion.

Ric watched the faces of the agents as they worked. When the news about KLAWS had broken, he had seen how agitated they were, searching the crowd for danger. His initial impression had been that they were looking for an exit, that the hunters had become the hunted. Yet here, in the midst of the chaos, they risked further exposure to help their fellow victims. Part of him wondered why he had expected anything else. Mohan had told him very little about the Tiger's Stripe, but somehow, Ric knew this was exactly what they should be doing. He knew because he could feel it himself, and his birthmark burned intensely as he surveyed the pain and devastation around him. He had to do something.

If I really am one of them, it's time to start proving it, he thought.

His bruised ribs made him wince, and there was a shallow cut on his cheek, but he managed to stagger to his feet. An agonised roar reached his ears, and he turned to see the lion from two gates over, leaning across his fallen mate. A heavy pillar lay across her torso, and even as Ric went to help push it off, it was clear from the amount of blood that she wouldn't make it. He put a hand on the lion's shoulder but couldn't think of anything to say.

Looking up, he saw the other members of the elephant family cowering on the far side of the terminal.

He waved to Rizzo and helped her guide the young one back where she belonged.

Rizzo nodded her thanks and looked beyond him. Ric turned to see Mohan standing at his shoulder. The wail of sirens drifted from outside, and emergency first responders were arriving on the scene.

"Help has arrived," the tiger whispered. "We've done all we can here; time to go. There will be a lot of inquiries from the local authorities that we'd rather not be involved in."

Ric understood, but he didn't like it. He had a feeling the tiger felt the same way.

Miraculously, none of them had anything worse than a few cuts and bruises, and they used a service ladder on the boarding ramp to climb down to the tarmac without difficulty. Their plane sat waiting to be loaded, and what was left of it was currently on fire. Fortunately, the nearby baggage cart had rolled away from the explosion and appeared undamaged.

Swarms of people were everywhere, some fleeing the burning terminal and others rushing to offer what assistance they could. The agents were not the only ones rummaging through the baggage cart, but in the confusion, it was uncertain how many were there to claim their own luggage and how many were already succumbing to a looter's mentality.

Vicki, Kitty, and Rizzo sifted through the disorganised heap. To Ric's knowledge, the agents only had carry-on bags, so he wondered what they were searching for besides his suitcase and Vicki's medical bag.

Vince called out and pointed across the tarmac; a few metres away, a gang of meerkats attempted to haul away three large stainless-steel trunks. Mohan was on them in a few long strides, roaring a challenge. Most of the diminutive *Suricata* scattered, but a small knot sneered up at him and drew short knives. The giant tiger punted the nearest one into his companions, knocking them over like ninepins. Their spirit broken, they scattered across the field.

Mohan threw one of the trunks over a massive shoulder as if it weighed nothing while Zed, Kitty, Vince, and Rizzo grabbed the others. Ric helped Vicki carry some of the loose bags.

"Where do we go now?" the lynx asked. "The airport has to be sealed by now."

"Just follow me," Mohan replied. He set a brisk pace for the warehouses at the airport's south end.

The journalist was out of breath when they arrived at the large white cinder-block building emblazoned with the Kaulsk Shipping logo. He remembered seeing the emblem on the side of the lorry he and his unfortunate photographer found themselves in the previous evening. Several identical trucks were lined up outside, as were several other vehicles that were clearly not from the shipping company.

Mohan held up a hand to stop them and waved them behind the cover of one of the trucks. Thanks to his height, he could look over the roof of the front cabin. The building was swarming with figures wearing the uniform of the Pytian army. Several employees were face-down on the ground while others argued with the officers blocking their path to the warehouse.

"Bollocks," the tiger muttered.

Kitty poked her head over the bonnet of the lorry. "This wasn't just about starting a war between Pytan and Barju. Somebody knew we were here."

"And they're doing everything they can to make sure we're out," Mohan replied.

A goat employee pressed against the bonnet of a police cruiser spotted them. He made a subtle jerk of his head and blinked twice.

Mohan nodded in response. "Right, back to the terminal. We're not getting out this way."

"I'm assuming they won't actually find anything at the warehouse," Ric said. "All your spy gear is already gone?"

Vince patted one of the trunks. "What do you think we got here?"

The lynx raised an eyebrow. "You put your weapons in checked luggage?"

"Why not?" Mohan replied as he led them back. "Big-game hunting is a tourist attraction in Pytan, and we had agents in place to help juggle some of the more…sensitive material. We've been planning this operation for a while and had lots of assets in place. You have to move fast and free in the business. Especially after things have gone Rollaroo."

"You've said that before. Rolla-what?"

The tiger chuckled. "Sorry, Plainsman expression. Eighteen fifteen, Battle of Rollaroo. Look it up when you get the chance. The short version is everything's mucked up."

They skirted the outer edge of the airport to avoid emergency vehicles and police. Eventually, Mohan led them to a rental agency sitting alone on the north end of the airport grounds. It was approaching noon, and the hot Pytian sun had climbed high into the sky, the pale-orange disc of Druna lagging behind it.

There was a police cruiser waiting there, and both jackal officers saw them. Mohan gave a curious sign with one hand, and the officers responded in kind.

"The Golden Eye," Mohan responded to Ric's unasked question. "Some of our allies in the region. Keep your distance; they'll be cautious of KLAWS thanks to the recent news, but they won't turn us in."

Cut, bruised, hot, and sweaty, the hunters collapsed resignedly in the shade of the building while Mohan went inside. Vicki retrieved her kit and began tending to their injuries while Zed went to scrounge up some water.

The rental agency was a squat structure; the walls inside and out were a pale yellow with a double red stripe running at eye level—or chest level for the tiger. The agency's red logo was emblazoned on the wall behind the front desk.

A concerned middle-aged gazelle was nervously watching the news of the bombing on the lobby TV. He looked up as Mohan entered.

"Sorry, we are closed due to the bombing," he said in Netib, waving his hands emphatically to shoo the tiger away. "We have no vehicles available at this time."

Mohan answered in passable Netib, "Is Rahja here? He's holding a convertible for me."

The clerk straightened slightly at this and glanced at the small group gathered outside. He scratched absently at his shirt, giving Mohan a brief glance at the Tiger's Mark tattooed on his neck just under the collar.

"No, he called in sick with the flu," the clerk said.

The tiger completed the countersign. "Well, I suppose an economy car will do. As long as it's something in...red."

The colour ending the phrase was variable, but in this case, the message was clear: agents in need of extraction.

The clerk lowered his voice and switched to accented Locken. "How many?"

"Seven, including a recruit," Mohan said, leaning casually against the counter and feigning interest in the news broadcast. "The warehouse has been compromised."

"Merciful Aaba!" the gazelle exclaimed. "Anyway, get in line. Clean-up started as soon as you reported last night, but we were barely half done when the bomb went off. And here I was hoping I wouldn't be needed."

Mohan knew what he meant; three operations were underway in Kairran, and his hunters were late additions. The rental agency was only a contingency if their primary extraction failed. Under normal circumstances, the clerk would have gone about his job as if there weren't any agents in the country at all.

"Hang in there, mate," he encouraged the gazelle. "Hopefully we'll make it out of this alive."

"We already lost three agents."

Mohan had to fight a sudden rush of anger. "Bloody hell. Who?"

"Raislin, Medev, and Gallows. They reported some suspicious activity just before the bomb went off. We suspect they found it and were trying to move it away from the terminal when it exploded."

"Gallows? Strewth, he's been pulling his weight all through this operation. He was a good man; they all were. Look, Mümtaz, right? Don't stay any longer than you have to."

The clerk smiled wanly. He shouldn't have been impressed that one of the hunter assets knew his name, but he was. "I've been fighting to find excuses to stay.

183

Local authorities have already been in here twice asking some very leading questions. I'm glad we got some of our Golden Eye friends to keep this channel open, but it's getting more dangerous by the hour."

Mohan nodded. "I have a feeling whoever started this whole mess knows we're here and why. Has anyone else reported in?"

Mümtaz pressed against a hidden compartment under the countertop and produced a small steno pad. "Rosa came through with our PR team, and the tracking assets have already cleared; the local PR is going to hate us after this. Especially since that news report flagged KLAWS. A few of our intel assets have volunteered to stay and support those being reassigned. Not surprising. Lunatics." This last statement was a good-natured jibe. Everyone knew their intelligence assets often had the most dangerous hands-on assignments and were damn good at it.

He finished checking off the list. "You should be the last ones."

"Good. Is Caz staying?" At the mention of the intel assets, Mohan thought about the burly bear who had done most of the intelligence coordination for the hunters.

"No, actually. Rishaad will be transferring from Barju. Cazimov will be meeting you at your next stop."

"Good. He deserves a break after this. What is the extraction plan, exactly?"

The clerk sighed heavily. "We're working on it; our doors have been closing almost as soon as they open. The airport is sealed, of course, but the east and west gates have also been closed. The navy hasn't sealed the harbour yet, but that probably won't last long." He reached beneath the counter and produced a set of keys. "But you get special treatment. Since our operations have been compromised, the Council has decided to pull our operatives out of Jar-Geshim."

Mohan accepted the keys with a grunt. "I didn't know we had anybody in Jar-Geshim. It's really as bad as that?"

"It was a long-term op; they were looking for political prisoners that the bandits might have apprehended. We have no choice now; the country will be shut tight in a matter of days. Gallows was going to handle it once Kairran was clear, but…"

"I understand."

"You'll have backup. Almost everyone heading out the south gate is being redirected there, myself included."

"A small team would be better."

"No choice, and no time. With war brewing, we aren't sure how the bandits are going to react. Safety in numbers. I just wish we had some heavier guns to send with you."

"So we're the heavy hitters. Right. Well, first, we need to get out of Kairran."

"Get to the south gate before fourteen hundred hours; our friends in the Golden Eye will hold it open as long as they can. With luck, I'll see you in Jar-Geshim. Otherwise, have fun supporting the intel team as this place tears itself apart."

Mümtaz made a show of typing some things into his terminal and switched back to speaking Netib. "Well, it looks like I might be able to help you after all, Mr Kazim. We have a Tracksman Hiker in lot D, fuelled and ready to go; it's the blue one. Our lot guards fled after the bombing, so just roll on through the gate. Thank you for choosing Authority Auto Rentals." He leaned in close. "I'll be right on your heels."

Mohan held out a paw, and the clerk clasped it at the wrist. "Good luck, mate. Strength and Honour."

"Wisdom and Justice," the clerk responded.

Mohan exited the rental agency and strolled over to his waiting team.

Ric was leaning against a light pole, arms crossed, and chatting lightly with the hunters he had only recently been introduced to. He looked up and nodded towards the rental lobby. "Clerks, rental agencies, airport warehouses—just how expansive is this organisation of yours?" he asked.

"Ours," Mohan corrected. "We have small pockets all over the world, but only a handful of large operations like this one are running at any given time. We've been moving assets into the region for almost two years;

breaking up the slave trading rings was a big priority long before we knew fiends were involved. Unfortunately, our resources aren't as limitless as they used to be."

"Really? Just how long has Tiger's Stripe been around?"

"Oh, about three thousand years," Mohan said with a grin.

Ric gave him a sidelong glance. "Are you having a laugh again?"

"Not this time. Come on, I got us a lift out of here."

The small size of the rental lot only highlighted how rare personal vehicles were in Pytan. Most of the cars were primarily for commercial use and safari tours. Lot D at the back end was no different, although the types of vehicles available were much larger than normal.

The rugged truck they eventually stopped in front of looked more like a powder-blue breadbox mounted on four large knobby tires with a spare strapped to the roof. Mohan appraised it with a gleam in his eye.

The Tracksman Hiker EX-380 C was an expedition vehicle designed for a wide range of wilderness terrains, and the rental agency kept several on hand for tourists venturing outside the city walls. Above the driver's cabin were four powerful floodlights. Mounted on the front were a heavy tow winch and hooks.

It was a massive vehicle that could easily and comfortably seat nine people of Mohan's size, three on the front bench—the centre seat was collapsible—and six in the rear. Sliding doors on either side provided access to the passenger compartment, separated from the driver's cabin by a set of storage lockers that created a narrow passage forward. Two rear-facing bucket seats rested against the lockers, and a pair of two-person bench seats were arranged on either side of the rear compartment, with a small collapsible table between them.

In the C model, the very rear of the passenger compartment was mostly empty space with a few built-in storage containers and wire racks on the side, most likely for securing hunting rifles and other equipment. The brochure in the glove box advertised models that could include anything from beds to extra seating or even a small kitchen.

The rear double doors had fuels can strapped to the outside and spare water jugs mounted inside.

"More like a half-sized RV than a truck," Ric said.

Vince stroked his goatee. "And here I thought usin' one of the warehouse vans would be too conspicuous."

Vicki rapped on the armoured panelling. "What did you rent us? A tank?"

They stowed the stainless-steel containers in the back along with their personal baggage.

"Well, at least they provided us with rations," Vince said, opening one of the built-in containers.

"Oh, I wonder what else is in there." Vicki eagerly started popping open the boxes.

Rizzo reached for the driver's door on the Hiker's left-hand side, but Mohan got there first. "Sorry, Rizzo, I'm driving!"

Clearly disappointed, the basilisk grudgingly climbed into the rear compartment with Vince, Vicki, and Zed. Kitty and Ric claimed the front bench, but the white tigress insisted on having the window seat.

Mohan turned the key, and the big diesel engine came to life with a satisfying roar before settling into a gentle purr.

Kitty caught the expression on her father's face. "Does mum need to get you one of these for your birthday?"

The tiger ran a hand over the leather-bound steering wheel. "She just might."

There were no guards at the gate, just as Mümtaz had said, and Mohan rolled right over the retracting spike traps guarding the entrance. He turned left out of the lot and continued north at the intersection; to the south, the front of the airport was a sea of emergency vehicles and flashing lights.

Vince called from the back seat, "Hey, if we can spare the time, how about lunch? I don't know about y'all, but all this runnin' around has made me a mite peckish."

Rizzo managed a humourless laugh. "I'd say that is the most sensible thing you've said all day, *non*?"

14 – The *Star of Carmen*

The luxurious *Star of Carmen* cruised through the calm waters of the Medean Basin. She was over seventy metres long with a beam of eighteen metres. Her hull was a traditional white, but each level of her four superstructure decks was a vibrant purple with gold accents. From stem to stern, the vessel symbolised its owner's thirst for opulence and power. Every lounge and cabin flaunted plush carpets, elegant crystal, and comfortable beds. There was even a helipad on the aft deck, although currently, it was devoid of one of the unique aerial contraptions.

Beside the second deck pool—just forward and above the helipad—a very angry Jirair al-Seif paced back and forth, his goatee waggling with each step, a bulky satellite phone pressed to his ear. The patient form of the mouflon's right-hand man and personal bodyguard, a melanistic panther named Abar Kami, stood nearby in the shade provided by the third deck.

"And you're sure the rest of the shipment had been secured?" al-Seif said into the phone.

The voice on the other end was as deep as the mouflon's was high. It also contained a great measure of fear. "Yessir! I Swear! We met with the contacts before we pulled into port and offloaded per your instructions. Only one asset broke containment, and it went over the side before we could contain it again. With the damage caused in the incident, the captain insisted—"

"Gods be damned what that blasted captain thinks," al-Seif roared, "as long as the remaining specimens were received undamaged. Where are you?"

"In Arbai, sir. I wasn't able to return to Pytan after they closed the borders."

"Well, I want you back down there! The Terrapin Holdings account must be closed by the end of the week. Without those papers, I cannot proceed with the next phase of my expansion, and I am holding you personally responsible for ensuring they get signed and delivered to me by then."

"Yessir, but how am I going to—"

"I don't care how you get your ass back into the country, just do it! Nahas and Weis are most likely already moving in, and I refuse to let this little war ruin everything I worked for." He disconnected the call, but the phone rang again before he could put it down.

"Yes?" he answered.

"Rashid here, sir," the calm voice of his market attaché said. "I wanted to inform you that the assets from your auction are secured and en route back to Khet. Shall I cancel the event?"

Al-Seif had considered this and was most pleased that the dromedary was taking the initiative. "No. My clients have paid for my services, and a cancellation may be taken in bad faith." He did not add that it may also be viewed as a sign of weakness. "I regret I will not be able to attend myself. However, I am most curious to see who actually turns up for the games."

"Very good, sir."

"Rashid, a moment," the mouflon caught him before he hung up. "Could you get to Arbai and back?"

"Of course, sir," the reply came without hesitation.

"Good. I want you to meet with Hamadi. He was overseeing a very special shipment, which has, regretfully, been delayed. Ensure he does not fail the remainder of his tasks."

Again, the mouflon disconnected, but again, the handset rang before it left his hand.

"Yes?" He was more annoyed than ever now.

A filter on the other end made the voice sound deep and mechanical; however, it couldn't mask the glottal amphibian clicks and the faint hint of a Locke accent. "I understand there has been an incident at the market."

Al-Seif's fury rekindled. For the past eight months, he had been dealing with the mysterious voice, to which

193

he was only given a single name: Freggs. The mouflon had been unable to determine who he worked for, but his best guess was one of the Aerenian crime syndicates.

"As if you didn't know, you bastard," al-Seif said acidly.

"Now, is that any way to greet your most generous benefactor? I trust you were able to contain the situation?"

"Contain? What is left to contain?" Al-Seif stomped between a deck table and the pool's edge. "I managed to salvage my gladiators and slaves if that's what you mean."

"Ah, then we have only minor collateral damage to worry about."

"Collateral damage?" the mouflon roared. "You never told me you planted demolition charges in the new arena. I hope they weren't intended to go off with me inside."

"Of course not!" The mechanical voice managed to sound insulted. "The security measures were a failsafe against the escape of your new…exhibit."

"Speaking of—"

"Just a moment," Freggs interrupted. "We believe part of the group that set off the security measures also had elements at your auction. Did you witness any peculiar characters?"

"Beyond what normally attends my events?" al-Seif scoffed. "No. If they were the mongrels that ruined my exhibition, I didn't get a good look at them. I was informed Nahas planted some thugs in the crowd, but he would never intrude on the warehouse. He's a guingin-headed ape, but he has some respect for his rivals.

"Which brings me to another issue: why, in the name of all the goat gods, did you bring *her* to my exhibition? And to have a sniper murder—"

"You were in no danger, I assure you," the calm, mechanical voice interrupted again. "You were paid— handsomely, I might add—to place a certain lot on display at an appointed time. From there, events played out as we had anticipated."

Al-Seif's patience was growing steadily thinner. "As you anticipated? You approached me with the grandest spectacle ever seen in the history of gladiatorial combat; you provided a new venue to house the event, and you provided a prime piece of merchandise to sweeten the festivities. And then your assassin stripped it away from me! For what? To start a war that was probably going to happen anyway? I assumed you were just as invested as I in this little venture."

"Please, Jirair. Everything will be revealed in time. It was necessary for us to…accelerate the situation in Pytan. Believe it or not, the peace talks were actually working. That would not have been good business for you or your interests in Medocci. Interests that, need I remind you, would not have been obtainable without the help of *my* employer."

The mouflon paused and wiped a purple silk handkerchief across his brow. From the start, Freggs had made it perfectly clear that he was employed by an entity that could move political mountains as easily as it manipulated crime syndicates. Al-Seif's ambitions were significant, but he had never aspired to political office. Freggs knew this, but he was still pushing him in a direction he didn't wish to go.

"No," the mouflon said finally. "No, of course I do not wish to jeopardise our further cooperation. Clients of your calibre are far too valuable to risk, but I do expect some form of remuneration."

"I'm certain that can be arranged. However, we will have to assess the damages. How much of the arena remained?"

"Nothing, it was completely destroyed. The warehouse was also severely damaged; however, we may still be able to recover the security tapes. Thankfully, the shipment had not yet arrived."

"Ah yes, the shipment. I understand there was an incident during the transfer process; one asset was lost. Was the vessel salvageable?"

"I do not know, nor do I care. That was your responsibility. I insisted on using my own resources, but you overruled me."

"And if we hadn't, you would have to explain to signor De Palma how one of his ships was damaged and several crewmembers killed."

"Even so, he will demand an explanation why I did not use his resources."

"Tell him what you will. Soon, they will be your resources."

"They are still not limitless. Those specimens were quite costly to obtain. Don't expect me to finance another expedition to the Saran Waste any time soon, especially with Barju and Pytan at war."

"I wouldn't concern yourself with that. I take it the ship is no longer proceeding to Kairran?"

"No, they diverted to Kalegos."

"Very well, we'll see to it. In the meantime, why don't you scout locations for an arena in Medocci?" It was an order, not a suggestion. "Estan has outgrown you, Jirair; let us handle it from here. Your holdings will be preserved, of course, but you are no longer required to directly involve yourself in the region until we have finished with it. Understood?"

Al-Seif wiped more sweat from his brow. "Yes, fine, but I refuse to change my timetable. Remember, it is not only fodder for the arena that you promised me. You claimed the shipment would be available within a fortnight, and I will expect something by then." He paused. "Even after what happened last week."

The voice sighed, producing a mechanical hiss that made the mouflon's fur stand on end. "Yes. We are attempting to recover at least some of the data. It will be months before our operations in the valley are viable again. However, we do thank you for creating inroads with the Marshal and providing us with the real estate for our...experiment."

"More valuable commodities that I doubt will yield any profit," al-Seif said.

"They may yet. We are already working on a solution to that problem. Stiff upper lip, my friend. You are a valued asset. I hope you don't forget that."

"I'd advise you to do the same," al-Seif responded.

He disconnected the call and tossed the handset as hard as he could over ship's side. "Bastard," he muttered angrily, but with less conviction than he felt. He called over his shoulder, "Abar, are we on course?"

The panther moved gracefully out of the shade. There was a fluidity to his movements that could be mistaken for effeminate, but al-Seif knew better. Abar was a practitioner of a brutal Busawn martial art known as chut-ri and held claim to several world-championship titles in many legal tournaments—and a lethal reputation in many more illegal ones.

He bowed respectfully to his employer and answered in a soft voice, "Yes, sir. We should be arriving in Pianure Rosso in a few days."

Al-Seif stared out at the glassy ocean, wishing his own internal struggles could be so at ease. "Good. If we have anyone left on the *Resthoven*, pull them off. Our associate" — he spat the word — "has other plans for her. And get me another gods-damned phone."

Abar Kami bowed and slipped silently away, leaving Jirari al-Seif leaning on the rail and gazing moodily at the sea.

15 – Escape from Kairran

Mohan and his Scrappers only had time for a quick lunch at an outdoor café, but even as they ate, the rumours of war were starting to spread. Murmurs came from the people around them. The local news showed reports of native Pytains assaulting the Barjans who had been their next-door neighbours just hours ago. The violence had not broken out into full-scale riots yet, but the agents knew it was only a matter of time.

When they returned to the Hiker, they intercepted a coded message from Mümtaz on Vince's radio. The clerk had reached the city gates and joined several others making their way out. The Scrappers were probably the last to leave.

As they drove south, they passed several military patrols, but there was no official declaration of martial law yet. Most of the additional security was headed towards the airport and the palace. The Scrappers could only hope they wouldn't be watching the rural farmlands as closely.

As the crowded buildings began to spread out and the hills blended into the fertile lowlands, the great bastion of the outer wall appeared mirage-like in the distance. Even several kilometres away, the fortifications were tall enough that they couldn't see the endless sea of sand and rock stretching beyond it.

Randomly spaced patches of cultivated fields dotted the land between them and the wall. Even in late Ferrus, grain, cotton, fruit trees, and livestock continued to thrive in this unique oasis near the banks of the Hutsepth Canal. With all the acres of sudden greenery, the Scrappers found it difficult to remember they were at the edge of the country's broadest desert.

When they finally approached the south gate, they were reminded that only one stage of their journey had ended, and another was about to begin.

The gate was a six-metre square at the base of the fifteen-metre-high wall. The doors were made of massive steel plates that recessed into housings on either side. Two cement structures protruding from either side of the opening housed the mechanical workings of the portal, and the fortifications outside were double-thick to protect these vital mechanisms. On the crown of the wall above the gate, a reinforced, air-conditioned control room monitored traffic going in and out of the city and kept a close eye on the horizon for signs of sandstorms and other threats.

Currently, a line of pedestrian and vehicle traffic backed up before the partially opened portal—trade convoys mixed with refugees wishing to flee in the face of the ensuing conflict. Most of the refugees appeared to be tourists and foreign contractors, hoping to purchase passage out of the country before it officially closed its borders. The Scrappers wondered if they realized the next closest egress was the port of Khet, nearly five hundred kilometres to the southwest.

Tiger's Stripe had more routes available than the public had access to, but they were all outside the city. The Golden Eye had been causing confusion to keep the exits open, but the Scrappers didn't know how much longer they could keep it up.

Mohan checked the dashboard clock: 13:30.

They were cutting it close; according to the Golden Eye's timetable, the gates would only remain open another half hour. However, the guards were taking their time screening everyone attempting to leave.

Ric sat up front next to Kitty again. "What sort of escape plan do you have to get through here? Did you actually manage to get agents in the city guard?"

"Not bloody likely," Mohan grunted. "The city guard is a more prestigious post than it is in 'safer' parts of the world, where they place new recruits—or even police—at the gates. Out here, the guards know what they're dealing with, and most have years of experience dealing with the dangers lurking in the wastelands. Countries like Locke or the WUK have found ways to spread their populations beyond their walls, but Estan is a whole different animal. The strength of the wall is the key to their survival."

Ric knew what he meant. Beyond the ramparts, there was no protection from sandstorms that could tear flesh from bone, packs of vicious and territorial wild animals who showed no fear even when confronted with modern weapons, or the bandit hordes who had abandoned society to pillage supply caravans and raid smaller settlements.

"Besides," the tiger continued, "the Golden Eye is handling things from here on out. They're good, almost as good as us, but I doubt they managed to get anyone on the wall. They'll try something different." He pointed at the figures busying themselves around the gate housings. "Like maybe arranging a little mechanical failure."

As they crept closer in the line of slow-moving traffic, Ric studied the figures more closely. In addition to the guards, a group of workers in orange-and-yellow vests swarmed like ants around the doors and the structures housing the gate mechanisms. He noted with interest that several of them were Hom-An ants, the one hundred twenty-centimetre sentient insects proving just as industrious as their tiny cousins. They were a curious sight walking around on the four legs attached to their lower thorax while their upper thorax bent upright so the remaining two appendages could serve as arms with pincer-claw hands.

Clearly, they were having trouble with the machinery, and Ric saw the crocodile squad commandant arguing with the crew supervisor about why they couldn't get the doors sealed as ordered. He was instantly reminded of the chaos surrounding the Kahmir District when he and Ed conducted their investigation.

"Nice work," Vince said, glancing out the window, "but it's not goin' to do us much good if things don't speed up."

A distant horn announced the top of the hour. The guards began to shift around.

"Guard change," Mohan said. "If the Golden Eye is going to try something, it'll be now."

Just then, a small economy car cut him off in line. Before Mohan could lay on the horn, the driver draped a feathered arm out the window and gave a curious sign.

The tiger leaned back to speak to the agents seated behind him. "This is it. Buckle up if you haven't already."

Ric heard a distant thunderclap and felt the vehicle tremble slightly. He put a hand on the dashboard to steady himself. "Did anyone else feel that?"

Rizzo poked her head up front, over Ric's shoulder. "Mohan, I think that was a bomb, but it came from *outside* the city."

A low rumble began to shake the big truck. On the wall, guards were suddenly waving frantically at the desert beyond. Through the open gate, Ric could see a cloud of sand beginning to rise off the crest of the nearest dunes. A klaxon began to sound.

"Sandstorm?" the journalist asked.

He was answered by the shouts of the guards nearest them. "Sandworms! It's a sandworm stampede!

Their panic was well-founded. They didn't lack experience handling the gigantic scyllian sandworms, but the gate, the weakest section of the wall, was still open. And they could not get it closed.

As the confusion around the gates grew, the once orderly exodus from the city dissolved into chaos. Many vehicles broke out of line and fled back to the city, as did most of the foot traffic. However, several cars and a few light trucks made a run for the gate itself.

The guards stood momentarily dumbfounded. Why would anyone still try to leave now? Only a suicidal lunatic would try to brave the desert during a sandworm stampede.

Whether by accident or plan, the crews at the gate mechanisms were no longer about to keep up their charade; with a great screech of metal, the giant portal began to inch closed.

Mohan gripped the wheel and pressed the accelerator to the floor, following in the wake of the Golden Eye vehicle in front of him. He pulled on the air horn, and guards and pedestrians alike dived out of the path of the speeding Hiker. Several guards finally gathered enough wit to try and stop them, opening fire with their rifles; the bullets did little more than scratch the paint—the safari vehicle's panelling was bullet-proofed against possible raider attacks.

The vehicle in front of them peeled away at the last second, and Ric winced as the Hiker raced through the narrow gap, the passenger's side mirror shattering as it clipped the closing gate. Vince quipped about losing the security deposit on the rental, but the clang of the steel plates shutting behind them drowned him out.

They had made it clear of the city and were instantly enveloped in a cloud of sand. The air filled with a sudden roar as of a wave endlessly crashing against the shore.

The scyllian sandworms burst forth from the ground, rising nearly as high as the fifteen-metre walls, and that was only half the creatures' actual length. Their tough segmented hides bristled with small cone-shaped horns that allowed them to push through the sandy soil as easily as a fish swam through water. A thick bony shell crowned their heads, split into three sections at the mouth.

Somewhere in his brain, Ric recalled that they used the hard, flattened ridges in each mouth plate to grind and pulverize the sedimentary and igneous rock upon which they fed. He didn't want to think about what they could do to the Hiker.

In their agitated state, the sandworms slammed their great bulks against the mighty bulwark protecting the city. It shuddered violently, but only a few minor cracks appeared in the superbly engineered structure.

The stampede didn't last as long as the journalist had expected. A guard turned a valve in the control room, and within moments, a thin spray of foul-smelling liquid coated the walls. The sulphur was a natural repellent that confused the worms' senses. The guards fired several well-placed RPG rounds into the ground around them, the explosions further distracting the creatures. Soon, the giant creatures backed off.

A sprinkler system delivered the same sulphur repellent over the paved road leading out of the city. Unfortunately, it lay directly in the path of the retreating worms, and the escaping vehicles were forced to abandon their only solid ground as the sandworms descended upon it. The lighter cars halted instantly as their tires sank into the soft sand. Four-wheel drives like the Hiker fared better, but they still had to dodge the worms themselves. The creatures were not interested in the fleeing people, but it only took one fatal misstep for some to meet their end under the crushing mass of the worms.

Ric couldn't tell if the roar surrounding them came from the worms themselves or the torrents of sand that rushed off their bodies as they rose and fell. So much dust clouded the air he wondered how Mohan could even see, and his stomach grew queasy as the tiger swerved left and right around the occasional vehicle and the tree-like bodies of the worms.

At last, they cleared the final wave of giant creatures and rediscovered the main road leading from the city. As the dust cleared, they breathed a collective sigh of relief.

Vicki turned to gaze out the rear window. "I hope our people made it out. They won't be getting the gate back open any time soon."

"Mümtaz said we were the last," Mohan said. "I think most everyone that dared the gates with us were just frightened civilians."

"That was quite a spectacular exit strategy," Ric said.

"Sandworms are usually pretty docile," Vicki said, "but they're particularly sensitive to seismic disturbances. Simple ground traffic can startle them, so traffic going in and out of the city is carefully regulated."

"But it doesn't take much to start a stampede," Rizzo added. "I still find it crazy that the Golden Eye would try something like that."

Mohan glanced in the driver's side mirror at the chaos still left across the road behind them. "Maybe they didn't, Rizzo," he said quietly. "Something tells me the Golden Eye were just going to try a simple dash for the gate when the guards changed. The stampede was a real corker for us, but I don't think it was intended to help, and I think the Golden Eye suffered some casualties as a result."

"Then we owe them a debt," Zed said.

The tiger nodded. "Too right."

"It doesn't look like the worms caused much damage to the wall," Ric said, glancing back at the city fading behind them.

"No," Vicki said, "they were already starting to calm down as we broke through. Give them a few minutes, and they'll go bury themselves in the dunes again. Repair crews will get right to work patching the cracks and getting the road repaved." She paused a moment. "And hopefully give those poor souls that didn't make it a decent burial."

She didn't sound very optimistic.

"Was there anything we could have done?" Ric asked.

"We're not magicians," Mohan said, keeping his eyes on the road ahead. "We're as much victims to acts of nature as anyone else. Believe me, sometimes I wish that wasn't the case, but sometimes you either survive or you die. It's bad business to leave corpses outside the gate; it attracts predators. But the city guard probably won't do much beyond hauling away the wreckage and digging a mass grave."

Vicki seemed very upset by the innocents harmed in the stampede and that she hadn't been able to lend any assistance. Rizzo put a friendly arm around her shoulder, and Vince, for once, didn't try to lighten the mood with one of his bawdy stories. Ric watched them for a moment and then turned to the surrounding dunes.

"Not a lot to see out here," he said. "Is all of this sandworm territory?"

"Pretty much," Vicki answered, perking up. "Sandworms are farmed for the silk they produce, but you don't see buildings outside the wall because Kairran learned a long time ago that constantly rebuilding can get expensive real quick. This is especially true because the worms are extremely temperamental. So outside the walls, the main road is the only thing kept in constant repair."

Naturally, it's their lifeline to the rest of the country, Ric thought, but he said nothing. The change of subject seemed to brighten Vicki's mood, so he let her continue.

Happy to find a captive audience, the bullfrog dived into a long recitation of a documentary she had seen about sandworms and their importance to the Pytain economy. Meanwhile, the Tracksman Hiker rolled along the cracked pavement, and the walls of Kairran faded into the distance.

16 – The Valley of Nefrit

Ric jostled awake at a sudden bump and realized he had been dozing. The sun and day moon were low on the western horizon, flirting with the ridge of a rapidly approaching mountain range that barred their passage south. He wondered how long he had been out.

The main trail had turned west towards Khet, and all the traffic that had escaped the sandworms went with it. They were the only ones still heading south. There had been few outlying settlements in their path, and apart from one or two semiabandoned oases, there was little greenery. The paved asphalt had ended some kilometres back, along with the sandy dunes, but a worn dirt path divided the rocky ground dotted here and there with scraggly brush and stunted trees. Soon, new patches of green began to appear, and as the Scrappers crested a rise, they could see the canopy of a vast jungle marching up the sides of the mountains.

The journalist yawned widely. "In Kairran, it's easy to forget the whole country isn't just one big desert."

Zed spoke up behind him. "Indeed. Although there are few places quite like the Valley of Nefrit and the slopes of the Nefrit Ishem Mountains, where things are truly green."

"I've heard of the valley," Ric said, peering out the window, "but I didn't think I would get a chance to visit it."

"Well, you may wish you hadn't," Kitty said with a snort. "It's jam-packed with all sorts of beasties, and at its heart, there's Jar-Geshim."

"Is that a city?" Ric asked. "I don't recall seeing it on the map."

"And you won't," Mohan said. "Despite being along the most direct route between Kairran and Det, it's pretty isolated. It's also something of an embarrassment to the government of Pytan, and they'd rather people didn't know it exists. Probably because it happens to be swarming with bandits."

Ric sat up a little straighter. "A bandit city? That's where we're going? Have you gone mad?"

"We don't have much choice in the matter," Mohan said. "We're pulling all assets out of Pytan and have agents there who need to be extracted. Besides, it's probably the safest place for us to layover. Bandits aren't the only thing prowling the jungle, and the Pytian army won't go near it."

"Even with the looming threat of war?" Ric asked.

The truck was silent, and Mohan gave him a knowing look. Clearly, the agents didn't like the thought any more than he did.

Geographically, the Nefrit Ishem Mountains rose through the very centre of Pytan. At some point in the ancient past, time had carved out the broad, deep Valley of Nefrit that split the western tip of the range from the longer, taller range to the east.

Despite appearances, the last light of the sun had time to vanish below the horizon well before the rocky lowlands ultimately gave way to the jungle. Midori poked its green face over the eastern mountains and bathed everything in pale light, but it wasn't long before their path vanished through a dark hole in the thick vegetation, and the light disappeared almost completely. Ric got the uncomfortable sensation that the jungle was swallowing them whole.

The road became a wide, worn path paved with gravel and loose stone. Even with the four-wheel drive of the Hiker, it was difficult to traverse as the low-hanging vines and branches occasionally tugged against the floodlights and roof-mounted spare tire.

As his eyes adjusted to the gloom, Ric saw that the moonlight filtering through the canopy wasn't the only illumination. Luminous plants blossomed around them, and soon, a blue-green glow that served almost as well as daylight lit their path.

"Beautiful," the lynx muttered under his breath.

Mohan glanced over and noticed that the journalist's attention may have been more focused on Kitty dozing against the window than the valley outside. They had only been stuck together a short while, but the tiger had to admit he was starting to like the journalist; however, that was still his oldest daughter the lynx was eyeing.

He cleared his throat. "And deadly," he said, not only referring to their surroundings. "The jungles of Pytan are probably even more dangerous than its deserts—"

Suddenly, he slammed on the brakes as a massive fallen log appeared around a bend in the path. Kitty instantly awoke and instinctively reached out to brace herself against the dashboard. Ric reacted in the same manner and accidentally brushed her hand. He withdrew it quickly when he caught the cold look in her eye. He looked away, suddenly feeling guilty and wondering if she had noticed him staring at her.

Vince groggily spoke up from the rear of the truck. "Hey, what's the big idea? I was enjoyin' a rather pleasant nap."

"*Oiu*," Rizzo grumbled. "It was wonderfully quiet for once."

"Log across the road," Mohan answered. "Everyone, on guard. I expected to find a bandit ambush when we were within cooee of the city, but we only just entered the valley. Zed, check the rear."

The tiger climbed out and unsnapped the safety strap for the holster of his massive pistol. He approached the obstruction carefully, looking intently to the left and right at the thick jungle growth that could easily hide an ambush.

There were several deep gashes in the side of the log, and it appeared to have fallen recently. Inspecting the broken end revealed it was splintered and uneven, clearly not cut. It lay across the road at an angle, and several smaller trees lay smashed down off to the side. Something heavy had fallen against them, and not more than two or three hours ago, the log lay over several sets of fresh tire tracks—no doubt made by the Tiger's Stripe agents who had proceeded them on the way to Jar-Geshim.

However, a single set of much older tracks came towards them around the bend, and they veered off into the jungle just before the tree. Several dark stains covered the ground nearby. Mohan didn't need his tracking experience to recognize dried blood. The odd thing was that both the tracks and the blood were several days old, as was the small clearing of trampled brush near where the trail vanished into the jungle.

Zed called from his post at the rear of the truck, "I do not see anything out of the ordinary back here, Mohan."

The tiger crouched to get a better view of the old tire tracks. "Well, there's definitely something shonky up here; come see. Rizzo, take over for Zed."

Rizzo climbed out, shotgun in hand, and Zed came forward to study the signs for himself. Mohan followed the tire tracks into the jungle. There, half buried in the vegetation several metres from the road, were the remains of an army-issue jeep retrofitted with a methane engine, a preferred method of transport among bandits since natural gas pockets were plentiful in the wastes. The vehicle rested in a wide swatch of trampled brush and trees, splattered everywhere with dried blood. Mohand returned to the road.

"I'm not sure what to make of this," he told the badger. "It looks like a regular patrol came up this way a couple days ago, but something knocked it into the bush. There was a hell of a blue back there." He motioned to the wreckage. "I'm guessing they got ambushed by a couple of ceravaags, who probably got miffed that one or the other was in his neck of the woods. The bandits got gobbled up for brekkie in the middle of it.

"Several of our own crew stopped by over the next couple hours—they'd been leaving Kairran in small groups all morning, so they didn't stop all at once. But each of them got out, did a cursory inspection and left. The log got knocked over later, after the last group came through. Maybe the ceravaags came back to investigate the noise?"

It was a logical assessment. Ceravaags grew to six metres long and were a metre and a half at the shoulder. They bore a passing resemblance to a Komodo dragon crossed with a rhinoceros and a crocodile—except for the fringe of long colourful feathers covering the neck. They were also extremely territorial, and most fights were often to the death.

Zed nodded at Mohan's evaluation and held up a handful of brass shells. "Indeed. But a ceravaag would not explain these. I count at least eight different loads, including a fifty-calibre machine gun. No ceravaag could withstand such firepower." He crouched near a splotch of crimson and gazed into the jungle. "All of this blood is Hom-An, and these animal tracks are strange to me. They are certainly not ceravaag prints. Whatever this creature was, it was powerful and trod lightly, leaving very little impression.

"Yet it is very strange. There are two sets of prints here, one larger and newer than the other. And yet, they appear to have been made by the same creature."

"So whatever it was had a growth spurt?"

The badger nodded. "And a significant one. Also, I do not believe this was a patrol; there was only a single jeep, and the bandits do not send patrols this far from Jar-Geshim. Something was chasing them, from the air."

He pointed to the path of broken trees. "It was an aerial creature that flattened those branches."

Mohan squinted into the darkness above them. "A quetzalcoatl?" he asked, naming one of several types of airborne fiend.

The badger shook his head slowly. "No, larger. Much larger, I deem. Perhaps even larger than an alkonost. Whatever it was, I have never tracked such a creature before."

"And the tree?"

"A curiosity. Perhaps after our friends passed through, the creature returned to inspect its territory? From the way this tree is broken, it does not seem it was intended to block the road. That is merely how things fell, as it were." Zed smiled at his own joke.

Mohan chuckled mirthlessly and set his shoulder against the log. "Oh sure, mate. Anyway, best keep an eye out. Gimme a hand with this, would you?"

It was the work of ten minutes for the huge tiger and the badger to shove the great log out of the road, and then they were on their way again. They had only driven a few kilometres when they found the remains of several more vehicles in another clearing.

There were four in total, including two flatbed trucks only a little larger than the Hiker. Both had probably been used for hauling cargo but were currently empty. They couldn't tell if that was because someone had retrieved the payload after the attack or the trucks hadn't been loaded in the first place.

As before, blood and spent brass lay everywhere. Unfortunately, carrion scavengers had spoilt the site, so finding any clear sign of the attacker was impossible. The only sure thing was that the attack had come from above, and their fellow agents had stopped to investigate and found nothing.

"You think it a mite odd they're so far away from Jar-Geshim?" Vince asked as he poked through the remains of a jeep.

"Indeed." Zed nodded. "The trucks bear no markings, as I would expect from bandits, but they were clearly on their way out of the valley with little or no cargo."

"Could they have been a raiding party?" Ric asked.

"Not if they were heading north," Mohan said, "at least not at this time of the year. The major supply caravans for Kairran and Khet don't start up until mid-spring. Both cities are too heavily fortified to attack directly, and with so few settlements in the desert, there isn't much worth taking for a raiding party this size. There are much easier pickings southward, around Det and Abaat-Khan, or maybe even as far as Ghadir."

"Think they might have been fleeing Jar-Geshim?" Vicki asked.

Mohan scratched behind one ear. "I don't think so, but we'll see."

220

"You sound pretty confident," Ric observed. "You think the bandits could actually fend off one of your fiends?"

"Not really, but you'll understand once you see the city."

Unable to learn anything new, the Scrappers piled into the Hiker again and continued to their destination.

Just as they passed under the canopy of trees, Ric thought he saw a dark shadow on the ground, as if some massive form had passed in front of the moon. But when he looked up, the sky was clear and cloudless.

17 – The Gates of Jar-Geshim

The sound of rushing water reached their ears, and it was only then that Ric realised how silent the jungle around them had been. There were no nocturnal avian calls or faint rustlings in the underbrush; even the chirp of insects was absent.

The broad river flowed down from the eastern mountain range, easing up parallel to the road, and the two ran side by side for several kilometres.

After about an hour, they rounded a sharp bend, and the river suddenly emptied into a broad crescent-shaped lake. The road followed the northern shore as it arched westward, and an orange glow appeared on the southwestern end.

"Sentry fires," Vince said. "Looks like the city is still alive and kicking."

"I take it Jar-Geshim doesn't have electricity," Ric said.

"I've heard there's an old hydroelectric plant on the waterfall between the north and south lakes," Vicki answered, "but if they actually have it running, I'm sure only those at the top of the totem pole get such luxuries."

"Our intel says they have a few scattered floodlights on the walls," Mohan added, "particularly around the main gate. But fire adds more than light to a city's defences out here."

"How exactly does a city like this get established in the first place?" Ric asked, his professional curiosity starting to kick in. "Wasteland bandits are such a chaotic group it seems unlikely they'd establish any sort of governing body."

"Even vagabonds need a refuge when night falls," Kitty answered, checking the ammo in her pistol. "I'm guessing our agents here were trying to figure out what makes them tick, but it's amazing what you can accomplish with an iron fist and some loyal muscle."

"Kings of the dregs of society," Vince said with a flourish.

"Lovely concept," the journalist replied, his whiskers drooping in a frown.

"Now, where's your objectivism?" Mohan asked rhetorically. "You've every right to let your personal bias out here, mate. Remember, these people haven't the slightest interest in what we would call polite society." He let slip a growl. "It's as close as you can get to total anarchy out here. Watch your back, or you'll likely get a knife in it."

"Who actually has the balls to try and rule over something like that?" Ric asked.

"All I know is they call him the Marshal," Mohan replied.

Not long after they started down the lakeside road, they heard the buzz of engines, and a pair of battered dirt bikes roared out of the jungle. Their heavily armed riders made no move to accost the Hiker, but they paced alongside it all the way to the city gates.

The walls of Jar-Geshim were ancient but no less solid and impressive than those of Kairran. The city could easily have held a population of over ten thousand Hom-Ans, but Ric doubted there were that many bandits inside; at least, he hoped there weren't.

Every few metres, a ramshackle turret of scrapped sheet metal formed a guard post along the top of the wall, and a wide area at least thirty metres across had been cleared between the base of the wall and the surrounding jungle. There was little chance of anybody or anything approaching without attracting attention.

About half a kilometre from the walls, the road pulled away from the lake, and they lost sight of the city behind the trees. The road came to a T junction, and one of the bikers swerved in front of them, forcing them to turn. The entrance to Jar-Geshim loomed before them beyond the jungle canopy.

The gate itself was made of sturdy wood bound in iron and flanked on either side by metal catwalks strung with banks of floodlights. It reminded Ric of a sports stadium.

Heavily armed guards of multiple species, including a few Hom-An insects and aquatics, swarmed over the catwalks as the Hiker rolled to a stop. Ric noted that the tropical fish wore crude bladder-collars and tanks, devices designed to filter recycled water over their gills so they could remain out of water for extended periods. Almost stereotypically, most of them carried spears or tridents in their webbed hands, and many had large scars that marred their bright colours.

While the bandits' clothing was dirty and stitched with many patches, the weapons held in paw and claw were clearly well cared for. Ric knew only a little about firearms from his academy days, but the Tiger's Stripe agents identified many Mosvian-made Karshov assault rifles, WUK military-issue pistols and shotguns from Chesterfield and Bonners-Harrington, and even a few Medoccian-made Ferreli submachineguns. However, less than half the bandits actually carried firearms; the primary weapon of choice was either long spears or wicked-looking curved swords.

A burly gorilla with a heavily tattooed face stomped up to the driver's door and glared at Mohan. He was shorter than the two-plus-metres tiger but could easily match him in weight. He grunted something Mohan couldn't understand.

"Sounds like Farse," Mohan said. "His accent's too thick for me to make it out. Zed, can you translate?"

The badger slowly opened the side door and exited with his hands raised; however, he made sure that the guard got a good look inside to see they were all armed.

"I am an interpreter," he answered the gorilla's silent query in Farse.

"A Soketh scavenger from the sands among the trees?" The gorilla laughed. "Tell me, does your striped cat always wander where he is not wanted and can't even speak with his benefactors? What is your business here, Striped One?"

"I take it he's not very flattering," Mohan said.

"He is wondering why we are here," Zed said. Then he turned back to address the gorilla. "We are hunters seeking shelter for the night."

One of the biker escorts—a mangy-looking wolf—leaned against the passenger window, leering at Kitty, but he couldn't hold the tigress's fierce gaze; he quickly looked away. Ric had kept both hands on the dashboard, and the bandit noticed the Tiger's Mark on his forearm.

"They bear the cat face!" the wolf cried.

The gorilla looked up sharply at this and broke into a wide grin. "Ha! More pussycats limping to our gate with their tails between their legs! We have had many of you call on us this evening. But I know you, *Soketh*." He spat the name. "You make things difficult for our kind in Nanca Fier and Kirque. But this is not your valley. I would sooner skin you and make your striped skull into a new helmet."

"Enough, Rahkim!" The bandits parted reverently as a tall figure exited through the gate.

As the ants at Kairran's gate demonstrated, Hom-An insects largely resembled their small, nonsentient cousins. Most wore loose clothing such as scarves and cloaks, averaging between ninety and a hundred fifty centimetres in height.

The wasp who approached them was a magnificent one hundred and ninety centimetres tall, taller than most of the bandits surrounding them. He wore blue and white silk scarves and a white turban, from which his antennae protruded out the top.

"You have your orders when admitting those who bear the Cat's Eye." Even without proper vocal cords, the wasp's raspy voice reverberated an air of command.

Rahkim was instantly cowed. "Yes, Seer Xereas." The gorilla sulked away from the Hiker.

Another difference from nonsentient insects was that the Hom-An variety had eyelids, and the wasp's narrowed as he approached. He addressed them in Netib. "So, more of you have come to the gates of Jar-Geshim seeking refuge from the coming storm. Yes, we have heard the news from Kairran; do not think us uninformed simpletons. The Marshal, lord of Jar-Geshim, has been lenient with you so far, but his patience wears thin despite your generous donations. However, if you are hunters, as you say, you may be able to repay your debt to him." He lowered his voice and switched suddenly to unaccented Locken. "Tread lightly, friends."

He turned his left shoulder to Mohan, and hidden within the pattern of his chitin was a small Tiger's Mark, barely noticeable unless you were looking for it.

"The Marshal was not expecting us—neither was I, for that matter—but he agreed to put up with us for a few days after supplying him with some much-needed parts and supplies. But that only gets us so far, and he'll expect further compensation for his continued hospitality. Truth is, he could use some hunters like you right now." Seer Xereas turned back to the gate, waving dramatically and switching back to speaking Netib. "Open! These are guests of the Marshal, and they are not to be harmed!"

Mohan slowly edged the big truck through the gate. Just beyond the portal was an expansive courtyard bordered on one side by a long warehouse of rusted corrugated steel and on the other by a large stone-brick barracks; it appeared to have once been a proper barracks for the ancient city but rebuilt as time wore away the old structure. A gatehouse on their immediate left housed the controls for the massive doors.

Xereas waved to the farthest warehouse door. "You may park your vehicle there. Several of your compatriots are already waiting for you inside."

Six agents were posted outside the doors; half had Tiger's Marks visible on hands or faces. They were dressed as civilians and armed with handguns and long knives or axes.

Xereas managed a snide wheeze. "You have posted your own guard. It's as if you don't trust us."

Mohan carefully backed the Hiker through the doors. The inside of their assigned warehouse section was surprisingly spacious, but it was still crowded with tool racks, piles of scrap, and numerous winches and chains. They found more agents gathered around a collection of sturdy vehicles. The Tracksman Hiker was by far the largest, but the others were equally rugged and well-suited for travel through the harsh wilderness. The agents were busy dismantling some of the smaller cars, but Ric didn't know why.

He also noted with interest that these agents were garbed like the guards outside, as civilians, and didn't appear as heavily armed as Mohan and his team.

Kitty climbed out and stretched sore muscles. "How many do you think we have?"

Mohan glanced over the agents gathered. "I'd guess only two dozen or so."

Ric found he was having difficulty keeping his eye off the lithe tigress and forced his attention elsewhere. "How many were part of your op to start with?"

"Our op specifically? Only ten, including us," Mohan answered, opening the rear door. "But we had a couple different teams working the area on other missions. Pytan has become quite a hotbed for underworld activity in the past two years. All told, there were almost a hundred and twenty agents working Kairran. That's all the intel gatherers, observation posts, extraction specialists like our clerk at the rental agency, and PR." He hefted a bag from the rear of the truck. "Only take what you need," he ordered. "The rest is safer here."

"PR," Ric said. "Is that your Public Relations team?"

"Public Restoration," Vicki answered, grabbing her duffel. "It's a much broader spectrum than what public relations would cover. Collateral damage kinda comes with the territory, as you've seen. We try to clean up as much of our own mess as we can, but sometimes time is of the essence. That's when PR steps in. If there's a problem with the local authorities or if we need emergency services, PR signs the paperwork and runs interference so our identities remain a secret.

"A lot of them actually live and work in the AO, which makes them easy to recruit and assign. Some of them aren't even our agents but work with allied organisations. Naturally, they think they're working with KLAWS the whole time; we never use the name Tiger's Stripe outside our most secure facilities. Honestly, PR is probably the most difficult job in our little spy world."

"I don't doubt it," Ric said.

He noticed Seer Xereas had followed them inside. On closer inspection, the lynx could see small scars and cracks that lined the wasp's chitin, possibly resulting from multiple physical altercations. Leaning close, he asked, "What is your role here?"

Xereas placed a clawed hand to his mandibles. "Shush! I and others have been working among the bandits for nearly ten years. Of course, it hardly matters now; we're folding our operations in Pytan. You're here to get us out."

"Are Naji and Awiti ready?" Mohan asked.

Xereas nodded. "Since the call came in. But the Marshal is highly suspicious; we must move quickly. Unfortunately, I have a feeling we may be delayed while you handle the Marshal's errand. I cannot say more now."

Once they gathered their gear, the wasp led them back outside and resumed his bandit persona. "I will show you to your accommodations. The Marshal has graciously put you up in one of our better hotels; they have electricity and running water."

Ric had travelled widely as a journalist, but he hadn't been sure what to expect inside a city made up entirely of the dregs of society. What most Amarthians—especially those dwelling inside fortified cities—knew about bandits was what they read in the paper or saw on TV, which is to say very little. Bandit attacks on outlying settlements were so common in almost every part of the world that they rarely made headlines.

What he saw as they started down the narrow street neither surprised nor disappointed him. The ruins of Jar-Geshim were old—several thousand years old, by the look of the mouldering stonework—but to Ric, it looked like the set of some cheap post-apocalyptic movie.

Several ancient sandstone- and brick buildings still stood, but most of the structures were haphazardly pieced together out of whatever rusted scrap the bandits could get a hold of—old cars and busses, loose sheets of corrugated tin, and even the fuselage and wing of an aeroplane had been used to build some form of shelter. Ric wondered idly if the plane had crashed in the city or if the occupants had dragged the wreckage inside.

The twisting streets were paved with loose, smooth cobblestones and fine sandy soil that was easy on their bare paws. Torches and gas lamps lined every lane, most adorned with odd fetishes made of feathers and nonsentient animal bones—or at least Ric hoped they were nonsentient. He wasn't sure if they were ceremonial or just decorative; his initial impression was the latter, but he guessed bandits could be just as superstitious as anyone else.

Some of the more prominent buildings boasted electric neon signs and decorative eaves, proof of the owner's affluence within the city hierarchy—Ric noted that most were brothels or bars.

As they passed shops and merchants, the journalist wondered what they used for currency, but after a second thought, he realised that maybe it was better if he didn't know.

What did surprise him was that Jar-Geshim's community looked and sounded as vibrant as the black market of Kairran, if much dirtier and noisier.

He wrinkled his nose and sneezed. And a hell of a lot smellier.

Even at this late hour, the streets teamed with bustling people indulging in all manner of recreation, from the benign to the outright lewd. In addition to the shouts and boisterous laughter, a gunshot or series of gunshots would frequently ring out, followed by screams, the crash of glass, or both. But these were largely ignored by those not in the immediate vicinity of such incidents.

The people themselves had the same mild diversity one would expect from any port city in Pytan. Most were local species of goats, horses, camels, canines, rodents, and desert felines. However, there were a few exotic representatives like bears and squirrels from

233

Aerenia, and Ric even saw a couple of beavers, who largely stuck to the West United Kingdoms. Clearly this bandit haven had attracted thieves and cutthroats from across Amarthia.

The denizens of Jar-Geshim wore everything from simple rags to patched remnants of what might once have been fine clothing. And the guards were not the only ones clad in some form of armour, whether it be pieces of padded leather or even segmented plastic sports pads that Ric could only assume they had looted from a Wook football team. It made the agents' own average street clothes look like Hayes of Barburry fine tailoring, and the Scrappers were all too aware of the covetous looks they received from the crowd. There was a distinct impression that even Mohan, towering head and shoulders above most of the throng, would have been a target if not for the presence of the Marshal's seer. All the same, they gripped their belongings close with one hand and kept the other firmly placed on their weapons.

"This seems pretty lively for a bandit city," Ric said, trying to make light conversation as he stuck close behind Mohan. He had no weapons to defend himself with.

"What else did you expect?" the huge tiger answered. "Mutilated bodies strung up in chains like in the movies?"

Just then, they passed a recessed shop occupied by an aged crow surrounded by unidentifiable objects preserved in glass jars of various sizes. Ric didn't look too closely, but several appeared to be organs of Hom-An origin. He started to wonder how the crow had obtained the fetishes when a gunshot rang out in the next street, followed by a scream and the crash of glass.

"OK, maybe it gets a little rough," Mohan said. "Remember, most of these people are seeking refuge from the hangman's noose, but even a villain understands the basics of economics. Unfortunately, some far better than most. If someone is willing to buy, there's always somebody ready to sell."

"Structure even in the midst of chaos," Ric said thoughtfully. "This Marshal character must have his hands full just to keep the place from tearing itself apart."

"The Marshal is probably the most enlightened mind in this sea of reprobates," Xereas said loftily, and Ric admitted he couldn't tell if it was an act or genuine admiration. "But is that what you see, cub? Only chaos? Perhaps these people have discovered a life that is truly free, self-dependent, accepting of the chaos that is life itself. He may be a tyrant, but the Marshal is all that keeps them from slipping into the madness of the feral beast that lies at the heart of us all."

Ric eyed him closely, but he found it difficult to read the expression in those compound eyes. *Is that his true opinion, or just the bandit disguise talking?* He thought. *Either way, perhaps the seer has a point. When life becomes meaningless, and you feel society has failed, what else is there but to embrace a life of chaos and debauchery?*

His journalist brain filed the thought away for future reference as they turned down one of the twisting alleyways into a broader throughway. Moments later, they stopped before a seedy hotel garishly lit in bright neon.

The lodging was a conversion of one of the larger ancient buildings. It had a narrow pyramid shape, and each floor above the first had a recess that formed a thin balcony overhung by the next level above. It was a design Ric had never heard documented in other ancient cities and looked almost modern in its approach. The stones were enormous, yet fitted so tightly it was impossible to believe they were crafted by simple hand tools. However, it was obvious from the pitted sandstone that it was very old; the metal railings on the balconies had been added later.

A broad hallway bisected the bottom level of the structure, and the current owners had walled it off with cheap pressboard to form a crude lobby for their hotel. Large holes cut into the front served as glassless windows, and a large hand-painted sign advertised in pictures the amenities available, which boiled down to a bed, electricity, and toilets. Tacked to the bottom was a yellow flyer for the nearest whorehouse.

"Well, it's not the Wellington." Vince snorted as he appraised the shabby structure.

"Oh, I would have thought you'd be quite familiar with any hotel that rented by the hour," Rizzo jibed.

Seer Xereas interrupted them. "You will stay here during your time with us, along with the rest of those who bear the Cat's Eye, compliments of the Marshal."

As they entered the lobby, a scruffy clerk who appeared to be the product of two different members of the weasel family shifted his bored gaze towards them. When he recognised the seer, he straightened slightly and pushed aside the dirty magazine he was perusing. And by dirty, that is to say, there was so much dirt and grime Ric couldn't determine what type of publication it was.

Xereas turned and spoke directly to Mohan in Locken, keeping his voice low. "General Durram and the others arrived several hours ago. He was the asset coordinator in Kairran, I believe?"

"Too right. Glad to know he'll be joining us."

"Ok. The Marshal wants to meet all the commanders tomorrow morning, so that includes you. I have an idea what he's going to ask as payment for letting you in, but keep your eyes and ears open. If anyone asks, the Cat's Eye are small-time smugglers based in Kairran. You fled when things got too hot and paid for your entry with a bunch of imported car parts and electronics."

The front bell rang, and the wasp paused as a drunken form staggered into the lobby, paused as if suddenly realising some mistake, and stumbled back out into the bustling street.

Xereas addressed the clerk in Netib. "These are guests of the Marshal. See they are situated on the third and fourth floors with the others. I will hear of it if they are mistreated."

The clerk gave a half-hearted salute and mumbled an affirmative.

"Rest well," Xereas said.

The seer bowed mockingly to the agents and vanished into the noisy street.

18 – Settling In

Once Seer Xereas had left, Mohan turned his attention to his weary team. "OK, everyone, get some sleep if you can. One eye open, of course." He turned to the clerk and addressed him in Netib. "We'll need three rooms and—"

The weasel clerk had picked up the magazine again and didn't bother looking up. "You get two rooms. Double beds, no spare cots available."

Mohan sighed, "All right then. Kitty, Ric and I will take one; the rest of you make do with the other. Vince, Behave."

The hare saluted smartly. "Sah! I am shocked you would insinuate I have anything but the best intentions!"

Rizzo squinted sideways at him. "Of course you do, *non*?"

"Why not just all the men in one room?" Ric suggested.

"Oh, it's not a modesty thing," the tiger answered. "We have this tradition; when a new recruit comes aboard, the agent that found them has to stick with them. So you and Kitty will be stuck at the hip until we get out of this."

Ric raised an eyebrow and couldn't help but glance at the tigress. "Really?"

"And that's why you also share the room with *me*." The tiger's tone was stern, but there was humour in his golden eyes.

The others began climbing the stairs, but Mohan returned to the clerk. "Is there a phone? I need to make a long-distance call."

The clerk still didn't look up from his magazine, but he answered smugly, "We have a satellite line, very expensive to maintain. It will cost you."

The tiger fished a large wad of caram notes out of his pocket. "I think you dropped this."

The clerk frowned and seemed displeased with the size of the bribe, but he quickly pawed the money and waved vaguely towards the back of the lobby. "There's a booth out the back. Maybe the dish is aligned today, maybe not."

Aren't you forgetting whether or not the satellite is in range? Mohan thought bitterly.

He ducked out the rear door and stepped out into a dirty alley. It was closed off at either end and accessible only through the back entrances of the buildings surrounding it. Consequently, there was little activity save for a few sleeping drunks. The muffled rowdy noise from the streets and a few pops of gunfire reminded him that perhaps the bodies lying there weren't sleeping.

The booth was small—especially for a two-plus-metres muscle-bound tiger—and consisted of little more than wooden panels that offered only the illusion of privacy and a handset connected to a crude rotary dial attached directly to a telephone pole. Mohan guessed the dish for the satellite phone was somewhere on the roof. He wondered idly how bandits got their hands on such a device and which satellites they were pirating off from, let alone who they would call, but at least it was something.

He dialled the number from memory and scanned the deserted alley while waiting for a connection. They had left Vince's radio transmitter with the Hiker, but he still needed to update Watch Command. Fortunately, when you couldn't call direct, Tiger's Stripe always had an emergency switch-board ready and waiting.

A brisk female voice answered on the fourth ring. "Blue Wing International Incorporated. How may I direct your call?"

"Repairs," Mohan replied.

After a brief dial tone and a series of clicks, a much deeper masculine voice spoke. "Line secure. Designation?"

"Hunter TS Three reporting. Stranded after Kairran airport terrorist attack. Reroute to Jar-Geshim successful. All team members accounted for, plus new recruit. Extraction proceeding, but unable to proceed with second phase of primary operation in Medocci. Has a substitution been arranged?"

"All acknowledged, Hunter TS Three. Hold, please." There was a brief pause. "Substitution arranged. Hunter TS Five has been assigned. Any changes?"

"Negative. Wish them luck."

"Will do. Report to General Durram until extraction complete. Good luck." The line went dead.

Mohan checked his watch, an expensive model that included a stopwatch and could display three different timezones—one of which was always home.

It was six o'clock in the morning in East Plains, Borne Bay. He picked up the phone again.

The connection wasn't as clear this time, but a gentle feminine voice answered on the third ring. "*Moshi Moshi, katoraru yashiki.*"

Mohan found himself choking with emotion at the sound of that voice. His wife spoke perfect Locken but always answered the phone in her native Ku-Song. He could almost picture the petite tigress standing in the kitchen of their homestead.

"It's me," he said.

"Oh, Mohan! I saw the news this morning. Are you all right? Is Kittina all right?" she asked, concern in her voice.

Singh Katral was only partially aware of the duplicitous nature of her husband and eldest daughter's work, even though her bloodline stretched back to the very foundation of Tiger's Stripe. Revealing your identity to trusted family members was at the agent's discretion, and Mohan felt obligated to tell her everything when they were married. Even so, she had asked to remain half in the dark for the sake of her sanity. Operational details were still strict secrets, and he could never say exactly where he was, but Mohan called home as often as he could when in the field.

"Yes, we're fine, luv." The tiger sighed. "I can't stay on the line long; I think the satellite might be getting close to a dead zone. I love you! We'll be home as soon as we can. Pray for us if you feel inclined." Though he attended the 1st Reformed Aabanite Church of the United Plains whenever he was home, Mohan had to admit his wife was far more religious than he.

"I will. I love you, my dear Mohan! My love to Kittina as well." She switched to Ku-Song, the musical dialect of the Ku-San Islands of East Benai. "*Yoi kaze ga ho wo mitashi, rampu ga takaku kakageraremasu yōni.*"

"*Anata no ami ga itsumo mampai dearimasu yōni.*" He completed the traditional islander phrase, but the line faded and disconnected before he could finish. In

243

Locken, the translation was, "May good wind fill your sails and the lamp be held high," to which one would respond, "May your nets always be full." He hung up the receiver with a sigh.

Wearily, he climbed the stairs to the fourth floor, passing by the broken icemaker and—from the smell—what passed for a latrine. The hotel was an interesting mixture of styles; the exterior was clearly the oldest, but some of the interior chambers that were now rooms had been carved out later. He found Kitty leaning on the balcony railing outside their room, smoking and gazing at the crowd below without really seeing them.

He stood quietly beside her, unwilling to test the flimsy rail against his weight. His nose wrinkled slightly at the scent of her cigarette.

"Don't start," she said after a moment.

"I didn't say anything."

She exhaled a cloud of smoke. "Yeah, but you were thinking it."

"So a father can't worry about his daughter's health?"

"We agreed. You have your cigars, and I have these."

He decided to test his weight against the rail, and it held. "And I could sure use one about now." He sighed. "But at least I don't smoke a pack a day."

"A week, a pack a week. Too few pockets to carry more than that, not to mention too bloody expensive."

They stood in silence for a few moments, neither looking at the other.

"I spoke with Mum. She sends her love."

Only the faintest twitch of an ear showed that she heard him.

"Something's bothering you."

"I keep thinking about that sniper I tried to run down."

"Maybe you ran out of breath from smoking too much?" He smirked. She gave him a dirty look, and he held up a hand defensively. "OK, OK, truce. I told you, it's no drama. He had a good head start."

She shook her head emphatically. "No, that's not it. He should have had more than a good head start. Where he shot from, the angle, the wind, him being on the fire escape when I spotted him. None of it adds up. It was a damn near impossible shot."

Mohan thought a moment. "And why didn't he run back through the apartment he shot from instead of climbing out onto the fire escape?"

"Exactly! He wanted to be spotted; he wanted to be chased. And then he gave me that thrice-damned bow when he got away…" she trailed off and gave an irritated chuff.

Mohan wanted to put a hand on her shoulder but thought better of it. "Just let it go. We'll track him down. If he's a professional, he may be in our database. Either that or he'll find us again."

More silence passed. The crowds below began to thin, and the noise died down to a tolerable level. It was well past midnight.

Mohan broke the silence. "TS Five is going to handle the freighter in Medocci for us."

Kitty angrily stubbed out her cigarette against the railing.

"I know you and Rothschild haven't seen eye to eye since training," Mohan said, "but we can trust them. She's good. Not as good as you, of course, but—"

"Don't patronize me," Kitty growled.

Mohan wasn't sure how her ongoing rivalry with TS-5's sniper had started, but she certainly wasn't pleased with the news. Best to change the subject.

"We're under Durram's command for now," he said. "I hope that old turtle has a better plan for getting us out of this than I do right now, 'cause I haven't got one."

"And our new recruit?" she asked, flicking the cigarette butt out into empty space.

"Not like we have much choice now. He would have had it easy just tailing us through Medocci; now he gets a real test." He straightened and turned to the door. "I think he'll make it; he's one of us."

Like that really makes a bloody difference, Kitty thought.

The room that met Mohan's eyes as he entered was the cheapest arrangement he had ever seen. The ancient walls of the twelve-foot room were so faded and cracked

246

that every surface had been reduced to squiggly grey fractures; it was impossible to tell what colour they had originally been. The only furniture was a double bed, two rickety end tables, and a single shade-less lamp. He was surprised to see actual glass and curtains in the window; the lower floors didn't have such luxuries. Lewd noises from the apartments below clued him in on the most likely reason the edifice was still in business.

Ric was leaning against the wall and peeking out the window.

At her? Mohan wondered.

The journalist straightened up quickly and asked, "Everything all right?"

The tiger looked at him a moment. "Fine, just fine. You'd better get some rest. I have a feeling our stay here won't be long." He laid a blanket on the floor and started fluffing a pillow. "These hotel beds are always too small for me. You'll have to share. You can keep your hands to yourself, right?" He squinted meaning-fully at the lynx.

"Swear to it!" Ric gulped. Then, he grew a little bolder. "For an overprotective father, you seem to actually want us to be together."

The big tiger grinned and lay down on the floor with a mighty yawn. "Only fooling, mate. I already explained our tradition with new recruits, but I think I've seen enough of you to know you won't try anything."

Ric lay down but couldn't sleep yet, and it wasn't just because the mattress was incredibly lumpy and uncomfortable. He tried not to wonder if there might be something living in it.

"Back at the airport this morning," he said to the ceiling, "you didn't run."

Mohan opened one eye. "How's that?"

"They didn't have your faces plastered all over the news broadcast, but they may as well have. And yet you stayed to help. The more I think about it, the more I'm wondering if you actually had a choice."

The tiger sat up and looked at him intensely. "There is always a choice, mate. But the one to do the right thing is always the hardest."

"I've heard that before, but I think you needed to help. I could see it on your faces. The thing is, I felt it too. Here on my arm." Ric patted his birthmark. "It's in our blood, isn't it? To face the danger and do what needs doing. Not many people can live up to that kind of pressure. In fact, I wonder if I can myself."

Mohan closed his eyes again and settled into his pillow. "You're already living up to it, mate. Just look at your career so far. You handled yourself well at the airport, especially considering whoever bombed it tried to blow us up specifically."

That made the lynx sit up. "What?"

"You saw the news yourself. They reported the bombing at the airport *before* it actually went off.

248

Whoever detonated it wanted us to know we were the target, and I suspect we weren't supposed to survive. We lost three agents in that blast; they were trying to remove the bomb. Oh yes, we were the target, all right." He let out a growl. "And believe me, we're gonna hang those bastards up by their balls when we catch them."

Kitty came in then, and without a word, she climbed onto the bed next to the journalist and lay with her back to him. Moments later, bother tigers were sound asleep, leaving Sedric Barnes staring at the ceiling, lost in thought.

19 – The Hunter's Task

Seer Xereas greeted the Tiger's Stripe agents in the lobby the following morning. Mohan took a moment to identify the leaders of each group that had arrived in Jar-Geshim before the Scrappers.

In addition to himself, as leader of the Hunters, the tiger saw Mümtaz—the gazelle clerk from Kairran—representing the extraction specialists in place of Gallows, his deceased superior; Gregor "Caz" Cazimov, a scarred brown bear slightly larger than Mohan, representing their intelligence specialists; Rosa Merchant, a petite koala who led Tiger's Stripe's PR assets; and Archimedes Durram, a stocky old hooked-beak turtle, who was the Operations Overseer for each team assigned to Kairran. By field-rank, each unit commander was a Major General (Mümtaz was promoted straight from Lieutenant). Durram was a full General and carried himself as proudly as his rank suggested.

Mohan was glad to see them, although he hoped their combined experience would prove unnecessary.

Xereas addressed the group in an official tone. "You are each permitted a single sidearm and/or blade for your audience with the Marshal. He likes his guests to feel on equal footing when they meet. However, know that should you draw a weapon against him, you will be dead before you ever get a chance to draw blood. This is not an idle threat."

The wasp turned to address the other agents who had gathered in the lobby, including the remainder of Mohan's team. "As for the rest of you, enjoy your stay. I am sure you will find Jar-Geshim offers many of the same luxuries a more civilised city has to offer and perhaps some that they do not."

"Not bloody likely," Mohan said, speaking directly to his team. "I don't expect this to take long, so keep out of trouble until I get back. Especially you, Ric. I just know your journo senses are tingling about now." Before the lynx could protest, Mohan turned and followed Seer Xereas out into the city.

The sun was just beginning to poke its head over the distant eastern mountains, and the streets were nearly empty. In the morning light, Mohan could finally grasp how big the ancient city was. Despite its twists and turns, the road between the main gate and the shores of the lake was easily two kilometres, if not more. It was also easy to see how sparse the population of the bandit city really was compared to its vast size. The previous night's revellers had slunk away to their hovels to nurse what Mohan assumed was one hell of a hangover. Only patrons who favoured the quieter morning hours still roamed the deserted streets, and store owners continued to service these less troublesome customers. Not that they were any less dangerous; Xereas's group witnessed no fewer than three standoffs at knife- and gun-point, but all were resolved without bloodshed as the combatants agreed to go their own way.

The daylight also revealed that Jar-Geshim was technically two cities—one on either side of the lake, separated by a shallow waterfall and connected by a wide bridge. Despite the vast amount of real estate, most of Jar-Geshim's denizens packed into the smaller southern city. The jungle had reclaimed the northern section, creating a haven for wild beasts and the so-called Wildmen—individuals who had succumbed to madness and reverted to a primitive, almost feral nature.

A sickly haze hung over the deeper sections of the crumbling ruin, and the bandits shunned it like a plague. They called it the Warren.

Through Xereas, the Tiger's Stripe had learned that the Marshal would often send victims through the gauntlet as some sick sport, rewarding them with freedom should they make it out alive. To date, he had not had to make good on that promise.

As the group approached the municipal centre for the southern city, the character of the buildings began to change. More solid—and more ancient—granite structures began to replace the tin and brick shacks. Many had the strange pseudo-modern design they had noticed at the hotel. They featured pillared overhangs and gravity-defying balconies that didn't fit the more simplistic designs found in classical ancient cities. Despite the humid jungle environment, the old stonework remained remarkably well preserved, reinforced here and there with the help of marble and concrete.

The narrow streets widened until they opened into an expansive public plaza, the smouldering remains of a huge bonfire occupying its centre. The cobblestones of the road merged into dirty, cracked tiles arranged in intricate patterns. Of course, it was mostly obscured by piles of trash and the bodies of numerous revellers who had simply passed out where they were after the previous night's party. Hunched forms moved among them, pickpockets boldly plying their trade in full view of the city guard.

Xereas and his charges entered from the west side of the square. On their left, a series of raised stone platforms displayed the true barbarism of bandit society: metal cages that held the victims of the Marshal's courts. The unfortunates within varied in status from the recently incarcerated to bleached skeletons. Around the cages, bodies impaled on metal spikes bore witness to the much crueller sentences. The agents' birthmarks began to tingle, and even Mümtaz and Rosa—who were only tattooed—felt sickened by the display.

Off to the right was a more familiar sight: a caged arena waiting patiently for its next round of would-be champions. Fresh blood stained the wooden floor, and the razor wire ringing the top of the cage walls still gripped ragged chunks of flesh from furred, feathered, and scaled victims. A bank of floodlights towered overhead so the spectators could see every brutal moment of the bloody contest at night.

The bridge dam and the upper structures of the hydroelectric plant built therein were almost directly across from them. The plant—and a natural-gas refinery downstream from the falls—were remnants of the Pytian government's failed attempt to re-civilise the city in the late 1930s. Unfortunately, they had seriously underestimated both the dangers the Warren posed and the tenacity of the bandits, who swiftly retook their home. Since then, the brigands had learned to maintain the dam and the refinery—albeit inefficiently—and use their energy to achieve total independence.

The bridge spanned four hundred metres from one shore to the other, and the falls plummeted a hundred metres to the lower lake, splitting the jungle to the southeast. A massive steel gate stood like a lone sentinel just beyond the power plant. It was every metre as formidable as the main gate to the city and reinforced with heavy iron chains. Guards patrolled the ramparts above it, constantly alert for anything that might slither out of the labyrinth of the Warren beyond.

But the crowning jewel of the plaza was the Marshal's palace, resting against the edge of the lake by the foot of the bridge. Long ago, the megalithic structure may have once been a temple or public forum belonging to a long-dead civilisation. Generations of bandit rule had transformed it into the seat of their own unstable little empire. Crumbling columns of smooth stone lined the front façade, braced by wooden frames and draped with red banners bearing a silver five-pointed star in a silver ring. Filigree and twisted figures etched the eaves under the low-peaked roof, so pitted with age it was impossible to tell what they once represented or what story they once told. Armed mercenaries patrolled the open second-floor balcony, bright and alert even at that early hour when the square's occupants showed no sign of wanting to do anything but sleep off the binge from the previous night.

General Durram nodded to the impaled bodies on their left. "The pinnacle of bandit justice."

Seer Xereas turned on him sharply. "Mind your tongue, General. Your reaction is typical of one who has been coddled in the arms of civilisation. You do not know what it means to embrace true freedom."

Mohan gave a derisive snort. "And those in the cages? I suppose their freedom is on hold?"

"You may not believe it, Striped One," the seer replied, "but we still have some laws here. Not many, it is true, but punishment for breaking them is swift and sure."

It was all an act, of course, bolstered by ten years of living among bandits. As one of the Marked, Xereas was as disgusted with the barbarity around him as they were. Secretly, he was glad it would all be over soon, but he would need to keep up appearances a little while longer.

The group passed between the tall wood-and-iron doors of the Marshal's palace and entered a long hall lavishly decorated in marble and gold filigree. Several paintings by semifamous artists from numerous periods lined the walls. Most appeared to be the genuine article, probably stolen from a private collector. They also had very morbid or disturbing overtones, the dominant theme being punishment meted out for some unknown crime. The method of execution ranged from public flogging to beheading to the gallows.

Xereas paused at a pair of large gold-inlaid doors. "The Marshal has not been in a good mood of late," he said quietly. "Our more recent raids have not been very prosperous, and allowing you and your agents into the city has caused some to question his judgement. Tread very lightly if you value your hides."

He pushed open the door, but instead of passing into another lavish room, they entered a sunlit courtyard lined with elegant gardens and hanging plants. Guards roamed the second-floor balconies, but Mohan noted several snipers in shadowed alcoves with an excellent view of the entire area; no doubt they believed themselves cleverly concealed. Four grassy terraces led down to a small amphitheatre ringed by three levels of stone benches around a raised stage. At the back of the stage, framed by pools with mounted gargoyle fountains, was a broad flat throne, upon which coiled a large cobra.

The Marshal.

The sentient snakes of Amarthia were quite different from their close cousins, the nonsentient wild serpents. Both had long muscular coils that could reach immense sizes, but Hom-An snakes had short necks attached to a narrow hominid torso with two arms that served as their only appendages. Their appearance often netted them the derogatory epithet "half-lizards."

The Marshal wore a long, fringed leather vest trimmed with turquoise beads and a broad-brimmed hat commonly referred to as a gambler. A ringed silver star was pinned to his left breast. It was difficult to determine age in reptiles and amphibians, but Mohan guessed he was close to his own from the flakes of moulting scales and the wrinkles around his burnt-gold eyes.

As Xereas had warned, his hood was up.

Another difference between snakes and their serpent cousins was the presence of eyelids, and the Marshal's narrowed sharply as he studied his reluctant guests.

"Welcome, agents of the Cat's Eye," he hissed in Locken. There was the distinct twang of a southwest WUK accent in his voice.

"Or is it KLAWS?" the cobra went on, but the agents betrayed no sign of recognition. "I've heard all about that airport bombin' in Kairran. Trouble is, I've heard about KLAWS, too. Don't strike me as your handiwork. And yet when the chips are down, you come runnin' to me. Kinda clever tryin' to masquerade as smugglers to barter your way in here."

"Your Locken is too good for this part of the world, hos," General Durram retorted, his own Northern WUK accent coming across very dry in the humid gardens.

The Marshal's coils shook with laughter. "That so? Not that it matters anymore, but I was from Carlin, good old WUK. City of Beauregard, if you want to be specific. Let's just say I found these jungles more to my likin' some time ago." His eyes glittered. "Now, what am I goin' to do with you?"

With a sudden leap, he was down among the agents, slithering between their ranks. Each of them met his gaze without flinching. He was five metres long but had to raise himself almost halfway to look into Mohan's eyes. This was uncomfortable to do without losing his balance; because of their pseudo-torso, snakes were often top-heavy.

"You, Big Fella. You brought those hunters in last night," he said.

"Too right," the tiger replied.

"Plainsman, eh?" The Marshal almost smiled. "Always liked you fellers. More shrimp on the barbie, mates!"

"I prefer snags," Mohan said. The Marshal cocked his head quizzically. "Bolvin sausage. Never cared much for shrimp."

The cobra's hood flared, but he returned to his seat. "I have a...problem. As my reluctant guests, that means *you* have a problem. You see, over the past week, every foragin' party I've sent to our fields on the northeastern cliffs hasn't come back.

"Except the last one had a survivor. Came up to the gates rantin' and ravin' about dragons blottin' out the sun and breathin' fire everywhere. Couldn't get much else out of him. You probably passed him on the way in—third spike from the north end, great spot to watch the fights from until you bleed out."

Again, nobody flinched at his comments.

"You're a bunch of tough bastards, I'll give you that," the cobra said. "Well, plain and simple, you're goin' out there, and you're gonna kill whatever it is that's been foulin' up my fields. We had a good crop

259

comin' in, and now everyone's too scared to go harvest it."

"And I'm guessing you don't like not being the scariest thing around here," Durram said.

Again, the Marshal shook with laughter. "Well, give the turtle a cigar!" His smile faded instantly, and he stared back at Mohan. "Three days. You kill it, bring its head back here, and maybe I can see about lettin' you leave in one piece. You don't, I skin the lot of ya and use your hides as throw rugs. You'd look damn good at the foot of my bed, Stripey." Mohan growled low in his chest, but the Marshal just made a dismissive gesture. "Right, off ya go!"

20 – Stay Out of Trouble

Not long after Mohan left for his audience with the Marshal, the rest of the Scrappers found themselves lying about the flat roof of the hotel. Several cheap plastic chairs and tables had been set up to accommodate guests, but it was obvious they hadn't seen use in many years. The patrons were likely too busy with other activities to even bother going to the roof. There was no shade, but a gentle breeze blew off the eastern mountains down into the valley and helped relieve the already escalating heat. Fortunately, the humidity was low and wouldn't really kick in until the spring and summer.

The hotel was one of the taller buildings on that side of the city, with an excellent view of the outer wall and the streets below. The lane was straight enough to see almost all the way to the city square, but the small group of Tiger's Stripe commanders had already entered the Marshal's palace.

"I strongly suspect these people will not tolerate our company long," Zed said, gazing at the slowly swelling crowd below. "They live far beyond any sense of law or honour."

Ric was also eyeing the crowd, but the gleam in his eyes was far different. "Look what they've built here," he said. "They can't be all bad."

Kitty lounged on a plastic chair with her eyes closed and hands behind her head. "You really are looking for a blue, aren't you?" she said, "There's a reason these people have cast off society to live out here, where the law can't get them. Don't think for a second that they have any scruples or remorse."

"That is something I can only prove for myself," the journalist continued, unfazed. "I'd be a poor journalist indeed if I only took your word for it when you're obviously biased."

The tigress cocked her head at him and raised an eyebrow. "You're not thinking what I think you're thinking?" she asked.

"It looks like things have quieted down since last night. Now might be the safest time to get a good look at life in Jar-Geshim. You know, from their perspective."

Rizzo sat up and clasped her hands together, a wide grin spreading across her face that revealed her cone-shaped teeth. "The simple lives of bandits? Now this I have to see!"

"Didn't Mohan tell us to stay put?" Vicki asked.

"No, I believe his exact words were, 'Keep out of trouble until I get back,'" Ric said. "I don't intend to get into any."

Reluctantly, Kitty rose from her chair. "Somehow, I doubt I'm going to be able to stop you. Well, short of beating you senseless. And you're not going anywhere without me, so I guess I'll just have to come along."

Ric wondered how much of the tigress's reluctance was genuine; she seemed as curious about the city as he.

Vicki bounced up and down with childish glee. "Yay, field trip!"

"As the ranking agent here, I must set some boundaries," Zed said. "We are not to stray far from the hotel, and each of us must remain extra vigilant. The last thing we wish to do is cause a confrontation in the heart of bandit territory."

They started descending the stairs, passing Vince, who was trying unsuccessfully to coax the broken ice machine to life.

"Heading out?" he asked hopefully. "I'm drivin' myself insane tryin' to get this workin'."

Kitty jabbed a thumb over her shoulder at Ric. "Mr Journalist here wants to get a unique perspective on how people can actually live here."

Vince winked. "Sounds fun. Hey, maybe some of these bandit women aren't so bad?"

Rizzo squinted at him slyly. "I always knew you preferred bad girls."

Since Mohan had ordered that they leave their hunting gear at the motor pool, they had only their personal sidearms for protection—Ric remained unarmed. They still wore their armoured shirts but knew the high-quality equipment would make them primary targets for would-be thieves.

Ric led the way, headed for what he hoped was the local market. The spell of the quiet morning was starting to break, and it wasn't long before the traffic on the streets swelled to a veritable throng, and the cries of shop vendors rang in their ears. The gunfire hadn't started yet, but there was an electric feeling in the air as if the milling crowds were waiting to see who would draw first.

They passed a group of mercenaries who bore the Marshal's star harassing a shopkeeper—undoubtedly part of a standard protection racket. Vagrants high on an exotic array of narcotics lay in the alleys, while those who retained enough wits rifled through their pockets. The journalist self-consciously checked his pockets before remembering that he had purposefully left his wallet at the hotel. Another look at the vagabonds around him made him wonder if that was the wisest choice; it probably wasn't any safer there than out here. Plus, the bandits might decide his lack of coin was decidedly uncharitable.

They walked and browsed for nearly an hour. Kitty was impressed that Ric could keep himself from gawking too much; nothing was more tempting to pickpockets than a wide-eyed tourist who wasn't watching where he was going. The journalist proved just the opposite, drinking in every detail while maintaining a neutral expression—except for a raised eyebrow now and then.

The people they passed on the street all seemed eager to get anywhere that wasn't there. Nobody would meet their gaze, and everyone gave them as wide a berth as the narrow street would allow. Apparently, word of the strangers had spread rapidly, and it was made known they were under the Marshal's care.

Vince tried his best to appear his usual charming self, but he was unnerved to find it wasn't working. Not that he was disappointed; few faces could be considered comely, even by his most open-minded standards. Scars, sores, dirt, and rotted or missing teeth were as common in the women as in the men.

Children were a rarity, but not absent, products of the rampant indiscretions so freely indulged by the immoral populace. Although one could argue that their mothers—if they even cared—were among the toughest bitches on Amarthia.

A group of young street urchins scribbled obscenities on the stucco walls of a local eatery. The proprietor came out to shoo them away but didn't bother cleaning the graffiti off.

As they scampered away, Kitty noticed that one child had drawn a crude daisy blossom. Again, she felt a sudden rush of emotion, as she had during the chase through the alley in Kairran. Again, the face of someone long dead and buried flashed before her eyes. She staggered and shook her head to clear it.

Ric turned to her, concern evident on his face. "Is something wrong?"

She shook her head and took a breath. "Just the air in here. I never understood how these people breathe."

"Have you been to many bandit cities?" he asked.

"Well, no." She walked swiftly past him to avoid any further questions. Her fellow agents seemed too engrossed with the sights around them to have noticed the brief panic attack.

Ric followed her lead, and they turned down an even narrower street, where a few food vendors had set up to offer confections of uncertain origin. This alley seemed a little more deserted than the one they had just left, and the lynx wondered if they should turn back. He paused to look at a drunkard lying in the shadow of a doorway. Closer inspection revealed that the meerkat would never wake again.

"Are you satisfied now?" Kitty asked coldly. "What do you see?"

The journalist was surprisingly good at maintaining his composure, but the sadness in his voice was noticeable. "I'm not sure what I see. There's a lot of bad choices here and very little, if any, hope. Yet no one seems to have the slightest inclination to try and change it."

"These are the lives of those who have chosen to live in misery and violence, regardless of the consequences," Zed said. "Or perhaps in some cases because of them. For many, only they know their reasons. They wish only to deal with what the Wheel of Fate has handed them."

Ric nodded. "I can see that now, but I still don't understand it. I'm still curious how anyone could choose to live like this."

A scruffy-looking meerkat was passing as he said this, and he turned to appraise the journalist with an odd gleam in his jaundiced eye—a tattered rag concealed the other.

"How could one not choose a perfect life?" he said with a grin that revealed he was missing several teeth. "There is only one law, friend: survival of the fittest. What greater freedom—"

In the blink of an eye, Kitty had the meerkat plastered face-first against the wall, one arm pinned behind his back. The other she jammed against the wall; in it, he held a long, wicked knife.

"And I'm sure this is what makes you the fittest?" she growled, her snout wrinkling in a vicious snarl, the lips curling back to reveal her sharp fangs.

"I only sought his purse, Striped One!" the meerkat choked as he struggled against her iron grip.

"And if you happened to relieve him of his life as well, who would miss another tourist?" Zed responded, his own teeth bared in anger.

Ric was still recovering from Kitty's lightning reflexes. *My God, she's fast!*

After a breath, he said, "He'd knife me in a group like that?"

Vince looked down a nearby side alley, and his ears drooped slightly. "Um, I don't think he planned to take us on alone."

When Ric turned, he noticed that the regular patrons and shopkeepers occupying the alley had mysteriously vanished. Several shutters could be heard slamming shut nearby. At least a dozen men and women of varied species, armed with knives and rocks, were snaking their way down an adjoining alley towards them. A dozen more appeared at the head of their own lane, and more blocked off their route back to the main street.

With unspoken precision, the agents squared off to meet these new threats. Rizzo and Vince took the narrow side alley, and Zed and Vicki faced the thugs ahead of them, leaving Kitty and Ric to face the group approaching from the main street.

Ric tried to take an equal stance with the tigress, but she forced him behind her. "Look," he protested, "I might be naïve at times, but I'm not helpless. I was training to be a cop, remember? I passed the basic hand-to-hand training."

"I'm responsible for you," she growled, "and I'll be damned if I let you get so much as a scratch on my watch."

Holding the superior rank of colonel, Zed took charge of the situation. "Kittina, as soon as you see an opportunity, take Sedric Barnes back to the hotel and keep him there. The rest of you are to create that opportunity. Try to keep maiming to a minimum. These fools are clearly unaware of our true potential."

Vince limbered up, hopping from one foot to the other. "Been a while since I had to square off against somethin' with only two legs, but we can handle these clowns—Hey!"

He ducked as a rock narrowly missed him from overhead. Looking up, they saw another half-dozen avian assailants circling above them.

Most Hom-An avians could only fly short distances before tiring; their wings were much better suited for gliding or, in this case, hovering. The exception was insects, which could remain in the air almost indefinitely.

A large bee, who appeared to be the leader of the gang, shouted down to them, "How about six legs, Long Ears?"

Rizzo frowned. "OK, this may be a problem, *non*?"

Vicki was monitoring the escalating situation with increasing apprehension. She refused to engage in physical violence unless absolutely necessary, but she wasn't about to let a bunch of bandits push her that far. She had to find some way to give her allies an advantage.

One of the approaching ruffians carelessly knocked over a cooking pot at one of the food stands, and when its contents hit the hot coals, they sent a puff of grey smoke into the air.

Suddenly, she had an idea. Spinning into the middle of the group, the bullfrog began rummaging through her pockets. "I got this!" she said. "Just hold them off for a minute!"

The first wave approached within three metres of the defenders and paused, gauging the strength of their prey.

With a sudden yell, they charged forward, raising their weapons high over their heads and hoping their sheer numbers would quickly overwhelm their prey. Against the average tourist, the tactic would've worked, but this rabble of ruffians was not prepared to tangle with a tight-knit team of highly skilled agents, each trained in a variety of martial arts.

Vince lashed out with his powerful legs, felling one attacker and knocking another back into his compatriots. A third tried to take advantage of the hare's recovery, only to find himself flattened against the wall by a vicious snap of Rizzo's tail. Then the basilisk laid into the next thug in line, showing off what happens when you combine Neuf Marisian jiu-jitsu with a whip-like tail and claws longer than the average mammal.

Zed squared off against the group in front of him, turning so that his broad shoulders appeared to fill the street. For the Soketh, conflicts were focused on manipulation and misdirection, often redirecting offensive manoeuvres of one opponent so they would hinder or maim themselves or another opponent. At its core, their strategies were about mastering the flow of battle and turning it in their favour. Naturally, their own unique brand of martial arts was the same.

A bandit lunged at Zed with a knife, which he dodged easily as he stuck out a foot to trip him. As the rat fell, the badger grabbed at the scruff of his neck, spun, and sent the tumbling rodent into the path of a lumbering bull. The bandit's short knife buried itself to the hilt in the bull's thigh, sending both of them staggering to the left, where the bull gored an unfortunate tree gecko on his single horn. While all that was happening, Zed lashed out and gave a quick yank on the striped antennae of a long-horned beetle. The insect gave a raspy shriek and staggered backwards, his senses momentarily overwhelmed. His movement caused the moon-faced macaque behind him to drop his large rock on the toe of the jackal beside him, and they all went down in a heap. With only two movements, Zed had clogged half the alley with living debris.

Opposite the badger, Kitty braced against the rush of ruffians from the main street, lashing out with a series of vicious kicks and punches. Ric recognized the boxing style as similar to what he learned at the Royal Police Academy, but she was far more skilled, and her reflexes were nearly twice as fast. A ragged-looking emu struck out with its beak but ate a striped backhand instead, followed by a powerful sidekick that sent a cloud of feathers into the air. As she brought her heel back, it connected with the jaw of a marten who tried to squirm in from the side.

Not to be outdone, Ric caught the next bandit—a scraggly lemur missing half an ear—with a solid right hook that sent the simian staggering. He shook his hand from the sudden jolt of pain; he hadn't really kept up his fighting skills as much as his running.

Suddenly, Kitty threw him to the ground and caught a coatimundi in midair as it jumped out of a second-floor window above them. Grabbing his shirt front, she sent the ring-tailed Nasua flying into the crowd of bewildered thugs.

The journalist lay there for a second, thinking maybe it was best he stay out of the tigress's way. In fact, the fight seemed to be going so well that the journalist almost felt useless. Then, a stray rock reminded him of their aerial assailants.

Picking up the rock, he leapt to his feet and launched it back with expert aim and skill. It connected solidly with a mottled robin and sent her crashing into her duck-billed neighbour. Both plummeted onto a nearby roof.

"Nice throw," Kitty commented. "Cricket?"

Ric nodded as he gathered up more ammunition. "College league. I was a pretty wicked bowler."

Vicki finally found what she was looking for buried in her pockets: a large plastic bottle labelled KNO3, liberated from the medical supplies she found in the freezer in Kairran.

"Get me to that baker's stand over there! She cried, waving off to Ric's left.

The group shifted, fending off blows and returning them with every step. Vince took a leap off the wall and propelled himself into the midst of a group blocking their destination. He knocked them all flat with a sweep of his leg and flipped back into formation before any other attackers knew what was happening.

"Work fast, darlin'," he said, "Or bodies are going to start bein' a problem."

When they reached the stand, Vicki grabbed a large clay pot and set it over the fire. The powdery contents of the bottle and a large handful of raw sugar quickly followed.

"Hella time to bake a cake." Vince panted as he traded blows with an irritatingly agile howler monkey.

"Just hold them a little longer," Vicki instructed.

273

"We're tryin', darlin'," the hare replied, finally getting the drop on the simian was a swift left cross that made him see stars.

The dapper hare wasn't wrong. For every thug the agents knocked down, two more seemed ready to take their place. Even with their superior training, the agents were beginning to tire. Plus, the unconscious bodies of their foes were starting to make footing treacherous.

The flyers returned with reinforcements, filling the air with the drone of insect wings as they dive-bombed the mass of bodies below. Fortunately, thanks to the manipulative skill of the agents, their missiles tended to fall on their fellow bandits rather than their intended targets.

Long blades and clubs began to replace the simple knives and rocks. Zed was forced to draw his axe to fend off a pair of sword-wielding foes, and Vince liberated a scimitar from another while Rizzo yanked a support from an awning to use as a quarterstaff.

Ric stumbled away from the heavy blow of a hammer-wielding orangutan, opening himself to a stab from the simian's ocelot neighbour. Kitty pushed the journalist away from the attack, taking it on her arm. The sleeve on her armoured shirt slipped, and she gritted her teeth as the knife scored flesh. She delivered a vicious back kick to the ocelot's midsection, and he crumpled with a gasp.

"Any time now, Vicki!" Rizzo said, parrying a blow with her pole. "If this keeps up, they'll eventually switch to guns." She didn't have to mention what their odds were if that happened.

The bullfrog reached up and tore a strip of cloth off the stand's awning. She used it to grab the pot. "Ok! Hold your breath and get ready to run for it!" She lifted the pot high above her head and smashed it onto the ground.

Almost instantly, the narrow lane filled with thick grey smoke. There were shouts of surprise from their attackers both above and below.

Ric coughed and choked on the scrid smoke screen, and somebody—probably Kitty—grabbed him by the collar. They stumbled down the alley for several metres before somebody called a warning. Vicki? Rizzo? He couldn't tell. The smoke stung his eyes to near blindness, and with only the noise of combat around him, he completely lost his sense of direction. Somebody was shouting off to his left. Another voice warned that the flyers were coming back.

How can they see through all this smoke? He thought.

Suddenly, a voice very close to him warned everyone to get out of the way. There was a tremendous crash, and he felt a sudden weight on his head and shoulders. Then everything went black.

21 – Monsters and Morals

Slowly, the room came back into focus, and Sedric Barnes became aware of voices around him. His head throbbed as if a hundred jackhammers were continually pummelling him. A face in black and white stared down at him. At first, he thought the blow had struck him colour-blind. Then, those hard blue pools came into focus.

Stoic indifference quickly replaced Kitty's look of concern, but the journalist was sure he had seen a brief crack in her frozen armour.

"Get up already," the tigress growled with annoyance. "It's not that bad."

Vicki was packing her medical supplies nearby. "Why do people keep saying that? Getting knocked unconscious for more than a few seconds usually means you've got a concussion or the flow of blood has been cut off to the brain. That isn't exactly 'not bad.'"

Ric reached up and touched the bandage around his head. His left ear itched terribly. "I'll live," he said groggily. "Just need an aspirin...or a really stiff drink."

Mohan was leaning against the doorway. "Not even an agent yet and already causing trouble. Thought I told you not to go mucking about?"

"I thought trouble was one of those things that finds us?" Ric replied.

The giant tiger broke into a grin. "Good on ya. That does seem to be the case."

Ric sat up gradually, well aware that he probably shouldn't move around too much or too quickly just yet. Slowly, he examined his surroundings.

"OK, back at the hotel. You're back. Sun is still up. What happened? How long was I out?"

"Only an hour," Vicki said, fussing over his bandages. "Some dirty buzzards literally dropped a house on us."

"If you can call one of those tin-plated hovels a house," Kitty said as she looked out the window.

"And these people do," Mohan grunted. "Had to call on the Marshal's guard to break up the fight and get you out of there. He's not going to be happy about that. Anyway, if you feel up to it, Ric, we're having a meeting on the roof in a few minutes."

Ric nodded slowly but didn't follow them immediately; the room needed to stop spinning first.

Kitty was the last one out.

Ric noticed the bandage on her arm. "I'm sorry," he said, "That was my fault."

"No drama," she replied curtly.

She paused in the doorway and stole a furtive look at the injured journalist before following the others upwards.

Several other Tiger's Stripe agents—including Mümtaz, Caz, and Rosa—had gathered on the rooftop patio for want of something to do. Some decided to join them, even though the meeting mostly concerned the Scrappers.

"So, what is the Marshal like?" Vince asked. "And what was the big favour Xereas kept hinting at?"

"Oh, the Marshal's got tickets on himself, for sure," Mohan replied. "Figures himself to be some kind of frontier sheriff, keeping the rabble in line. Even says he's from bloody Carlin, if you can believe it. But the job is right up our alley, unfortunately. You remember that wreck we came across in the jungle?"

"Ah, some beast has been terrorising the bandits," Zed said. He was examining the city's exterior defences through a pair of binoculars.

The tiger nodded. "I suppose we should have seen that one coming. They haven't got a bloody clue what it is, only that it sure as hell isn't your typical ceravaag or jungle bahnger. Our gracious host has given us three days to hunt it down and deliver its head to his throne. We'll head out tomorrow morning."

"He's got a throne?" Vince said, but they ignored him.

Ric slowly emerged from the stairwell and gingerly seated himself at the table. Mohan nodded at him encouragingly and filled him in on the mission.

"We don't really have a choice in this, do we?" the journalist said.

"Much as they are the dregs of society, I suppose even bandits don't deserve to be slaughtered like bolvin," the tiger answered, looking up at the westering sun and checking his wristwatch. "Not to mention I have a nasty feeling that whatever this thing is, we don't want it roaming rampant across the countryside."

"Do you think it's a fiend?" Vicki asked.

"Perhaps," Zed answered. "However, it may only be an escaped denizen of the Warren." The badger had since turned his binoculars in that direction.

"Which probably has a fiend or two lurking in it," Vicki pointed out. "We've all heard the rumours, but nobody's actually gone in there to check it out."

"Or made it back alive," Kitty muttered.

Mohan shrugged. "Whatever it is, we still need to kill it. We should only be so lucky if it's just a wild beast." He looked up to the other agents. "Caz, Rosa, you think we've got time for this?"

Rosa rubbed at her chin a moment. "Can't say for sure, Mo.' She had a Plainsman accent similar to the tigers. "We only need a few more hours to get the trucks ready, but then it's all about timing."

Caz nodded and spoke in a heavy, rolling Mosvian accent, "*Da*, that is true, but we must also be wary of other assets in play. Your report say third party killed the ambassador's daughter, *da*? We had not much time to follow up on this information. It is possible this third party has followed us here. Much as I do not want to think of that."

Mohan nodded. "I hadn't forgotten. Mümtaz, don't be a wallflower, mate. What's your opinion as our extraction specialist?"

The gazelle looked momentarily flustered, uncomfortable with being put on the spot. Then he straightened up and said, "Three days will only give us more time to prep an escape route or three. Breaking out of the front gate isn't going to be easy, but my guess is it will be a lot safer than trying to get through the Warren. Rosa is right; it's all going to be about timing. You should be ready to go as soon as you get back with the Marshal's prize."

The tiger nodded again. "We will. Now, we noticed that you found those wreckage sites on the way in here. Tell us what you found."

The agents explained what they had learned for the better part of the next hour and corroborated it with what the Scrappers suspected. Then, they compared it with the account of the missing scout parties the Marshal had given them.

Ric listened patiently as the group speculated on what type of creature they could be dealing with and how to combat it. However, the journalist felt out of place during the discussion; his only experience with the strange creatures had been almost by accident, and even then, only from a distance.

When they appeared to be wrapping up, Ric cleared his throat and asked, "While I appreciate the courtesy you've given me, I'm afraid I must remind you I still know very little about these fiend creatures."

The tiger slapped his forehead. "Strewth, mate, I keep forgetting you haven't been properly initiated. Well, if you want the whole story, you'd have to browse our library at the Sanctuary; the short version is we think they came through a portal from another dimension."

"You mean like demons?"

Mohan laughed heartily. "God, no! Although I admit you might think that to look at one, I wouldn't try splashing holy water on it. They're living creatures like you or me—almost as intelligent, too."

A small avian creature fluttered down and perched on the railing on the other side of the roof.

Mohan pointed to it. "Look there. What do you see?"

Ric studied the avian. It was small enough to fit in the palm of his paw, and the brightly coloured feathers on its oblong body were reminiscent of a parrot. The similarities stopped there, of course; a short, scaly neck curved up from the body and supported a broad reptilian head dominated by two large, bright opaline eyes.

It snapped up a small nonsentient beetle into a wide mouth lined with tiny cone-shaped teeth. Like the head and neck, the creature's tail was reptilian and nearly as long as the body, yet it ended in a narrow, fanned plume of iridescent feathers. It clung to the rail with four long lizard-like claws attached to thin, scaly bird legs.

The lynx looked back to the tiger. "It's a galradon. They're pretty common around here."

"Yes, but what does it *look* like?" Mohan pressed.

Ric looked again. "Well, not to offend anybody, but it looks like a cross between a parrot and an iguana."

Rizzo cocked her head to the side but said nothing.

"Bonza!" Mohan said. "That's my point. Every creature native to Amarthia looks like something else, right? Like bahngers almost look like pumas or panthers mixed with crocodiles, or hargaers look like bears mixed with owls." Caz grunted, and one of the other avian agents ruffled the wings on her back. "I'm not one to speculate why, but the point is it's something we can relate to—as unnerving as some similarities might be at times. Fiends are entirely different. They don't look like they belong here. There is something…alien about them. You said you've seen one."

A cloud passed over the journalist's face, and he nodded. "In Barju near the border of the Aizlgeist. I'm not exactly looking forward to repeating the experience. But you're right; whatever it was, it didn't belong here."

"That's because they don't," Mohan growled. "They may not have come from hell, but it's our job to send them there. But you'll see that for yourself tomorrow."

"So I'm coming with you." It was more a statement than a question.

"I think you'll enjoy getting to see how the real work is done."

"And it'll keep me out of any more trouble in the city," the lynx said with a lopsided grin.

"Too right, mate," the tiger said with a wink.

After the meeting, the agents lounged around the roof for a while. Now that talk of monsters had died down, Ric pondered other questions about the Tiger's Stripe and saw some opportunities opening.

He sauntered over to the koala. "Hello! Rosa, right? Mohan tells me you're with what you call the public restoration team."

She was almost a head shorter than him and looked him over with wide brown eyes. "Too right. And you must be the new recruit Mo picked up in Kairran. I must say they get handsomer every year."

"You're too kind." He took the compliment in stride. "But I think that would be obvious as the new face around here. I am curious, though. From what Mohan

283

told me, I'd imagine that public restoration would involve more paperwork than actually being in the field."

Rosa laughed easily and scratched at her bulbous nose. "And don't I wish it was that simple! No, mate, sometimes you need to get your hands dirty to fix the damage that's already been done. Kinda like a medic, right Vicki?"

The frog nodded enthusiastically, but she was only half listening and didn't interject anything.

"You see, mate," the koala continued, "TS does a lot of cross-training. Have to since our numbers are so few. You might see most of the pencil pushers at the Sanctuary, but rest assured, every agent is combat-ready, even those of us who prefer not to mix it up. And being PR means you need to think quick on your feet, especially in an environment like this." She gestured to the city below. "If we get in a tight spot, I'm the one who will need to tell our heavy hitters—that's Mo and the Scrappers—what *not* to shoot."

General Durram summoned her before Ric could pose another question, and he turned back to the railing. He gazed out at the people below and scratched absently at the bandage on his head. He had never seen a place so alive and yet so dangerous. The random gunfire had started again, but it did nothing to faze the throngs of people below. To them, this was a normal day. There really was an organisation to the chaos.

"Why do you do it?" he asked suddenly of nobody in particular.

Caz was standing nearby, and the massive bear leaned on the railing. "That is question with many answers, Mr Barnes."

The journalist nodded. "Call me Ric. Rosa was just telling me it's her job to tell you not to shoot if these bandits turn on us. And something inside me is inclined to agree. I'm still asking myself why; I mean, these people haven't been quite hospitable towards us. It's exactly like Zed told me; they care nothing about law or order. And yet, I can't bring myself to try to change them. I don't want them to hurt anyone else, but I can't deny that it's their right to choose such a destructive life. Is that really in our blood?"

Mohan came up and leaned against the railing next to Caz. Ric panicked briefly when the iron bar shifted, but it held the weight of the two large agents. He was also grateful Mohan stood on Caz's other side instead of sandwiching the journalist between their towering forms.

"What does anyone truly know about what is right and what is wrong?" the tiger asked.

Ric thought a moment. "I suppose with so many cultures, it is difficult to say one view is more correct than another."

The tiger shook his head. "Does that excuse murder? Extortion? Slavery? No! Yet why do we view such things as wrong?"

"By virtue of our existence, I suppose," Ric said.

Caz grunted. "But doesn't Pytan Common Law teach that purebloods are better than half-breeds? Or that those who show strength hold dominion over the weak?"

"Or that women are to be subservient to men? I see where you're going with this." Ric shook his head. "But who says we have the authority to change that because our blood compels us to seek 'justice'?" He used his fingers to create air quotes.

The burly bear put a massive paw on his shoulder. "That is right question, Ric. That is why we live by code."

"But who interprets that code?" the journalist pressed.

Mohan sighed and looked to the sky. After a moment, he looked back to the lynx. "I suppose history, but then they say history is written by the victors. How do you make someone believe what you say is truth? What if I were to say the sky was yellow?"

"I'd say we were in the middle of a sandstorm."

The tiger chuckled. "Good one, but let me put it another way: what if I *believed* the sky was yellow?"

Ric thought a moment. "I think I understand. It's not about language or words; it's about reality. No matter how hard you believe it, it doesn't change that the sky is blue."

A nod. "And even if I insist it was different, knowing full well the difference between blue and yellow, the sky would still be blue. No matter what you believe, it doesn't make it different. That's how we see the difference between justice and injustice. There are things in the world that are inherently wrong, and we understand it more strongly than most. It doesn't matter what nations or treaties say; it is and always will be wrong.

"But that leads back to the question of whether or not we have the authority to change it. To be honest, TS has kept itself in check by focusing on the issues that are obviously wrong, no matter how you look at it. Things like slavery or extortion and the preservation of life. The most important thing is that we never seek power, only to make right that which is wrong. Free will, for all its possible faults, is very important. None of us are perfect, and we must tread very carefully to avoid falling into the trap of believing we're right all the time." Mohan paused as if remembering something.

When he remained silent, Ric asked, "Can an imperfect mind truly comprehend what is good and evil?"

Mohan smirked. "I thought I asked that already? You see? Now we're starting to talk in circles. I was never big on philosophy and theology. I only know that when I see a sixteen-year-old girl chained to a post and paraded in front of a muscle-bound gladiator, my blood boils. And it does the same when a fiend threatens a community who just wants to get on with its day-to-day life."

Ric pointed to the crowds below. "Even when the day-to-day often means killing your neighbour over a crust of bread? Or just because you felt like it?"

Caz nodded slowly. "That is problem: which problem you must fix first? Do you let monsters eat bandits? Or do you save them and hope you find other means of stabilising their society?"

Ric looked up at him. "But if we aren't in the business of assuming power, who decides which means are best? Surely, not all governments are fit for that responsibility."

The bear understood his meaning and let out a hearty laugh. "I am no communist. I was taxi driver in New Port before being recruited. My family left Mosvia when I was teenager. I never lost accent."

Ric smiled. He had guessed as much when he first met the bear, but his journalist instincts drove him to pry. For all the Mosvian government's talk of a classless society, giving political and socioeconomic power to the state had not proven to be the utopia its doctrine professed. On the flip side, it wasn't much better than living under the fascist rule of the Dollan Empire.

While he was no philosophy major, Ric could see that neither system meshed with the "free will" values espoused by Tiger's Stripe, at least as far as Mohan and Caz explained them. But he felt he had a long way to go if he ever wanted to understand the inner workings of an organisation three thousand years old.

The sun sank low on the horizon, and the noise of the street rose to fill the silence that had fallen on the agents. Mohan yawned widely, and Ric found himself following suit. With all the excitement that had happened that day, he suddenly felt exhausted, and his bandaged head throbbed again.

"Right," the tiger said. "It's about time we all got some rest. Gotta get up early to head out to the farms."

The journalist watched as, one by one, the agents of Tiger's Stripe retired to what passed for their quarters. He listened to the noisy life of the bandits for a while longer, then looked to the sinking disc of Druna, the day moon.

He thought the western horizon appeared to be an unnaturally deep shade of red.

22 – Minion Management

While the Scrappers rested in Pytan, night had already settled in over the nation of Medocci, a thousand kilometres and more to the northwest. Unlike most countries, which shared contiguous borders, Medocci comprised two landmasses divided by the Tharsian Sea, a large tributary of the Medean Basin. As such, it was also one of the few nations with territory on two continents: Aerneia and Estan. Despite the wide watery barrier, the provinces of Pianure Rosso and Mata remained united through industrious trade and a rich shared culture. Such was the variety of its history that Medocci laid claim to being both one of the oldest nations in the region and the birthplace of many modern philosophies, both political and economic.

However, there were dramatic differences between the two provinces. While Pianure Rosso held claim as the home of the Amarthian Catholic Church of Aaba, its cousin served only the religion of the dekon, the local

Medoccian currency. In Mata, all faiths were welcome as long as you lined your purse with enough coin.

The fortified port city of Kalegos was a prime example of this worldly faith. Inside the walls, the glittering lights of the beach resorts mirrored the glow of large cruise ships floating at anchor in the bay, a testament to the city's vibrant nightlife.

This was all too obvious to the watchmen posted on the deck of the *Resthoven*, who would much rather have joined their captain and the rest of the crew currently partaking of those pleasures.

Little activity surrounded the *Milo Sabbanti Porto Internazionale* this late into the evening. The long piers reached into the bay like the fingers of a spider monkey, but only two still glowed with light as the workers laboured to unload ships that had arrived late that afternoon. Heavy cranes on steel tracks ran up and down as they loaded and unloaded containers from all over the world.

One of the watchmen on the *Resthoven*'s bridge wing turned a lazy glance northward, where smaller piers offered shelter to tugboats and pilot ships. It was equally as dark and lonely as the maze of stacked containers, large warehouses, and stumpy cinder-block office buildings that marched away from the docks.

The ship groaned gently beneath the lookouts' feet as the tide pushed it against the buffered dock. The markings on the *Resthoven*'s hull claimed her registry was Dolchester in Locke. She was three hundred metres long with a beam of thirty-two metres and grossed sixty thousand dead-weight tons.

The burly goat leaning on the railing lowered his binoculars. "What the hell 're we doin' 'ere, Eddie?" he asked his companion in a thick burr straight from Oakbridge in the Faith Islands.

The wiry tabby cat blinked as if half-asleep. "Eh, whatcha say, Rocko?"

"Och, ne'er mind." The goat went back to idly scanning the docks through the binoculars. For what, he didn't know; there had to be something to break the monotony of the evening.

Of course, maybe it would be better if nothing happened at all. This had been one of the strangest cruises for the crew of the *Resthoven*, marred by the unexpected death of several of their friends and cohorts.

They were no strangers to illicit cargo, but the captain steered clear of drugs and guns. Live cargo was a rarity, and for good reason, as they had experienced only a few days ago.

"Oi, you 'ear that?" Rocko asked.

Eddie yawned widely. "Oh, knock it off, Rocko. You've been paranoid ever since we pulled into port."

"An' I dinna know why you ain't paranoid, 'specially with that lot who came on halfway through the cruise. Then they up an' leave straight as we get into port."

Eddie grunted. "Good riddance, I say. I'm telling ya, Rocko, there was something funny about those blokes. Scary even. Never seen a bunch of mercs like them. And did you see the way they kept fussing about the centre hold?"

"Dinna remind me," the goat said with a shudder. "And then Jones gone and got 'is arm chewed off."

The tabby shuddered as well. "Aye. And it got MacDugan, too. Fuck me, but if we ever do live cargo again, it'll be too soon. Nobody who saw those marks would believe it was a crane accident. Torn to shreds they were." He made a religious gesture, both for swearing and for the horrific memories the conversation brought up.

Both crewmen suddenly felt a presence behind them and turned. Out of the shadows stepped a broad-faced sun bear with fiery red long-fur. He was dressed all in black and wore tactical webbing, much like the mercenaries they had just talked about.

"Thank ye, gentlemen." Meyrick Keir's Faith Islander burr was formal but not as heavy as Rocko's. "Ye've been very informative."

In a lightning movement, the sun bear delivered two powerful blows that left the crewmen out cold on the deck. Another figure appeared and helped drag the lookouts into the pilothouse, where they dropped them unceremoniously next to the unconscious form of another crew member.

The sun bear's companion had the stocky build and blunt head of a groundhog, but his body-fur bore the rust-coloured markings of a chipmonk. Most prominent was the black Tiger's Mark in the fur on the back of his neck, just below the hairline of his cheek-length blond long-fur.

The bear pressed the transmit button on the radio strapped to his webbing. "All clear here. What's it look like out there, Rothschild?'

From the control cabin of one of the large cranes, a ferret scanned the dockyards through the scope of a large sniper rifle. A strand of golden long-fur escaped from beneath her black knit cap, but she ignored it.

"Still good, Kier," Terry Rothschild said, her voice carrying the distinct nonaccent of someone who moved around a lot as a child. "Terrell just got the last of them on the forward deck."

The mink in question flashed a thumbs-up in her general direction. Crystaldawn Terrell's long-fur was platinum-blond, but she hid it under a knit cap like Rothschild. The mink's body-fur was still white for the winter season, but she had used special grease paint to mask most of it with black stripes. The effect reminded Rothschild of a certain white tigress who probably wished she was in her place right now. The ferret allowed herself a brief smirk.

"Bloody beautiful," Keir said. He also gave a slight smirk but for different reasons.

As the leader of Hunter TS-5, the sun bear expected such efficiency from his hand-picked team; each of them had served in some branch of their respective country's armed forces, and Keir had moulded them into an effective hunter team.

Of course, they didn't usually hunt other Hom-Ans.

They were busy tracking rumours of a miraj pack in the wilderness south of Sweisæ Alps when the call to redirect had come in. Keir would be sure to remind Mohan Katral that the tiger owed him one after this.

He spoke into his radio again. "OK, some of the crew mentioned taking on mercenaries while out at sea, but they left when they got into port. They must've been hired by that al-Seif character TS Three was after. Terrell, it sounds like they were keeping the special cargo in the centre hold. Check it out, and I'll meet ye there."

The sun bear turned to the chip-hog. "Völundr, check the chart room and see if ye can find the ship's manifest. My guess is the captain scrubbed all the records of his illicit trading, but ye never know. At the very least, see if ye can track where this ship's been during the last few months. Maybe we can find out where they loaded the live cargo. We're on the clock; let's move, people."

Even if she was a smaller freighter, the *Resthoven* was still a big ship with plenty of places to hide things you didn't want found. Keir's experience with the Locke

Coast Guard had taught him a lot about where those hiding spots were, and the watchmen's conversation about the centre hold was a good enough starting point. Unfortunately, they still weren't exactly sure what they were looking for.

Terrell met the sun bear on the second deck of the hold. "Hate to say it, Keir," she said in her pleasant singsong Midwest WUK accent, "but things look pretty normal so far. You see anything on your way down here?"

Keir shook his head. "Nay. But the watchmen Völundr and I took out on the bridge seemed mighty agitated about the mercenaries they took aboard. I believe 'scary' was one of the terms used."

"Yah," the mink replied, "they did seem a bit shook up, eh?"

As they made their way to the bottom of the hold, Keir asked for a status report from his team.

"Nothing new," Rothschild reported, a little curtly. As much as she would enjoy ribbing Kittina Katral about doing her job for her, she had to admit she didn't like covering for TS-3. She was also getting cramped up in the crane control booth.

"Steady, Rothschild," Keir admonished. "I don't think those miraj are going anywhere. We'll be back in Pianure Rosso by morning. Just keep your cool."

"It's already too chilly up here," she said flatly but not into her radio.

Völundr's report from the chart room was more helpful. "According to the logs, the ship was transporting computer parts and foodstuffs from East Benai." The chip-hog had a rough Norsen accent that instantly summoned images of broad-shouldered warriors sailing ships adorned with dragon heads on the prow. "However, the charts show they went south around the cape of Coasta Blanco instead of west up the Adrakar Strait and the Hutsepth Canal."

"That's a long way to go for a vessel this size," Keir replied.

"They might've been trying to avoid the commercial tariffs from Adrakar," Terrell suggested. "Or the pirates, take your pick. There's a huge territorial political mess surrounding those waters."

Völundr ruffled some pages. "But I thought they had a mercenary escort? By the way, there's no record of when they came on board."

"I'm not surprised," Keir said. "Keep me posted."

The sun bear and mink stepped off the stairway onto the deck of the centre hold. The light was dim, and they had to watch their footing even with their powerful torches. Stacks of shipping containers rose all around them. Kalegos was not the *Resthoven*'s intended destination, so it was no surprise that it hadn't been unloaded.

Keir rapped on the side of a container with a knuckle. It sounded hollow. He aimed his light up and counted the decks they had descended.

"That's odd," he muttered. He pressed the button on his radio. "Völundr, once yer done there, get down into the centre hold with Terrell and me. Something is wrong 'ere."

The chip-hog acknowledged and finished taking pictures of the charts for later analysis. However, before leaving, he took a final look at the chart table. He had also served in his nation's coastal patrol and had learned that smugglers never kept their plans out in the open. He ran his foot paw along the wooden baseboards and was rewarded when one of the panels came loose and fell off. He quickly bent down and drew out a rolled map.

Spreading it over the tabletop, he discovered a duplicate chart of the Adrakar Strait and the eastern coast of Mwungo to the Cape of Coasta Balnco. Grease pencils had been used to mark several locations in the middle of the Green Sea and along the deserted coast of the Saran Waste between the shores of Bozambwe and Coasta Blanco.

He spoke into his radio. "I found something, Keir. There was a hidden compartment under the chart table. They must use it to hide the charts for their smuggling routes. Not only did they make the trip around Coasta Blanco, but they made several stops along the way, some off the coast of the Saran Waste. If these dates are correct, they loitered there for several weeks, went back up the Adrakar Strait to anchor off the Aizlgeist, then went back to the Saran Waste before continuing up the west coast to Gat Bahar."

"Out and back and out again," Keir said. "Not a very efficient travel route, even for smugglers."

"So much for Terrell's theory about tariffs," Rothschild commented.

"Perhaps not," Völundr said, scratching the mark on the back of his neck as it started to itch. "The marked route looks like they were trying to avoid official patrols. And even the boldest smugglers try to avoid the coasts of the Saran Waste and the Aizlgeist."

"Fiver on what they were really picking up at those locations," Rothschild said.

"Nay bet," Keir replied. "But I don't think that locker in the chartroom is the only secret compartment on this ship. Terrell and I are standing on the lowest deck of the centre hold, but by my count, we should still have two to go before we hit her keel."

"That is a lot of space for a secret compartment. On my way."

While they waited for the chip-hog to arrive, the sun bear examined the containers more closely. Most were average, except that they were empty. Decoys that could probably be explained away as ballast to inquiring inspectors; their location in the centre hold helped balance the ship. However, there was one that felt different. It rested flush against the outer bulkhead, and no other containers were on or around it. The metal also sounded different when knocked on, as if the echo lasted longer.

Keir pointed it out to Völundr when he arrived.

"I don't think this container is meant to be moved," the chip-hog said after looking it over. "There are scrapes and scratches on the deck around it, but they don't follow a consistent pattern."

"Like they were put there to make it look like the container was moved?" Terrell asked.

Völundr nodded. "I also think this container is built right into the hull. See how close it sits against the outer bulkhead? You couldn't even slip a piece of paper through there."

"And the doors are strange, too," Keir said. "No chain, but these latches are locked tight. Almost like there's some kind of mechanism inside keeping it shut."

"Magnetic locks?" the chip-hog suggested. "There must be a way to disengage them."

"What about that?" Terrell said, pointing to a large red button on the bulkhead. It was labelled as a fire alarm, but no sprinkler heads or other emergency equipment were nearby.

"Hidden in plain sight," Keir said. He pushed it.

There was a surprisingly loud *clack* as the lock disengaged and the door popped open a fraction. The sun bear opened the container to reveal a large piece of machinery mounted on a pallet.

"A bust?" Terrell asked.

"Maybe not," Keir said. "Völundr, see if you can find a jack."

The chip-hog reached out and gave the mechanical object a tug. "I don't think we need one; the pallet is mounted on casters."

None of them knew what type of machine it was, but it was likely only meant to dissuade further investigation should prying eyes make it past the door. When the pallet was pushed out, they discovered that only half the floor was part of the container. The rest was a narrow stairwell leading down. After stepping through, they closed the doors behind them, and the lock re-engaged with another loud *clack*.

"Glad we knocked out the crew, eh?" Terrell said, "You can hear that through the whole ship."

"Aye," Keir said. "Proceed with caution."

As they descended, they felt a change in the atmosphere, and Völundr noted that they must have passed beneath the ship's waterline. They could hear the water lapping at the side through the outer bulkhead. At the bottom of the stair, a corridor led back into the ship and ended at a dual airlock. Keir guessed they were about amidships.

"Seems like there's still a lot of wasted space here," Terrell said as they waited for the lock to cycle.

"I think I know why," Keir said. "It's a pressure space designed to keep the ship from flooding."

They couldn't see much in the darkened room; the only light came from a large pool at the centre. Closer inspection revealed that the pool was open to the sea below. Völundr found a bank of light switched near the airlock and flipped them on one by one.

"A moonpool," the chip-hog said. "A big one, too."

Despite the pressure hull built around it, the hidden loading bay easily occupied the missing two decks from the hold above. A machine shop near the airlock served the small two-man submersible that hung from the ceiling. On the opposite side, at least six large steel cages were stacked against the far bulkhead; they had a peculiar, almost egg-like design and were nearly five metres in diameter at the longest point. The space next to them may have held much larger cells at one point. Cranes at each corner of the pool could move the submersible or a cage into place over the water.

Something had reduced one of the cranes near the cages to little more than a twisted hunk of metal.

"A lot of this looks new," Keir said. "That layover near the Saran Waste must have been when it was installed."

Völundr nodded. "But if that's true, it means someone has a working drydock along the Saran Waste. Which also means there's a hole in the dead zone."

Keir drew a breath and blew it out his nose. "Aye. But that's something for the Elder Council to worry about. We have a job to do 'ere"

"Those cages could probably hold something big and powerful," Terrell said, "like a ceravaag, eh?"

"Or and ahuitzotl," Keir replied, examining the cages more closely. "They're watertight with their own air supply. They probably use the sub to tow them through the water. It looks like they can remove the watertight shell and use the metal cage for land transport."

"Maybe that's why they swung back to the Aizlgeist?" Terrell said. "After they built the moonpool and loaded up on cages, then went to pick up specimens."

"They scrubbed this place pretty clean," Völundr said. "No blood, no spore. I'd be tempted to say they hadn't even used this equipment if I didn't smell bleach everywhere. And the broken crane, of course." He moved to take a closer look at it. "Look at the gears; the teeth are stripped clean, and the pneumatics bent. Whatever they were trying to haul with it put up a hell of a fight."

Terrell aimed her torch towards the ceiling and gasped. "My God, look at that!"

Above the pool near the broken crane, several long, jagged gashes marred the bay's roof. At a guess, the widest was nearly fourteen centimetres across and sunk deep into the steel hull. The blow had ripped through the cross-beams as neatly as someone would scratch a claw through the dirt.

"That," Völundr muttered, "was not caused by any kind of industrial equipment. And it wasn't a ceravaag or hargaer, either."

"Not even an ancient grendel has claws that large," Terrell said breathlessly. "What the hell were they transporting?"

Keir frowned. "Unfortunately, it doesn't look like we're going to find out 'ere. Much as I hate to admit it, I wish we had Ezekiel 'ere; he could make more sense of these markings. Take some pictures; we'll see if somebody at the Sanctuary can get anything out of it. Rothschild, are we clear for extraction?"

"So far."

Up in her perch, the ferret carefully swept her scope around the yard, moving from the active piers to the *Resthoven* to the warehouses and back. She straightened slightly. "Hang on," she said. A train of three black off-road vehicles was approaching the north gate.

The guard exited his shack and approached the lead driver's window. Seemingly satisfied with the driver's ID, he turned and opened the gate. Before the guard returned to his kiosk, Rothschild saw him give two quick jerks and collapse to the ground. The vehicles proceeded through.

"Shit! Heads up, we got company. Someone just rolled up and took out the gate guard."

"Shit!" Keir responded. "Is our boat clear?" He was referring to the inflatable craft they had used to approach the shipyard.

The ferret watched as the line of ORVs headed directly for pier three. "It is for now, but hurry up. They are definitely here for the freighter. I'm guessing they're the clean-up crew."

The vehicles pulled to a stop along the quay, and several black-clad figures climbed out, four per truck. Despite the masks, Rothschild identified a mix of canines, felines, and at least one reptile. Within seconds, eight of the figures were already approaching the gangway of the *Resthoven*. Rothschild saw the suppressed flash of their compact weapons as they put a bullet through a pair of crew members her teammates had gone out of their way to render unconscious. The remaining four figures headed for the admin building, probably to erase any trace of the *Resthoven* from the harbourmaster's records.

"They know something isn't right," Rothschild said into her radio. "They found the crew you left on the pier. They shot them. You're gonna have company shortly."

"Slow them down if you can," Keir ordered. "We're almost done 'ere."

Rothschild took careful aim and sent a bullet right through the skull of a canine figure as he approached a stack of fuel drums near the gangplank. The tungsten-coated .50 calibre rounds—the same ones Kittina Katral wanted to test—had been designed specifically for hunting large armoured fiends in the wilderness; against an unarmoured target, the effect was incredibly messy.

The other mercenaries dived for cover behind the containers and equipment lined along the dock. Rothschild had suppressed her rifle, but the pop of the large calibre round was still loud in the control cabin of the crane. Even so, she was too far away for the enemy to hear which direction the shot had come from, and they assumed they were under attack from the ship. The sniper saw several flashes as they fired on the empty decks, unaware of the danger behind them.

She climbed down the crane as swiftly as she dared. The first rule of sniping was never to shoot from the same spot twice. It wouldn't take them long to figure out they were shooting at nothing, and she didn't want to get pinned at the top of the crane with no egress.

The mercenaries began cautiously approaching the ship again. When she reached the foot of the crane, Rothschild lined up another shot and took out the first target to reach the top of the gangplank. This time, her opponents caught on much faster, and she ducked as a spray of bullets ricocheted off the crane's support girders.

Two mercenaries split off from the main group and tried to flank her hiding spot. However, when they arrived, a small explosive wired to a proximity motion trigger greeted them.

Keeping low, the ferret used the explosion to sneak behind a nearby container and approached the mercenaries' ORVs. The figures that had entered the harbourmaster's office were still busy inside, but the commotion would draw them out soon enough. Rothschild quickly and quietly planted a candy-bar-sized explosive on each vehicle.

A quick peek around the corner of the last vehicle revealed that her path was clear, and she crept carefully down to the lower docks, where they had moored their inflatable.

Down in the *Resthoven*'s hidden moonpool, the three remaining agents of Hunter TS-5 could feel the deck beneath them rumble to life.

"They're taking the ship out," Keir growled.

"We'll probably never see her again," Völundr said as he started for the airlock. "They'll either scuttle her or give her a complete makeover to alter her appearance."

He stopped when they heard the *clack* of the magnetic locks on the container door disengaging.

"Damn, they've already reached the container," Keir said. He looked to the only other egress. "Right, into the pool!"

The three agents secured their weapons and dived into the water, swimming out the bottom past the ship's keel.

Moments later, two of the assassins passed through the airlock and began a sweep of the room. They couldn't see the agents in the dark water, but they fired several volleys in case they were hiding beneath the surface. When nothing floated up, they turned and continued their search of the ship.

The sun bear, the chip-hog, and the mink had all trained extensively in the water and could hold their breath for a long while. Finding their sense of direction was the greatest danger in the black water, but they didn't surface until they were out of sight in the shadow of the neighbouring pier. The *Resthoven* was slowly pulling away from the dock.

The agents dived again and swam away from the departing ship to the far side of the pier. Rothschild approached in their own boat and helped drag them out of the water.

"Those bastards murdered the entire crew," the ferret said.

"Only those left on watch," Keir corrected. "But I've a feeling those who went into town won't live through the night. If they went through all this trouble to secure the ship, they won't leave any loose ends."

Rothschild looked back to the shore. The remaining mercenaries had returned from their mysterious trip to the harbourmaster's office and were busy loading the bodies of their fallen into the ORVs. No doubt they planned to drive away with the last traces of their mess. The ferret flipped the switch on her detonator.

Three simultaneous explosions lit the night sky as Rothschild turned the boat out into the waters of the Tharsian Sea.

"Now they're even," she muttered.

Keir stared after the fleeing freighter, then turned to the flames on shore. "That were messier than I would have cared for," he said. "We'll call Watch Command as soon as we get back to shore. I hope they can get in touch with Hunter TS Three. Call it a hunch, but I don't think those mercenaries belonged to al-Seif. They unloaded something big from that ship, and we have no idea where it's headed."

* * *

The *Star of Carmen* dropped anchor off the coast of Pianure Rosso. Jirair al-Seif had set his sights on Medocci for only two reasons: a potential alliance with the mafia and because it was the birthplace of his mistress, Carmen Abbatelli.

He informed the captain he would remain in the country for an extended period. Then he reached for the phone to call his lawyers in Medocci. The handset rang before he could dial.

"Yes?" he answered.

He heard the timid, deep voice of Hamadi, the lieutenant he had sent back to Kairran. "S-sir, it's about the *Resthoven*. I just received word the captain was found dead in a Kalegos brothel."

The mouflon looked eastward towards the distant shores of the eastern province. "Is that so? Well, let Freggs deal with his thrice-damned ship." It occurred to him that perhaps this was why he had been told not to use a De Palma vessel. "As long as the shipment arrived on schedule..." he trailed off meaningfully.

"Our courier team took delivery just hours ago. They are en route to the final drop-off now, sir."

"Who was assigned?"

"Santini and Raphello, as per your earlier instructions."

"Good, at least I can count on their reliability. Speaking of which, what about the Terrapin Holdings account?"

There was a pause.

"I...the city is locked down, sir. I—"

A gunshot cut the speaker off. A moment later, another voice answered.

"Rashid here, sir." Al-Seif recognized the mild manner of the dromedary. "I will be inside Kairran within the hour to secure your accounts, and I will have the necessary documents to you by Taursday."

Al-Seif smiled. "Very good, Rashid. I am pleased to see you taking the initiative. And keep an eye out for those mongrels who interrupted my auction."

"Of course, sir. However, I believe they were last spotted leaving the city through the south gate. There was no word from your facility in Khet, which has led me to believe they are headed further south."

The mouflon frowned. "South? To the valley? How could they know about that?"

"I am unsure, sir, but rest assured, I will look into it. Also, I should inform you that Mody Nahas is already inquiring about the status of your other assets."

This angered al-Seif, but he recalled the words of his benefactor. "Leave them for now. I have a feeling that bloated orangutan may soon wish he had also fled the country. Keep me informed about what happens in the valley. Freggs promised he would look after my assets; I am curious how he intends to do that."

Rashid acknowledged and hung up. Al-Seif momentarily wondered why he hadn't promoted the dromedary earlier. He had only been in his employ a few years but had already proven his worth when finding new exhibitions for his arena. It was he who had first informed al-Seif about the monsters in the abandoned Barjan mines and later in the Kahmir District.

Al-Seif resumed dialling his lawyers.

"Hello?" a sleepy voice answered. The mouflon could almost picture the large, bleary eyes of the marmoset on the other end of the line.

"Lukas, it's Jirair."

The speaker was instantly awake. "Yes, sir! I take it by your call you have arrived in Medocci?"

"I have. Have the assets been transferred?"

"Yes, Jirair. However, the notary will not be able to sign until there is confirmation of the liquidation of your Terrapin Holdings account."

"I will have it to you by Taursday."

"Then there is nothing to worry about. Syris Industries has already been dissolved and can only be reinstated by your signature."

"Very good," al-Seif replied and hung up.

Leaning against the railing, he stared out at the Tharsian Sea. Few ships were moving through either way

at this hour, vague shadows betrayed only by the lights running along their hulls. He wondered idly if one might be the *Resthoven*, with a crew of Freggs' own thugs stealing her away for some other purpose.

"You are troubled, sir," came a soft voice behind him.

Al-Seif turned to see the tall form of Abar Kami silhouetted against the superstructure.

"Disappointed is all, Abar," the mouflon said. "I feel like a fool for having fled when my empire is in danger. Does this strike you as weakness?"

Kami's eyes glittered. The mouflon had executed his old master and taken possession of his assets, but the panther had slipped away unnoticed. Through observation, Kami became impressed with al-Seif's strength of will and, instead of seeking revenge, offered him his service. There had always been an understanding that if the mouflon ever sank to the level of his old master, Kami wouldn't hesitate to kill him.

"A man cannot carry the weight of the world alone," the panther said. "You cannot fault yourself for the things that are beyond your control."

"And what do you think of Freggs and his employers?" al-Seif asked.

The panther thought for a moment. Then he said, "He does not play games of chance. Each move is calculated with purpose and the knowledge of its outcome. Against this opponent, no move you make will be unexpected."

Al-Seif nodded. "That is what I thought. But everyone has a weakness. The trick is to hide it long enough so that it's too late by the time it's found. Freggs is intent on not giving us enough time to find his. One thing I know: his resources far exceed my own."

He leaned on the railing a moment longer before silently descending to the yacht's launch and riding it to shore.

The next morning, during breakfast, he read that a fire had broken out at one of the piers at the *Milo Sabbanti Porta Internazionale* in Kalegos, Mata. The office of the Port Authority had suffered extensive damage, and many records were lost. Port officials blamed the fire on the improper storage of fuel drums, but al-Seif knew a cover story when he read one.

He also noted that the article was near the back pages, which nobody ever read.

And that was it. The *Resthoven* had vanished entirely without even a record of her passing. Freggs had very deep influence indeed.

23 –Jungle Fields

The sun was still several hours from rising when Mohan and his Scrappers rolled out of the gates of Jar-Geshim on their errand for the Marshal.

The cobra had only given them vague directions to the fields. They were somewhere between the eastern edge of the north lake and the base of the eastern mountains. Mohan was more than a little surprised that the bandits would cultivate land so far away, especially when they had farmlands established near the base of the falls along the edge of the south lake. Actually, he was surprised they had cultivated land at all. Bandits weren't much for farming; why would they be when it was easier to steal from those who did. Then again, stealing enough food for several thousand people couldn't be easy. He wondered what kind of people worked those fields. Were they bandits who got some pleasure through toil or slaves captured during their raids?

There was no way past the Warren on the south side of the lake, so Mohan retraced their path along the north road. At first, he considered trying to find which way the wrecked convoy had taken, reasoning that they had likely come from the hidden fields. This was discounted because the wrecks were several hours from the lake in the wrong direction, and there was no guarantee of finding the path in the dark. He settled for crossing the river at the first shallow ford, which was little challenge for the rugged Tracksman Hiker. However, few trails were large enough for the heavy expedition vehicle on the other side. It was slow going through the thick jungle brush, and he had to stop frequently to cut the clinging vines away.

The tiger and his fellow agents didn't encounter any of the jungle's nocturnal hunters, which was more than a little odd, and aside from the growl of the Hiker's diesel engine, the forest was strangely silent.

Mohan kept more or less parallel to the lake shore until they reached the eastern tip and then used the compass built into the dashboard to chart a course towards the mountains. When they finally discovered the fields, the night was already old. Ordered rows of corn, wheat, and sugar cane marched up a steady rise; however, most of the crops consisted of small plants that hadn't yet flowered.

"Poppies." Mohan frowned. "I guess I shouldn't have wondered why the Marshal was so insistent on getting the vermin cleared out."

"We have an opportunity here," Vince said, looking out the side window. "Maybe we could squeeze in a little collateral damage?"

The tiger shook his head. "Much as I'd love to muck up this little operation, I can't think of a quicker way to get us skinned."

"Oh, come on," the hare pressed, turning to Rizzo, seated across from him. "I'm sure you could whip up some kind of delayed incendiary device. Wasn't us; we weren't even there!" He gave a sly wink.

The basilisk thought for a moment. "*Oui*, I think I could cook something up."

"I don't like the thought of leaving explosives lying around for some unwitting farmer to step on," Vicki admonished. "Even a bandit farmer."

"I am all too certain the bandits use slaves to cultivate their fields," Zed added

"No, we won't be leaving any surprises behind," Mohan insisted. His mind drifted unbidden to his time in the United Plains Army during the Caandian Conflict; the socialist revolutionaries of the Khai Longshoon were all too fond of mining farmlands.

At the crown of a rise, they found the remains of a large greenhouse, and the tiger eased the Hiker into a clearing nearby. Very little of the structure remained, save for a lone panel or two and the rough frame outlining where the other walls once stood.

"How about I go half and half?" Rizzo suggested, still eager to talk about explosive ordinance. "If we have agents here, I could leave the reactive elements with them, and they could trigger it later."

"No, Rizzo." The tiger sighed as he climbed out and headed towards the rear of the Hiker. "Did you forget we're here to rescue our agents? I'm sure you'll get to blow something up sooner or later."

Ric climbed out with the rest; he still had a bandage around his head. "What happens after you're—we're gone? I'm still trying to guess what our agents were doing here in the first place, but is it really wise to burn our bridges?"

"The torch was lit and set to the wood as soon as we entered Jar-Geshim," Zed answered, staring at the lightening sky. "The Marshal is far too crafty from what I have heard. This hunt may be a ruse to give him more time to determine our true motives. At this point, we are merely soaking the wood to keep the bridge up as long as possible."

"An interesting metaphor," Ric said. "I hope you're not all planning to go down with the bridge."

"Don't be a dag," Kitty said.

Mohan unlatched the rear doors and started handing out equipment. "No, with war coming, we've got bigger things to worry about than bandits. But the

Marshal is an unstable element in this mix. If he becomes a problem, we might have to replace him."

Ric paused. "Replace? You mean assassinate him?" he asked.

"Not exactly," the tiger answered. "But we could arrange for him to end up in a weakened position, easy prey for a successor of our choosing."

Ric felt a little sick at the thought. After the conversation yesterday and witnessing their compassion at the airport, the lynx found it disturbing that the same organisation could resort to that type of "diplomacy" — even against people as unscrupulous as bandits. He felt a hand on his shoulder and saw Zed gazing intently at him.

"Do not fret, Sedric Barnes," he said gently. "This is not a power we delight in using. The Elder Council will not make such a decision without stiff deliberation. It is not uncommon for us to forfeit our own interests in order to save lives, but sometimes it is necessary to sacrifice some to save many more."

"I think I've heard that line before," Ric said. "In the TV show *Space Journey*. But they phrased it 'the good of the many outweighs the good of the few.'"

Somebody began to hum a tune, obviously catching his reference to an old science-fiction serial that had exploded in popularity when it went into syndication. When he turned, he was surprised to see it was Kitty. She looked away, embarrassed.

The team retrieved the outfits they used on the dark streets of Kairran's slums. Ric borrowed one of Vince's spare hybrid-mesh shirts since they were about the same size. He found the armour surprisingly comfortable.

"I've never seen this material before," the journalist commented. "Something Tiger's Stripe invented?"

"You bet!" Vicki answered. "It might look as supple as cotton at a glance, but put it under a microscope, and you'll find a hybrid polymer mesh. It's as good as chain mail against knives and can even stop most common pistol rounds."

Ric ran a hand over the shirt again, hoping they would never have to test those qualities.

Mohan made a radio check and ordered a quick sweep of the greenhouse area. The scorched ground and debris covered several metres around the building's footprint. Obviously, something volatile had gone off inside, obliterating the structure, but they found little else of interest besides a few surviving planters containing unknown saplings.

Vicki gathered a few samples for testing, and then they gathered in a circle near the greenhouse's former doorway. Mohan crouched down to one knee, and Ric felt like they were getting ready for a rugby match.

"Right, everyone, take a look around," the tiger instructed. "We've only got about an hour before sunup, but we don't know if this thing's a night hunter or a day

320

one. Kitty and Vicki, spread out on the west side. Rizzo and Vince, take the east. Zed will take the north, and I'll go south. Ric, normally, I'd keep you with Kitty, but I need to break tradition here and keep you out of her way. You don't have any of our tracking experience, so it's safer if you stuck with the Hiker. If you think you can stay out of the way, you're welcome to tag along with me." They acknowledged their orders, and Mohan nodded. "Right. Strength and Honour."

"Wisdom and Justice," the five official agents responded.

Ric raised a questioning eyebrow. "You do that every time?"

Kitty frowned, clearly embarrassed. "I know. It's very corny." She handed him a compact submachine gun. "You know how to use one of these?"

"For the most part," he said. "I did pass the basic firearms qualifications before I quit the academy."

It was the same weapon the journalist had procured from the market in Kairran, newly oiled and cleaned. He checked and cleared the gun as the Royal Police Academy trained him: carefully, keeping the weapon aimed at the ground, downrange, and with his finger off the trigger.

It turned out to be the right move. There was a brief flicker of respect in the tigress's eyes. Clearly, she was more impressed that he hadn't tried to play it cool and perform the action quickly like a movie star.

321

Vince hopped past on his way to his assigned post and gave the journalist a wink. "Just don't go shootin' yourself in the foot, right?"

Kitty cuffed the hare over the ears as he passed and turned back to the lynx. "He's right. Keep that finger off the trigger, mate." She took off in the direction of the west fields.

Ric watched her a moment and found his eyes straying down her frame. He shook his head to clear it of any foolishness and quickly turned to follow Mohan to the south. The tiger's stride was much wider than his, and he wasn't half the tracker, but he managed to step only where Mohan stepped. He was sure never to get in front of the tiger and his wicked-looking assault weapon.

The south fields were mostly poppy plants, which wouldn't mature until spring arrived.

"How often do you have to track like this?" the lynx asked, slipping into journalist mode.

"In the jungle? Rarely," Mohan answered. "We're really supposed to be all about urban pacification. You use different techniques depending on the territory you're tracking. I haven't seen jungle like this in…in a long time."

Ric caught the pause. He wondered what kind of memory could make the giant tiger hesitate, but something told him now wasn't the time or place to pry further. It went against his journalist instincts, but their survival depended on everyone keeping a clear head.

"What exactly are we looking for out here?" he asked instead.

"Hard to say, honestly," Mohan replied. "Spore, footprints, that kind of thing. Zed says he's never tracked a beast like this, so we don't really know what we're up against."

"Is it a new type of fiend creature?"

"It's possible. We've built a pretty large catalogue, but new hybrids pop up every couple of years. Of course, researchers are also discovering new native species the further we push into the frontiers. People seem to forget how little we know about our own planet. Civilisation spent thousands of years looking after its own interests, and it's only been within the last two hundred years that we've put more emphasis on exploring the unknown. There are still whole regions of Amarthia uninhabitable and unexplored because of all the natural hazards they present.

"For instance, about a thousand klicks south of us are the Saran Wastes, which have no less than eight million square kilometres of unexplored territory smack in the middle of the continent of Mwungo. Eight *million*. And that's tiny compared to the Aizlgeist, Porozhnij, Lugar Nenhum, or the Caiman's Desert. Hell, geographers and cartographers suspect the Caiman's Desert alone makes up two-thirds of all West Contéga."

He didn't have to mention that maps of these regions were primarily guesswork because no aerial or ground expedition that tried to map the territories ever returned.

"This sounds like a hobby," Ric said.

Mohan chuckled softly. "A bit. I've always loved to travel and got to see a fair bit of the world over the years. I grew up around the Uuwanip Plains People, basically the Soketh of the United Plains. They have a lot of stories and legends about Amarthia's ancient past."

"I've heard their entire religion is based upon some of those legends—what do they call it, the Great Inventor?"

The tiger nodded. "Mbektar. That's one of the keys that ties the Uuwanip to the Soketh. It's an odd religion, but not too far off from Aabanism, just much older. No mistake, there are a lot of strange secrets buried in our past, mate. And some of them, I think even people like us weren't meant to know."

Ric considered this in silence.

Vicki hopped along cheerily in the western fields next to the ever-stoic Kitty. The primary crop here appeared to be a thin bean plant that grew as tall as their knees.

Kitty glanced over her shoulder, curious about what the journalist and her father were discussing.

"He's probably trying to figure out how we do things," Vicki said.

"We should split up," Kitty said, pointedly ignoring her comment, "to cover more ground."

"You know, he's kinda cute," the bullfrog said. "For a lynx."

The tigress wasn't biting. "Why, Vikci, I didn't know you liked fur."

"No, I mean, haven't you noticed how he looks at you?"

"He's given us all a good once-over. Probably wants to get all the details right for his next fluff piece."

"And he is a nice piece of fluff." Vicki winked.

"Gawd, you sound like Vince."

"Oh, come on. I saw you hovering over him when he got knocked out." Vicki grinned widely, but Kitty refused to face her.

"Of course I was. If that damned fool had gone and got himself killed on my watch, there'd have been bloody hell to pay." She grew increasingly agitated with this conversation, but she didn't want to fly off the handle at Vicki; the medic was only trying to be friendly.

"No, I think...oh, never mind. This isn't going anywhere, is it?"

"Nope," Kitty said flatly. She veered off into the southern part of the field. "Keep your eyes peeled; some of these sprouts have been trampled recently."

The tigress moved away quickly. She didn't want Vicki to see the faint trace of a tear in her eye as she forced back painful memories that she refused to let go.

She fished out a cigarette and stuck it in her mouth, careful not to light it because the scent and flicker of light would give her away. A few budding flowers had sneaked their way between the crops. As she passed the white-petalled blossoms with their yellow crowns, a ghostly face flashed before her eyes again.

But it was a different face this time. A face with luminous green eyes.

On the opposite side of the field, Vince and Rizzo pushed their way through tall stands of sugar cane. The basilisk noticed that the hare's hops became a little less enthusiastic as they entered the field, and she wondered if he was feeling homesick. Unfortunately for her, it did nothing to shut him up.

"Ah, morning dew on the cane fields," Vince said, gazing wistfully at the sky. "Aside from this damned humidity, I can almost see myself back at the family plantation in Banton."

"*Mon Déesse*," the basilisk muttered. "Not another one of your scandalous stories."

"Scandalous?" the hare said, a look of mock surprise on his face. "My dear Emperatriz, I would never dare besmirch my beloved brothers and sisters."

Rizzo frowned and muttered an apology.

"Well, you're right, darlin'," Vince continued, unfazed. "I'd rather talk about somethin' else anyway, like our new friend back there."

"Barnes? Why? Something wrong with him?"

"Not at all! I just wanted to know what you think."

Rizzo thought for a moment. "I haven't encountered many new recruits in the field," she said. "He seems to handle himself well enough; I thought this is normal. He is almost as talky as you sometimes, but at least he has something intelligent to say."

"Ouch," the hare replied with a grin. "You know I really don't mean to get on your nerves, darlin'. You just make it so easy sometimes. Besides, I've heard you've got some stories of your own from your Revolutionary days."

The basilisk frowned. "That's none of your business! *Oui*, I have a few past indiscretions, but I grew up. Someday, you will too."

"Never!" Vince said with a defiant flourish.

"*Mon Déesse*," Rizzo muttered again. "Let's go back to being homesick."

"As you wish. I do admit these fields make me think of the old homestead," he replied. "How about you, Rizzo? They have cane fields in Neuf Maris?"

"*Oui*," she answered, "but mostly they grow coffee. Acres and acres of coffee."

Before the hare could dive into this new topic, their radios clicked.

"Mohan," Zed's voice said, "I think you had better come see this. Everyone else as well."

The north fields were set aside for tall banana trees arranged in ordered rows roughly a metre apart. Many had been smashed in half, and ragged fronds littered the ground. Several corpses lay scattered about the roots of the trees. From their state of decay, they appeared to be several days old.

Vicki was crouching over the nearest one. "They just left them here. Left them and ran."

"Probably didn't have much of a choice," Mohan said, frowning. "When you're up against something you can't fight, you're only option is flight."

"Flight doesn't seem to have worked either," Ric said, picking up a severed branch. "Are you sure *we* can fight it?"

"Well, we're bloody well going to try," Kitty snapped at him.

Ric started at her sudden vehemence.

Mohan held up a paw. "Kittina, don't do your block. Vicki, what happened here? The bodies haven't wasted away, so do we have to worry about Daeminox?"

Ric shuffled nervously; he had almost forgotten that deadly aspect of the alien fiend creatures.

Vicki studied a couple of bodies before pausing at one near the base of a larger banana tree. "Tough to say. Most of these guys were bitten in half, so at least it isn't spread through saliva. Some of them suffered some kind of blunt-force trauma; their rib cage or head's been crushed." She pointed along the injuries as she spoke. "Take this one, for example. These markings on the chest? I can't quite place them."

The individual in question might have been a bear or other large mammal — he had been at least as broad as Zed. It was difficult to identify because there was so little left of him. A series of broad parallel impressions lined the torso, each about fifteen centimetres across. They weren't ragged like claw marks, but only tremendous force could have embedded them in the victim's flesh.

"They're finger marks," Ric said quietly.

Vicki looked up at him. "What?"

The journalist made a crushing and twisting motion with one hand around his other wrist. "He was crushed like this, with a giant hand. Those are finger marks. Really big finger marks!"

The medic looked again. "You're right! Look, you can see the scale pattern on the muscle fibres. Looks fiendish, all right."

"You're tellin' me this thing had fingers as thick as my hand?" Vince whistled and turned to the journalist. "Pretty sharp observation. What tipped you off?" The hare picked up a ripe banana that had dropped to the ground and started nibbling it while Ric answered.

"Ed and I witnessed al-Seif unloading a shipment of slaves a few weeks ago. Ever watch a three-hundred-pound gorilla drag a half-emaciated slave girl around by the arm? He left marks like that. Of course, al-Seif made sure he never did that again."

"Tch, tch." The hare clucked his tongue. "I bet it didn't turn out well for the slave girl either."

"It didn't."

"Damaged goods," Rizzo spat.

"Bastard'll pay," Kitty growled.

"Eventually," Mohan said. "But he's thousands of clicks away, and we have bigger fish to fry."

"Lucky none of us are fish," Vince chided.

Rizzo glared at him but accepted a banana, which she promptly began to munch on. "Hmph, these are surprisingly good."

"Aren't they?" the hare replied, peeling a second fruit.

Zed was busy climbing an unbroken tree several metres away. "The attack came from the north," he called down. "These trees were flattened as the creature rested on them and attacked the ground."

"There's quite a lot of damage here, Zed," Vince said. "You sure it didn't just thrash around a bit."

The badger climbed down and paced out several trees to his right, then to the left. Finally, he came back to the group.

"No," he said, "not based on the damage I see here. Kittina, would you stand at the base of the tree behind you, please?"

She did so, and the badger motioned to Rizzo and Vicki to follow him. He had them stand at the bases of two more trees and placed Vince and Mohan twenty metres to either side. Lastly, he put Ric in front of Kitty, near a section of trees smashed right down to their roots. They had the highest concentration of bodies scattered around them.

"What did you find, Zed?" Mohan asked.

"Do not move, please!" the track instructed. "It is a footprint, if you will."

He instructed them to take the electric torches from their harnesses and hold them as high as possible; the morning light was dim even with the sun rising. Then he climbed an undamaged tree near Ric and produced an instant camera.

After snapping several shots of the agents below, shaking out the glossy squares and placing them in a pocket, the badger climbed down and motioned for them all to rejoin him.

He laid out the pictures, placing the agents in a rough diamond pattern. Then, he gathered a few small sticks and laid them out like the bones of a skeleton. A large outline began to take form.

Very large.

"Bloody hell!" Kitty gasped.

"Strewth, the size of it!" Her father concurred.

"Indeed," Zed said. "I believe the distance between Kittina, Emperatriz, and Victoria is the approximate length of the creature—roughly fourteen metres. From the damaged trees along that length, I estimate its girth is about four metres." He pointed to the stumps where Ric was standing in the photographs. "I believe this damage was caused by the head and neck swaying back and forth; this also explains the concentration of bodies in the area. And this lighter damage between Mohan and Vincenzo was likely caused by its wings as it balanced itself over the trees."

Rizzo stared at the pictures. "*Mon Déesse*! Are you telling me this thing has a wingspan of over forty metres? Merciful Maiden Buru'Nadi!"

"Guess it is enough to make anyone religious," Vince said.

The basilisk shot him a glance, but she couldn't do anything since he was on the other side of the group. She turned a pleading gaze to Kitty, who promptly cuffed him across the ears.

"Hey, watch the hat!" the hare whined.

Ric gazed apprehensively at the stick skeleton connecting the pictures. "And you're still planning on hunting this thing down?" he asked.

Mohan looked off to the eastern mountains. The sun was just below the edge, lighting the sky with orange and yellow. "We haven't got a choice," he said. "Our extraction from Jar-Geshim depends on pleasing that bastard Marshal. Any ideas, Zed? It's too bloody big to be a quetzalcoatl."

Zed also turned his gaze to the mountains. "I am afraid not, my friend. It may be an alkonost that flew down from the Aizlgeist or possibly a karkadann up from the Saran Wastes. Even my people, who make such wastelands our home, have not dared to go far beyond those borders."

Something caught Ric's eye, and he rummaged through a pile of refuse that was more metal and plastic than body parts—probably remnants of the greenhouse explosion. He uncovered the remains of a large white plastic container. The top half was missing, and it was heavily scratched and scuffed. Block lettering identified it as the property of Terrapin Holdings, and beneath the moniker was a bright red biohazard symbol.

"Hey, look at this. Maybe it's a clue."

Mohan took the container and examined it more closely. "Bonza find, mate! Unfortunately, I've never heard of Terrapin. Not much left of the canister, either; there's no telling what was inside it originally."

Kitty had been about to light the cigarette in her mouth, but on seeing the container, she thought that probably wasn't a good idea.

"I've heard of Terrapin," Ric said soberly. "It's a distribution company owned by Jirair al-Seif. They supply chemical compounds and equipment to a wide variety of research companies. They're based in Medocci."

"So we've got him then?" Vince asked.

Ric shook his head. "Unfortunately, no," he replied. "They're just a distributor; they don't do any research themselves. Just because al-Seif's materials ended up here doesn't mean he was using them. And since this is a bandit farm, he could just argue the shipment was stolen."

"Which it probably was," Kitty added. "What better way to cover up that you're working with bandits than to stage a theft? You think they were lacing the crops with it?"

Vince and Rizzo glanced at the peels of the bananas they had just eaten.

"I don't think so," Vicki said. "You wouldn't want to contaminate crops you wanted to eat." The basilisk and hare gave sighs of relief. "But maybe they were modifying the crop somehow? Growing them faster, making them tastier. They would have kept the chemicals in the greenhouse."

"Uh, modifying?" Vince mumbled.

Mohan tossed the piece of plastic away. "What else were they modifying, I wonder?" he muttered. "But you couldn't do that here. That greenhouse wasn't big enough for all the genetic equipment you'd need for an experiment like this. Zed, what's your guess on this thing's range, a thousand kilometres?"

The sun peeked over the mountain ridge, and the badger reexamined the corpses in the dawn light.

"No," he said at length, "such a distance would cover half of Pytan, and the creature is still in the valley. I believe this creature has marked out a territory between these fields, the wrecked convoy, and the jeep we found." He turned and pointed to the distant cliffs. "And this is only a radius of it. Those mountains are riddled with caves and gorges that would provide excellent nesting ground. That is where we will find the centre of his domain."

"Or lab space," Vicki added. Then she snapped her fingers. "That's it! That's why this field is so far away from the city!"

Mohan caught her meaning. "It isn't a food crop for the city; it's for a lab."

Ric stroked his chin thoughtfully. "But a lab for what? If they engineered fast-growing food to supply the lab, what were they—you don't think they actually created this creature, do you?"

"I didn't want to consider that," Mohan said with a sour face, "but at this point, it's a possibility."

"But who else besides you knows these things exist?" the lynx asked. "And why would they want to even try?"

"Money, weapons, entertainment, maybe even just to see what happens," Kitty answered as they returned to the Hiker. "Bloody lunatics trying to play God."

"It has been a struggle to keep this secret as long as we have," Zed said, "but with the creatures starting to appear more frequently, it should not come as a surprise that someone else has taken an interest in them."

"It's the weaponising part we're most concerned about," Mohan said as he stowed their gear. "Biological terrorism is becoming the new MO among tin-pot dictators and your aspiring supervillains. Threaten to unleash your own incurable plague on the general populace and just watch the money pour in."

"Or just watch the chaos unfold," Ric added.

"Charmin' sentiment, ain't it?" Vince said as he opened the side door for Rizzo and Vicki. "You think our Marshal was in on it?"

"Perhaps not all of it," Mohan answered, climbing into the driver's seat again. "He definitely knew something was going on here, but he wouldn't be asking us to kill this beast if he had anything invested in its creation."

"He was probably more interested in these poppy fields," Ric said. "But why? He could just as easily plant a crop nearer Jar-Geshim."

Mohan started the engine and pointed the Hiker towards the mountains. "I don't know, but I have a feeling we'll find out if we can find that lab."

24 – Encounter

There was a clear trail leading east from the fields. They only travelled a few kilometres before the jungle faded away into rocky foothills, and the ground rose sharply.

The Nefrit Ishem Mountains were the tallest in the region, roughly three thousand metres at their highest peak. From a distance, they appeared like a series of rolling waves of rock with a few sharp peaks scattered in for good measure. Up close, they rose from the ground in jagged steps, some as tall as a hundred metres or more.

As Zed had pointed out earlier, they were pockmarked with depressions and hidden gorges that could appear without warning. Even in the lower foothills, Mohan had to slow considerably to navigate a path that was barely wide enough for the heavy exploration vehicle. However, he noted that the trail had seen some use.

The morning was already old when the tiger halted the Hiker in a relatively flat clearing. The shelf was just wide enough to fit the exploration vehicle with room to turn around. Below them, the ground sloped away gently towards the edge of the jungle canopy. Above them, the cliffs began to rise steeply, and no path was wide enough for the Hiker. A few small trees provided shade near the clearing's edge for those brave enough to step out that far.

Zed poked his head into the forward cabin. "Does our trail end here, Mohan?"

"For the Hiker, at least," the tiger replied. "I think they marked this clearing as a parking area of sorts." He pointed to the cliff's edge where a series of white stones were set in neat rows, too ordered to be a natural occurrence.

Ric studied the clearing outside the window. "Maybe not just a parking area. Does that pile of rocks dead ahead look natural?"

"Good eye, Ric," Mohan said. "No, it doesn't. There may have been a tunnel into the mountain here, but it's collapsed." He pointed off to the left. "We don't have the tools to dig through it, but that trail looks promising."

The lynx searched for the path the tiger saw among the rocks and scrub brush. It was little more than a series of narrow shelves cut into the rock, partially obscured by a cascade of loose dirt from a recent minor avalanche.

It climbed at a steep angle for about thirty metres before disappearing into the cliff face. A rope guideline ran through metal anchors set in the rock every three metres.

Vince squinted at it. "You call that a trail?"

"It is as good as a city thoroughfare." Zed grinned and slapped Mohan on the shoulder.

Again, they climbed out of the Hiker and distributed the gear. Before moving on, they ate a light breakfast of trail rations thoughtfully provided by the rental agency—or at least the Tiger's Stripe agent who had prepped the vehicle. Vince had thoughtfully gathered more bananas to save their dried fruits, but the carnivores enjoyed a few strips of cured meat. Vicki snatched up a few beetles from under the rocks and grinned satisfactorily; then, she picked up one of the bananas.

"These are unusually tasty," she said, turning it over in her long, webbed hands.

"Yeah, about that," Vince mumbled around a mouthful before swallowing. "You said something about 'modifying'?"

The bullfrog stashed one of the fruits in her bag. "Oh, I'm sure it's fine. Like I said, they probably enhanced the growth cycle to provide food for the lab—it must be a pretty big staff for a field that size. I'll get one of these shipped off to our lab guys. Might help the hydroponic labs at the Sanctuary."

When they finished breakfast, Zed examined the parking lot. "At least two of the convoy trucks were parked here. There are several deep ruts from the tires, and the tread matches."

"We're on the right track then," Mohan said, producing a few lengths of stout nylon rope and various bits of climbing gear. "Not sure about that guideline's condition. Best to be prepared."

Ric stared at the steep stairway and scratched at the bandages around his head. "This doesn't look at all safe."

"Oh, you'll be fine," Vicki said, reaching up and smacking his hand away. "Don't scratch."

Vince began to ramble again as they lined up to make the steep climb. "This reminds me of a trip I took to the Oryote Canyons in Carlin. The painted deserts out there are just gorgeous. Our guides were this old native prairie dog and his daughter, Taneya; she was as pretty as the landscape."

At that moment, his companions knew exactly where the story was going, and they began to wonder about the hare's actual rock-climbing experience.

"Your guide must have been one of the Kaanehe," Zed said. "They are the Soketh tribes who dwell on the frontiers of West Contéga."

Vince continued in his most enthusiastic voice. "In the evenin', we'd sit around the campfire, and old Greyfoot—that was the guide—would go on about the spirits of the land while his daughter would perform cultural dances. Then, one night, Taneya and I did a little private moon dancing of our own." He gave a salacious wink to Ric.

The lynx wasn't sure how to process this unsolicited information, so he changed the subject. "Well, this reminds me of the week I spent with the Cliff People of Gom in eastern Barju. Are they also Soketh, Zed?"

Mohan had already started up the steps, the long bulky belt-fed machinegun strapped to his back. Zed went after him, followed by Vince.

The badger looked over his shoulder. "No," he said, "Although they have many interactions with the tribes who dwell in the region and have thus adopted many of their customs."

Vicki stepped onto the wall to follow Vince. She asked over her shoulder, "Remind me again what you were doing so close to the Aizlgeist?"

"It was part of my research into al-Seif's criminal underworld," Ric answered as he waited behind Rizzo for his turn, "back when I knew him as Assad Alabwaq. There had been rumours of people disappearing from the border villages, so I assumed he was raiding them for slaves. I was only half right. He was recruiting— more like abducting, really—hunting parties to send into the Aizlgeist. Nobody would say why."

"Probably because nobody ever made it back out," Rizzo said, pulling herself up to the first step.

"Maybe." Ric started his climb. "But they didn't go far. I took a risk and followed one of the parties to an old mining camp just beyond the borders, where the dead zone didn't take effect yet. I learned that Alabwaq was the owner, but he certainly wasn't doing any mining. I never figured out how he found out about the place, to begin with, but I'll never forget what I saw down in that pit." He shivered at the memory. "That was the first time I saw one of your fiend creatures."

"Describe it, please," Zed called down.

"Well, I only caught a glimpse of it, but it was big, almost as big as the Hiker. Blunt head, broad shoulders, horns coming out of the chin, splayed feet, and no tail. I do recall that the teeth were flat, and the eyes were blue with a star-shaped pupil."

"Sounds like a wendigo," Mohan answered. "Believe it or not, they're one of the slightly less dangerous fiends. Al-Seif would probably have gotten some good sport out of it and wouldn't risk infecting anyone with Daeminox—wendigoes don't carry it. What happened to it?"

"One of Alabwaq's men panicked when it started to gore the capture team and killed it. I still wonder if there was anything else he was interested in over there."

Kitty was the last to start the trek up the steep staircase. "There's rumoured to be a smuggler trail that starts in Barju. Assuming they can actually make it through the Aizlgeist, they could turn south into Busawar or travel along the border into East Benai."

"I doubt that," Mohan said, bracing himself against a narrow cleft in the path as he helped Zed climb to the next step. "From Barju to Busawar is almost a thousand clicks, and it's another fifteen hundred to East Benai. Even a heavily armed convoy couldn't make that trip. I know those jungles."

Ric found it curious that the tiger didn't elaborate.

"Perhaps they bring the goods to ships waiting on the southern coast," Zed suggested. "The Adrakar Strait borders those shores."

Mohan paused as he approached the top of the rocky staircase. "Risky. The trade routes are thick in the northern strait, no mistake, but they tend to avoid the reefs along the Aizlgeist; it's a ship graveyard. They don't call it the Land of Ghosts for nothing."

The stairs levelled out at a small landing. There wasn't room for the badger and the giant tiger, and they had to watch their footing. At first, Mohan thought they had reached a dead end; then, he spotted a narrow cleft leading into the rock. He couldn't tell how deep it was, and he had to remove the machine gun from his back and turn sideways to squeeze through.

About three metres in, he paused suddenly and drew a deep, shuddering breath.

"Are you all right, my friend?" Zed asked, concern showing on his face.

The tiger breathed again. "Yeah, yeah. I think it opens up in just a few more metres."

Ric glanced down at Kitty. "Bout of claustrophobia?"

The white tigress frowned. "You're two metres tall and crammed in a space less than a metre wide. You do the math."

The lynx nodded.

As Mohan had hoped, the narrow cleft opened into a cave or ravine roughly three metres wide. The walls, worn smooth by ancient water runoff, curved up to the ceiling. The roof had cracked ages ago and allowed the hot Pytian sun to dry it out, leaving nothing but the sandy stream bed lit by a thin beam of light. The slow joining of stalactites and stalagmites had formed narrow pillars along either side of the narrow gap in the roof. Now and again, a branch would shoot off from the central passage. Signs of heavy foot traffic marred the sandy ground, but it was several days old.

Zed followed the tiger, followed by Vince, Vicki, and Rizzo. As Ric prepared to squeeze through himself, his eye caught a glint over Kitty's shoulder. He could see the Hiker parked far below, and just beyond it, on the trail leading up to the clearing, a pair of shadowy figures were attempting to hide themselves among some large boulders.

Kitty shushed him before he could speak and half shoved him through the cleft in the rock. "Get through there and keep quiet. They've been on our tail since the fields."

Ric followed orders but asked quietly, "The Marshal's men, I assume?"

Rizzo helped him through the last part of the gap. "*Oui*, most likely. They probably left the city just after we did. But with all the jungle growth, we didn't notice them until the fields."

Once inside the cave, Ric saw Mohan seated on a low rock shelf, his eyes closed and his breathing slow and deliberate. The lynx was surprised to see the big tiger in such a vulnerable state; the narrow squeeze through the cleft really must have shaken him.

Mohan regained his composure after a moment and turned to Kitty. "How many did you see?"

"I only spotted two, but I suspect at least four."

Mohan nodded and rose. "A full jeep, but my money is on two; the Marshal isn't taking any chances with us. I hoped to lose them in the jungle, but the Hiker isn't much for stealth. They're probably just keeping an eye on us; we're here to do the shooting, and they're here to make sure we don't mess up."

"Or to keep us from seeing something we shouldn't," Ric said.

The tiger chuckled. "You watch too many spy movies, mate."

"Like they could stop us, anyway." Rizzo snorted. "You think they will follow us in here? Maybe there's a branch further in we could use to ambush them. I would feel much safer if they were—"

A horrific, blood-chilling screech cut her off, and a black shadow briefly blotted out the sunlight coming through the cracks in the roof. A rush of wind whistled through the cave, and outside, they heard distant screams of terror followed by sporadic gunfire. Another keening screech assaulted their ears, and they thought they heard the rev of an engine. There was a groaning screech of metal, and a chorus of panicked screams suddenly cut short. Moments later, the ground shook beneath them, and they heard a terrific crash followed by more groaning metal. Another metallic crash and the rumble of rocks shortly followed.

And then there was silence.

They stood quietly at the mouth of the cave. Even Vince had ceased his prattling.

"What the h—?" Ric breathed before Kitty clamped a hand over his mouth. She removed her hand and held a finger up to her mouth for silence.

Five minutes passed, and still, there was no sound from outside. Mohan pointed to Kitty, and she nodded, carefully edging her way back through the cleft, her rifle at the ready.

The scene that met her as she eased silently onto the shelf looked like something out of a war movie. Blood and the dismembered pieces of several bandits spattered the cliffside below. There had been two jeeps, as Mohan had suspected, and the remains of one had somehow smashed into their Tracksman Hiker, tumbling the heavier vehicle onto its passenger side. The jeep's engine had caught fire, sending a plume of oily black smoke drifting into the sky. The second jeep lay crumpled further up the hillside, also on fire.

Kitty couldn't clearly assess the damage from up on the shelf, but their exploration vehicle appeared little worse for wear. A small rockslide had half buried the first jeep and the Hiker, ironically protecting their vehicle from the fire.

The tigress started to edge out further for a better view and stopped suddenly. The fur on the back of her neck rose, and she felt a warning flash through the birthmark on her chest and arm. She heard a heavy snort, and a wave of hot, fetid air ruffled her long-fur. She turned Sharply and raised her rifle in the same motion.

The monstrous angular face that stared down at her reminded her of a scaly, featherless buzzard with a razor-edged beak. Four glittering, pupilless red eyes stared down at her from a head covered with so many twisted black horns it appeared to be wreathed in ebony fire. The head met a serpentine neck that coiled around until it blended into the shoulders of a sleek body that seemed to stretch forever until it finally ended in a pair of twin forked tails. The fiend had four massive limbs folded beneath it, but Kitty could see one gigantic five-fingered hand peeking out as it gripped the side of the mountain. Long serrated claws crowned each digit. Its enormous leathery wings spread like a shroud against the cliff face, and the broad scaly plates of its thick hide had a dusty brown or mottled yellow hue that blended almost perfectly with the rock.

The blood-soaked beak parted, and Kitty could see several rows of serrated teeth lining its jaws. Another wave of fetid breath washed over her as she squeezed the trigger.

Inside the cave, the remaining agents and their recruit heard the sharp crack of a rifle round, followed quickly by another. Again, the terrible keening screech shook them to their bones.

Ric urgently stepped towards the cleft, but Mohan held him back. A rush of wind swept over them, and the ground shook violently.

Kitty staggered back through the cleft, blood soaking through the right sleeve of her shirt.

"Run!" she shouted.

Chunks of rock began to fall from the ceiling above them. They could see the dark shadow of the creature outside as it beat furiously against the mountainside, trying in vain to reach the prey trapped in the cave.

"What is it, Kitty?" her father asked as they followed the riverbed.

"Fuck if I know," she panted, "but it's big. Really fucking big! I got two shots off, point blank. It didn't even blink!"

The cave widened to form an archaic hall of natural pillars, several recently shattered or toppled against the walls. The sandy floor turned to rock, and it was difficult to tell where the foot traffic they had been following led from there. The chamber ended ahead at a wall of solid rock.

"Aw hell no!" Vince said, kicking at a loose stone. "We can't be trapped."

"I do not believe so," Zed said, his voice surprisingly calm. "The stairs we climbed were deliberately carved into the rock face, and they led into this fissure. There must be an opening or hidden door somewhere."

Seeming to sense their plight, the creature outside pounded more insistently on the weakening roof of the cavern. Each blow sent larger and larger chunks of rock tumbling down on them, and the gap in the ceiling grew steadily wider.

Mohan raised the machine gun and ordered everyone to hit the deck. The heavy-calibre ammunition slammed into the creature's exposed flesh, but he expended half his ammo box before the beast finally began to back off with an enraged screech.

The barrel began to glow, and the tiger eased off the trigger to prevent the weapon from overheating.

"Well, that bought us all of ten seconds," he growled.

Zed was clambering around the back wall, scraping furiously at the base of one of the fallen pillars. "Mohan!" he shouted. "There is a draft behind this pillar!"

The badger heaved his weight against the rock, and a dark crack began to appear. Mohan dropped the assault weapon and grabbed the pillar in both massive paws. The muscles of his arms and shoulders bulged as he strained against the weight. Slowly, the crack widened.

The creature returned with a vengeance, sensing its prey might evade it. Vicki couldn't contain a frightened shriek as it beat furiously against the rock. The crack in the ceiling opened wide enough to reach a thick, powerful arm inside, and they ducked beneath the searching claws. Kitty, Ric, Rizzo, and Vince opened fire with their lighter weapons while Zed added his weight to the pillar. Between the gunfire and the creature's bellows, the noise was deafening. With agonizing slowness, a passage appeared. It went only a short distance before it ended in a steel hatchway of the type used on naval vessels.

It was open.

"Go! Go!" Mohan cried as he strained against the rock.

One by one, they squeezed through the gap. Ric had the foresight to grab the tiger's discarded weapon. Zed was the last to squeeze through, but he turned to hold the weight of the stone for Mohan.

With a final blow, the creature created a gap big enough to squeeze its head through. It snapped viciously at the tiger, and he ducked out of its reach, almost dropping the pillar.

Mohan twisted to shoulder the weight of the rock and drew his heavy revolver. The creature lunged for him again, and he fanned three rounds point blank into its gaping mouth. The beast screamed in pain and fury, thrashing violently in the narrow cave. Mohan and Zed gave the pillar a final heave and dived into the passageway beyond, the pillar falling back in place behind them.

Cries of fury echoed off the walls, and the world shook as the creature smashed the tunnel entrance to oblivion. The agents moved further into the concrete passageway, and Mohan dogged the hatch shut, throwing them into complete blackness. The creature's fury seemed endless as it threw blow after blow against the cavern walls. The rocky passage that had been their salvation was obliterated under a storm of heavy boulders.

After several long minutes that seemed like hours, a deathly silence settled in.

25 – In the Dark

"Think it's gone?" Vicki's voice drifted out of the darkness.

"It's awfully quiet out there," Ric responded.

There was a feminine shriek, and Rizzo's voice cried, "Vincenzo!"

"Wasn't me, darlin'," the hare protested from somewhere close.

Mohan snapped on his torch, and they blinked in the sudden hundred-candle brightness. As soon as their eyes adjusted, Rizzo promptly smacked Vince across the face.

"You guingin!" she spat furiously.

"I said it wasn't me! Look." He pointed to the remains of a skeletal form propped against the wall, reaching pitifully for the door. Rizzo, standing in front of it, must have brushed against it in the dark. Then, they noticed the faint but distinct odour of decaying flesh in the air. The basilisk muttered a half-hearted apology.

Vicki tended to Kitty's bleeding arm—the same one that had taken a knife for Ric during the market brawl—then examined the journalist's bandages.

"I'm fine," the lynx protested.

"Oh sure," the frog said. "Really, you shouldn't be doing so much running around with a concussion. But it looks like you'll be fine. Keep that bandage on, though."

When she finished, she hopped over to examine the corpse.

"Meerkat, I think, or in that family at least," she said. She carefully reached down to check the pockets of the faded jumpsuit, but it disintegrated at her touch. "Weird, the body hasn't been here long, but the clothes and flesh are all rotted away. Left arm is broken, but I can't determine the cause of death without an autopsy. Looks like he might have been wearing a lab coat over the jumpsuit."

"Know any chemical compounds that could do this?" Mohan asked. "Should we be worried?"

"I know several, but most of them oxidise quickly. He's been here a few days, so whatever it was has probably dissipated by now. He might have been splashed with something and managed to stagger all the way out here before succumbing to his wounds. A very bad way to go. I don't smell anything—well, aside from him—so we should be OK."

"Cockatrice breath could do that," Kitty said quietly.

"I was trying not to think that," Mohan replied.

"Cockatrice?" Ric asked. "Another mythological creature that actually isn't?"

"That happens quite a lot, actually," Mohan answered. "A lot of those old myths are or were types of fiends. Or at least our historians adopted their names; they fit disturbingly well. Anyway, the cockatrice is one of the fortunately few fiends with toxic breath. Very nasty. I recall the Marshal saying the only survivor fled a fire-breathing dragon, but here's hoping he was just panicky."

Zed examined the steel hatchway. The concrete was cracked and crumbling around the door, which had buckled inward. He tested his weight against it with no result. "We will not be leaving the way we entered," he said. "And I believe we should move further into this installation. The integrity of this entryway has been compromised."

The narrow tunnel was made of smooth concrete braced with steel ribs every few metres; they had a peculiar bell shape that reminded Mohan of the science-fiction serials he watched on TV as a cub. Iron pipes ran along the ceiling, and cage lights hung on the walls. Most of the lights had blown out, and the Scrappers had to carefully step around pools of shattered glass.

They removed the rubber-soled sandals from their pouches and slipped them over their bare paws for protection. Mohan was about to apologise to Ric for not having a spare when the journalist produced a leather pair from a vest pocket.

"It's not that uncommon for one to own a pair of footwear," he argued. "Besides, in pursuit of a story, I tend to travel over rougher terrain than your average citizen. Although I admit yours look a bit tougher than mine. I take it you didn't buy them at Barrows."

Mohan chuckled and shook his head negatively.

Zed and Kitty brought out their torches, and the group cautiously made their way down the tunnel. The floor transitioned from concrete to a rusted metal catwalk raised a hand's breadth above the floor; old cables and pipes now ran above and below them. There were no branches, and they encountered several more skeletons along the way, all of which had the same melted flesh and rotted clothing and had been attempting to flee toward the hatch. The stink of rotting corpses almost overpowered them in the close air.

The tunnel seemed endless, and Mohan was just starting to feel the itch of claustrophobia again when the passage finally connected to a much broader corridor. Again, the curved shape of the doorways and the ribbed uniform structure of the hallways reminded the tiger of a '50s sci-fi film. A broad green stripe was painted halfway up the corridor walls, and large block lettering in chipped white paint announced they were on level six. Smaller signs pointed the way to various points of interest.

"Written in Locken," Ric observed. "Is that a good sign or bad?"

"Hard to tell," Mohan said. "But at least we'll know where we're going."

He shone his light further down the wall, revealing a faded black-and-blue emblem. The banner depicted a wolf's head angled skyward and swallowing a crescent moon.

"Foresight," he said with a frown.

"A competitor?" Ric asked.

"The Foresight of the Twilight Moon," Zed answered him. "They were not a very pleasant cabal in their day. Their particular interests were nuclear extortion, political assassinations, and divination."

"Divination?" The journalist raised an eyebrow. "You mean like literal magic?"

Kitty snorted. "Black magic hoodoo voodoo. It was all parlour tricks, but they believed they were destined to fulfil some ancient nature prophecy or some shit back during the Atomic Age. They were more an occult group than a proper spy organisation."

"Fascinating. Are they still around?" Ric asked.

Mohan shook his head. "Not for many years; we saw to that. But they got pretty big in the late fifties and early sixties."

"Hence the snazzy décor." Vince grinned. "You ever go against them, Mo?"

The tiger chuckled. "No, that was just before Zed and I signed up. Shame though, could have been fun." He scratched his head. "But it's odd; if I remember my history, the Foresight mostly hung around Aerenia. This is pretty far from their home turf, and this place wasn't shut down by us."

"How can you tell?" Ric asked.

"Because if we can't repurpose a facility, we destroy it completely," Vicki answered. "You'd be surprised how many secret bases pockmark the globe. Some even we haven't found yet, and I'm pretty sure we invented the concept."

"You know, I've been meaning to ask about that."

Mohan held up a hand to stop him. "It'll have to wait. If things had gone as planned, you'd be off to the Sanctuary right now, but things got a bit mucked up if you haven't noticed. If we ever get the time between here and there to have a decent cuppa, I'll tell you everything you need to know."

Ric noticed the tiger's use of "need to know" versus "want to know," but he was beginning to accept that he would just have to wait if he wanted more information.

Rizzo spoke up. "Wait, if this place was built in the Atomic Age, is it nuclear?"

Mohan fished a small box out of a pouch and checked the readout on its face. It clicked gently, but the needle remained in the green.

"Not likely," he said, stowing the box again. The Foresight were nuclear extortionists, but part of their beliefs was the halt of nuclear proliferation. Ironic, hey? Most of their schemes involved turning a nation's own atomic devices against them, and they didn't keep or manufacture any of their own. About the only positive thing they did was pioneering the use of geothermal generators in their facilities. They're bloody efficient; we even adopted their design for the Sanctuary."

Ric thought for a moment. "If they used geothermal, why is this base here? The Nefrit Ishem mountains aren't volcanic."

"Indeed," Zed said, "but if one digs deep enough, one can find a thermal vent to power a generator."

"That's really deep, though," Vince added.

Vicki was examining several boxes stacked along the wall. "Look at this. Some of this equipment is practically new. From the dust, I'd say it's only been sitting here a couple days. No markings, though. Looks like somebody else already repurposed the facility."

Mohan nodded. "Based on the recent activity, I'm pretty sure this is the lab we were looking for, but I'd be more interested to learn how they found it in the first place. Foresight definitely wasn't in the fiend game. Kitty, what exactly did you see out there?"

The tigress rubbed her bandaged arm and shuddered slightly but went into as clear a description as she could remember. "It seemed to blend right into the mountainside," she added in closing. "I only saw it because it moved. It…it tore the Marshal's goons to pieces; they were scattered all over the place."

A change came over Kitty as she recalled the horrific event. This was only her second encounter with a fiend in the field and her first direct experience with the carnage they could create. For a brief instant, she felt as small and scared as a cub.

Mohan placed a hand on her shoulder. "Are you OK?"

For a moment, her father was the man she remembered growing up on the frontier outside of East Plains, and her frozen armour began to melt. Then she remembered where she was, how she got there, and most importantly, whom she had lost along the way. An image from her past flashed before her eyes, and the curtain of ice snapped closed again.

She drew away suddenly. "Fine," she said. "As for the Hiker, that beast smashed one of the jeeps into it. I couldn't tell how badly it was damaged, but they are built pretty tough. If we can get it back on its wheels, we should be able to roll right out of here."

Mohan straightened. He felt the gulf widening between them again, but now wasn't the time or place to bridge it. He cleared his throat and turned to the signs on the wall.

"We'll deal with that when we need to," he said, but he wasn't sure which issue he was referring to. "I think our first task should be to see if this place still has power. Then we'll see if our flying friend really was born here."

The floor they were on was laid out in a rough square ring, with various labs, offices, and storage areas branching off the main corridor. A corridor bisected the ring, with a shaft at the centre housing elevators and a stairwell. As the agents descended, they noticed that the doors to the other levels were sealed, and they felt that the facility was much larger than they had suspected.

They found more disintegrated bodies along the way and wondered if the whole facility had been flooded with chemical gas at some point. Corpses became fewer the deeper they went, and by the time they hit the lowest levels, the bodies disappeared altogether, as had their stench.

It also got increasingly warmer the lower they went, and eventually, the stairwell ended in a cavernous space that could only be the main generator room.

The block letters on the wall read "16."

Four large turbines formed the central focus of the gigantic cave; they looked like the shells of enormous snails laid on their sides. A massive cave-in on the far side of the room had pulverised one of the giant motors and left a second partially buried, but the remaining two still appeared to be in working condition.

Vince played his light along the rubble. "Well, there's your problem."

"The cave-in must have caused a power surge through the whole facility," Vicki said, hands on hips as she eyed the turbine. "It's recent too, only a couple of days old."

Mohan's light caught a battered control booth off to their left. "Think we can get these other two up and running again?"

"Oh, let me look!" Vicki said cheerily, hopping into the control room.

Several large consoles covered in buttons, switches, and gauges lined the wall under the main window. The cave-in had partially knocked out the safety glass and lay over the switchboard. More banks of switches and dials lined the rear wall. Scorch marks, burnt panels, and exposed wires clearly showed severe electrical damage.

"You're not exactly screwin' in a light bulb, Vicki," Vince said. "But what the hell, worse that can happen is the power stays off, right?"

Vicki set down her large bag and slowly turned, studying each panel. Then she crawled under the main console, pulling cables and removing fried circuits. She hummed as she worked, clearly enjoying the opportunity to be of some use besides medical. Her teammates watched the growing pile of damaged electronics with increasing apprehension.

"You sure you know what you're doin', darlin'?" Vince asked.

"Just watch!" Vicki answered.

Several snaps and sparks of arcing electricity echoed through the cavern. A dull whine began to come from the turbines, and the lights flickered to life.

However, Vicki's triumph only lasted a few seconds before a sharp crack came from one of the boxes across the room, and the lights blinked out again as the motors hummed into silence.

"Drat," Vicki said, crawling out from under the panel. "Sounds like we blew a fuse."

She was greeted by a cloud of smoke when she opened the box. Waving the screen away, she studied the old cylindrical tubes that were the fuses. Without a word, she returned to her pack and rummaged around until she pulled out a thin sheet of aluminium foil.

"Baking a cake again?" Kitty asked, amused.

The frog waved the sheet around. "This is what happens when you watch too much TV."

She popped out the blown fuse and carefully wrapped the foil around it, covering each connector end. After replacing the fuse, she dived back under the panel. She fiddled with the circuitry, and again, the crackle of electricity filled the control room as the turbines whined to life. The lights flickered more brightly this time and stayed on.

"How about that!" Vince said and slapped the old console.

There was a sudden bright surge of electricity, and the panel began to smoke. Vicki gave a startled yelp and pushed out from under the console, her shirt smoking slightly.

"Terribly sorry, darlin'!" Vince said.

She waved him off with a smile. "I'm just glad I don't have fur," she said. "I'd look like a puffball right now!"

"How did you do that?" Rizzo asked.

The frog shrugged. "I watched too much *MacTavish*. We're lucky this panel had a lot of redundant parts I could swap out for the broken boards. But be careful with it; if it goes again, that's all she wrote."

"All right." Mohan chuckled. "Enough wagging about. Now that we have power, we can do a proper search."

Rizzo had already started with the cave-in. There was scattered construction equipment partially buried in the rubble. She examined some of it and sniffed at the air. "It looks like they were expanding the cavern," she said, "and they hit a natural gas pocket."

Mohan rubbed at his whiskers thoughtfully. "Expanding for what, I wonder? Enlarging the power grid, maybe?"

"I bet the power surge was how the monster got loose," Ric added.

Mohan nodded. "Keep your eyes peeled, everyone."

They began their sweep with the floors they had passed on the way down. Only half the lights were working, and they still needed their torches. Except for the generator room, the lowest levels hadn't been touched in decades and were mostly storage for equipment and supplies, much of it left over from when the Foresight had been the primary occupants. Above these levels, they found the loading bay and the other end of the collapsed tunnel that led to the clearing where they parked the Hiker. It didn't show any signs of use other than as a convenient entry into the base; several skeletons were caught in the rubble, and it was obvious that when the initial escape route was cut off, everyone turned and ran for the other exit. The agents hoped these two were not the only ones.

The living quarters and cafeterias showed the most recent signs of activity and had the highest concentration of skeletal remains, especially in the corridors. It appeared that the former tenants had dropped everything and tried to leave in a hurry. Fortunately, the facility's ventilation system had kicked in and significantly lessened the stench.

The research labs started on level six—where they had initially entered the base—but none contained the equipment necessary to breed a monster. They did find some botany labs that included the equipment needed to alter the poppy and banana plants, but a fire had destroyed much of it. After examining the scene, Rizzo announced that it had been an accident caused by the fleeing workers.

"I've noticed the facility's layout is fairly uniform," Ric said as they mounted the stairwell to level four. "Is this setup typical as far as subterranean bases go?"

"Well, I've never been in a Foresight base till now," Vicki answered, "but, yeah, I'd say this is a pretty normal arrangement. Believe it or not, there's several contractors out there who specialise in this kind of thing, and each has their own style."

"Contractors for building secret bases?" Ric said. "I suppose I shouldn't be surprised."

Kitty laughed derisively. "Says the journalist talking to a bunch of super secret agents who hunt alien monsters while standing inside a facility once owned and operated by their adversaries."

Ric shrugged. "I see your point, but how does any of this even work?"

The door to level four was jammed shut, and Mohan shoved against it. "At some point, mate," he grunted, "you're just going to have to accept that everything you knew about the world has changed. Now, for our Sanctuary, we did the work ourselves. Even so, the good-guy contractors have a code of their own and take precautions so they don't know the exact location of where they're building."

"And the bad guys?" Ric asked.

"Oh, well, they just kill everybody and hire a new team for the next job," Vince answered. The lynx didn't think the hare was joking this time.

Mohan chuffed irritably, but it was uncertain if it was at Vince or the blocked door. "Anyway, I'd say this place is about average size. They probably had as many as three hundred people working here at one point. The Sanctuary is a bit bigger but much more spread out."

"And constantly under construction," Rizzo grumbled.

"Changing with the times," Mohan said.

He finally got his fingers through the crack in the door and gave it a yank. Zed got on the other side and added his own weight. Between the two, the door didn't stand a chance.

"Regular maintenance is essential to a facility's health," the badger said as he stepped into the corridor. "This base is over forty years old, and you see the deterioration that has already occurred. The Sanctuary is more than twice that age."

Ric swept his light around aimlessly. "Only eighty years? You must have changed locations multiple times if Tiger's Stripe is really three thousand years old. Are there any older permanent facilities?"

"There was," Zed said with sudden solemnity. "The Tiger Temple in the mountains of East Benai was our original home. Sadly, it was destroyed some five hundred years ago." He sighed wistfully. "From the histories I have read, it must have been quite beautiful. After its destruction, Tiger's Stripe roamed all across the globe before we found a suitable location to build a new Sanctuary."

"Which is?" Ric prodded.

"Ah, ah!" Vince wagged a finger at him. "Don't want to spoil the surprise."

Mohan chuckled. "Too right! You'll just have to wait and see." He checked left and right down the elevator corridor. "Right, same sweep as before.

26 – The Experiment

Level four had the largest labs yet, but their purpose remained unknown until Ric made a crucial discovery. He, Mohan, and Kitty were sweeping through their half of the ring when the journalist peered through a porthole into a preparation room of some sort. Several clean-suits still hung in recessed alcoves. The airlock on the far side had been forced open on both ends, and he could see the lab beyond was a mess of broken test tubes and overturned chairs. Papers and scientific equipment he couldn't identify lay strewn across the top of a large central counter. A dim glow drifted through the double doors at the rear of the lab.

The glow of daylight.

"Mohan, I think I found something!" he said, pushing past the prep room into the lab.

Mohan got on the radio and called the rest of the team in from their sweep.

The papers on the counter meant nothing to the journalist, but Vicki found several quite interesting. Mohan cautiously approached the double doors, and the stench of death and decay assaulted his nostrils as he entered the cavernous space beyond.

The doors exited onto a small observation platform overlooking the lab floor below, the railing still mostly intact. The old Atomic Age punch-card machines, reel-to-reel computers, and switchboards rested against a far wall covered in plastic. In their place were much newer banks of computers, arc coils, and wires surrounding a shattered glass containment cylinder; Mohan guessed its volume was easily twenty thousand litres. Hoses and heavy cables linked a chain of large stainless-steel vats, each bearing a bright red biohazard symbol; most were dented or torn open. Sunlight poured into the room through a gaping hole high in the wall beyond the containment cylinder. Dirt and rubble formed a crude ramp up and out. Skeletal bodies lay everywhere, particularly around the shattered cylinder.

"So this is where you make a monster," Ric said grimly, wrinkling his nose at the stench.

"Indeed." Zed frowned.

Vicki set to her regular task of examining the corpses while Kitty and Rizzo sifted through more discarded notes.

"Well, it's not Frankenstone's lab," Vince jibed as he prodded some broken machinery. His reference was to a popular old thriller novel that spawned a series of black and white films, which not only created the horror genre but also inspired the look of mad-scientist labs the world over.

"That tank isn't near big enough for the creature I saw," Kitty noted.

"They probably pumped it full of growth hormones," Mohan said. "Once it fed, it probably practically exploded in size."

"A healthy diet of mad scientists," Vince chortled. This time, Rizzo was close enough to cuff him over the ears.

"We have two sets of victims here," Vicki announced. "The lab techs show the same level of decay our friends in the rest of the facility have, but the rest are probably victims from the farm and the convoy. They aren't melted like the lab guys. Also a few animal corpses thrown in; he made sure the jungle knew who owned the block now."

"Indeed," Zed said. "We may be able to rule out cockatrice breath as part of its arsenal."

"So what happened to the rest of the facility?" Ric asked.

"My guess is whatever chemicals they were dealing with got into the ventilation system," Kitty said. "Or it was a security measure in case one of their specimens got out."

"My God," Ric said. "All those skeletons. What could they have been messing with that could melt flesh like that? And why?"

Vicki looked up, the colour draining from her green face. "Mohan, Daeminox could do this in a concentrated form."

Everyone backed away quickly, the sudden thought of contamination foremost in their minds.

Mohan was the first to recover and carefully stepped around bodies as he moved to get a closer look at the hole in the wall. "If it was a concentrated dose, we'd all be infected by now. And don't forget that Daeminox gets rid of the bones, too. Whatever it was, let's be thankful it evaporated after the containment system failed."

Vicki snapped her fingers and wagged her index digit in the air excitedly. "It all fits! The cave-in shorted out the generators, right? That disrupts their containment grid and sends a jolt through the system, but instead of killing the creature, it jump-started it, bringing it out of whatever hibernation state they kept it in. It woke up, got pissed, tore up the lab and broke through the wall."

"It had help," Rizzo said. She used her shotgun to lift the twisted remains of an RPG from a tangle of corpses. "There's a couple of them here, all fired."

Mohan played his light around the edges of the hole. "There are a lot of blast marks here. Either it was moving too fast, or they had the worst aim ever."

"They must have hit the vats containing the decay agent," Zed suggested, "and ended up flooding the entire facility."

"First they can't kill it with grenades, and then they can't kill it with chemical agents?" Vince shuddered. "What the hell is this thing?"

Kitty picked up a stack of dot-matrix printouts half buried in glass shards. "I think I just found out."

She handed the printout to Mohan. Each line had a base letter string, which he recognized as DNA, followed by a chemical compound and percentage graph. The column on the far left had a common name offset from the scientific jargon.

Mohan let out a breath, "My God. Quetzalcoatl, grendel, chimera, camazotz, cockatrice. Is there anything they didn't mix with this thing?"

"I take it those are all fiend types?" Ric asked.

The tiger nodded. "Mostly flyers, although the grendel and chimera are land-bound. And we think the chimera is a naturally evolved subspecies, not a pure strain."

Vicki looked up sharply. "Mo, some of those are known carriers of Daeminox syndrome."

"I know." He turned a concerned gaze to Kitty.

She rubbed at the bandage on her right arm. "Ugh, we just went through this for the whole group! I'm fine. It's just the knife wound I took for pencil boy over there. Tore it open against the rocks when I was scrambling back into the cave. None of us would be standing here if that thing could spread Daeminox so easily."

Ric's ears flattened slightly; he wasn't sure he appreciated the moniker "pencil boy."

Zed glanced over Mohan's arm at the printout. "It appears they used an alkonost as the base. That at least explains the creature's size. These notations are quite detailed; they may be useful to our database."

"Too right," the tiger agreed. "Stow them, would you, Vicki?" He handed the printouts to the frog and turned to the lab doors. "Let's finish our sweep. Some of these bodies are fresh, and we should get out of here before—"

An all too familiar screech cut him off.

"Bollox!" The tiger waved hurriedly to the entrance and hissed, "Back in the corridor. Quick!"

They rushed back through the lab and preparation room. Mohan paused inside the double doors and watched through the window as the Frankenstone beast landed on a lip of rock outside and slithered through the hole in the wall.

He squinted as he carefully observed the details of his adversary for the first time and suppressed a shudder. His breath caught as he watched its skin shift from mottled brown to grey and black, blending with the machinery and debris inside the chamber.

The creature paused and raised its head, the narrow nostrils flaring as it caught the lingering scent of intruders. Slowly, it crept further into the chamber, moving towards the doors, its head swaying from one side of the room to the other as it sniffed. Mohan backed away slowly, keeping his machine gun levelled before him. The beast's massive jaws nudged against the double doors just as the tiger ducked back into the prep room and waved everybody to get out of sight.

The enormous, jagged head of the creature barely fit through the doors, filling almost the entire lab. The fiend shoved the centre table aside with an annoyed snort, the solid wood and steel crumpling like cardboard as the bolts holding it to the floor snapped and popped. It sniffed at the open airlock doors leading to the prep room for several tense moments before it grunted and slowly backed out into the main testing chamber. It was too big to proceed any further into the facility.

They heard the scrape of scales on rock as the creature slithered back out into the noonday sun.

Slowly, Mohan backed out into the main corridor to join the rest of the Scrappers, and they breathed a sigh of relief.

"Could we not do that again?" Ric asked.

"Bloody oath!" Mohan agreed. "Sorry, mates, that was my fault. I knew we'd walked right into the bloody nest, but we had to gather what information we could while it wasn't around."

"That's twice now," Kitty growled at him. "Next time, why don't you do it on your own."

He snorted but let the comment slide. "What colour was that thing when you first saw it?" he asked.

The white tigress shrugged. "Kinda brown and blotchy, like the rock face. Great camouflage."

"Too great," Mohan said. "I saw the scales shift as it crawled inside. This bloody thing has chameleon abilities."

"I take it that's not normal," Ric said.

"Too bloody right. We've never seen that in a fiend in all the three thousand years we've been hunting them." He turned to the frog. "Vicki, how much juice you think is left in those generators?"

The medic thought a moment. "I'm not too sure, Mo. We only have the two up and running, and that patchwork job I did won't last forever." She squinted up at him shrewdly. "But maybe enough to kill it?"

Mohan nodded grimly as he glared back at the lab door. "Enough to kill it."

27 – To Kill a Monster

Before they made any more preparations, the agents finished their sweep of the facility. They needed an inventory of every available asset and a complete understanding of the base's layout. Most importantly, they needed to find out if there was another exit besides the lab.

The levels above them contained mostly admin offices. Level one was a cave where the facility's roof served as the floor. They guessed it had once been a small motor pool from the markings on the concrete pillars supporting the natural ceiling. Now, it contained crates labelled with the logo of Terrapin Holdings. Again, they lamented the nature of the company and the lack of proof that Jirair al-Seif was directly connected to the facility.

At one end of the cave, an angled concrete shaft housed a cargo elevator large enough to fit two or three Tracksman Hikers; the signage suggested it led to a heliport on the mountain peak. The heavy gears and hydraulic pistons supporting the platform gleamed like new, and it was evident that this entrance had seen much use up until the accident. Narrow ladders along each side of the shaft provided the only other access to the surface should the platform malfunction. Fortunately, while the lights had blown out along the steep angle shaft, the lift was still intact and powered. At the top, they found a heavy steel blast door sealing the tunnel. A body lay half crushed beneath it.

Vince immediately went to the control panel off to one side. He dug several tools from the pouch at his hip, and after crossing a few wires, the door rose with a protesting screech. The afternoon sun was all that greeted them on the other side.

The cave extended another twenty metres before bending to the right, where they could see sunlight shining through the unseen cave entrance. Two small guard booths fit into alcoves on either side of the blast door. More large crates and several pieces of machinery covered by rotting tarps and cargo netting lined the walls. Most of it appeared to be antique Foresight paraphernalia, displaced to create room for the equipment distributed by Terrapin Holdings. The remains of several bodies were scattered along the floor, but not as many as they had expected. Unlike the corpses inside the facility, it was clear that the beast had mauled these.

"I believe they were trying to get back into the facility after the monster escaped," Zed said after he examined the tracks.

"Looks like the only ones who escaped were the ones who made it to the convoy trucks," Ric said.

"And they didn't make it far either," Kitty reminded him.

"It is clear the creature knows of this exit," Zed said. "The helicopter landing must be just outside the entrance."

"Shall we take a look?" Ric asked, taking a step towards the exit.

Mohan held him back. "We're not ready to leave yet," the big tiger said. "Best to remain out of sight until we want to draw attention to ourselves." He turned back to the cargo lift. "We have an exit. Let's go kill us a monster."

As they descended, Vince asked, "What if zappin' it isn't enough?"

Rizzo's eyes lit up. "I saw an explosives storage room on one of the lower levels. If the shock doesn't kill it, it should stun it long enough to vaporize it!"

"Do it," Mohan ordered. "But try not to bring the mountain down on top of us."

When they reached the bottom of the elevator again, Ric looked up the shaft. It was easily thirty metres to the top.

"When we electrify this thing, we're probably going to lose power to the rest of the facility," he said. "I don't know about you, but that's an awfully long climb to the surface."

"Especially with an explosion behind you," Vince pointed out.

"Indeed," Zed said.

"Oh, it won't be that big," Rizzo scoffed. Then she added, "I think."

"All of us don't need to be inside when we spring the trap anyway," Mohan said. "Rizzo, you can insulate the explosives so the trap doesn't set them off, right?"

The basilisk gave an insulted snort. "But of course! However, most explosive compounds are highly unstable. If the beast thrashes around too much, they may go off on their own. I'm more concerned about giving Vicki enough time to climb all the way up here from the generator room."

"Oh, I thought of that already," the bullfrog said. "The Foresight had the *foresight* to put auxiliary stations all over the base." She chuckled at her own pun, but the others just frowned.

"Anyway," she continued, "there's a substation on level six, right next to the elevators. We can crank up the generators to full power and trigger the discharge from there. I still have to get past the lab before you trigger the bomb, but you know how quick I can move when I have a purpose."

"What about the blast doors?" Ric asked.

"They've got a mechanical safety lock," Vince answered. "Once the power's out, the doors are locked in position; we'll just make sure that they're open. I can disable it to close them, but only from the inside. Fortunately, the hydraulics will lower it slowly."

Mohan nodded, satisfied. "OK then. We have a plan; let's get to it."

Preparing the trap consumed what remained of the afternoon.

After many assurances, Rizzo managed to coax Vince into opening the explosives store room. Inside, barrels stamped with chemical labels for Baratol, barium nitrate, ammonium nitrate, and TNT were stacked into carefully sorted pyramids from one wall to the other. A giddy expression spread across the basilisk's face as she gazed at the explosive compounds and started cackling like a schoolgirl. Her companions exchanged nervous looks.

Unfortunately, many of the compounds had become inert after sitting so long, but Rizzo quickly pointed out those she could still use—and warned against the unstable ones that they shouldn't go near. Ric and Vince carefully loaded the barrels onto sledges to haul them up to the beast's lair on level four—an agonizingly slow process with the elevators out of commission.

Rizzo went to work creating a package that wouldn't go off when they triggered the shock trap. It wasn't an easy task, considering the whole point of a detonator was to deliver an electrical charge that would detonate the compound. The challenge awakened old memories from her revolutionary days, and the expression on her face was almost euphoric. Her companions heard her singing Marisian pop songs to herself as she worked, giving her a wide berth if they had to pass by.

Vicki scrambled over the generators and control panels, double-checking the fuses and relay switches to ensure she used every ounce of voltage. She estimated she could coax at least two megawatts out of the motors before they burned themselves out for good. Two million volts ought to be enough to fry anything, but there were always Rizzo's explosives.

Mohan and Zed fed lengths of heavy power cable through the central elevator shaft, connecting the generator to the substation on level six and then to the lab on level four. Running the line directly ensured they would avoid any breakage if they used the facility's internal wiring. They checked each length for corrosion but didn't know how long the cables remained locked away in storage; hopefully, it would hold the charge without shorting.

Kitty was put in charge of the delivery system. One good thing about the old Atomic Age machinery was that it was heavily copper-based, and she set to work stringing strips of scavenged metal and copper wire into one of the cargo nets that was still in good condition. The final product was roughly sixteen square metres, nowhere near enough to cover the creature. However, its purpose was only to deliver the electrical charge, not to actually tangle the beast.

Once work on the lab began in earnest, Mohan and Zed kept a constant vigil on the hole in the wall and the landing beyond while the others worked; the last thing they needed was for the beast to return early.

Vince assisted Kitty with suspending the net from the ceiling of the creature's lair and attaching the power lines, a feat made all the more harrowing because they had to climb the containment vats just to reach the rusted latticework beams that crisscrossed the roof. They smashed several old computer units and scattered the copper pieces across the floor to improve the charge's conduction.

Rizzo supervised the placement of the last explosive barrels. Most of them had to be lined around the edges of the room because of the shock trap, but between her and Vicki, they picked out some of the weakest structural points in the room. If they couldn't blow the creature up, maybe they could collapse the lab on it.

Night had fallen, but the fiend had not made another appearance. It was troubling, to say the least. Avoiding the creature's detection while they worked would have been difficult, if not impossible, but they would have at least known that their quarry was still watching.

When the work was complete, Frankenstone's lab transformed into a giant superconductor with a surprise explosive finish.

Mohan examined their handiwork through the windows of the double doors. "Rizzo, just how much explosive force is that, exactly?"

She smiled sweetly and batted her eyes. "Oh, just enough to level the whole mountain."

Ric and Vince took a couple steps back as if the added distance might save them. Mohan just frowned.

"You are no fun," the basilisk pouted. "Honestly, I am concerned it will not be enough. All told, there are only about fifty pounds of explosives, and they had to be spaced around the room."

"We'll make it work," Mohan said. "OK, Vince and I will be the bait. Vicki will stand by at the substation. How far away can you get with that detonator, Rizzo?"

"I've run a cable all the way to the parking garage on level one," she replied. "I wish I could have done it by remote, but there is too much rock and concrete in the way."

The tiger nodded. "Don't hit that trigger 'til I give the word or you see us coming out the stairwell. I want the rest of you already waiting for us at the top of the lift; we'll pile anything we don't need to carry outside the blast door. Got it?"

They all nodded, and Mohan ordered everyone into position. It was time to draw their target's attention.

The forest swept beneath the creature in a blur of colour. The ones who hunted it could only imagine how the world looked through its eyes. Even at a great distance, the details of the veins in the leaves below leapt into pristine clarity, and yet the world was awash in halos of deep blues and greens, with the occasional splash of yellow from rocks that still held the heat of the day.

Its own hunt had not gone well. With each passing day, its hunger grew; with each passing day, there were fewer morsels to satiate it. Eventually, it would have to venture towards the great light in the southwest. That territory was already claimed, and it made the creature uneasy whenever it approached. Something ancient and powerful was buried in the great city's ruins, something that attracted and repulsed it like a spinning magnet.

The wounds it had received that morning were already starting to heal, a trait that would have stunned its hunters. However, the inside of its mouth still burned where three hot projectiles had lodged deep in its flesh. Time wouldn't force them out to regurgitate them, like the fiery spines from past victims; these wounds would remain, a constant reminder of the prey that had escaped through the ravine and cavern.

The greatest insult was that this quarry had invaded its lair! In the primitive recesses of its animal brain, the instinct for revenge flared with renewed fire.

A regular pounding disturbed its thoughts. It didn't have ears, but it sensed the disturbance in the air and arched its neck northward. A small red speck stood out against a pool of blue, ringed on all sides by the fading yellow of the mountainside. It was still too far away to make out the details clearly, but the creature's instincts picked out familiar landmarks, and it realized the growing speck was standing at the mouth of its own lair.

A primal rage filled the creature, and it let loose a screech of hate as it beat its wings harder against the air, picking up speed. The time for its vengeance had come.

Vince stood outside the hole in the wall of the test chamber, pounding on a plastic bucket with a pipe. He saw the black shape against the night sky and heard its cry of rage.

The mountainside spread its sheer walls in all directions from the landing; there was no escape save back into the lab.

Still, he didn't move. If their plan was going to work, he had to cut it as close as possible. He just prayed he wouldn't underestimate the creature's speed.

Once he could hear and feel the beat of the creature's wings, he dropped the bucket and dived feet first into the chamber. He still clutched the pipe firmly in one hand, but it was more because his fear-numbed fingers wouldn't let it go than because he thought he might actually need it.

He had been elected as the bait because of his superior agility, and he put every ounce of his abilities to the test as he bounced from one surface to the next down the crude ramp, hitting the floor below at a dead run. The room shuddered as the beast crashed onto the landing behind him, snarling and screeching furiously.

The nimble hare bounded up over the rail of the observation deck, and the creature snapped at his heels, getting a mouthful of railing for its efforts; the six-centimetre metal bar snapped like a toothpick. Its clawed feet scraped and slid over the uneven mess of metal plates and pipes scattered on the floor.

Vince dived through the double doors where Mohan waited, and the tiger gave a mighty pull on the ropes in his hands. The catches released, and the metal-laced net fell over the beast's folded wings. It screeched in rage and struggled to unfurl them but only succeeded in getting itself more tangled.

A copper ring rebounded off the doorframe with a dull *ping*. The flimsy mesh wouldn't hold the creature for long.

Mohan shouted into his radio, "Now, Vicki! Do it now!"

Down on level six, Vicki posed dramatically with one hand pointed to the sky as she cried into her radio, "Throw ze svitch!"

With the other hand, she jammed the circuit into the On position and leapt back as sparks flew. With her task complete, she dashed out of the room and began climbing to level one.

In the test chamber, the creature screeched in pain and fury as two million volts of electricity coursed through it. It arched and twisted and smashed against walls, computers, and vats. Its scales began to blister and scorch as smoke rose from its body. Thankfully, none of Rizzo's explosives went off prematurely as the creature writhed. Electricity flashed through the air as it arced between the netting and the bits of metal underneath the beast. Mohan and Vince averted their eyes from the blinding light, and their fur stood on end from the static in the air.

And yet, after a full thirty seconds, it was clear that the creature refused to die, and a shudder from deep beneath their feet told Mohan and Vince that the generators had gone out for good, punctuated by the lights in the corridor behind them winking out and throwing the facility into darkness. The creature was staggered, but Mohan suspected not for long. He waved Vince out, and they dashed towards the stairwell. Vicki blinked in the light of their torches as she came up from level five.

They were halfway up level two when they felt a shudder and heard the screech of twisting metal far below.

"It's tearin' into the facility itself," Vince shouted above the din, "tryin' to chase us."

"Now, Rizzo!" the tiger bellowed into his radio. "Blow it to hell!"

The basilisk jammed the button on her detonator and heard the roar and shudder of the explosion beneath her, but it was staggered and uneven, not the single blast she had hoped for. Smoke started to billow out of the stairwell, but she breathed a sigh of relief when she saw Mohan, Vicki, and Vince race out soon after. Together, they dashed to the elevator shaft.

They kept a steady pace through the steep climb but were only halfway up when the mountain began shaking violently.

"The creature!" Vince shouted

"*Non!*" Rizzo gasped. "*Mon Déesse*, something's triggered a chain reaction through the facility!"

"Climb, mates!" Mohan shouted. "Climb like it bloody means something!"

With less than five metres left to go, they heard and felt the heavy cargo lift tear away from its mounting. Mohan fought the urge to look back even as he felt the heat of the approaching fireball, keeping his eyes steadfastly on the feet of Vince in front of him, breathing hard as he forced himself to reach from one rung to the next. He was glad he kept himself in decent shape.

Rizzo reached the top first, followed by Vicki, and with the help of the others, they dragged Vince and Mohan over the lip. They rushed as a group towards the open blast doors. The fireball from below shattered the lift platform and raced towards them at an alarming rate. Already, flames were belching over the edge of the shaft behind them.

Once they were all through, Vince tripped the safety switch and rolled under the closing portal. He kept a firm hand on his lucky hat, not wanting to drop it in the excitement. It was a good thing, too. The door snapped shut much quicker than he anticipated, and tongues of fire lashed through, singeing his tail and ears in the process.

The heavy blast door shuddered as the facility's last fiery breath pounded against it. The thick steel began to buckle and glow from the intense heat. Just when it looked like the blast would actually melt through it, there was a sharp *crack* of rock, and the violent shaking gradually stopped. The stone roof of the cave proved thinner and weaker than the blast doors, and the explosion vented into the night sky—no doubt this would have troubled the facility's original designers.

The agents stood in the tunnel for a while, breathing hard.

Ric turned to Mohan. "Can I ask a favour? Let's never do that again, either."

"No shit," Kitty agreed.

Mohan stretched and grinned. "No promises. Rizzo, what happened back there?"

The basilisk shook her head. "I'm not sure. Perhaps my charges ignited another gas pocket somewhere."

"Through the whole facility?" the tiger said. "No, that was a demolition blast."

Rizzo thought about this a moment. "*Oui*, that could be so. C-Two charges, maybe a little thermite for incendiary work. The failsafes must have triggered when the generators blew."

"We encountered similar countermeasures in al-Seif's arena," Zed said quietly.

The tiger nodded. "We did, but I still think it doesn't fit his profile. Either he's changed tactics, or whoever financed his new arena also used this facility." He paused and let his eyes wander over the collected crates and equipment. "We'll have to try and recover something off the creature. Not much chance of that after the explosion, but the Marshal wanted proof."

His eyes stopped on a long, low object against the far wall, and he wandered towards it. "Now, what's this doing here?" he said under his breath.

As the others milled about shaking off the adrenaline rush, Vince began to chuckle suddenly.

"What's so funny?" Rizzo asked.

"Throw ze svitch!" the hare chortled, imitating Vicki's horrendously overdramatic Dollan accent.

The frog flushed. "I always wanted to say that."

They all laughed, partly to relieve the tension but mostly just thankful to be alive.

Ric borrowed Vince's torch. "I wonder what side of the mountain we're on," he said as he headed towards the bend in the tunnel. "If there is a helicopter pad, too bad we—"

He leapt back suddenly as the head of the Frankencreature lurched through and snapped at him. The hunters gasped in shock and stared incredulously at the mangled beast.

On half the face, yellowed bone gleamed beneath tattered flesh; both eyes on that side were missing entirely. The other two burned with deadly purpose. The explosions had severed both wings from the body and reduced one foreleg to a bloody stump. Electrical burns blackened what scales it still had and scorched the rest away, revealing the knotted muscle and bone beneath. Orange ichor leaked from its wounds to coat the stone beneath it.

"Won't this fucking thing stay dead?" Kitty snarled, her ears flattening.

They backed towards the sealed blast doors, which Vince was furiously trying to get open again. Zed raised his bracer to engulf the agents in its mysterious protective shield.

Suddenly, they heard Mohan let loose a roar of challenge and turned. He was standing beside an old cannon mounted on heavy rubber tires. The black maw of its forty-eight-inch muzzle pointed straight at the creature's head.

"This science experiment is over!" the tiger bellowed.

The thunder of the cannon drowned out the beast's screech of rage, and it staggered back as the heavy shell tore through its serpentine neck, severing its head cleanly and blasting a large crater in the far wall. The body tottered back through the cave opening before collapsing with a shudder. Silence settled over the mountainside.

28 - Evidence

Vince stuck a finger in his ears, trying to stop them from ringing. "Is it really dead this time?"

"I'd like to see you live without a head," Rizzo said and spat on the corpse.

"I'm sure he'd manage somehow," Vicki replied.

"What the bloody hell did you hit it with, Mohan?" Kitty asked.

Mohan patted the heavy piece of ordnance. The barrel had split and curled at the end like in a cartoon; it would never fire again, but it had done its duty.

"A blast from the past," he said.

"Literally!" Vince said, and Vicki couldn't stifle a laugh. Rizzo cuffed him across the ears.

Mohan ignored him. He stared at the old cannon, lost in past memories. "It is—or was, rather—a forty-eight QF Short Ordnance, standard field artillery for the United Plains back in the day. I haven't seen one since the Caandian Conflict many years ago. How this one got here is beyond me; the Foresight must have used it for defence."

"Well, we're bloody lucky it did," Kitty said.

"Indeed," Zed agreed.

Ric frowned. "Well, I suppose it would be tacky to look a deus ex machina in the mouth."

Mohan brushed off some of the dirt from the mangled barrel to reveal the name Isabelle painted on it. "Thanks, Belle," he said quietly. "Rest easy, old girl."

Vicki found a box of old aerosol cans and tested one experimentally. "Hey, Riz, you got some fire?"

The basilisk and the frog hastily whipped together some burning torches and used the aerosol to create small flamethrowers, which they used to burn a safe path through the pools and spatters of poisonous orange blood. Though more than confident the fiend was quite dead, they had not forgotten that its creation involved fusing several very toxic creatures.

Once outside, they approached the corpse cautiously. The twin tails lay mangled and partially severed at their base. Burns covered more than 80 per cent of the body, but it appeared that without the aid of its camouflage, its skin was originally a mottled red.

Vince scratched his head. "You weren't kiddin', Kitty. That's really big! We already established that's not normal, right?"

Mohan folded his arms across his chest. "No, it's not. Even an alkonost doesn't get this large. I wonder if that may have something to do with the growth hormones they were experimenting with. But first things first. Rizzo, you still have some incendiaries left?'

"*Oui.*" The basilisk nodded.

The tiger heaved a sigh and absently thumbed his trophy necklace. "Right. Destroy it."

Kitty gave an unsurprised chuff.

"Do you believe that is wise, Mohan?" Zed asked.

The tiger shook his head. "No, I don't, actually. What we should do is pack it up and ship it back to Sanctuary. But we have no way of doing that, and it's far too dangerous to leave the corpse here. In fact, when morning hits, we should scour the cliff face and try to clean up as much blood as we can. With as much mixing as they did, it's almost certain this thing is carrying Daeminox syndrome. Unfortunately, we need to save the head as proof for the Marshal."

"With any luck, maybe he'll catch it," Kitty said under her breath.

"If this thing carries the sleeping sickness, how are we even going to get close enough to clean it up?" Ric asked, backing away from the corpse.

"You didn't tell him?" Vicki asked. She had retrieved her backpack and was rummaging through it.

"You didn't tell me a lot of things," Ric replied. "What should I know now?"

Mohan looked at him evenly. "I already explained the Tiger's Mark is in our blood. Well, it also gives us natural resistance to Daeminox and other diseases. Think about how often you've had to call in sick from work. Not often, right? Zed here is actually the most at risk since he isn't birthmarked."

"Just avoid the blood," Vicki said. "We aren't completely immune. The disease isn't airborne but can be absorbed through skin if you're not careful." She pulled out a small vial of bluish liquid and several syringes. "And take one of these."

"What is it?" the journalist asked, holding up the filled syringe he was handed.

"Belladonna's Elixir," the frog responded, "a fancy name for a serum composed of several enzymes with very long and complicated names. It's not a cure, but it's the only thing we've found that will keep the disease from infecting a host."

"I take it there's a reason we didn't take these before?" Ric asked.

Vicki sighed. "This is all I have, and the formula is so low-yield that the effect only lasts a short time—usually long enough for us to hunt, kill, and clean up. It's also extremely expensive to manufacture because the materials are very rare.

"We—that is Tiger's Stripe—already distribute as much as possible to frontier hospitals in the hopes they can avoid a pandemic." She hung her head sadly. "But like I said, it's not a cure. Once you're infected, there's nothing we can do."

"Yet," Rizzo said quietly, reassuringly shaking the frog's shoulder.

Once they had all taken the inoculation, Vicki examined the corpse more closely while Rizzo prepared her charges, and Zed took photos with his camera. The others scouted the area. The clearing for the helicopter was just outside the cave entrance, but Mohan judged it had been several weeks since it had been used. During their exploration, Vicki gave an excited cry.

"Mohan! Come look at this!" She waved him over.

She was examining a portion of the hip where the flesh burned away to the bone. There, grafted onto the exterior of the pelvic bone near one of the rear leg sockets, her light flashed off a metal plate. A closer inspection revealed the etching of a mouflon horn wrapped around a globe with Pytan as the focal landmass. Underneath was an inscription in Netib.

"Syris Industries International," Ric translated. "I'm not familiar with them."

"But we are," Mohan growled, ramming a fist into his palm. "We got him! We've finally got the slimy bastard!"

Kitty stuck a cigarette in her mouth, lit it, and answered the journalist, "Syris Industries is a chemical company with a lot of shady connections." She took a drag and exhaled a cloud of smoke. "Mostly, it's a drug operation owned by Assad Alabwaq."

"Whom we can prove is Jirair al-Seif," Mohan said. "And since Terrapin Holdings is owned by al-Seif, we now have our connection to him meddling with fiends. This is a real corker. Proof that al-Seif is into some really serious shit. Bag it and tag it, Vicki. Let's get the rest of this cleaned up."

Midnight was drifting past as the Scrappers began rummaging through the crates in the entrance tunnel. They found one big enough to fit the creature's massive head and carefully packed it. Vicki then had the brilliant idea of stripping the QF Short Ordnance down to just the wheel carriage and mounting the crate in place of the cannon.

"Going to need something to preserve it," the frog mumbled to herself and wandered back towards the guard booths. She returned a moment later with a fire extinguisher and a canvas bag. "Hold this a minute, would you?" she asked Ric, handing him the extinguisher.

She sifted through her backpack and came up with the insulated gloves borrowed from al-Seif's warehouse and a roll of duct tape. Accepting the extinguisher from Ric, she placed the nozzle in the mouth of the bag and taped it closed.

"Hope this thing still has a charge," she said, squeezing the extinguisher's handle.

She was rewarded with the *whoosh* of pressurized gas, and the bag began to expand. It also got very cold.

When it reached maximum capacity, Vicki removed the nozzle, grabbed the bag by the neck, and shook it vigorously. Removing the tape, a puff of pale smoke drifted out.

"Homemade dry ice," the frog said, smiling widely.

She carefully dumped the frozen crystals in the box around the creature's head and repeated the process with the bag and extinguisher twice more.

Rizzo continued her task of destroying the beast's corpse, but not before Vicki produced a bone saw and carefully removed the incriminating metal plate along with a good chunk of the hip bone. She slipped it into a large yellow plastic bag stamped with a biohazard symbol, sealed it, and stowed it in the dry ice alongside the creature's head. Later, she would have to find a proper way of storing and shipping it back to the Sanctuary for testing.

Finally, they began the trek back to the Tracksman Hiker, with the burning corpse of the monster quickly reducing itself to ash behind them. Kitty took point, followed by Mohan and Zed pulling the makeshift cart with its grisly prize; the rest followed.

Vince started up a rousing dialogue on what they should call the creature. "I mean, seriously, Frankenbeast is perfect!"

"I don't know," Vicki chimed in. "Margret Kelly's *Monstroso* was about a stitched-up monster. I think

Verne Well's *Moreau Island* fits better. We could call it a Moreaudon!"

"She has a point, Vince," Kitty agreed. "This thing was mixed through genetic manipulation, not surgical a procedure."

"But Frankenbeast sounds better," Vince argued.

"It doesn't matter anyway," Mohan grunted. "The scientists always get to name these things; you know that."

"Yeah." Vince sighed. "They'll probably pick somethin' stupid like 'wyvern' or 'thunderbird'. Would it hurt them to read a piece of popular literature for once?"

"You do know some of them write popular literature, right?" Ric smirked. Caught up in the thrill of their victory, he was beginning to feel like a proper team member.

The conversation continued as they hiked down the mountain. The helipad entrance was near the summit on the opposite side from where they entered, but the trail leading in that direction had obviously been built with vehicle traffic in mind. It was still a steep road, and they had to be careful with the modified cart. The sun was rising behind them by the time they reached the wreck of the Hiker. Ironically, the damage caused by the monster attacking the cave had settled into a shallow ramp they could easily cross. Nothing had disturbed the rockslide that half buried the vehicle, and the burnt-out shell of a bandit jeep rested not two metres away. Mohan and Zed set down their burden and went to take a closer look at the heavy truck.

"Axels are still intact, but all the windows are smashed," the tiger said as he poked his head through what was once the front window. "On the whole, it's amazing she's still in one piece. We're very lucky the gas tanks haven't leaked."

"I've heard they built them to run upside down if they had to." Rizzo beamed, her appreciation for the rugged vehicle temporarily rivalling her love of explosives.

"Like they say, 'Tracksman, beyond the end of the road,'" Vince said, quoting the company slogan.

Mohan, Ric, Vince, and Zed went to work getting the toppled Hiker back on its wheels, the rope Mohan had originally packed for climbing finally seeing some use. Kitty, Vicki and Rizzo saw to the remains of the bandits and their jeeps. They needed to burn the bodies in case any trace of the creature's venom had infected them. They could only hope that, while they lay there, no carrion animals had taken a bite and been infected.

In the shade of some trees, Kitty found a sturdy insulated ice chest—the kind used to store ice before freezers were invented. She guessed it had tumbled from the jeep when the Frankenbeast—they agreed it sounded better—dropped it. The seal was tight, and she cracked it open curiously. A grin spread across her face.

Behind her, the four men gave a final heave, and the Hiker rolled back on all four tires. They collapsed in the shade of one side, panting heavily; even with Mohan's and Zed's strength, the vehicle was a real beast.

"Oi, catch!" Kitty called over as she tossed something towards them.

Mohan caught it and examined a can of domestic beer; it was still cold.

"Ramses?" he read the label uncertainly.

"They had a whole case of it, but I don't think they wanted to share. They were using one of those old-fashioned ice boxes as a cooler, so there's still some ice left."

The tiger took a swig. "Eh, not bad. Not Eckland Black, but better than nothing."

They were more than exhausted after the last thirty-six hours, and after a breakfast of dried rations from the Hiker, washed down with the domestic beer, they decided to get some much-needed rest. Zed took the first watch; the Soketh seemed to need very little sleep.

As the agents rested, the familiar sounds of the jungle wildlife began to return. The terror that had threatened them for so many days had ended, and life could return to its usual, chaotic self.

29 – Merchant Conspiracy

Pianure Rosso—the western province of Medocci—was little different from its sister Mata, just across the Tharsian Sea. Nestled within a shallow cove almost directly across from the port of Kalegos was the affluent city of Pacé Acqua. The beaches and resorts were still enclosed by protective walls, but there were those with the courage—and the money—crazy enough to build small compounds along the cliffs, leaving the city to the tourists and the upper-middle class.

Many of the cliff-side villas of Pacé Acqua were marvels of engineering, ranging from neoclassical fortresses to sprawling ultramodern edifices, each almost a self-sufficient kingdom unto itself. And if it weren't for the small armies of private security their owners employed, they would be prime targets for the bandits that roamed the nearby forests.

Jirair al-Seif's villa was one such compound.

The main house and facilities sprang from the southern face of the cliff, each tiered rectangle rising like uneven postmodern steps up the hillside. Deep ochre paint coated the walls of the main structure and its surrounding fortifications, while the windows were tinted slate grey. The lush gardens, blossoming with various flowers from across the Medean Basin, appeared empty; al-Seif's security forces had been hand-picked and trained by Abar Kami to remain unobtrusive as they patrolled the grounds.

Pacé Acqua meant "the Waters of Peace," but there was no peace in the heart of Jirair al-Seif that afternoon. The troubled mouflon leaned against the railing of the south balcony, which swept out over a narrow, private beach of white sand. Even at the end of winter, the weather was pleasant, and he had swapped his pressed linen suit for a pair of khaki pants and a white silk shirt, but the ever-present purple feather remained pinned in his lapel. He gazed out at the magnificent view without really seeing it, a thin, dark cigarillo dangling half-forgotten from his lips.

It had been four days since the incident at the market, and in that time, he had been able to do little to keep his criminal empire from unravelling. Already circumstances forced him to dispatch a trusted lieutenant who turned out to be a spineless guingin—though his replacement may yet prove better than his word.

His mysterious benefactor had also remained disturbingly quiet since their phone conversation on the deck of the Star of Carmen, which now lay at anchor in the bay just below the villa.

The cordless phone on a nearby table interrupted his brooding with a harsh mechanical beep.

He picked up the bulky handset and answered sharply, "Yes?"

The respectful voice of Rashid spoke to him at length, and al-Seif rubbed a hand across his brow.

"By all the goat gods," he said hoarsely. "Is there anything left?"

"No, sir," Rashid answered. "The internal security systems were offline, but my source claims the facility and the asset were completely destroyed. I am hesitant to remind you that it was Mr Freggs who assisted with the refit of the facility. I believe he used the same security measures he installed at the arena in Kairran."

"Gods-damnit all!" Al-Seif pounded a fist against the railing. "Could you confirm who was responsible?"

"Not clearly, sir, but their description was close to the individuals seen on the security footage from the arena."

The mouflon swore again. "How did they survive that? What about our other shipment?"

"I received a call from a representative of Mr Freggs, who insisted it is on schedule, though I have not heard from our couriers directly. I admit I find this disturbing, but if I may be so bold, sir, I would encourage you not to worry. Santini and Raphello have proven their worth many times before. The shipment should arrive at the prearranged drop in Kolovania this evening."

Al-Seif frowned but said nothing. It was only natural that Freggs also had minions to deal with minions, but he didn't like having to be informed of their movements second-hand. There were too many moving parts that he wasn't aware of. Freggs insisted that his team handle the transport between the freighter and the crime lord's mercenaries on shore, leaving a wide gap where al-Seif didn't know what was happening. And if that wasn't enough, once the shipment was delivered, his benefactor demanded that they plot a course through the Kolovanian mountains that was not one of his regular routes.

"Our staff in Medocci have also been reassigned," Rashid continued. "However, there has been no sign of the *Resthoven* since it vanished from Kalegos."

"Fine. As far as I'm concerned, that bastard Freggs can sink with that blasted ship," al-Seif said, pacing angrily from one end of the balcony to the other, his horn tassels waggling with each step. His temper flared at every mention of his supposed benefactor.

He stopped by the table and said fiercely, "Now, I want you to call up that useless snake in Jar-Geshim. I want those meddlers taken care of once and for all. Tell him he can name his price, but they are not to leave the city alive. Understand?"

He disconnected the call and tossed the handset on the table, from which it promptly skittered off and clattered to the ground. The mouflon turned again to the stunning vista and leaned heavily on the railing.

A soft voice called behind him moments later, "Is something wrong, my darling?"

He turned to see a lovely middle-aged female ibex standing in the doorway. She wore a floral-print bikini with a matching sarong wrapped around her slender waist, the bright colours standing out sharply against her melanistic body-fur. She was still damp from swimming in the ocean below the villa, the dark ringlets of her black long-fur clinging to her delicate cheeks. Al-Seif sighed, and a faint smile even touched the corners of his mouth.

"No, Carmen, my love. Just some...business arrangements."

Carmen Abbatelli was the one shining light in his dreary world. She was only a few years younger than he, but she retained the youthful beauty of the day he met her, sitting in some smokey bar in the port of Khet. The whirlwind romance of those days had been short-lived. Carmen went on to further her education in Locke, and al-Seif began building his empires, both legal and illegal.

That had been almost twenty-six years ago.

The villa was his gift to her when they reunited years later, but he confessed it was also her prison. Losing her again would be a pain he could not bear.

He embraced her and kissed her passionately.

She pulled away smiling, but her expression quickly changed as she remembered something. "Oh, your wife insisted on seeing you this afternoon."

Al-Seif's mood darkened instantly.

"Bitch," he said, ignoring the irony of the insult. "Apparently, the news of my recent shortcomings has finally reached her. Fine, we'll discuss it over lunch. You need not attend, my dear."

Carmen smiled bitterly. "You are too kind."

She watched him fume silently for a moment and then gently took his face in her hands. "It pains me to see you like this. Does it not torture you to keep living like this? You are certain you can't just leave her?"

He sighed. This wasn't the first time the subject of his marriage to Yursa De Palma had come up. He rubbed her shoulders gently and said, "I admit there have been…setbacks. Unfortunately, I will need her assets in the coming months. But soon, my love." He kissed her forehead and pulled away. "Soon, I'll hold the reigns of De Palma Shipping and will be able to get rid of this dead weight around my neck."

Carmen shivered involuntarily. "You know I don't like it when you talk like that."

Al-Seif nodded. "I know; forgive me. You know I have kept no secrets from you. Many times, I am surprised you still love me."

"There are no angels in this world," she answered softly, "only the demons we create for ourselves."

They stood holding each other silently for several moments. Then al-Seif asked, "Has Delshad arrived yet?"

"I am here, Father!" The voice came from the doorway behind them.

When Carmen had rediscovered al-Seif, she held the hand of a young boy. Now, in adulthood, Delshad al-Seif was a more youthful but slightly taller version of his father, yet he possessed the ibex horns of his mother.

Theirs had been a strained relationship at first. Discovering he had a son brought home all the painful memories of al-Seif's abusive father. However, he made a promise he would not be the same man.

"The plane arrived ahead of schedule," Delshad said, grinning.

A new smile spread across the elder al-Seif's face, and he embraced his offspring warmly. "As well it should have! You used one of my best pilots."

Leaving one arm on his son's shoulder, he turned and placed the other around the waist of his mistress. "Good. For a little while, at least, I can be happy in the company of my son and his loving mother."

Their moment of bliss was not to last. Abar Kami gave a polite cough from the balcony doorway.

"Mrs De Palma to see you, sir," he announced softly.

Moments later, a tall canine stepped brusquely onto the balcony. Yursa's father, Vigo, was a deerhound, but she took after her wolfhound mother. If Delshad was an example of obvious mixed breeding, Yursa was a perfect example of how only a blood test could reveal such heritage. She towered above the three *Caprinae* and glared down at them with deep grey eyes. Her silky fur had only seen the finest groomers, and she kept her rust-coloured long-fur pinned up in a severe yet fashionable bun. Her dark blue suit and skirt were of an expensive cut found only at the finest Medoccian tailors.

"I thought I might find you here with your whore," she said, the lips of her long, pointed snout curling in a sneer.

Al-Seif felt his son and mistress tense under his grip, but he stepped forward before they could respond. "What do you want, Yursa?"

"Want? Your manufacturing facilities in Libris, but we both know that was not part of our prenup. Neither was the usage of third-party transport when conducting our business arrangements."

"Leave us," al-Seif commanded his son and mistress.

They obeyed silently, but Carmen delivered a withering glare to the taller Yursa as she passed. The

410

wolfhound glared right back, restraining herself from snapping at the retreating ibex.

The mouflon seated himself in a wicker patio chair. He did not offer the other to his wife, but she took it anyway.

"For your information, I was not facilitating any of *our* business ventures." The mouflon spoke slowly, lighting another cigarillo. "The client wished to use one of our storage facilities but his own transport. As a condition, I requested that the package be handled by our own employees. They needed to abandon the ship's company after an…incident occurred on board."

It was a flimsy excuse but laced with enough truth to allay suspicion. De Palma didn't buy a word of it.

"Only it never arrived, did it?" she said, her already high-pitched voice rising even further with her anger. "In fact, I don't believe that shipment was ever supposed to arrive in Kairran."

"I'm beginning to wonder that myself," al-Seif muttered.

His wife's voice dropped suddenly to a low growl. "My father agreed to this marriage on the understanding that it could mutually benefit our interests. He would not appreciate discovering that you were trying to strike out on your own."

He laughed at her. "And what 'interests' are you referring to? The Favera? Or perhaps the Costellianos? Don't take me for a fool. I know your father only agreed to my proposal because he saw a potential to expand into the Pytian market, away from the increasing tension with the other mafia families here."

He puffed on his cigarillo. "It just so happened I wanted to expand in the opposite direction. We've both been waiting for the other to make a move for a long time now."

Yursa rose swiftly. "But now your assets in Pytan are frozen behind a war. Your hand was forced, and you retreated to our territory. You have no choice but to capitulate, Jirair."

The mouflon exhaled a steady cloud of smoke. "Your Pytian assets are in as much jeopardy as my own. Your father must know that. I had hoped to discuss it later this week. Perhaps over dinner?"

Her eyes narrowed, but she had never been able to read him. His inscrutability had been one of his finest business qualities.

She turned to leave. "I'm sure it can be arranged."

He rose and snuffed out the cigarillo. "I suppose that means I will not be seeing you for lunch this afternoon."

"I have a prior engagement," she called over her shoulder. "Enjoy your whore."

"Bitch," he muttered under his breath, again not caring about the irony of trying to insult a female canine as such.

He stepped up to the patio bar, poured himself a double shot of expensive bourbon, and downed it in a single gulp. He stared at the facetted crystal for a moment, watching the sunlight glitter through it. Then he threw the empty glass against the concrete base of the balcony railing, where it shattered into a million pieces.

30 – Family Matters

It was late afternoon when the Scrappers were ready to head back to Jar-Geshim. Mohan hitched the makeshift cart to the Hiker, and Vicki added the remaining beer ice to the box containing the creature's head, finishing off the charge in the extinguisher to make a final batch of dry ice. They wished they had better packaging, but at least the flesh wouldn't rot away before they returned to the Marshal; then, it was his problem.

Everyone except Mohan and Kitty piled into the rear compartment; the two tigers rode up front. Vince broke into another of his bawdy stories as they got underway.

Mohan took it slow. The poor Hiker had been through a lot, and he wasn't sure how far he could push it. The rockslide had cut off their original path back to the fields, so the tiger plotted a route northward along the foot of the mountain.

The sun had begun to set by the time he found some less dense jungle foliage to push through; it must have been what was left of the path the lab convoy had taken when they fled the mountain. There was another shallow river crossing, and Mohan hoped that, once on the other side, they could find an easy path back to Jar-Geshim.

Vince reached the punchline of another tall tale. "So my friend Terry turns to me and says, 'Well, you wanted to bring the orangutan in the first place!'"

Even Rizzo laughed at the story. They were all still riding the high of a successful hunt; bringing down something as nasty as the Frankenbeast was a significant feather in their caps.

Mohan chuckled heartily, but when he looked at Kitty, she was staring stoically out the window.

"Liven up, Kitty," he said. "We scored a victory here."

A bare twitch of an ear.

"Something wrong?" he asked.

She was silent for a long moment.

"What happens now?" she asked without turning.

"Now? We take the Marshal's trophy back and hope General Durram has everyone ready to get the hell out of this godforsaken country."

She turned to him. "I meant with al-Seif. We spent almost two years trying to nail this bastard. Now it looks

415

like we got him by the short hairs. What do we do with him?"

The big tiger frowned. He had a general idea of the procedures that would follow, but he knew what his daughter meant. They might have the evidence, but al-Seif wouldn't go down without a fight.

"He has nowhere to run anymore," he said slowly. "With war coming, we might not get anyone in to see what's left of the Foresight facility, but as far as we're concerned, the job's done. Between the gladiator games, the slave ring, and now bioterrorism, we have enough to get Jirair al-Seif thrown in a nice dark hole to rot like the filth he is."

"What if no one prosecutes him? What if he's been working this angle for a while and knows exactly how to cover his tracks? We can't let him get away. Not after all the lives he shattered. Not after Rijay-din-Aden. He doesn't deserve a cell."

Mohan's frown deepened. He knew how the conversation was turning, and he didn't like it.

"That's not our call," he said. "We're hunters, not assassins."

Kitty turned back to the jungle rolling past. "I thought Justice was one of our pillars?"

"So is Honour," he growled, "and there's none of that in cold-blooded murder! We've got to trust that people like al-Seif will be held accountable to the law."

"And what if the law won't do anything about it?" she snapped. "What if people like al-Seif *are* the law? We already know he would never be tried in Pytan; he's got too many high-powered allies. You think Medocci actually has any honest lawyers left, especially with al-Seif's De Palma connections? For all we know, he could already have distanced himself from Terrapin Holdings and Syris Industries by now."

"And we have PR and intel teams that will poke holes in those boats once we get them what we've found."

"More wasted time." She slumped against the door. "Time for that bloody bastard to worm his way out again. Especially with his resources."

"What would you have us do?" her father growled.

She stared out the window. "I don't know." A long silence followed. Then she said, "The Council has made sanctions before."

"In very specific and unavoidable circumstances. Drop it, Kitty."

The white tigress was silent for several minutes again. Something stirred inside her every time she thought that al-Seif might get away with his crimes, something that longed for vengeance.

"There's always the Black Talon," she said quietly.

Mohan nearly brought the vehicle to a halt.

He turned to her and roared, "Kittina Rin Katral, I said drop it! Don't you ever bring up that band of misanthropic death dealers again. Do you have any clue what kind of fucked-up way of thinking that is? We're going to do things the *right* way, and that's the last I want to hear of it!"

The rear of the Hiker had gone quiet, but both tigers ignored the others; this was a family matter. Mohan jammed on the accelerator, and they lurched forward again.

After several minutes of silence, Ric quietly asked Vince, "What's the Black Talon?"

The hare shook his head slowly. "An assassin league. Started in Medocci some five or six hundred years ago. Despite the name, they're a bit of a grey area as far as we're concerned; they only go after the really nasty guys. Still, Tiger's Stripe believes in society's ability to fix its own problems—with a little nudge in the right direction. The Black Talon thinks a bullet is quicker."

Ric nodded thoughtfully. After a moment, he said, "Mohan mentioned that Tiger's Stripe has sanctioned assassinations under extreme circumstances. Like what exactly?"

The agents were silent for a long moment before Vicki answered, "There's a delicate balance of power in the world. Now and then, you get a genuine supervillain, someone with the power and influence to tip the scales really quickly. If we didn't take them out fast, they would send everything spiralling into chaos.

And I mean in a big way. Fortunately, it's very rare, and we've got enough experience we can kinda see the signs before it gets out of hand."

"Signs like the assassination of an ambassador's daughter?" the lynx said pointedly.

The agents remained silent as the Hiker rolled into a clearing, and the last rays of the sun vanished behind the cliffs on the far side of the valley. Father and daughter ignored each other for the rest of the trip. Some kilometres away, the distant lights of Jar-Geshim winked on, a solitary beacon in a sea of dark green.

31 – Special Delivery

Santini squinted at the heavy fog surrounding them, his scraggly squirrel tail twitching in agitation. The fog had settled in with disturbing rapidity as soon as the small convoy of trucks had entered the forest outside a Prapusk. Not that fog was unusual at the foot of the Kashkeya Mountains, but you didn't want your visibility hampered in this type of country.

The squirrel looked over at the driver, Raphello. The badger-marten was drumming his fingers nervously on the steering wheel and trying not to keep glancing at the rear-view mirror and the object in the rear bed of the heavy transport truck. Even with the massive cage covered by a heavy tarp, they both recalled their brief glimpse of the horrific creature the black-clad mercenaries had loaded aboard nearly twelve hours ago.

Their journey had started on an isolated beach outside Paznegrov, on the western edge of Kolovania.

From there, they had been forced to keep to back roads and side lanes, skirting the capital of Wahlrest until they could finally turn south for the border of Kirque.

Their employer, whom they knew as Assad Alabwaq, was paying them double for this transport. Santini and Raphello were the ones who drew the short straws for the truck, and they had only specialized tranquillizer rifles to arm themselves. It wasn't their place to question the boss, but they would be more than happy to dump this cargo over a cliff and get back to running guns as usual.

Raphello knew which roads to take to avoid the Kashkeya bandits and military patrols, but they still had felgheists and other predators to deal with. A pack of feline-like mountain bahngers had attempted to ambush them not an hour ago, but when they got close, the creature in the cage began to howl like a mythical banshee. The predators backed off instantly, and even the mercenaries had been tempted to flee the safety of their vehicles. The sound was most unpleasant and made the air around them feel heavy.

Santini had used multiple tranquillizer darts on the creature to shut it up, but he had no idea how long they would last. He didn't want to know what that thing might do to its cage if it woke up fully. On the flip side, he didn't want to overdose and kill it and face the wrath of his employer.

"Where the fuck are we?" he asked Raphello. "Shouldn't we have been there by now?"

Raphello gripped the steering wheel until his knuckles turned white—quite a feat considering the dark fur on his paws. He flipped on the windshield wipers as if they might wipe away the fog.

"Not much further," he said. We should be nearing the Kirque border somewhere east of Nove Mishka."

They drove in silence for some time before the sudden glare of a searchlight blinded them.

Raphello slammed on the brakes, and Santini winced as their companions in the jeep behind them swerved to avoid a collision. Thankfully, the beast did not awake from the sudden jolt.

"We can't have hit the border already." Raphello frowned.

Santini's expression asked why the driver had said they were close an hour ago if they really hadn't been, but he said nothing.

Concrete barriers blocked the road ahead. The figures behind them certainly looked military, with their black and grey tactical gear and camouflage-painted assault weapons. Still, it was obvious they were not regular army, Kolovanian or otherwise.

In the glare, Santini couldn't quite make out any features, but he saw at least one rhinoceros with a long, sharpened horn and the long neck of an ostrich or possibly an emu. The rest appeared to be feline or canine.

A single tall canine with black and tan markings and sharp features approached them.

He was almost two metres tall, broad-shouldered, and he wore the tall-peaked cap of a Dollan officer, but in place of the more familiar Zeichmacht army emblem, there was only a simple white shield with a black canine paw print in the centre. A long grey trench coat fastened with polished silver buttons heightened his imposing appearance. The only insignia on the coat was a slanted badge on the collar that must have been his rank—four silver diamonds arranged in a diamond pattern on a black field and a patch on the left breast that was the same as the shield on his hat.

"We have been waiting for you," the shepherd-dog said in a basso voice with a heavy Dollan accent. "Please exit the vehicles."

They did as instructed and came forward.

The officer removed his hat and ran a hand through his closely cropped black long-fur. It was then that Santini noticed he had a patch over his left eye and was missing half of his left ear. The patch didn't completely conceal the jagged scar running through his eye.

"You are ahead of schedule," the shepherd said, slipping his ear and a half through the holes in the hat's crown as he replaced it. "*Sehr gut.*" He called over his shoulder, "Fritz!"

An ocelot in a similar uniform came forward with a radio—Santini noticed that the emblem on his collar was a single lightning bolt.

The canine removed the handset and handed it to Raphello. "Inform your employer that the shipment has arrived."

Raphello dialled the frequency given by his employer, and the voice of Alabwaq's new lieutenant, Rashid, answered. The badger-marten informed the dromedary that they had delivered the cargo as ordered, and after receiving further instructions, he handed the receiver back to the ocelot.

He turned to Santini. "Payment will be waiting for us in Nove Mishka," he said, and the squirrel nodded.

The shepherd's smile was not at all friendly. "We will take it from here."

"You're welcome to it," Santini said. "I hope I never have to see one of these things again as long as I live."

The officer paused halfway back to the barricade. "*Ja*? Well, I don't think that will be a problem."

In the blink of an eye, a pistol was in his paw. Two shots rang out as he put bullets through Santini and Raphello's skulls. Before their compatriots from the jeep could react, the mercenaries behind the barricades gunned them down with short bursts from their own weapons.

"Pity," the shepherd-dog said without much conviction.

He stepped over the lifeless bodies of Alabwaq's hired guns and stood before the cage on the rear of the transport truck. In one swift motion, he yanked the tarp away to reveal the sleeping beast inside.

Horns and scales covered the entire creature. Two lidless eyes, each possessing two parallel black pupils, stared back at them. Even in the glare of the floodlights, it was difficult to judge its length, but it must have been at least six metres from snout to stubby tail. The bottom jaw was split in two, and each side—lined with razor-sharp teeth—hung limp as the creature slumbered.

Fritz, who had remained close to his commander, let out an involuntary gasp at the sight. The shepherd didn't so much as blink.

"Does it frighten you, Fritz?" the officer asked.

"*Ja, mein Major*," the ocelot said. He knew there was no sense in lying to his superior.

The major studied the beast a moment longer and then returned to the barricades. "*Gut.*"

His mercenaries were already clearing the concrete barricades from the road, and teams moved on the transport truck to cover the cage with the tarp again.

The shepherd stopped at a four-wheel-drive utility vehicle hidden in the trees and motioned for Fritz to hand him the radio. There was no acknowledgement when his call connected.

"We have received the package and are ready to begin," the major said. Then he disconnected.

32 – Unwelcome Guests

The doors to the Marshal's courtyard burst open, and Mohan and Zed strode boldly across the threshold into the warm morning sunlight. Behind them, Kitty, Vince, Rizzo, and Ric dragged the massive head of the Frankenbeast on a tarp, with Vicki trailing behind. She had a lighter and an aerosol can and was burning away small bits of flesh that might slip off the macabre sledge. All of them—except Vicki—had drawn their weapons but were careful not to provoke the guards. They were through playing the Marshal's games and had unanimously agreed they would present themselves from a position of strength.

The cobra's hood flared violently at having his morning routine interrupted, but he waved his guards down. After the hunters had left on their errand, there had been several altercations—similar to what Ric and company had experienced—between some of the more brazen citizens and the remaining agents. The bandits had not fared well during these encounters, and the Marshal was beginning to understand how dangerous his guests could be.

When he saw the size of the bloody object Mohan and his hunters were dragging across his marble floors, his fears magnified.

They stopped before the Marshal's throne, and the tiger presented the prize before the dais, being very careful not to spatter any gore about.

"One giant monster head, as ordered," Mohan said. "I hope you like it well down. Don't touch the blood; it's toxic."

The Marshal leapt from his chair and circled the head curiously. After a moment, he slithered back up on the dais to gaze into Mohan's eyes. "I'm impressed. I gave you three days, and you delivered on time. Cuttin' it close, sure, but you're quite the resourceful bastard."

He slowly began to slither among the agents, hoping one of them would flinch, but even the diminutive pacifist Vicki met his gaze with solid defiance.

He spoke as he moved. "I sent eight men to track you. I take it they're dead?"

Mohan watched him steadily, his grip tightening on the butt of his revolver. "That tends to happen when you make yourself into a nice fat piece of bait."

The cobra paused near Vince's shoulder. "How convenient."

"Your local beer isn't half bad, by the way," Vince said casually.

The Marshal's hood flared, and with sudden lightning speed, he dashed past the hare towards the guards at the door. His fangs flashed and buried themselves in the necks of the simian on the left and then the canine on the right. The other guards stared in horror as their compatriots screamed and writhed while the cobra's venom coursed through them. In seconds, they were nothing but lifeless, twisted heaps on the floor. The Marshal produced a paisley silk handkerchief from a vest pocket and cleaned the blood off his fangs.

"What do I pay you morons for?"

His hood lowered slightly, and he turned back to the agents. "Sorry you had to see that. Good help is so hard to find these days. You delivered on your half of the deal. I'll...deliberate about my half this afternoon."

He waved them off dismissively, but Mohan didn't move.

"How long have you been associated with Assad Alabwaq?" he asked evenly.

The Marshal whirled on him, and his eyes narrowed sharply.

The tiger returned his gaze. "You knew all along what we were dealing with. What we would find out there. That lab was nice and secluded, but there was no way they could bring in all that equipment without your knowledge. Not through *your* jungle. Hell, I bet you even offered to transport half of it for a price. Maybe you didn't know exactly what they were making up there, but I'm sure a crop of genetically enhanced poppies did wonders to smooth things over."

He tossed a withered sample of the plant on the dais. "Of course, once the beast was loose, you couldn't get anywhere near it to collect. That is, until we came along."

The cobra stared at him for a long moment and then gave a little shrug. "You're right; I didn't know what kind of mad science they were up to up there. But you have no idea how useful such a potent strain of heroin can be. Alabwaq has a lot of clients who enjoy his gladiator games, many with particular tastes. Some of them are even pretty high up in the Pytian government, like, say, Governor General Agabe Hassan. Let's just say I supply their cabinet with heroin, and the military doesn't set foot in *my* valley."

"And the sultan?"

"Sultan Abdülkadír wasn't completely unaware of the corruption within his own government, but he was naïve enough to believe he was actually winnin' his pathetic fight against them. Hell, he probably wouldn't have believed it if someone told him his own son was one of my finest customers. The sultan was nothin' more than a puppet who provided a smilin' face for the media. Hassan is the real power, and our deal was to leave me alone. Or at least, that was how it was supposed to work."

The Marshal returned to his throne and pressed a button concealed on the armrest. A bulky TV sitting in a nearby alcove switched on. The image portrayed an international newscast, but from the lines on the screen, they could tell it was a video recording of an earlier broadcast. A watery-eyed sheep read his reports in a thick Locke accent.

"The continent of Estan was rocked earlier this morning as Barju unleashed a series of artillery strikes on targets in and around the city of Meshim on the northeastern border of Pytan. The sovereign kingdom of Kirque has yet to issue a statement on its position in the conflict. It claims it was unaware that Barjan forces had invaded their territory to set up positions in the Gen-Yeshif Desert across the border from Pytan.

"The continent of Estan has been growing increasingly unstable following the assassination of Rijay-din-Aden, daughter of Barjan Ambassador Abdul-bin-Aden, and a retaliatory bombing of the Nayhadjin International Airport by Barjan nationals three days ago." The agents noted that KLAWS was not mentioned. "Despite the previous efforts of Sultan Abdülkadír to stem hostilities in Pytan, late yesterday evening, reports were issued that his royal motorcade was attacked, and the monarch was confirmed killed. News of his death has sparked surgical bombings by

Pytian insurgents in the Barjan cities of Kesher, Sarat, and Yam Fashem. Early this morning, Pytan's Governor General Agabe Hassan released the following statement."

The image of an elderly markhor with polished ebony horns appeared on the screen. He wore a dark green Pytian officer's uniform adorned with many ribbons and medals. The royal Pytian crest—a cluster of wheat sheaves encircling a hollow ram's horn filled with fruit and topped with a crown—emblazoned the podium he stood behind. He spoke Netib in a strong, clear voice that was obviously as familiar with issuing commands as delivering public addresses. An interpreter repeated his words in Locken.

"It is with the deepest regret that I must announce the death of our beloved Sultan, Abdülkadír Rijan. Survivors of the attack on the sultan's motorcade confirmed that Barjan insurgents were responsible for this most heinous crime, enacted as our sovereign was being moved to a secure location. The seat of the monarchy now falls to his son, Aluk, who was away on a diplomatic tour of the Marisian Alps."

"Of course he was," Vince commented slyly.

The young prince was a well-known stereotypical billionaire playboy; the hare had no doubt that this "diplomatic tour" involved more than a few female companions.

"Unfortunately," the general continued through the interpreter, "as many of you know, there was an avalanche in the region last week. While our sultan never gave up hope, it is believed that Prince Aluk was a victim of the disaster, although his body has yet to be recovered.

"In light of these terrible events, the General Council has elected me to the position of regent until such time as the prince can be found or hostilities with Baju abate, and a new sultan can be crowned. I assume this post with great reluctance and appoint my trusted aid and loyal compatriot, General Rousel Ach'eman, to the position of Governor General in my stead.

"I wish the people of Pytan to know that we will not handle this injury to our culture, to our very way of life, as meekly as bolvin. Our beloved sultan will be avenged, and we will not falter in our resolve. Thank you. May Great God be with us in these troubled times."

The Locke reporter appeared again and commented further about a state funeral for the sultan, but the Marshal switched off the TV before they heard any more details.

"A lot can happen in three days, eh, Stripey?" He sneered at Mohan. "Rumours are already spreadin' that Hassan may conveniently forget his arrangement with us in light of these...escalated tensions, as it were. Not to mention, our benefactor, Alabwaq, seems to have vanished to who knows where.

432

"Now, I'm not sayin' any of this is your fault, but you have to agree the timin' just sucks, don't it? You comin' here just as this whole shitstorm really gets brewin'? It wouldn't be far-fetched to say your bargainin' power just got a bit skewed." He coiled himself atop his throne and again waved dismissively. "I think you've got enough to think about for the rest of the day. Bye-bye now."

As they walked through the streets towards the hotel, Mohan and the Scrappers couldn't help but notice the air of apprehension that had settled over the city. Even here, the threat of war hung above the bandits like a storm waiting to break. The narrow lanes were nearly empty, and the bark of vendors seemed muted despite the clear air. What bandits they did pass glared at them with open hostility, and it was clear that the Marshal's protection of them was reaching its end.

Once they reached the hotel, the agents went straight to the roof to discuss their next move. The bandit guards' presence on the exterior wall and rooftops had increased significantly in just a few hours, and the agents grew increasingly uncomfortable under their watchful eyes.

"Well, what the bloody hell do we do now?" Kitty asked as she leaned against the wall next to the roof access, arms folded and an unlit cigarette dangling from her lips.

Mohan leaned on the railing and gazed in the general direction of the Marshal's palace. When he finally spoke, it was with restrained anger. "We find a way to wipe that smug grin off the Marshal's face, that's what. Vicki, did you repack that sample?"

The bullfrog sat on a dilapidated beach chair with her long legs crossed. "You bet. Managed to scrounge up another ice box and get some real ice to keep it cool; should last a few days easy."

Mohan nodded. "We're not going to be here that long."

"You can say that again," General Durram said as he stepped onto the roof. The old turtle looked hunched and weary like a great weight rested on his shell. "But whatever we do, we must consider our plan very carefully."

"What news, General?" Mohan asked.

The elderly turtle sat in a chair with a sigh, and Ric noted the old scars that crisscrossed his tough shell. "I received word from Hunter TS Five and their recon work in Kalegos." He recounted what happened on the *Resthoven*, the hidden moonpool, and the clean-up crew that stole the ship.

"So it's gone then?" Mohan asked when he had finished.

"Vanished like a ghost," Durram said.

"What about al-Seif," Kitty asked.

"Holed up in his villa in Pacé Acqua. Hasn't budged an inch, although he recently met with Yursa De Palma." He shifted forward and clasped his hands together, resting his elbows on his knees. "I'm sorry to be the bearer of such unsatisfying news, but we have more pressing concerns now. I take it you noticed the bandits are keeping a much closer eye on us now."

"Indeed," Zed said. "I assume the Marshal does not intend for us to leave?"

Durram nodded. "Correct, but that's not the half of it. Xereas intercepted a message from one of al-Seif's lieutenants. It appears he's pretty pissed that we've been meddling in his affairs. He wants the Marshal to see that we're out of the picture permanently.

"As if that wasn't enough, it looks like the Marshal has even more incentive to rub us out." He scratched absently at the weathered scales on his head, which bore the stripes of his Tiger's Mark. "There's a report out of Kairan that two military convoys are prepping to leave the city even as we speak. The larger one is headed for Meshim to bolster the nation's ground forces. They'll have a hella time pushing back the Barjans, but logistics were never easy in this charming little corner of the world. Things are going to get real popular over there."

"I take it the other convoy is heading here," Ric said.

The general nodded slowly. "This valley is still rich in natural resources, and waging war is expensive. We suspect they'll try to take back the city and get that dam

435

up to full power again. Hell, if they upgrade it with modern improvements, they could feed power to half the nation without relying on the oil fields in Dhamaq or Abaat-Khan."

Kitty and Rizzo swore, and Mohan rubbed his chin thoughtfully.

"So much for the Marshal's allies in Kairran," Vince said drily.

"Indeed," Zed said.

Ric gazed out at the city. "The bandits will fight. They're too independent to bow to government forces."

"And they'll lose," General Durram said with a shrug. "They have the strength to control this valley, but the military won't underestimate them like they did decades ago. Not this time."

"What will happen to them?" the journalist asked, meaning the bandits.

"Most likely, any survivors will be conscripted and sent to fight in the desert. If any escape, they'll probably just go on with life like they used to."

Ric smiled mirthlessly. "These aren't exactly the kind of people who take orders from anyone. Well, except maybe the Marshal."

"Cannon fodder," Rizzo said. "Those bastard royalists pulled the same stunt in Neuf Maris during the revolution. Put the undesirables on the front lines and leave your best troops to defend more strategic targets."

"But there's still the issue of control," Ric pointed out.

"The heroin," Vicki said. "Maybe al-Seif's botanists added something besides growth hormones and heightened potency?"

Rizzo arched an eyebrow. "Like something to make them more malleable?"

Ric almost laughed. "Mind control through heroin? What the hell, I'll add it to the list of all the other insane things I've seen in the past few days."

Mohan wasn't smiling. "I've seen stranger. But Vicki might be on to something. A doped-up bandit is much less resistant than a sober one."

Kitty lit her cigarette. "I seriously doubt Hassan will waste his cut on doping bandits," she said.

General Durram coughed. "As amusing as this conversation is, perhaps we should get back to—"

He was interrupted as Rosa scrambled through the door. The koala's large brown eyes were even wider with concern. "General! We've just heard that the *Alqarmizi Alhulm* has been sighted in the city!"

"*Mon Déesse!*" Rizzo breathed.

Everyone but Ric mirrored her sentiment.

"The Scarlet Dream," he translated. "Another competitor like the Foresight?"

Mohan unholstered his pistol, checked the chambers, and scanned the nearby rooftops with renewed intensity. "They're a particularly nasty bunch;

437

Tiger's Stripe has had to tussle with them on several occasions when working in Estan."

"Did al-Seif send them?"

"Probably not directly. Al-Seif has connections with Regent Hassan, who has been known to use them as his own personal hit squad, but officially, they're almost on our level."

"So technically, they don't exist." The journalist nodded in understanding. "And even if al-Seif called in a favour, he probably doesn't rate high enough in the spy game to know about them."

"He catches on quick." Vince grinned.

"Well, not entirely," Ric said. "If al-Seif didn't send them, why are they here?"

"Someone's been hunting us ever since Kairran," Mohan answered. "We thought we could shake them here; obviously, we were wrong. General, whatever plan you came up with to get us out, I think it's time we used it."

"We were only waiting for you to get back," the turtle said, and he rose from his seat. "The plan was to wait for the bandits' nightly revelry to kick in, but I don't think we have that much time now. However, with the bandits packing on extra guards, we'll have a hella time getting through the front gate."

"What about the Warren on the east end?" Vince asked.

"Same problem, but we may not have a choice; however, I wouldn't wish that escape route on the bandits themselves." Durram shook his head.

"What's in there, anyway?" Ric asked.

"Everything," Mohan replied. "Large predators, carnivorous plants, maybe even a fiend if that haze over the centre is any indication. But that isn't the half of it. You know how the bandits are the outcasts of civilized society? Well, the Warren is home to the outcasts of the outcasts, the half-feral Wildmen."

Ric needed no further explanation. Becoming a bandit was one thing, but losing one's mind and becoming feral was the worst fear of every rational Hom-An, civilized and bandit alike. However, feral power was intoxicating. To completely abandon the chains of civilization and run free, even as a beast, was a constant temptation for bandits and gladiators.

"It's also a literal maze of ancient structures," Mohan continued. "Not exactly a piece of piss to get through, day or night. But if we don't leave now, I don't think we'll be leaving at all."

Durram nodded. "I'll spread the word. Meet up at the motor pool in an hour, and let's hope to God even that isn't too long."

They all exited the roof and went to gather their belongings. Ric had only his backpack, and he waited by the door as Mohan and Kitty swept up their baggage and cleared the room of any trace they had been there. In moments, they were ready to leave.

"You're not going to fall apart on us, right?" Kitty said as she passed. "You kept it together pretty well fighting the Frankenbeast; be a shame if you bolted now."

The journalist raised an eyebrow. "Um, thank you?"

"She's right," Mohan said. "You've been through a lot in just a few days, but you've got a level head on your shoulders."

"Well, I still don't exactly know your expectations," Ric said. "Unless this has all been some kind of elaborate test?"

The tiger gave him a reassuring grin. "She'll be right, mate. We've been in tougher scrapes before."

"No, we haven't," Kitty called over her shoulder.

They met the others in the lobby, and together, they pushed out into the street, which had partially recovered some of the everyday hustle and bustle of its chaotic life.

Several minutes after they left, another figure, clad head to foot in black biker leathers and helmet, entered the lobby from the rear entrance. The weasel clerk jerked his head in the direction of the departed agents and held out a hand.

Instead of a wad of carams, the figure produced a silenced pistol and put two bullets in the clerk. Then he turned and vanished into the crowded streets.

33 – Escape from Jar-Geshim

The guard on the gate was double its regular contingent, and more than half had their attention focused inside rather than out. The tattooed gorilla, Rahkim, was in command, and he paced heavily back and forth across the top of the gate arch, occasionally casting a hateful gaze towards the motor pool.

He stood up a little straighter when he noticed many agents entering the warehouse but not returning. When Mohan and his team entered the courtyard, the gorilla quickly disappeared into the gatehouse. The agents didn't need a psychic to guess he was calling the Marshal.

Preparations for their escape had been in the works from the moment the first team was shown through the gates. Ric remembered that the agents initially arrived in small groups with several vehicles, and their escape convoy would consist of only a fraction of them: the beat-up and surprisingly reliable Tracksman Hiker and four lighter diesel trucks. The trucks were designed for cargo transport, and while the open driver's cabin was armour-plated on the sides, only low wooden panels with canvas tops protected the rear bed.

Looking at them now, Ric finally understood what the agents had been doing when they arrived several days ago. Each truck was fitted with a crude suit of armour scavenged from the panels of the other vehicles and a few thin metal sheets the agents found stacked in a back corner of the garage. The plating on the transports was much lighter than what was on the Hiker, and Ric wasn't sure how much protection it would offer against the bandits' automatic weapons, but it was better than nothing. The agents had stripped the remaining vehicles of any useful parts or identifying marks and rendered them inoperable; with luck, this would help them avoid a chase no matter which route they took. The bandits had their own vehicles, of course, but they clearly didn't use them inside the city.

Ric had noted on their first day that Mohan and the Scrappers were the only ones with heavier firearms, the other agents having little more than pistols and blades at their disposal. They had tried to fix this during the Scrappers' absence, but the bandits' open hostility towards them had made making a deal for weapons almost impossible. Once the bandits started shooting, it would be up to the Scrappers to bear the brunt of the attack and protect their more vulnerable companions.

They refuelled with whatever they could find; diesel was in short supply since the bandits primarily used methane engines. Hopefully, it would be enough to escape the jungle and make it to their rendezvous in southern Pytan.

Despite their need for urgency, the sun was approaching noon before all the remaining agents gathered, and they were ready to leave.

The last to arrive was Seer Xereas, followed by a short rhesus macaque with a chipped ear and a lanky hornbill; the bright orange casque on the latter's head curved upwards, almost comically resembling a rhino horn. Xereas introduced them as Naji and Awiti, respectively, the other agents he had been working with in Jar-Geshim. Each carried a cloth-wrapped bundle and a smaller parcel of personal items.

"I do not suppose you have room for three more?" the wasp rasped.

General Durram nodded soberly.

"What about your mission here?" Ric asked. "Will anyone pick up after you're gone?"

An insect's expressions are difficult to read unless you know how, but from his slumped shoulders and the tilt of his head, it was easy to see the wasp felt as if a great burden had finally been relieved. "Our work is finished. If things cool off, we may return, but for now…we spent ten years in this, pardon the expression, shithole. These are not exactly the kinds of people you make friends with."

"So why were you here?" the journalist asked.

Xereas turned and gestured out the warehouse door as Awiti closed it. "Many people from many walks of life end up in a city like this. Some are political exiles; some just don't want to live under the thumb of an oppressive government. But they aren't made for the chaos and anarchy of bandit life, even if they somehow survive it. Our goal was to find those weary souls and try to get them somewhere where they could live peaceful and productive lives.

"A day may come when the bandits are all but extinct. The Marshal didn't know it, but what he established here was the first step towards teaching these vagabonds how to value something other than their own personal gain. We still don't know where he came from; he keeps his past close to his chest. Something happened to him many years ago that drove him away from the WUK. He never talks about it, but it inspired him to try to find order in chaos.

"They've got a long way to go, but Jar-Geshim may yet become a respectable city and the Warren reclaimed. I just don't think we will be here to see it."

He turned back to Ric. "I must confess we are not loathed to leave them now. We are agents of Tiger's Stripe, and ten years is too long to spend apart from your roots."

The journalist thought he understood, though, after his own experience on the streets of Jar-Geshim, he was curious to meet a bandit who might be reformed.

The large bundles the faux bandits carried turned out to be small caches of carbines. There were only enough to assign two per truck and very little ammunition, but it was a welcome boost to their meagre arsenal.

"So, we are going to shoot our way out of this," Ric said flatly.

Mohan glanced towards Kitty, but the tigress was too far away to hear them. "Yes," the elder Katral answered. "It's going to be kill or be killed now. Believe me, I wish we weren't in that situation, but the bandits won't give us that option. Can you do it?"

The journalist hesitated, which seemed to answer the tiger. He gave the lynx's shoulder a reassuring shake before moving away.

They loaded six agents to a truck, with Mohan and his Scrappers taking on two extras in the Hiker. Xereas and his companions offered to take command of the first truck behind them, and the other Tiger's Stripe leaders dispersed between the remaining vehicles: Mümtaz in the second, Caz in the third, and General Durram rode shotgun in the fourth with Rosa.

All of the drivers acknowledged they were ready. It was now or never. The extraction specialists had built all their plans around what they knew of the bandits' strengths and weaknesses, but the addition of the Scarlet Dream had thrown almost all of that out the window. They knew where their exits were, but now their very lives depended on the element of surprise and a lot of luck.

And it all went to hell as soon as Mohan jammed his foot on the accelerator and burst through the garage door.

Mohan heard the first sniper's bullet *pang* off the Hiker's armoured panels harmlessly, but a glance in the rear-view mirror revealed that a second round struck the agent riding shotgun next to Xereas in the open cab of the first truck.

The shots had not come from the gate or guard barracks as they had expected but from one of the ramshackle buildings overlooking the courtyard. An RPG round soon followed, erupting centimetres in front of the Hiker. Mohan yanked hard on the wheel to careen around the crater left by the blast. Another sniper attempted to pick off Rosa in the fourth truck, but she swerved at the last moment, and the bullet shattered the driver's side mirror.

Bandits were notoriously clumsy, disorganised, and blunt in their approach to combat, especially when they tried to launch a surprise attack. These strikes were too meticulous, too well-timed. In those first tense moments, the agents of Tiger's Stripe knew who had hit them first.

"Shit!" Kitty growled, her ears flattening against her head. "It's the Scarlet Dream."

Mohan gripped the wheel with grim determination. "Should have guessed as much. Once in the city, they probably watched the motor pool like a sevviks."

To Ric's surprise, Kitty unslung her rifle and aimed out the shattered side-door window, bracing herself against the inside panel. She compensated for the motion of the Hiker, let out a slow breath, and squeezed the trigger.

The *crack* of the rifle was deafening in the confines of the exploration vehicle, but as the journalist looked in the direction she was aiming, he saw a figure topple from the balcony of one of the shacks. It was a short-lived victory. The bandits were not as surprised by the agents' desperate ploy as they had hoped, and they began peppering the convoy with small arms fire from the gate.

Mohan wished the Frankenbeast hadn't blown out the glass, but the Hiker's thick panels took the brunt of the onslaught. Zed offered a little more protection by activating his bracer's shield. However, it required a great deal of concentration and manipulation on the badger's part; forming a dome was simple, but creating a barrier to the dimensions of the front windows was not.

The lighter armour protecting the vehicles trailing behind them proved less effective. Two more agents fell as they returned fire, and it rapidly became clear that, between the Scarlet Dream and the bandits, they would never make it through the city's main gate.

Mohan cut the wheel sharply to the right, veering towards the gap between the wall and the city's outer buildings. He gave three pulls on the Hiker's air horn, and the trucks behind him acknowledged with two horn blasts. They would follow his lead, and he saw only one path before them.

Ric ducked involuntarily as bullets peppered the thick roof of the Hiker. "Where do we go now?" He shouted over the din.

"Only one place to go," the tiger answered calmly. "We're gonna push through the Warren."

As with most ancient fortifications, the outer row of buildings was reasonably spaced from the wall, but that still left little room for the broad exploration vehicle. Ric winced each time they scraped against a wall or rumbled over a dustbin. Fortunately, these back alleys weren't heavily populated, and those citizens they did encounter dived back into the doorways from which they had come.

Mohan knew it was only a matter of time before they hit an obstacle the vehicle's raw power couldn't overcome. As they rounded the curve of the alley, that obstacle appeared as an outlying building constructed right up against the city wall. The tiger cut a sharp right turn, smashing his way down the next closest lane. As the Hiker bounced against the far wall, the driver's side mirror tore from its mounting with a crash of glass. It had survived the escape from Kairran, the gripping vines of the jungle, and the wrath of a Frankenbeast, but fate had finally decreed that it would join its opposite number. Vince was too busy keeping tabs on their pursuit to make more quips about the security deposit.

This alley felt even narrower than the one they had just left. As the buildings began to close around them, Ric silently prayed that they wouldn't wedge themselves between the walls like some horrible slapstick comedy. At least the gunfire had eased up, and the journalist looked over his shoulder to see the trucks carrying their companions doggedly trailing behind. Their canvas tops were shredded, and the makeshift armour was riddled with large bullet holes. He couldn't tell how many they had lost in the initial assault, but they were mercifully out of the guard's range.

He became aware of a faint buzzing sound echoing off the walls around them. Unconsciously, he rubbed his head, remembering the attack in the alley just days ago—Vicki had cleared him to remove the bandages that morning. He checked the sky above them, half expecting to see a legion of flying insects ready to drop another hovel on top of them, but the air was clear. As the noise grew louder, a mechanical rattle became more prominent, and the pitch seemed to rise and fall regularly. He knew that sound: the whine of dirt bikes.

They appeared across from the agents as the convoy entered a wide intersection. There were seven of them, and immediately, it was obvious the riders were not garden-variety bandits.

The drivers—four male and three female—wore padded black leathers and black helmets with blacked-out visors hiding their faces. Ric could identify a mix of goats, felines and canines from the tails, the helmet-ears, and horns protruding from the costumes. Each bike had a pair of long, curved scimitars mounted behind the rider, and each rider brandished a compact sub-machinegun in gloved hands. Each had a blood-red silk scarf tied around the left arm.

Agents of the Scarlet Dream.

They charged forward, and the occupants of the Hiker ducked as a fresh burst of gunfire peppered the convoy—Zed's shield kept them from any real danger. Mohan cut a sharp left, and they heard a satisfying thunk as the lead attacker collided against the rear panel. The glancing blow sent the canine biker careening towards a fruit stand, but he braked hard and prevented himself from crashing into it.

Ric saw their hotel zoom past and realised the convoy had somehow wound up on one of Jar-Geshim's main streets. They didn't have to worry about getting stuck between buildings anymore, but the pedestrian traffic had increased dramatically. Mohan pulled on the horn, and the people scattered in fright, diving for the cover of the nearest alcove or shop.

Glancing out the rear window, Ric could see the bikers weaving between the trucks behind them, trading gunfire and blows with the barely protected agents following them. He saw one attacker go down, thanks to the rifles provided by Xereas, and he felt a grim twinge of satisfaction.

It didn't last long; another attacker—goat horns poking through his helmet—sent a hail of bullets their way, and Ric heard a soft grunt as something warm splashed his face. The prairie dog agent beside him slumped in his seat, a pool of red spreading on his shoulder. Vicki tended to him immediately, bracing herself against the centre table as the Hiker bounced along.

Behind them, Xereas swerved to the right and clipped their attacker's rear wheel, sending him flying into a market stand. Ric heard Vince give a grim chuckle, satisfied by the display of wood splinters and feathered skull fetishes flying everywhere.

The journalist watched as another assailant sprayed the third truck with bullets, and another agent went down. At the rear of the convoy, a biker managed to clip Rosa, and her vehicle began to slow.

While her companions helplessly watched the fourth truck fall behind, Kitty saw another biker coming up on the driver's side of the Hiker. With no side mirrors and all his focus on avoiding the pedestrians in front of him, Mohan couldn't see the danger approaching. It was time to bring the fight to them, and it only took her a split second to decide a course of action.

Ric turned at the sudden rush of air and saw the tigress's feet and tail disappear onto the roof of the Hiker from the passenger side; Rizzo closed the door behind her without a word.

Once on the roof, Kitty drew a knife from an ankle sheath and waited, staying low to avoid the assailant's attention. The goat-horned biker—a female this time—sped up towards the driver's window and raised her SMG, but she never got off a shot as Kitty deftly leapt onto the bike behind her.

The goat struggled to balance against the sudden additional weight, attempting to butt her attacker off with her horns even as Kitty's momentum sent them to the ground. The biker was dead before her body tumbled to a stop, Kitty's knife having found purchase between her ribs.

The tigress wasted no time picking up the bike as Xereas's truck rumbled past her. She pointed it toward her beleaguered colleagues and kicked the engine to life.

Only two Scarlet Dream agents barred her path.

The first was hovering around the second convoy truck. In a single swift motion, Kitty drew a sword from one of the sheathes with her left hand and swung. The head of the biker parted from his shoulders cleanly, sending the bike crashing into a storefront as the body of its rider tumbled to the ground. A leopard head rolled out of the severed helmet.

Kitty wasn't so lucky with the second assailant, who was busy assaulting the third truck. Seeing the coming counterattack, the Scarlet Dream agent swiftly raised her arm to deflect the blow as the white tigress came roaring towards her. The blade clanged against a metal plate sewn into the padded leather jacket, stopping further injury but throwing both riders off balance.

Kitty gritted her teeth at the pain and dropped the blade from her throbbing hand, downshifting and applying deft pressure to the brakes to steady the bike. She recovered before she could career into a stand loaded with knives and similar sharp instruments. With a low growl, she looked over her shoulder briefly to check on her opponent.

The biker might have recovered if she hadn't swerved closer to the truck she had been attacking. Caz reached out from the rear bed and grabbed her around the throat with one giant bear paw, lifting her bodily off the dirt bike. The helmet came off to reveal a calico tabby, her eyes burning with defiant hatred. The burly brown bear roared in her face and gave one violent shake, snapping the biker's neck like a twig. With another roar, he tossed the lifeless thug away, and the corpse crashed into a pile of refuse stacked outside a bar.

Kitty gave the agent a thumbs up and continued to the last truck, which had almost stopped and now trailed the convoy significantly.

Two bikers, both canines with cropped ears protruding from their helmets, assailed the agents inside. But it appeared both parties had run out of ammunition; one biker had drawn his sword, hacking away at the agents in the truck bed. The other attempted to do the same, but one of the Tiger's Stripe agents tossed a small axe into his chest, and he crumpled to the ground.

Two agents lay dead in the rear bed, and the others were trying to assist the stricken driver, who was clutching a bleeding arm. General Durram attempted to keep the wheel steady from the passenger's seat as Rosa bravely tried to keep pressure on the accelerator, but the koala was weak from blood loss.

The remaining biker circled the truck like a hungry shark, striking out any time the agents exposed themselves and using his superior mobility to keep out of the agents' reach. He was not paying attention when Kitty rode into his path and rammed the second sword from her bike through his face mask.

Kitty braked and made a sharp U-turn. She took a quick mental count of the bikers she had seen fall. The lead bike, the one Mohan had clipped with the Hiker, was still missing.

The remainder of the convoy was approaching the city's main plaza and the Marshal's palace, beyond which lay the bridge-dam and the gates of the Warren. If they were going to escape, they had to do it together. Even at that distance, Kitty could see the forms of dozens of bandits flooding the square, attempting to cut off their retreat; they needed to close the distance fast.

Kitty came up next to the driver's side of the general's truck; it was a Locke model, so that meant the righthand side. By now, the vehicle was rolling along at a walking pace.

"Where'd the last one go?" she asked.

General Durram shook his head.

The agents in the rear helped the injured Rosa out of her seat, and the turtle took her place. The Hiker and the remaining trucks entered the square, and they could hear a voice shouting angrily over the loudspeaker; the Marshal was clearly not amused with their little stunt.

The general accelerated to catch up, but Kitty paused momentarily, scanning the nearby alleys for an ambush she knew had to be there.

Suddenly, she heard the whine of an engine above her. The seventh and final biker came crashing down from the roof of a low building just behind her, curved sword in hand. She dived to her left and drew her pistol in the same movement, firing in the direction of her attacker. His blow severed her bike in two near the rear wheel, narrowly missing the tip of her tail as she rolled away.

The biker landed hard, nearly throwing himself from his bike, but the canine managed to hold on with skill and determination to rival the tigress's own. He spun the back wheel towards her, kicking up dirt and temporarily blinding her. Then, he turned and popped the front tire off the ground, attempting to smash her, but Kitty rolled behind a market stand. She fired wildly as she furiously tried to wipe the dirt from her eyes.

When she could see again, she reloaded and leapt up, but her attacker was already speeding away from her—and away from the convoy.

She roared with rage, and the white-gold-plated .357 semiautomatic thundered as she fired round after round, her target ducking and weaving as he sped away. Pottery and glass shattered in the wake of her rapidly retreating target until, with a sharp *click*, the slide locked open.

"Shit!" she breathed.

She had allowed herself to lose count of her ammo in her rage. Now she stood in the middle of the street, completely exposed. The biker revved his engine and pulled a sharp turn to face her less than thirty metres away.

And just stood there.

Another biker rode up next to him—the goat-horned male Xereas had sent into the market stand. Kitty crouched low, ready to dive away from the coming charge. She could see a faint trickle of blood dribbling down the canine leader's right arm.

Got you, bastard! She thought, and a slow, satisfied smile pricked the corners of her mouth as she waited, tensed.

The other rider raised his submachine gun to fire, but the leader held up a hand to stop him. He touched the blood spreading across his arm and looked at his stained fingers. Then he rose slightly from his seat, gave a short bow, and sped off down the alleyway. His companion hesitated, then followed.

34 – Bloodlust

Kitty felt her blood freeze. She had seen that exact gesture before, delivered by a tall, thin canine on the back of a fleeing speedboat. Her thoughts returned to the chase through Kairran's black market. She saw the tipping flower cart, the face of someone long dead flashing in the curtain of daisies. A flood of emotions swept over her.

She didn't know how long she stood there frozen, but the next thing she knew, someone was shaking her by the arm.

"Agent eight! Lieutenant, snap out of it! Agent Katral?"

Was Vince playing name games again? So many titles. Do they mean anything?

She glanced dazedly at the speaker, but it wasn't Vince. It was one of the agents from the fourth truck, a mouse.

Do I even know his name?

Her mind was still fuzzy. She blinked to clear it and found that General Durram had backed the truck up to get her. The Hiker and the other three trucks had already cleared the plaza and were fast approaching the sealed gates of the Warren. A sea of the Marshal's thugs was beginning to fill the gap between them; they would not make it through without more casualties.

The torrent of emotions began to melt away, leaving only one: fury.

"I need another bike," she said, her voice deathly calm.

She strode purposefully towards the dirt bike belonging to the rider she had impaled and waved for the general to keep going. Moments later, she was racing past them again, sword drawn and pistol reloaded.

When she was sixteen, she had scored her first Hom-An kill, a bandit who had ambushed one of her uncle's transport convoys on the infamous Rummer run. The incident had awoken something inside her, a quiet, cold voice that somehow knew all the crimes the bandit had committed and explained them to her in excruciating detail. It made it easy to pull the trigger.

She felt that voice returning.

There is a dark place buried in the hearts of all Hom-Ans. A place where the lust for blood and the desire for survival clouds all judgment and reason, even in the most docile of species. A place where the animal within takes control.

For most people living within the safety of walled cities, suppressing this instinct has become a subconscious act, allowing society to live civilly together. Many didn't even know they were capable of unleashing such feral power, and those who did were quickly shunned and removed.

Al-Seif's gladiators understood this bloodlust; mastering it was their reason for living. The bandits understood it; they exploited it for their own selfish gain. The Marshal understood it; he maintained his power by keeping it in check. But enough was enough, and these interlopers would pay; now, his little empire was in jeopardy. He allowed his followers to gather in the square, whipping them into a frenzy and preparing them to unleash the beast from its slumber.

They were not expecting one of the outsiders to do the same.

Kitty descended upon the bandit horde with a roar fuelled by fury and suppressed grief. Most of them focused on the fleeing Hiker, and the white tigress tore into their flanks like a whirlwind, the razor edge of her scimitar severing limbs and bathing the courtyard in fresh blood. She had transformed into a fabled black knight, and the dirt bike was her fearsome steed; everywhere she turned, a wake of death followed.

This one murdered ten people yesterday for scraps of food. That one is a rapist from Det who now deals in narcotics. She murdered her own children by tossing them over the dam. He raped and murdered a whole family during a recent raid.

One after the other, the cold voice egged her on, a countless litany of criminals who fled from the hands of Justice. But Vengeance had come for them, and the white tigress was the executioner.

The agents in the truck behind her watched in fascinated horror as she practically danced from one cluster of goons to the next. She was so fast the bandits couldn't seem to touch her; they would raise their weapons to strike, only to find she was behind them — and they no longer had arms to raise.

Her companions recovered from their shock long enough to retrieve some of the weapons dropped by Kitty's victims. As she swept through the bandit hordes, they moved in behind her, protecting her flank.

She was only one lone fighter against dozens, but something supernatural seemed to give her strength and speed beyond anything the bandits had ever seen. Less than a third of them carried firearms, but this living devil moved so fast that they couldn't track her, and they fired wildly into their own crowd. The Tiger's Mark on Kitty's arm and chest burned with an intensity she had never felt before as she dashed first one way and then the other, the blade in her hand rising and falling among her enemies like a reaper's scythe.

Near the central bonfire, a stocky boar tried to halt her advance with a charge of his own. She leapt off the bike, hurtling herself over the boar's head and into the unfortunate huddle of feathered bandits trying to advance behind him. The tigress slashed through the four of them with a single blow, then twisted the blade and jabbed it behind her to impale the boar as he whirled to face her. She pivoted on her heel, grabbed the blade's handle with both hands and yanked it free of the still-standing corpse, using the blade's momentum to cleave through a leopard and a gecko who strayed too close to the fray.

Murderer. Rapist. Drug peddler. Serial abuser. The cold voice echoed in her mind.

General Durram and the last truck pulled forward as she picked up the bike and raced ahead to the next unfortunate bandit troupe. In this manner, they pushed through the horde, Kitty clearing the path ahead and the truck rolling over the bloody ground behind.

At the gates to the Warren, Mohan brought the escape convoy to a halt. Rizzo and Zed climbed out and headed for the small shack that housed the gate controls, and the rest provided covering fire.

The guards offered little resistance, and soon, the thick chains fell to the ground, and the heavy steel doors began to creep open. The only thing left to do was wait for the last truck.

Mohan leaned out the window to look back towards the courtyard. His jaw dropped as he saw the bloodbath his daughter was wreaking through the ranks of the vagabond hordes. His grandparents had taught him many family legends, and many more were on his wife's side. White tigers were something of an omen for both the Katral and Ruo-Shang lines, but he had tried to ignore that when Kitty was born. Now, he was witnessing one of those legends become manifest.

His anger flared suddenly, and the Tiger's Mark on his back burned; this was exactly the situation he had hoped to avoid by keeping Kitty at a desk in the Sanctuary. He swore and struck the interior roof hard enough to pound one of the dents back out. He was about to climb out and march into the fray himself when the fighting seemed to stop abruptly.

"Stand down!" the Marshal's voice roared over the loudspeaker. "That's enough! Let them pass."

Kitty and the last truck had reached the foot of the bridge-dam, and the thin line of bandits guarding it melted to the sides as ordered.

Kitty paused astride the dirt bike as the truck drove on past her. She and the vehicle were soaked in blood; red stained every exposed patch of her body-fur. Crimson droplets snaked down her blade, and the nearest bandits flinched as she gave it a violent shake to get the blood off.

The Marshal appeared on the balcony of his palace overlooking the carnage. "You really are some vicious, cold-hearted bastards, Stripey. More like us than you want to admit, but have it your way. You want out? Go! With any luck, the Warren will get you in the end. I hear that bug-eyed freak Xereas was one of yours, along with some of his friends. Shame, I almost liked him as an adviser. If any of your kind ever step paw in my valley again, they're dead."

"A whole city couldn't take thirty of us," Vince mumbled. "Imagine how much damage just one could do."

Ric looked at him and raised an eyebrow. "I think that's supposed to work the other way around."

Mohan growled low in his throat, "He hasn't got a bloody clue."

General Durram and Kitty drove up next to them; Ric noticed Kitty refused to look her father in the eye. However, she did look at him, and the haunted look he saw behind those cold blue eyes chilled him to the bone.

"We should move before he changes his mind," General Durram said.

Mohan nodded. "How many did you lose?"

"Taylor and Jensen. Rosa, Duke, and Korshev are injured, but they'll make it. Guess I'm the only one who somehow didn't get a scratch." He tapped the side of his hard shell. "How about you?"

"Solomons took one in the shoulder; otherwise, everyone in the Hiker is accounted for." He paused to take a breath. "We lost Kahlil, Jacobs, and Tunin in the initial attack. Griggs, Karloff, and De'Naren carked it when we broke through the plaza. Wallas was winged, but he'll make it."

The general shook his head. "Too many. Far too many. We'll regroup once we get through the gate. We don't want the Marshal thinking we changed our minds."

Eight dead and five wounded. That left twenty able bodies to face the Warren.

Mohan and his Scrappers established a rearguard while the trucks drove through the partially opened gates. When they were safely through, he sent Kitty ahead on her dirt bike, ordered everyone back on board the Hiker, and followed.

It was nearly a half hour before one of the bandits gathered enough courage to approach the gatehouse and reseal the gates. They would have remained open longer if the fear of what lay beyond that massive steel portal hadn't overcome their fear of the bloody angel of death who had just passed through them.

35 – The Warren

Immediately on the other side of the bridge were the remains of a once-grand public park. Over time, creeping jungle vegetation had reclaimed it, the trees hoary with hanging moss and vines. The waist-high grass had nearly obliterated the ancient stone paths, leaving a carpet of green everywhere.

A listening silence settled over the agents of Tiger's Stripe, and even with the late afternoon sun high overhead, the ancient city seemed wrapped in deep shadow. There was an unwholesome feeling in the air, \ as if some primordial evil had draped its withering shroud over the crumbling ruins.

At the centre of the park, still within sight of the gate, a broad circle of mossy paved stones had managed to escape the relentless march of the jungle grass. A long rectangular pool dominated the centre, stretching out before them like a marker pointing the way deeper into the ruin. They parked the caravan near the water's edge, and they all got out to stretch their legs and catch their breath.

Gargoylish fountains perched on the outer rim of the pool. The twisted statues bore a disturbing resemblance to many Hom-An species but in bestial quadrupedal forms. Ric tried to tell himself they were just caricatures of rix, dolvag, bolvins, or bahngers. However, the facial features were so unlike those familiar wild beasts that he discarded the thought almost immediately.

The thought was so disturbing he turned his attention to the ancient waterworks and what kept the fountains functioning. He wondered if perhaps the Marshal kept it going to serve as a staging ground for the victims he threw to the Warren.

Last water for the rest of your life, he thought grimly.

Several of the fountains were broken, and they sent showers away from the pool. Ric watched as Kitty parked under one and began to wash the blood from her fur.

There were so many strange and deadly things to see in the world, but seeing someone give in to the inner animal was one you never wanted to experience. History was rife with stories of great battles where the ancient bloodlust had caused acts of unspeakable violence and tragedy, decimating the bloodlines of families and even causing the extinction of entire species.

The feral nature of the bloodlust made him think of the grotesque fountainheads. Perhaps the ancient builders were more in tune with a bestial ancestry that modern civilisation had long forgotten. Observing the statues again, he wondered if that was honestly such a bad thing.

He was so lost in thought that he didn't realise Kitty had stripped off her shirt, heedless of the mixed company, and begun wringing the blood from it. He turned away, embarrassed, but not before his eyes got a good look at the Tiger's Mark covering her left breast. Mohan's cryptic words, spoken nearly a week ago in the journalist's hotel room in Kairran, echoed back to him: the Tiger's Mark always takes the form of a full tiger's face.

Like the one on her father, Kitty's birthmark seemed to push her stripes aside so the face stood out among the tangle of black squiggles. There appeared to be a little bleed-off down her side, but Ric could clearly see the two halves of the Tiger's Mark come together when she held her left arm down. It almost looked like someone had taped her arm to her side and taken a giant stamp to both arm and chest, leaving the excess ink to run down between her arm and torso. The sudden cartoonish image elicited an involuntary chuckle, which he quickly stifled.

"Somethin' funny?"

He turned and saw Vince looking at him with a peculiar expression. Gone were the jovial banter and wistful smile. Instead, he looked stern, even protective, like a brother who had just caught the neighbourhood peeping Tom looking at his sister.

"No, sorry. I was thinking about the mark, actually," Ric said, holding up his marked forearm, but the hare's expression didn't change. "Not her mark! Just…I meant no disrespect."

"Want me to pull my pants down and show you mine?" Vince slapped his right leg. His tone was still serious, but it had lost a little of the accusatory edge.

"Don't up yourself, Vince," Mohan said as he strode over. "We all know it's not that impressive."

Now, the playboy attitude reappeared, and Vince feigned a hurt expression. "That's not what that cute otter doe said the other night."

"I walked right into that one." Mohan sighed. He rested a massive paw on Ric's shoulder, and the journalist was suddenly very conscious of how much taller and broader the tiger was than him.

"Just let it go, mate," Mohan said. "The Mark is a curious thing. Even after three thousand years, we don't fully understand it. Right now, we're all in the shit and no mistake. And we're not out of it yet."

The tiger's calm response mildly surprised the journalist. He had expected to have his head removed for such a breach of the tigress's privacy, especially

469

when he noticed that the other agents had respectfully avoided looking in Kitty's direction until she had finished cleaning up and put on a fresh pair of clothes.

That brought to mind something else. Ever since Ric joined the company, he had noticed the easy camaraderie the agents shared. In many ways, they acted much like a family, as opposed to a secret army tasked with hunting monsters.

The ease with which he had become a part of them surprised him. Ever since the room in Kairran, Mohan and his Scrappers had treated him as if he was already a colleague, even when reminding him he wasn't officially an agent yet. And Ric had seen nothing to indicate that this wasn't perfectly normal.

Given al-Seif's criminal empire, Jar-Geshim, the Frankenbeast, and the assault by the Scarlet Dream, the journalist was starting to understand what they meant about the world resting on the edge of a knife. He also thought he understood how easily the scales could topple to one side or the other.

But there were still so many unanswered questions. He had barely scratched the surface of just how hard Tiger's Stripe worked to maintain the balance.

How can I even begin to tell such a story? Ric thought, and then another occurred to him. *Should I even tell it?*

Despite his desire to learn the truth, he had never fully believed in the precedent that the public had a right to know everything. His father had been killed because information had been kept from him; perhaps more would have died had it been freely known.

He shook his head to clear it. Right now, he should focus on surviving to make that decision later. Whatever his ultimate destiny with this strange group, he was damn well sure he would live to see it through.

He felt a peculiar tingle in his birthmark that told him maybe he had made the right choice. The thought made him feel better.

While Ric was pondering these revelations, Mohan approached his daughter.

"Will you be all right?" he asked, genuine concern reflecting on his face.

Kitty let out a shuddering breath and nodded.

The huge tiger paused a moment. "Do you understand now? Understand why it's so important not to take vengeance into our own hands?"

She turned her back to him. "What's done is done," she said with cold finality. "They would have done the same to us given the chance."

"We don't know that," her father attempted to argue. Then he stopped himself. "OK, yes, we do, but we should never assume that, even from bandits. What we do, what we're capable of, it's in our blood. It's the strength behind the Tiger's Mark. In some ways, it borders on the super-Hom-An. That's why we take such great pains to minimise casualties. It's as much to protect ourselves as to protect the general populace."

She faced him directly, traces of cold fury still burning in her eyes. "Well, it's done now."

She tried to move past him, but he stopped her.

"Hold on," he said gently. "Kitty, I need to know you're OK. I need you to promise me you understand what's happened."

She refused to look into his eyes, but her voice lost some of its edge. "I'm fine. We should get moving."

Mohan sighed. "Don't sheathe your claws just yet. The Warren is where we will need them the most. All of us may need to release our inner beasts to survive it."

He turned away, but Kitty called after him, "He was there." He turned back. "The sniper, from the market. He was in Jar-Geshim."

Mohan frowned. "You're sure?"

"He was the lead biker, that one you clipped with the Hiker at the intersection. Bastard bowed at me the same way he did when he got away in Kairran." She went to fish out a cigarette, realised the pack was empty, and threw it away carelessly.

"And he got away again?"

Kitty paused. "No. No, he let me go." Her father raised an eyebrow. "My mag was dry, and he was thirty metres away. I was exposed, outnumbered. I should have been dead right there. And he just gave me that bloody pompous bow again and drove off."

The elder tiger pondered this for a moment. "There's something wrong here. Somebody is moving pieces on the board." He growled low. "And I hate feeling like a bloody pawn."

He walked back to the Hiker and began rechecking his equipment, more to take his mind off his daughter's troubling news than because he actually needed to. Despite his team's importance, they were pretty low on the totem pole regarding the real spy games.

Information was shared pretty freely within Tiger's Stripe but be prepared to get a cryptic answer that might not answer your question right away—if at all. The Elder Council never revealed exactly what part you might play in the bigger picture, but if you had the patience—or wisdom, as they would say—you might be able to figure it out.

Still, Mohan wondered if they knew what was happening this time. They ran into new players all the time, but opponents with this level of intrigue—and arrogance—were extremely rare.

He shook his head and refocused on the task at hand. They had much bigger concerns in their immediate future.

Their goal was to make it to the ancient gate on the city's eastern side, but with the crumbling state of the walls, the agents hoped to find some other egress much sooner—hopefully before nightfall.

There was a short debate about what to do with their fallen companions, but they quickly decided they couldn't leave their dead to be desecrated by who knew what. They left Kitty's commandeered dirt bike behind; a stray bullet had severed the fuel line, and the tank was practically dry by now.

She took it to the edge of the bridge and tossed it—swords and all—into the water, where the torrent swept them over the falls; she didn't want any reminders of the terrible bloodbath she had made with them. Unfortunately, she couldn't make her fur grow any faster; it would remain pinkish for at least a few days.

As the dirt bike vanished into the mist of the falls, Kitty thought she heard a cold voice retreat with a satisfied laugh, slinking away to hide in the darkest corners of her mind. Gone, but not forever.

General Durram offered to drive the truck carrying their dead. Undoubtedly, the fresh blood would be like a magnet to the denizens of the Warren, so he took up position directly behind the Hiker for added protection.

They stuck at least one member of Hunter TS-3 in each vehicle because their experience—and heavier weapons—would no doubt prove invaluable, although their ammo was running dangerously low. Mohan and Zed led in the Hiker; Rizzo rode with General Durram in the first truck; Vicki followed in the second, where they also put most of their wounded; Vince was in the third; and Kitty and Ric brought up the rearguard. Vince also deployed his receiver unit to link each truck by radio, but the signal was weak and fuzzy; they would need to stay close or risk losing contact.

"You sure you want to hang in back?" Kitty asked him as she climbed into the last truck. "It's the most likely to get attacked in an ambush."

The lynx nodded. "I can see the whole column from here, which I'm sure is why they placed you and your rifle here. But you'll need a spotter."

Kitty eyed him up and down. Ric still had the loaned SMG, but he would have to acquire his own hardware if this became a regular thing. As much as he could handle himself, a part of Kitty hoped it wouldn't.

"I saw that shot you took outside the motor pool," Ric said as he checked his magazine. "From a moving vehicle, no less."

"Hmph," she grunted. "I missed. I hit him in the shoulder. The fall off the balcony killed him."

"Well, you still need someone to watch your back," Ric said, unperturbed.

"There are four other agents with me."

"Didn't you tell me back in Jar-Geshim that you'd be damned if you let anything happen to me on your watch?"

She paused mid-response. "Dammit," she muttered, and the journalist smiled thinly at his small victory.

Without the bandits' ramshackle tin houses, the true character of the ancient city now marched before them. Few buildings reached higher than the crumbling twenty-metre exterior wall, but the trees and clinging plants that had taken root in the mouldering sandstone towered high above them, spreading dark green canopies over the roads and rooftops. Every structure bore the peculiar semi-modern design they had noticed in Jar-Geshim. Whoever the ancient builders had been, they certainly loved balconies, arches, and pillars.

From the street below, the air felt very close, and the convoy moved forward as quickly as they dared. All eyes swept from left to right, constantly vigilant for the first signs of the Warren's fabled denizens.

The first assault came from the jungle itself near the outer edges of the park. *Drosera capensis* was a common enough carnivorous plant whose tentacle-covered leaves didn't grow much larger than three and a half centimetres. *Drosera mammothopus* was its monstrous and far more dangerous cousin.

The sticky vines that lashed out at them were almost twenty metres long, at least half a metre thick and covered with bright red tentacles as long as Mohan's forearm. They wrapped themselves around the Hiker, but the vehicle proved too heavy for the plant to move. The agents inside hacked away at the clinging vines, Mohan and Zed being the most effective thanks to the tiger's large kukri and the badger's broad axe. The air filled with a raspy hiss and chitter that was more than the mere rustle of leaves.

"What I wouldn't give for a flamethrower," the tiger growled as he tried to drive and slash simultaneously.

476

A vine whipped through the window, and he nearly lost his knife to the sticky tentacles as he tried to chop them away.

More vines appeared to molest the other vehicles in the column. They seemed focused on the second truck, which carried Vicki and their injured companions; the live meat apparently was more appealing than the dead.

A massive tendril grabbed Rosa, and the koala screamed helplessly as it lifted her into the air. Her fellow agents tried in vain to assist her, but more clinging tentacles forced them back.

A trio of vines swiped at Vince's truck, and Caz began cutting at them with a shortsword he had purloined from the bandits—rusted as it was, it was sharper than his bear claws. Tendrils wrapped around his waist and arm, and he roared in frustration. His companions grabbed him, trying desperately to keep the bear from suffering the same fate as Rosa.

From the rear truck, Kitty swept her scope down the length of the vines until she spotted the giant bulb of the plant's mouth lurking in the shade of the trees. Her rifle cracked as she squeezed off a round into its centre. The mammoth sundew hissed as bright yellow plant matter spattered the foliage behind it.

The plant didn't have a proper brain, but Kitty must have hit some kind of nerve cluster because the tentacles released their prey and retreated into the underbrush. Free of their tormentors, a pair of agents rushed to rescue Rosa. The experience had shaken the koala, but she suffered only minor bruises.

Mohan gunned the engine and drove into the shelter of the nearest buildings, the trucks behind him swinging out to give the mammoth sundew a wide berth as they followed.

"Everyone all right?" Mohan asked over the radio. Everyone reported affirmatively.

"It's goin' to take more than a plant to stop us," Vince said.

"Thanks." Rizzo groaned. "We're doomed."

"Lucky we have the trucks," Vicki said. "That plant would have ripped us apart on foot."

"Too bloody right," Mohan replied. "Everyone, keep your eyes peeled for more. And look out for pitfalls; looks like the foundation itself has fallen away in a couple spots."

The tiger's warning was only too accurate. Several times they had to turn around because the street had fallen away completely, and there was no path forward. To skirt a massive sinkhole, at one point, they risked driving right through the lower floor of what might have been an ancient apartment building. The last truck clipped a support column, and the entire structure collapsed behind them.

"Fingers crossed we didn't just seal ourselves in," Mohan mumbled.

He kept them pointed eastward as much as possible, but with all the twists and turns, they felt driven inexorably southward towards the city's centre. What disturbed him even more was that the only dangers they had encountered were the pits and the plants.

The sun was sinking towards the western horizon when the bahnger pack appeared.

Various species of the sleek, almost puma-like creatures were common in nearly every forest across Amarthia. Of course, all resemblance to a mountain lion ended at the body and legs. Their heads had more in common with an alligator, except the snout was short, and their eyes were still feline. The angular head appeared too large to be supported by the lean feline body, which nature had balanced by providing them with long, thick tails that twisted gracefully with the beast's every move.

On average, they grew up to two metres in length and wore coats of spotted downy feathers in various blue-grey or tawny colours. The feathers were broken only by a strip of short fur down their spine and the backs of their legs.

However, these Warren bahngers were slate black, and the smallest was no less than three metres from snout to tail. At least a dozen came slinking out of the ruins around the convoy, their cat eyes glittering like pools of gold in the half-light. They paced the trucks for several blocks, none straying too close to but neither too far from the tender flesh inside. The agents held their fire, not wanting to waste precious ammo.

"It is as if they are waiting for something," Zed said.

Mohan nodded. "Has anyone seen the pack alpha?" he asked into the radio.

"Not yet," Rizzo and Vince replied almost simultaneously.

"Wait, I got him," Kitty said. "Your ten o'clock, Mohan."

The beast that glowered down at them was three and a half metres long if he was a centimetre, heavily scarred, and perched atop a cleft of rubble coming up on the left. The jet-black fur down his back bristled in a universal sign of aggression. Something glinted around his neck.

Kitty was about to ask if anyone else had noticed the strange charm when she heard a sudden horn call. The pack alpha looked up expectantly, then arched its head to the sky and bellowed. The bahngers surrounding the trucks answered the howl and backed off, slinking back into the shadows of the surrounding buildings.

"What was that about?" Vince asked.

"I think I have an idea," Mohan replied. "Look ahead."

As they approached a wide intersection, they saw several fetishes of bone and sticks lining either side of the street. Unlike the ornaments in Jar-Geshim, many of these were clearly from the skulls of Hom-Ans. They

480

also noted that fences of thick sharpened logs blocked several of the side streets.

"This does not bode well," Zed said.

"I didn't exactly see another path," Mohan said. "Did you?"

"I did not."

The path forced them along until the road dipped sharply, and they travelled down a long ramp. At the bottom, they entered a broad square similar to the one in Jar-Geshim, where the bandits held their nightly bonfires; at the end, they even saw the remains of a temple, sister to the one in which the Marshal had established his seat of power. However, this once-mighty edifice had collapsed almost entirely, leaving nothing but a dark cave where the grand entrance had once stood.

Tall walls of stone and thick logs fortified every side of the square. Halfway up, a jagged ring of sharpened logs angled into the arena, ensuring nothing could attempt to scale them and escape.

A counterweight released as the last truck crossed the threshold, and a heavy gate, as formidable as any of the walls, swung shut behind them. Mohan parked the Hiker in the centre of the square, and the trucks fanned out beside him.

The air had grown steadily thicker as they were pushed towards the city's centre, the sense of dread and sickness increasing with every metre. Now, it hung about them so heavily they could almost see it, like a colourless haze that blotted out the sun above. Those agents with birthmarks felt them throb as if danger was approaching, and those without felt their guts tighten with unease.

It was quiet for several long moments before they heard a general murmur fill the air. Suddenly, writhing figures began to fill the top of the walls and surrounding buildings. The murmuring became shouting, but none of them understood the guttural language.

"Wildmen," Mohan growled.

Most appeared to be mammalian, but several reptiles, amphibians, and avians could be picked out among the crowd. They were naked save for jewellery and piercings made from slivers of bone, most likely trophies signifying the owner's status within the tribe. They were all terribly dirty, fur matted and ungroomed, feathers unpreened, scales flaky and unshed.

"Ladies and gentlemen, time for the main event!" Vince said in his best announcer's voice.

"Shut it, Vince," Mohan ordered. "I don't think this is a gladiator match."

"No," Zed said, "it appears to be a ritual sacrifice."

The figures began to sway in unison and chant in the unknown language. A figure appeared on a balcony beside the gate they had entered. The wild boar must have been a shaman; he wore an ornate bone headdress

482

and had more fetishes and piercings than anyone else in the crowd.

He chanted to the crowd at length in the language of the Wildmen, and the women began to wail and writhe as if possessed while the men stamped their feet and waved their hands in the air around them in curious ritual. Drums began to beat with the movement of the multitude, and the noise rose to the point that the agents wanted to cover their ears against the din.

Finally, the shaman bellowed, *"Rattuteh, Grun'garr!"*

There was a long, low horn blast, and the crowd fell to their knees, chanting the final word repeatedly in hushed reverence.

Grun'garr. Grun'garr. Grun'garr.

A smaller gate opened at the base of the wall near the temple steps, and several ceravaags rumbled into the arena. They were the largest specimens Mohan had ever seen, fully eight metres from their rhinoceros-horned Komodo-dragon-like heads to the tips of their tree-like tails and at least two and a half metres at the shoulder. Their thick scales and plates were coloured in bright shades of green with yellow and red stripes.

At the base of each feather-covered neck was a figure bound upright by the shoulders to a leather-and-wood harness. On closer inspection, Mohan could see that the riders also had crude spears tied in their hands but not in a position where they could use them. He was even more interested to note that each wore a tattered white lab coat.

There was a half-dozen prisoners in total, four male and two female. As their mounts began to circle the parked trucks, Mohan identified the females as a squirrel and a rabbit and the males as a newt, a gopher, an ibex, and a mountain goat. Only the last two looked like natives of the region.

"I think those prisoners are from the lab," the tiger said.

"Guess we'll just have to rescue them and find out," Vince said.

"Oh, *oui*," Rizzo said, the sarcasm dripping from her voice. "I'm sure that squirrel and rabbit doe will be very grateful to you, *non*?"

"Not now, you two," Mohan growled.

A deep coughing bellow issued from the temple cave and silenced any further banter. The ceravaags halted their circling and looked towards the dark portal. Ric thought he saw fear reflected in their large eyes. The chanting of the Wildmen stopped, and most threw themselves prone.

Slowly, a form began to rise from the shadow of the temple. Instantly, Ric could tell this was another of the mythic fiends hunted by Tiger's Stripe, and he shuddered involuntarily at the horrific visage. It definitely didn't look like anything that had been born on Amarthia.

The face of the creature was blunt and triangular, almost like a railroad spike. On each side of the narrow face was a wing that vaguely reminded the journalist of a hammerhead shark, but the golden eyes—all six of them, each with twin verticle pupils—were set into the front instead of at either end. Numerous horns protruded from the head, pointed outward like the horns of a bull. A spike of bone jutted down from the chin; at some point in the creature's life, it had splintered in battle, leaving only a jagged edge. Its mouth had no lips, and the dagger-like teeth grinned at them as if it was laughing at some hellish joke.

Two rows of long, bony spines ran down the length of its arched back to the tip of its long tail, which ended in a knotted cluster of spikes like the head of a medieval morning star—several protrusions had broken off in ancient battles. The leathery skin—once a dull red—had faded to a pale grey over long ages, and it bore the scars of many fierce battles.

"I guess that," Vince mumbled, "is Grun'garr."

"What is it?" Ric asked.

Mohan's response was hushed. "It's a grendel."

"A very ancient one," Zed added, "perhaps even one of the first."

"Wait, you mean that thing could be several thousand years old?" The journalist was incredulous.

"Maybe," Mohan answered, gripping the wheel of the Hiker. "We're not really sure how long these things live in the wild."

The grendel bellowed again, the echoing cough sounding eerily like the chant of the Wildmen.

Gruuuun'gar!

The fiend wasn't quite as large as the ceravaags, only seven metres long and two at the shoulder, but it was powerful and wickedly fast. Within moments of bellowing its challenge, it leapt upon the nearest of the rhinoceros-dragons, its jaws opening much wider than Ric had thought possible as it bit into the ceravaag's neck and nearly severed its head from the body. The grendel's horns impaled the unfortunate ibex riding on the ceravaag's back.

Mohan floored the accelerator and drove straight for the fiend, smashing into its side and sending it staggering. He was damn lucky the heavy exploration vehicle could withstand rough encounters, or he probably would've shattered the engine block against the fiend's tough hide. The bonnet still sustained serious damage, and his hands tingled from the vibration of the impact.

Zed activated his bracer's shield and let fly with Mohan's heavy machine gun, the bullets sending shimmering ripples through the field as they passed through from inside. However, even at point-blank range, the 7.62mm rounds couldn't penetrate far into the monster's skin. The new gashes oozed noxious orange blood, which snapped and sizzled against the Soketh shield, but the badger failed to cause any significant damage.

The other trucks pulled out of formation. With Mohan and the Hiker busy distracting the fiend, the remaining agents set themselves to rescuing the helpless riders strapped to the ceravaags. The grendel could easily have torn the lighter trucks to shreds, but at least the ceravaags—even ones of such tremendous size— were an equal match for them.

The rhinoceros-dragons had panicked, darting in every direction. General Durram ordered the agents to split up and try to corral the frightened beasts together.

Kitty aimed and squeezed off a round into the nearest ceravaag carrying the rabbit doe. Ceravaag scales are tough but not nearly as tough as a fiend, and the .308 round punctured the hide easily. The massive beast lurched forward and lay still.

Vince leapt out of his truck, cut the rabbit's ropes, and spirited her back to the convoy; he even took the time to tip his hat in the process.

"Show off," Kitty muttered.

The squirrel and gecko were not so fortunate. Their mounts attempted to scale the arena's walls, only to be hindered by the ring of sharpened logs jabbing at them from above; their riders were crushed when the beasts came crashing back to the ground.

487

As the scent of fresh blood filled their nostrils, instinct took over, and the ceravaags turned on each other. The Wildmen lining the arena walls cheered and prostrated themselves as their gods violently tore into one another.

Meanwhile, their chief "god" turned to face the threat of the Hiker and the soft meat inside that pelted it with fire breath. The grendel bellowed a challenge and leapt upon the exploration vehicle, the long claws of its six-fingered hands puncturing the thick steel of the side panels as it bit at the front cab.

Fortunately, its jaws couldn't get purchase for long with Zed in the front seat shooting hot lead down its throat. It screeched in pain and spun away from the line of fire, forcing Mohan to give chase. The tiger didn't need to look at the gashes in the side panels to know they couldn't take many more hits like that. Their only hope was to keep the pressure on and hope they could wear the monster down.

"Rizzo," Mohan bellowed into the radio, "gimme something!"

The basilisk searched through her bags. Not having been able to resupply since the Frankenbeast, she was running low on explosives. She found one large brick of Semtex and a couple of flashbangs, anti-personnel grenades designed to stun rather than kill. The hints of an idea began to take form.

"Vicki," she said into her radio, "find me a weakness in the arena wall!"

The bullfrog answered affirmatively, and she ordered her driver to circle the arena while she scanned the fortifications.

Nearby, Vince and Kitty had managed to corral the last two ceravaags, and the tigress put one down with her rifle—it was her last round. The hare and several agents dismounted their vehicle to rescue the gopher strapped to its back, firing wildly at the remaining beast to keep it away.

Suddenly, the truck Vince had been riding in exploded in a shower of steel shrapnel as the grendel barrelled into it.

The agents scattered before the fiend, but one mighty swipe of its claws felled three of them, including Mümtaz, the brave gazelle clerk from the rental agency in Kairran.

Gregor Cazimov, the most imposing member of their group next to Mohan, was pierced by shrapnel from the truck. It was a mortal wound, but he stood his ground and roared a challenge, raising his sword to strike. The grendel lunged forward, and the sword struck deep into the creature's hide, but with a violent twist, it was torn from the bear's hands.

The grendel turned to snap at Caz, and he grabbed onto two of the horns, answering the beast's snarl with one of his own. But he was growing weaker from the loss of blood, and a sudden jolt of pain caused him to stagger. The grendel lunged forward again and neatly severed the bear's head with a snap of its jaws.

The gopher captive shrieked in terror and would have run headlong into the path of the final ceravaag if Ric hadn't grabbed him by the collar and practically thrown him into the back of the truck with Kitty. As the journalist climbed in, General Durram and Rizzo pulled alongside to assist those thrown from the wreckage of Vince's truck, including the rabbit doe the hare had recused moments earlier.

The remaining ceravaag trampled two more agents in its panicked flight, but Vince managed to jump up and grab the harness trapping the unfortunate mountain goat.

He unslung his SMG and emptied several bursts into the base of the wild creature's skull before it staggered to a halt. The hare was busy with the mountain goat's bonds when the grendel loomed above them.

Vince gritted his teeth and levelled his SMG at the monster in a feeble act of bravado, but the fiend never got a chance to strike as Mohan rammed the Tracksman Hiker into its side again.

Zed braced himself against the seat and unloaded the last of the heavy machine gun's ammo box into the grendel's side while Vince and the mountain goat captive scrambled into Vicki's truck. They looped back away from the Hiker and fiend.

"Rizzo," Vicki radioed in, "over here, the wall near the temple!"

The spot the frog had chosen was near the gate where the ceravaags had entered. Rizzo instantly spotted the cracked stonework and frayed bindings on the wooden spike wall. She bounded out of the truck as it rolled to a stop and started setting up the charge at the base of the wall, waving for General Durram to clear the area.

"Mohan," the basilisk radioed as she worked, "get over here and bring that damned fiend with you!"

Mohan acknowledged and turned the Hiker towards the wall; the grendel bellowed and followed. The tiger was thankful for the lack of side mirrors so he couldn't see the hideous bloody maw of the fiend just centimetres behind them. As he neared the wall, he prayed his demolitions expert knew what she was about and ordered Zed to open the side door.

"Watch your eyes, everyone," Rizzo called as they hurtled towards her.

Mohan yanked on the wheel, veering away at the last moment, and Rizzo leapt for the open side door. Zed caught her by the straps of her harness.

There was a blinding flash followed by a deafening boom as both flashbangs went off behind the basilisk, right in the grendel's face. The monster shrieked in pain as its senses were overwhelmed, and its momentum sent it crashing headlong into the wall.

Rizzo only paused long enough to make sure everyone was clear before she flipped the detonator switch for the Semtex. The explosives went up practically underneath the fiend and sent it flying into the air, right into several sharpened logs that ringed the arena. There was a loud crack as the wall section tilted forward and came crashing down, driving the wooden spikes deeper through the fiend's tough hide.

When the dust cleared, the grendel lay still.

For long ages, it had ruled the Warren, worshipped by the primitive Wildmen. Now, it was no more. The Wildmen looked on in stunned incomprehension.

Slowly, a chant began to rise from the crowd.

Grun'garr. Grun'garr. Grun'garr!

"let's get the bloody hell out of here," Mohan said.

They gathered their dead and placed the rescued lab workers in the Hiker, where Zed could keep an eye on them. They might be grateful now, but they had once been employed at a repurposed Foresight facility.

Unfortunately, Rizzo's explosion hadn't created an exit like they had hoped; solid stone walls lay behind the broken wooden fortifications.

They circled the arena once, the chanting of the Wildmen rising until it reached a fevered pitch. Finally, Mohan headed for the temple cave.

"Do you think there may be an exit that way?" Zed asked.

"Only one way to find out," the tiger responded grimly. "Gredels usually claim a wide territory. I'm betting this one wouldn't just let itself be confined to the arena like this."

"Let's hope you're right," General Durram radioed from behind them. "Here they come!"

Mohan looked out the window to see Wildmen beginning to pour into the arena, tossing down vine ropes to scale the wall like a wave of ants. Spears and stones began to fall around the fleeing vehicles, a vain attempt to avenge their fallen god. He pushed the battered Hiker to its severely reduced limit and was relieved when the large vehicle cleared the threshold of the cave with plenty of room to spare.

The ground sloped down below the original floor of the temple and descended into a broad stone tunnel that must have taken the creature many years to carve out. The remaining trucks followed him into the darkness, and the Wildmen halted their advance abruptly, unwilling to cross into their former god's sacred dwelling.

They cursed and stamped and cursed again at the fleeing agents until the last pair of taillights vanished.

Slowly, they turned away from the blackness and set themselves to the task of building a funeral pyre for the body of their slain deity.

36 – Casa De Palma

Vigo De Palma's study was an exercise in subtle refinement. No item in the room was expensive or cheap; instead, he had focused on objects of good, sensible quality. The walls were oak wood panels with a marble stain, a careful blend of light and dark. He had converted one wall into simple, sturdy bookshelves; half the titles were Medoccian and Locke literature, while the others consisted of light fiction and a few bibliographies from acclaimed economists and business magnates. A large oil painting depicting an ancient Medoccian temple overlooking the Medean Basin hung on the opposite wall; a local artist, not one of the old masters, had signed it. A modest wooden desk was pushed against the wall under the painting, the bulky twelve-inch CRT monitor of a personal computer perched on one corner.

In fact, the only genuinely exceptional pieces in the room were the four rich leather chairs arranged in the centre and the elegant Benese carpet they sat on.

Vigo liked the room's openness; he felt it set him apart from the other families. It was almost stereotypical how they flaunted their plush offices and hid behind their massive desks to intimidate their guests. The head of the De Palma family wanted his visitors to feel at ease when they talked to him. There were far more effective ways of demonstrating your power without showing it off.

The deerhound sat in one of the chairs, which was turned to face the patio doors so he could see the Medean basin. Sunset was the time he enjoyed the most, and he made a point of being in his study to watch it as often as possible.

The sun and the pale-orange disc of Druna actually set on the opposite side of the house, but he loved watching the day moon's nocturnal cousin, Midori, as it rose in the east. The colours it cast on the landscape reminded him of the painting on the wall, although the temple it depicted was several kilometres away in the middle of a national park.

The only object that tarnished the view was the purple and white yacht anchored in the bay further down the coastline.

The *Star of Carmen*.

It had been ten years since he had agreed to the marriage of his daughter Yursa to Jirair al-Seif. Money laundering and smuggling—anything but narcotics—were the basis of the De Palma's power. Aligning with al-Seif—and his alter ego, Assad Alabwaq—allowed them to expand their operations further than he had ever dreamed of.

And it had all been Yursa's idea.

There had been a lot of friction from the start, especially with al-Seif's aggressive strong-arm tactics versus Vigo's subtle, more refined manipulations. Al-Seif had also tried to goad the De Palmas into the drug and slave trades, which Vigo outright detested. The De Palmas may be criminals, but they were still Aabonite catholic, and there were some things you just didn't do.

Vigo often questioned why he allowed the alliance, but then he recalled all the profits they had made from gun running and textiles.

But does that excuse his faults? Vigo thought to himself.

As if to further remind him of his troublesome son-in-law, his labrador manservant announced that his daughter was here to see him.

As Yursa De Palma entered, he rose and embraced her in Medocci fashion, with a kiss on each cheek. He silently remarked on how much the wolfhound looked like her mother.

"Wonderful to see you, *mia cucciola*." He always called her "puppy", even well into her thirties. His voice was deep and rough but with a gentleness that he reserved only for family. "To what do I own this pleasure?"

"I'll give you three guesses," she said as she collapsed heavily into one of the chairs. A strand of her rusty long-fur had escaped the bun and lay over her brow, but she ignored it.

The De Palma patriarch sat again, adjusting the legs of his finely tailored slacks, and smiled grimly. "I take it you didn't find out anything new while in Kalegos. I can't say I'm surprised." His daughter had taken a brief trip to Mata to inquire about his son-in-law's most recent venture.

"He's a slimy bastard," Yursa growled. "There was nothing, not a hint. The harbourmaster didn't even know the ship was berthed in his port. The gate guard was murdered the night the *Resthoven* disappeared, but all the evidence pointed to a different theft, not one involving an entire freighter. Jirair's up to something, Father. And I fear our necks are a part of it."

Vigo leaned forward and clasped his hands, placing an elbow on each tall kee. "That is most disturbing. I did not believe Jirair had gained such influence in Medocci, especially under the noses of the Voréas." He referred to the syndicate controlling the majority of Mata's criminal enterprises. "However, this damned war between Barju and Pytan has put us both in a weakened position. The entire continent of Estan has been sealed off, which will make even legitimate trade more cumbersome. They were already suspicious of our foreign business interests; now they're on a veritable witch hunt. Any foreign investor is being accused of assisting one side or the other. Still, al-Seif lost more than we did when the border closed. I think we should use that to our advantage."

"Don't underestimate him. Our holdings in Estan may have been less important, but I think he saw this coming. I believe he's transferred more of his power base here than we've caught on."

"Hmm, very true. Especially if he was able to erase all traces of the *Resthoven*." Vigo shrugged. "It's also important that we keep our head up. Grego Favera has been asking some pointed questions about our most recent losses, and word is getting out that al-Seif refused to use our shared assets for his last venture. This reflects poorly on our existing fleet."

"Hmph," Yursa chuffed, clearly unimpressed. "Let him ask. And the Costellianos and the Saventes, too, if they want. We're still the dominant family in Medocci."

Her father shook his head. "Now it is my turn to tell you not to underestimate them. I have always admired your spirit, *mia cucciola*, but perhaps you should tail your brother Tito around more?"

Yursa actually smiled. Her elder brother had indeed inherited his father's knack for the careful juggling act that was running a crime family. As she looked out into the bay, she caught sight of the *Star of Carmen* and frowned as she suddenly remembered something.

"Jirair wanted to discuss the matter over dinner," she said flatly.

The elder De Palma considered this for a moment. "*Bene*. I think perhaps we should make a few preparations then. We'll make him an offer, keep him under our wing but on a very short leash. He must be reminded where he stands in Medocci." He rose and went to his desk. "Why don't you go say hello to your mother and sisters? I have a few phone calls to make."

Yursa rose and nodded, taking one last look at the lights of al-Seif's compound as they winked on further down the coast.

Lukas Mikelos stood by the taxi door in the courtyard of Jirair al-Seif's villa. The mouflon who employed him sifted through the notarized papers he had handed him moments ago. His employer was particularly focused on the marked dates.

"It's all there," the lawyer said. "Terrapin Holdings has been absorbed into D'Verant Industries, and all of Assad Alabwaq's ties to Syris Industries have been dissolved. Congratulations." The praise came out flat.

Al-Seif looked up at him and nodded. Without another word, the marmoset got into the armoured taxi and left for the safety of the city.

As al-Seif entered the foyer of his home, Abar Kami approached him with the phone handset.

"Your wife," the panther said coolly.

The mouflon accepted the phone. "Yes?"

"My father has agreed to dinner on Faerday evening," came the curt response. "I trust you will be there." The line went dead.

Jirair al-Seif looked from the phone to the papers in his hand. "Absolutely," he said, a wicked grin spreading across his face.

37 – Beneath the Warren

Mohan had no idea how far they had travelled since entering the grendel's lair. The pinpoint of daylight that was the cave entrance had vanished long ago, and before him, he could see only the rough carved walls of the tunnel.

The battle with the grendel had smashed the Hiker's headlights to uselessness, and of the four floodlights mounted on the roof, only one was still operational. Zed held out two powerful hundred-candle torches to help light their path.

"We've got to be several kilometres beneath the city by now," the tiger said as the Hiker crawled along at a feeble thirty kilometres an hour; he didn't dare push them any faster under current conditions.

"By my estimate, we have barely covered two kilometres," Zed said.

"Well, I'll trust your judgement then."

Finally, the rough stone walls broke into an even wider passage of ancient brick; they had rediscovered the city's old sewer system. The green, slime-covered walls arched six metres above them, intersected by smaller runoffs every twelve metres. The smooth floor dipped slightly in the centre, and a thin stream of water flowed down the channel. Dark-furred munski skittered away from the invading lights of the convoy.

"Oh, look," Rizzo said over the radio. "Some of Vince's cousins are at home."

"Now that's just mean," the hare responded.

The basilisk was referring, at least in part, to the munski's long ears; however, their heads were more shrew-like, and their bodies more closely resembled a small bloated lizard with a rat's tail.

When they were safely out of the convoy's path, the small rodent-like creatures turned and glared at them through large, luminous eyes.

The sewer line twisted and turned for at least another kilometre before emptying into a large natural aquifer. Even the powerful beams of Zed's torches couldn't penetrate to the far side of the cave.

A broad road bordered the pool's edge, and they could see several artificial pillars assisting the natural ones supporting the roof.

Mohan pulled to a stop parallel to the lip of the landing and leaned out the window. The water's surface was several metres below them, but he couldn't tell how much deeper it might still be.

"Mo," Vicki's voice said over the radio, "shut off the light and have everyone else do the same."

Darkness blinded them for a moment, and then a faint blue glow began to fill the cavern. Soon, even the far wall became visible in the bioluminescent glimmer.

"It's beautiful!" Vicki breathed. "It was a long shot, but I thought I recognized some of the algae build-up here as the kind that offers its own light. Neat!"

Mohan chuckled. "OK. Let's change up drivers to ones with better night vision; the drivers could use a break anyway. Bad enough, we have to deal with the engine noise, but at least we won't advertise our presence with the lights."

"Advertise them for what?" Vince asked. "We haven't run into anything but munski since we came down here."

"True," the tiger said, "but there's plenty of cave serpents who love this type of environment."

"Not to mention our friends on the surface," Zed said. "They may overcome their fear of venturing into their dead god's home before we find a way out. At the very least, they may send that pack of bahngers after us; they have no fear of the dark and will probably be even bolder now that the grendel is dead."

Mohan checked the dashboard compass in the Hiker. Despite the cracked glass, it was still functional, although he was not surprised to see it spinning erratically right now. He confirmed it by digging a second compass from a vest pocket.

"Lot of magnetic interference down here; it's making my fur stand on end." He didn't have to mention the faint tingle in his birthmark, which the other marked agents also felt. "If we ever get the chance, we'll have to get a research team down here to check it out."

"Indeed," the badger agreed. "There may be one or two Soketh from the Opal Claw who would assist you. This aquifer deserves exploration; there is a source of power here that may require cataloguing."

"You mean it's one of those artefacts that your people excavate?" Ric asked, suddenly excited.

"Perhaps so. The past holds many secrets, Sedric. I did not think Jar-Geshim was a Tetzuma city, but there are many of their influences here. Perhaps it is one of their newer settlements, built towards the end of their power."

"Tetzuma?" Ric repeated. "That's the supposed 'first civilization', correct? The one the Soketh claim predates every known ancient culture on Amarthia?"

"Indeed," Zed answered. "The Soketh have discovered several remnants of their technology in the wastes. If this city is one of theirs, it could provide a wealth of information to both anthropologists and historians." He did not add that only the information the Soketh chose to release would reach the general public.

General Durram cut in. "I agree, but our first priority is finding a way out. Not even the Pytian military would dare step in the Warren. I think its secrets will remain safe until we can return."

"Yessir," Mohan said. He switched places with Zed, and they pulled away from the lip of the aquifer, slowly making their way in the direction they hoped was the east side of the city above them.

They came upon another massive sewer line emptying onto the aquifer; this one was nearly dry. The air drifting out of it was slightly less foul, but it still bore traces of something that even Zed could not yet identify.

Again, the walls of green slime closed around them as they snaked upwards. The bioluminescence of the algae remained, and they proceeded in a surreal blue glow.

The tunnel branched several times, and Zed had to step out and carefully sniff the air currents to choose their path. Eventually, it felt as if they had travelled at least as far up as they had down, but Mohan couldn't see an end in sight. It was well past midnight, so they probably wouldn't see the tunnel exit until they passed right through it.

Eventually, the blue light faded. Mohan and Zed switched places again and turned the Hiker's light back on, but he ordered Zed to keep the torches off for the moment.

Despite the diesel fumes coming from the battered Hiker's engine block, they could sense the air getting steadily fresher as they travelled upwards, and with it came the earthy stench of a serpent den. Yet they found nobody at home when the tunnel finally ended at a large cave.

"Well, that's lucky," Mohan said.

"From the shed skins, I would say that a Kregor's viper occupies this cave," Zed said. "Fortunately, they are night hunters."

"Are they dangerous?" Ric asked.

"Less so than a fiend," Mohan answered, "but still extremely territorial. But if you leave them alone, they tend to do the same. Unless they're hungry, of course."

They exited the cave beneath the imposing edifice of ancient Jar-Geshim's exterior wall, and the agents were relieved they didn't have to face yet another battle before they were finally free of the city.

That is until they saw the massive red and green scales of the forty-metre serpent coiled just outside the entrance.

They held their breath as the giant lidless reptilian eye gazed at them, but the beast didn't move. It seemed content to enjoy its last meal and watch the line of trucks slowly disappear into the jungle.

"Must have had a good hunt tonight," Mohan breathed when they were safely beyond it.

"Indeed," Zed said.

There were still many kilometres to traverse before they reached the southern desert and their predetermined rendezvous. Still, when the last trace of the city vanished behind them, they felt comfortable enough to stop and adjust Vince's radio for a long-range transmission. Watch Command needed to know they had made it through the Warren safely so it could signal the transport.

"Glad to hear it," the familiar voice of Andrew Kane said after General Durram finished his report. "What's your ETA?"

Mohan glanced at his watch. "One sec. Kane, give me a time check."

"Sure. Pytian time is…Taursday, Ferrus the twenty-fifth. On my mark, it will be oh-two-nineteen hours…mark."

The tiger and General Durram reset their watches. Whatever they had encountered beneath the Warren had slowed them considerably.

"Very interesting," Durram said. "Kane, make sure you get that flag on the Warren sent out. I think we've definitely found an artefact here."

"Yessir," the operator responded. "We always suspected there was somethin' in there. Now, about the ETA?"

"Not 'til tomorrow evening at the earliest," Mohan answered. "I'm afraid we're pretty banged up. I wouldn't push our Hiker any more than fifty-five clicks an hour."

Kane whistled. "I thought those things were built like tanks?"

"Bloody right they are, but they aren't grendel proof."

"Got it. What about personnel?"

The tiger paused a moment. "Twelve dead, eight wounded, and three prisoners. We'd like to send the dead home."

Kane was silent for a moment. "Will do. The Council is a bit anxious to get you squared away; kind of unusual to keep an uninitiated recruit in the field this long. You're going straight to Locke to get Barnes packed and ready to ship off back to the Sanctuary."

"What about al-Seif?" the tiger asked.

"Elder's discretion, but you could take a short detour to Medocci. If you've really got the proof we need to take that bastard down, our team there will handle all the details. I know it's not the same as gettin' to hogtie him personally, but at least he's going down. By the way, he's still laid up at his villa, keepin' his head down."

"Thank you, Watch Command," general Durram said. "Hunter TS Three and Guardian Four over and out."

After ending the call, the general interrogated their prisoners. They confirmed most of what Mohan and his Scrappers had guessed up to that point. Except for the ibex, who was now dead, they had all been employees of Assad Alabwaq. They didn't know who the ibex's employer was, but they didn't like working alongside them. All they would say is that they were "scary people"—general Durram asked his agents if the body had been recovered, but someone mentioned it was stuck under one of the ceravaag carcasses.

The genetically engineered poppy plants were not only payment for the Marshal but also designed by him; apparently, this was a part of his history that even Tiger's Stripe hadn't learned yet. The cobra had found the old Foresight facility long ago but never had a use for it. When Alabwaq and his associates expressed interest in the region, he thought he had found a way to make it mutually profitable.

Much to Vicki and Rizzo's disappointment, there were no mind-control substances in the plants. The botanists found the idea amusing but agreed that the potent strain would be an excellent incentive for conscripted bandits. However, neither Hassan nor the Marshal would be happy to discover the creature had destroyed most of the hybrid plants; the budding crops were the control group.

The lab techs insisted that their particular group was only involved in cultivating the poppies, although the dead ibex seemed to have ulterior motives for the plant. Alabwaq's employees didn't know what their associate was working on, but it required almost half of their crop. They also didn't know about the creature—that is until it broke free. They had been working in the fields that day, probably saving their lives.

When the Frankenbeast—they thought the name appropriate—attacked, they fled toward Jar-Geshim instead of heading to the convoy trucks. At first, they thought they were safe; over a dozen had escaped the carnage. Then they went into the Warren, where they were captured by the Wildmen.

They refused to talk about the horrors they had witnessed at the hands of those feral savages, but they were eternally grateful for the rescue. So much so that they agreed on the spot to testify against Alabwaq.

General Durram ordered a short rest before they continued out of the jungle.

Mohan leaned against the Hiker, arms crossed, listening to the sounds of the jungle without hearing them. He was grateful for the testimony of the lab techs but reminded himself that they might change their minds once they reached civilization again.

And they still had to convince the Medocci courts to prosecute al-Seif.

He looked up to see Kitty in the shade of a tree on the other side of the clearing. She had bummed a cigarette off another agent, and all he could see was her silhouette against the faint orange glow.

What if she's right? What if al-Seif does own all the courts?

He shook the thought away angrily. No, justice would be served. The right way.

38 – Dinner Engagement

The long 1954 Baronville Regalia rolled up to the gate of the De Palma estate, a gentle purr issuing from its eight-cylinder engine. The superb Zeichlind engineering would function at peak performance even in the desert sands of his homeland. The elegant vehicle was the most luxurious in Jirair al-Seif's small collection. He disdained the use of motor vehicles as a status symbol, it was a trait his father reveled in and thus something he had struggled hard to avoid. However, it only took one look at the Regalia's gentle curves for him to fall in love with the car.

The evening air was pleasant—not surprising for the region—and al-Seif had decided to take a dare and leave the reinforced canvas top down. Many cliff-side patrons would be driving about on a Faerday evening such as this, each with their own security. The bandits in the surrounding forests wouldn't appear until after midnight when the residents were drunk and a little more careless.

The reinforced gates opened, and he pulled slowly up to the house beyond. Several sleek Medoccian- and Locke-made supercars occupied the sweeping drive. They were as heavily armoured as the Regalia, but al-Seif found them ugly with their sharp angles and broad, nearly flat panels. The exception was the Jaguar R-Type, but he thought naming an automotive company after a particular Hom-An species was silly. Still, none of them could match up to the seductive lines and shining chrome of the Regalia. He intended to show-up the De Palmas as much as possible, and he thought he was off to an impressive start.

However, he did have to give them credit for the house itself.

The De Palma estate had a more classically designed structure than his ultramodern villa. Red terracotta shingles lined the low-peaked roofs and nicely offset the orange stucco walls. Large glass windows looked over a vast front lawn carefully manicured to mimic an ancient Medoccian temple garden, complete with life-sized statues of mythological heroes and Aabonite saints. Naturally, the saints had more prominent placement— the De Palmas were very Catholic.

Al-Seif sat in the car for several minutes, mentally preparing himself before shutting off the engine and walking up to the front door. This was a business dinner, but he would have to observe certain pleasantries first. He doubted he would be leaving on good terms afterwards, but the De Palmas could do nothing to him. Not anymore. If they didn't accept his more than generous offer, his assets were in place to ensure they wouldn't remain so dismissive for long.

His wife greeted him at the door. She was almost pretty in a blue, low-cut evening gown, and she had loosened her long-fur from its confining bun. But his anger began to rise as soon as she opened her mouth.

"Ah, you grace us with your presence at last," she sneered. "We were about to start without you."

"Forgive me, *darling*," he replied. "Yours was not the only party this evening, and traffic was quite heavy."

Yursa led him through a foyer decorated in glass and white ash wood. Thick Barjan carpets lay sparingly over a dark slate floor; as a Pytian, he wondered if the De Palmas had intentionally laid them out to insult him. The rear dining room looked over a large swimming pool and the bay beyond. He could see the distant lights of his yacht lying at anchor and the glow of his own villa on the far hills. What he wouldn't give to be there now, enjoying dinner with his lover and son instead of his in-laws.

Al-Seif had expected to eat at a crowded table; "family" was more than just a business pejorative to the De Palmas. In addition to the patriarch was his wife; his six children, two of whom were under twelve years old;

the wives of his two adult sons; and his young grandchildren.

Al-Seif had not expected three of De Palma's lieutenants to join them—the only attendees besides himself who were not canine. If Vigo had meant to shake him with their presence, he didn't show it.

Vigo De Palma rose and smiled as they entered. It was a businessman's smile but much warmer than his daughter's. Al-Seif had enjoyed working with Vigo, but he reminded himself that the tall deerhound could be just as ruthless as he was. Their dealings had been masterful duels, each seeking to score a point on the other. Tonight, al-Seif was determined to be the one to draw first blood, if not end their battle entirely.

"So glad you could make it!" De Palma's voice boomed as the mouflon seated himself. "Don't trouble yourself with being late; I know the Gainsboroughs down the hill are also hosting this eve. Damn Wooks are always so boisterous with their parties; they have no sense of class. Let us hope they don't attract any unwanted attention."

Al-Seif smiled agreeably, not missing the veiled reference to the bandits in the surrounding forests. The mouflon had no real cause for alarm; he knew Vigo's private security forces were every bit a rival of his own.

For the next hour, there was nothing but small talk. The meal was quite delicious; al-Seif had developed a taste for pasta since moving to Medocci, and although he and one of the lieutenants couldn't eat the meat dishes, his host had thoughtfully prepared a wonderful course of cooked fresh vegetables, though perhaps a little heavy on the garlic.

When they had finished with dessert and the servants cleared the dishes away, the younger members of the family and the women excused themselves from the table—all except Yursa. Vigo's two eldest sons and his three lieutenants also remained, along with four bodyguards at the corners of the room.

Al-Seif smirked. They wouldn't have been any challenge for Abar Kami had he brought him along.

"Now," the elder De Palma said as he leaned back in his chair and gazed at his guest, "I regret that we must follow such a wonderful meal with such tawdry dealings, but I understand there have been more than a few concerns regarding our shared assets in Pytan."

Al-Seif betrayed nothing, though he resented the implication of De Palma's words. "Yes," he said, "but I would not worry about it. As you have no doubt heard, the entire region has become quite unstable. None of our current business ventures stand to gain any viable profits in the next few months, or perhaps even years."

Vigo squinted at him. "That puts you at quite a disadvantage. With our base of operations here, I believe we hold the controlling interest." He paused. "But we can get back to that. First, I wish to ask why you made a shipment to your warehouse in Kairran yet refused the generous use of our fleet?"

The mouflon let the question hang for a moment. He had an answer planned but wanted it to appear he was considering how to proceed. "We have had many successful ventures, Vigo. However, we both operate on our own when we wish. I have never questioned you about the alcohol you smuggle to Coasta Blanco; we know their government has an embargo on all Medoccian goods. You know I have access to some of the finest brandy this country has to offer, but I have not complained that you ship a different brand." He didn't need to mention that Carmen's father was also a distributor of Colleté brandy throughout Estan.

The deerhound let out a slow breath. "Very true," he said. "However, we are both usually aware of who our competitors are. This time, your benefactor has remained a mystery. I do hope you are not considering selling out our partnership. It would be...inconsiderate not to allow us to make an offer. You would be quite welcome here. I can even get you a vice chair at one of our subsidiaries."

Al-Seif had expected this. They wanted him trapped like a fly in a spider's web. He reached into his coat pocket and pulled out a sealed envelope.

"Actually," he said evenly, "I was wondering if you might sell to me." He slid the envelope across the table to the deerhound.

Slowly, Vigo opened it and reviewed the documents inside. The frown on his face deepened sharply.

"Is this some kind of joke?" he spat, dropping the papers in disgust.

Yursa picked up the papers and read through them carefully. She glared at the mouflon with an intensity he hadn't thought possible. "You vicious guingin bastard!"

"That is correct, my dear; I am a bastard." Al-Seif steepled his fingers. "And thanks to some carefully invested capital, and a few minor strings pulled, I also own seventy-nine per cent of the controlling stock in De Palma Shipping Lines." He stood slowly. "But I am nothing if not generous. You still know more about the management of the shipping line than I, and I wish to retain you as consultants."

"And if I refuse?" Vigo asked, cold fury burning in his amber eyes.

The mouflon produced a second envelope and pushed it across the table. The De Palma patriarch scanned the document inside.

"I don't understand," he said, looking up.

"That, my dear father-in-law, is a contract stating that D'Verant Industries, your less well-known and less legal entity in Pytan, has recently acquired the assets of one Terrapin Holdings Inc. Which, thanks to certain parties I have been in contact with, is poise to be investigated for the manufacture and sale of biological weapons, not to mention the development of a

518

particularly potent and addictive strain of heroin. That is, unless you concede to my terms."

Of course, the part about the heroin was a bluff, thanks mainly to the creature that had destroyed the crop, but De Palma didn't need to know that.

Before Vigo could sputter a reply, the phone in the living room began to ring. A servant answered and brought the bulky cordless handset into the dining room.

"It is for Signor al-Seif," the servant replied, handing him the phone.

"Yes?" al-Seif asked sharply.

"The meeting is over," the familiar amphibian voice said through its robotic filter. "You have two minutes." The line went dead.

The mouflon stared at the handset for a moment and then returned it to the servant. He adjusted his jacket, bowed politely to his host, and excused himself from the table.

His sudden rudeness left the De Palmas shocked and not a little upset. Yursa waved her father and brothers down as she stormed out after her husband. She caught up with him just as he opened his car door.

"Just a fucking minute, *stronzo*!" she roared. "I don't know what kind of game you think you're playing, but I can assure you it ends right here."

"Oh, it most certainly does, my dear."

He looked towards the front seat. There was a pistol hidden underneath, if need be, but he had longed planned to make her demise look like an accident.

"You see, I no longer need you. As the majority owner of De Palma Shipping, I no longer feel any need to keep up with this disgrace of a marriage."

A regular throbbing sound that he couldn't quite place probed the edges of his hearing. He climbed into the driver's seat, but Yursa leaned on the door before he started the engine.

"I'll bleed you for this, Jirair. You and your whore and your bastard son. You think you can move in on our territory just like that? The De Palmas have fought generations of Medocci families. The Savantes, the Favera, the Costellianos, none of them have been able to stand against us. If you think for one moment that an upstart Pytian bastard like—"

The sound of the helicopters had been growing steadily louder, and now they cut off Yursa's tirade as they buzzed close overhead. There were three of them, each painted solid black; the bulbous blacked-out windows of the pilot's cabin made them look like giant insects.

They positioned themselves evenly around the main house, and the occupants inside found themselves blinded by the glare of their searchlights. Vigo's bodyguards stumbled onto the rear patio, aiming their weapons at the intruders. There was a mechanical windup and a high-pitched *spurt* as one of the helicopter's twin-mounted miniguns riddled the dining room with bullets. Its escorts followed suit, peppering the estate with lead.

They fired wave after wave across the entire compound. Glass and shrapnel flew in every direction, the stucco walls providing no protection against the onslaught. A few bodyguards tried to help the other family members escape through the garden, but the snipers in the helicopters gunned them down.

A light shone down on the Regalia, and al-Seif held up a hand against the blinding glare. It hung there for several tense moments, but no bullets followed.

There was a deafening boom as the compound's gates blew inward off their hinges, but nothing came through from the dark forest beyond.

The attack was over in less than a minute, and the helicopters vanished into the night. The gas furnace of the compound had ruptured, and a fire was quickly consuming everything.

Al-Seif started the car as calmly and deliberately as his trembling fingers would allow and sped off down the drive, leaving his wife staring dumbstruck at the devastation.

Slowly, Yursa De Palma stumbled around the outside of the ruin until she came to the pool. One of the bodyguards had fallen in, his blood staining the waters red. When she found her father's body, she collapsed to her knees. She sobbed uncontrollably as she clutched her deceased patriarch to her chest.

"You bastard!" she screamed into the night at the fleeing Jirair al-Seif. "You bastard!"

39 – Desert Flight

The agents' journey out of the Valley of Nefrit was uneventful. Nothing hindered their progress through the jungle once they regained the road south of Jar-Geshim. The Hiker stalled only once, but by the end of the day, they reached the forest's edge. Mohan and Zed switched places so they could drive through the night; the tiger had a bad feeling that if he shut off the Hiker's engine, it would never start again, and eventually, they reached the Khet-Ef Zaid Desert of southern Pytan.

To call it a desert was unfair. Though the soil was rocky and ill-suited for crops, it was still abundant with scrub brush and thin trees that provided a little shade for the herds of wild ghuskas—cousins to the bolvin—and the horse-like ecquai.

When morning came, the drivers switched places again. However, instead of continuing to follow the road south towards Det, Mohan turned the convoy east, skirting the southern edges of the Nefrit Ishem

Mountains until they reached a broad land where the trees were much sparser.

They drove all day through these empty lands.

As the sun began to set behind them, Mohan suddenly brought the convoy to a halt and ordered everyone to get out slowly.

Ric was tempted to ask what was happening, but his experience over the last few days told him it was best just to wait. He exited the battered rear-guard truck with the others and stood patiently nearby.

The daylight disappeared entirely, and still, they just stood there.

Eventually, the journalist thought he saw a light on the eastern horizon and peered at it curiously. He took a step forward, but Kitty forced him back against the side of the truck and raised a warning finger.

Zed stepped forward and called into the darkness, "The sands of Mbektar reveal your friends!"

A voice, surprisingly close by, answered him, "And grant blindness to your enemies. Approach, friend!"

Ric caught his breath as five figures rose ghost-like from the rocky ground practically at their feet. Each wore clothing similar to Zed's: a loose-fitting thawb of cotton under a rugged canvas cape and a keffiyeh that came in various colours wrapped around each head.

Beneath the keffiyeh, they wore peculiar hooded masks made of brass and thick leather plates and fitted with dark-tinted goggles.

Each also carried a long rifle that reminded Ric of old muzzle-loaders used by the ancient Turrecks, the civilisation that had given birth to the current nation of Pytan. But these were no museum pieces; the curiously and wonderfully carved weapons, with their multi-lensed scopes and barrel-mounted stabilisers, appeared both ancient and futuristically advanced simultaneously.

"If I didn't know any better, I would think those were some form of laser rifle," the journalist said offhandedly to Kitty.

"Don't be stupid," she scoffed. "The lasers being developed right now require massive battery packs too heavy to carry around. They're just projectile weapons. Although I admit, I've always wanted to get my hands on one. The Soketh fashion and care for them themselves. They say they have some extra features you won't find on a conventional rifle and are accurate at over two kilometres."

She didn't have time to explain further as Zed turned to the nearest figure, also wearing a sky-blue keffiyeh, and spread his arms wide.

"More than friend," he said. "I know that voice!"

The figure handed his rifle to another Soketh and removed his mask. Ric couldn't be sure because of the low light, but it looked like the hood had simply melted away from the figure's face and down around his neck. The Soketh was also a badger, probably in his mid-twenties, and his facial features and markings were practically identical to Ezekiel's.

The two embraced warmly, and Zed waved his companions over.

"Come, come," he boomed. "These are my people. Allow me to introduce Nada, my eldest son!"

"How did they move up on us like that?" Ric asked Kitty.

"They've been waiting for us for several hours," the tigress answered without looking at him. "We were waiting for the signal that the plane was almost here."

"You mean they were just lying there when we rolled up?"

"Yeah." She smirked. "You didn't see them?" She decided not to tell him that Zed was the only one who had, and he told her father when to stop the convoy.

As they shared introductions with Zed's son, several other Soketh were busy lighting torches a hundred metres away. As Ric watched, he realised they were outlining a crude runway nearly two kilometres long.

It was then that he heard the drone of a plane. No, two planes, and one significantly larger than the other.

He couldn't see them until they were practically on top of the group when they suddenly switched on their landing lights. They were flying low—too low, it seemed to him.

What kind of crazy pilots would fly blind over a rocky desert with only a few torches to show them the runway? He thought. *Probably ex-military. Or maybe even active military, now that I think about it. Tiger's Stripe seems to have people everywhere.*

Ric wasn't far wrong. The first plane was a large, blunt-nosed twin-engine military cargo transport—a Baern Avionics AC-130 unless he was mistaken. Painted on the nose, he could just make out the image of a curvy pika pinup rolling a pair of dice at the viewer—"Fuzzy Dice" was written underneath it in flowing script.

After taxiing off to the side, the second aircraft landed. It was also a twin-engine craft manufactured by Baern Avionics, but the long, sleek Corvair 882 passenger plane was only half the size of the military aircraft.

Once they cleared the runway and their engines slowed, the agents gathered their gear from the trucks.

As they approached the cargo plane, a short female pika greeted them. Even with the bulky flight suit, it was easy to see who the artist's inspiration had been for the pinup on the aircraft's nose. When she removed her helmet, Ric could see the Tiger's Mark on the back of her right ear, standing boldly against her bobbed red long-fur.

"Generals," she greeted them with a wide grin and a thick lilting Eisben Fens accent, "glad to see you all safe I am."

"Your timing is impeccable as always, Ms. Belle," general Durram replied.

"Hello again, Susan!" Mohan grinned.

The second pilot, a weathered female golden eagle, approached them. Those who recognised her instantly bowed their heads. She wasn't much taller than Vicki, but she commanded respect with every centimetre she had.

Ric also couldn't help but notice that the front of her flight suit was partially unzipped, showing off just a hint of feathered cleavage.

He had read an article somewhere that certain scientific circles debated at length whether mammalian breasts on nonmammals served any practical purpose other than to make the female form more appealing to potential mates. Curiously, the article concluded that the results were inconclusive, and additional funding was required to "conduct further research".

Regardless, it was not uncommon for nonmammalian females to take advantage of current advances in reconstructive surgery. The mammalian breast augments could not and did not need to lactate, but they were eye-catching, to say the least.

Ric thought the practice rather odd and maybe even a little unnatural, but there was no denying that the golden eagle before him had hired an excellent surgeon. He found the intended effect to be more than a little distracting, even if she was clearly several decades older than he. Interestingly enough, Vince completely ignored it, although whether from respect for her rank or personal familiarity with her, Ric couldn't tell.

"Elder Tyrsus," Mohan said, "I didn't expect to see you ferrying us around."

The soft corners at the base of the Elder's beak turned up in a tired smile.

"You should not be so surprised, Major General," she said in accented Locken. "As the Council's leading expert on international laws in this region, it is only fitting that I should come up here personally to observe the situation."

She didn't mention that she was also a native of Kirque and was deeply concerned about how the budding war between Pytan and Barju would eventually affect her homeland.

She turned to the journalist. "And you must be Sedric Barnes. I am Basira Tyrsus, Elder of the *Loahu Tiaowen*." She used the formal Benese name. "I must say your personal file is interesting, as are many of your articles for *LBC World Press*. No doubt, since we were unable to whisk you away to the Sanctuary, you have proven yourself valuable to us already?" She cocked her head at Mohan.

The tiger grinned broadly and slapped him on the shoulder. "Too right, he has. He might think he asks too many questions, but he's sharp, and he's been a great help so far."

Ric shuffled his feet nervously.

"No, don't sell yourself short, mate," Mohan said. "This is all new to you, and you've absorbed everything like a sponge. And you were a big help setting the trap for the Frankenbeast. Couldn't have done it without you."

"I'm honoured to meet a member of the Elder Council I've heard so little about," Ric replied, trying to change the subject.

"It's not often we get to leave the Sanctuary," she answered with a gleam in her eye. "In fact, several others wanted to come, but as I mentioned, I was the most qualified."

After the introductions, preparations for their departure proceeded rapidly. The support agents, General Durram, the prisoners, and the bodies of their fallen companions were loaded into the cargo plane. The Soketh were already in the process of scrapping the trucks to repurpose them for their own use. However, Mohan hadn't let them touch the exploration vehicle.

He stopped Susan Belle as she supervised loading the cargo plane.

"You wouldn't have any extra room for the Hiker, would you?" he asked.

The pika looked at the battered vehicle.

"Yeah," she said doubtfully, "but she looks done for, *a dweud y gwir*." Belle had a habit of breaking into her native Fenspeak; roughly translated, she meant "to be honest."

"She is." The tiger sighed. "But she's been through a lot. I want you to ship her off to the Playground, see if they can learn anything from her battle scars. Maybe we can get us a new breed of field vehicle. Plus, I'm fond of her."

"Willing her body to science," the pika said with a smile. "All right, I'll squeeze her in the middle."

"Thanks, Susan. Fly safe!"

"*Tara 'wan!*" she waved.

Midnight was approaching by the time everything was loaded. The pilots primed their engines and taxied to the end of the runway. The AC-130 went first, followed shortly by the Corvair 382.

Ric wondered where the other plane was headed or if he would ever see the other agents again. For the moment, their paths diverged He was flying with Mohan's Scrappers and Elder Tyrsus to Hempsford, in Locke, where they could catch a train to Grettasburg.

Home.

It felt strange to call it that after so many months in another part of the world.

They circled once above the desert, and Ric watched as the torches of the makeshift runway winked out one by one until the ground below was plunged into darkness. The mysterious Soketh had vanished as silently as they had appeared.

It was a surreal feeling to realise they were finally escaping the country after many days of terrorist

531

attacks, bandit lords, and Frankenbeast monsters. He recalled Mohan's time check with Watch Command and pictured a calendar. It was Faerday night, and fully eight days had passed since Kitty had rescued him from the bloodbath at al-Seif's slave auction and discovered the Tiger's Mark on his arm. So much had happened since then. He wondered how he would explain any of it to his editor.

Or even if he should.

Somewhere in the back of his mind, Sedric Barnes knew that really his adventure was just beginning. Maybe It would be best if he didn't say anything until he had more details. After all, that would be best if he wanted to maintain some semblance of journalistic integrity.

He settled back into his seat as Elder Tyrsus flew them northwestward, and the two aircraft vanished into the night with their precious cargo.

For the first time in eight days, the lynx slept peacefully.

Epilogue – The Hunted

East Benai, the seat of the Great Eastern Empire. A land whose rich history is drenched in ancient warlords, feudal states, and mysticism. Among its most important contributions to the world is the invention of gunpowder, rice, and sushi.

Most importantly sushi!

At least, that's what Chen Rogers thought as he staggered from his favoured eatery in the heart of the Quan-Sung District of the Imperial City. Sure, it was a seedy part of town, and they didn't often look kindly on foreign-born immigrants like himself, but he got by. A healthy swig from the rice wine bottle in his striped paw might have had something to do with that.

The small tiger's bloodshot eyes stared blearily at the neon signs around him, and he blinked as a splash of water hit him just right. It had been raining steadily all day, but the closeness of the surrounding buildings made it rare that a drop ever touched the streets—at least not directly. Now, the hour was late, and few pedestrians were out unless they were drunks like himself.

He leered at a pair of hookers in heavy makeup. Both were long-necked cranes. Normally, he would have preferred something with fewer feathers, but in his current state, he didn't much care. They rolled their eyes in disgust and mocked him in Benese. He staggered on.

It was for the best. Between the Red Eagle, the Hikigaeru, and the Fire Dragon Star, who knew which syndicate the pair might have been working for? Not good business to service just any old drunk off the street. Not that he considered himself any old drunk.

Chen tottered to the side as a figure rushed past him. "Heywatchitbub!" he blurted out in Locken.

The figure darted around the corner and paused only a moment at the next intersection. He was a middle-aged ferret wearing the chains and plastic jacket of one of the local street gangs. The coat was bloodied and torn, revealing a peculiar mark on the fur of his back. He was bleeding profusely from a large gash in his forehead, and his right arm hung limp and useless at his side.

He spotted the pay phone on the corner and stumbled towards it. The handset didn't want to stay in his hands as he fumbled around with his one good paw. He dialled as quickly as he could, his breath starting to come in ragged pants.

"Blue Wing International Incorporated," the operator droned. "How may I direct your call?"

"R-repair," the ferret gasped. "Repairs! Q-quickly, p-please!"

There was an agonizing pause, and the voice changed. "The line is secure."

"R-red," the ferret choked. "Agent...two four nine. R-red—"

A watery gurgle replaced the rest of his words as a small crossbow bolt pierced his throat. The ferret collapsed to his knees, the receiver still clutched in his dead paws.

"Agent two four nine, do you copy?" the operator asked urgently.

A feminine canine figure removed the phone from the dead agent's hand and held it to her pointed ear.

"Agent two four nine?"

The line went dead.

The figure ejected the change, redeposited it, and hit redial.

"Blue Wing International Incorporated. How may I direct your call?"

"Repairs?" the figure asked.

There was a pause, and the operator hurriedly replied, "I'm sorry; the department you have requested is no longer in service." The line went dead again.

The figure smirked and turned to see the drunk tiger she had passed earlier blinking at her from across the street. He saw the body lying by the phone and dutifully turned away; the same thing happened every day down in the Quan-Sung District. Best not to get involved.

Pity, she thought, but her lips curled up in a wicked grin as she raised the small crossbow pistol and put a bolt through the back of his head. Then she turned back to the phone and dialled a new number.

The call connected, but there was no salutation.

"It's done," she said to the silence on the other end. "The loose end has been tied off. Our operation is safe. As a bonus, one of their drop numbers is out of service as well. The number was registered to a Blue Wing International Incorporated. It wouldn't surprise me if they were halfway done cleaning out their physical call centre already."

"Very good," a heavily filtered voice answered. Unlike Freggs, this speaker spoke in a manner that obliterated all traces of an accent. "And their agent?"

She yanked the dart from the ferret's neck. "Dead."

"Skin him. You know where to send the pelt. The board is set. We will let them know it's their move." The line went dead.

The assassin hung up the receiver and snapped her fingers. Two hooded figures detached themselves from the shadows and picked up the dead Tiger's Stripe agent.

Carefully, the assassin taped a small ruby pin under the phone; it depicted an eagle in flight.

With another snap of her fingers, the trio melted back into the shadows, and a sudden downpour from above began to wash the blood into the overflowing gutters.